Praise for *The Dead Circus:*

"Enough plot for any crime novel . . . The reader is compelled to turn the page to find out what happens next. . . . Once the novel's momentum takes hold, [Gene Burk's] pursuit becomes ours."

—David Ebershoff, *Los Angeles Times Book Review*

"A suspenseful page-turner." —Judith M. Redding, *The Baltimore Sun*

"*The Dead Circus,* a fine new novel by screenwriter and director John Kaye, pulls some of the dregs of Manson's dark legacy into the light. . . . Kaye . . . explores two of the most tantalizing unanswered questions about Manson." —Jeff Baker, *The Oregonian* (Portland)

"Los Angeles is where noir was born, and with good reason; it's where most dreams go to die. . . . *The Dead Circus* . . . cements the author's reputation as an expert on L.A.'s seamy underbelly. . . . In the hands of a lesser writer, so many clichéd characters and fortuitous coincidences would doom a novel. But Kaye pulls it off by humanizing everyone who makes an appearance in *The Dead Circus,* from the leads to the cameos. . . . Kaye's characters' misfortunes put the lie to the myths of eternal sunshine and happy ever after." —John Schacht, *Creative Loafing*

"A portrait of Los Angeles filled with rock stars, private detectives, good-fellas, and, well, evil. . . . [A] modern noir thriller . . . Suspects abound in this multilayered mystery, as do icons of recent history."

—*The Daily News*

"Kaye has a knack for weaving rumor and innuendo into the fabric of history . . . and utilizing the theory of six degrees of separation to create compelling stuff out of the stuff of happenstance and coincidence. . . . *The Dead Circus* . . . is a fictional walk through history that ultimately may not be true, but is most certainly accurate. Hopefully, we will not have to wait another five years for its sequel, though any wait, no matter how long, will almost certainly be worth it."   —Joe Hartlaub, *Bookreporter*

"Evocative . . . Richly atmospheric . . . Masterfully creating and sustaining a palpable, pure, elegiac paean to lost hopes and dreams, Kaye seems to suggest that the human impulse toward yearning and hopefulness can exist unmarred by and side by side with rampant corruption and pure evil. . . . [*The Dead Circus*] never feels forced and is entirely unpredictable."
                    —Joanne Wilkinson, *Booklist* (starred review)

"A seemingly ordinary tragedy plunges an ex-cop-turned-detective into the murky, bizarre world of the Manson family . . . [A] riveting noir thriller . . . Kaye populates his novel with enough suspects and shady Hollywood characters to fill two murder mysteries, but the story remains reasonably tight. . . . This book packs a major wallop."   —*Publishers Weekly*

The **Dead** Circus

ALSO BY JOHN KAYE:

Stars Screaming

The **Dead** Circus

a novel

John Kaye

Grove Press
New York

This is a work of fiction. Names, characters, places, and incidents are either the product
of the author's imagination or are used ficitiously. The resemblance of fictional characters
in this book to actual persons living or dead is purely coincidental. The appearance of
certain public persons in this work of fiction is without their permission and does not
imply any endorsement of this novel.

Published simultaneously in Canada
Printed in the United States of America

FIRST GROVE PRESS EDITION
Library of Congress Cataloging-in-Publication Data
Kaye, John.
 The dead circus : a novel / John Kaye.
  p. cm.
 ISBN 0-8021-4017-3 (pbk.)
  1. Police—California—Los Angeles—Fiction. 2. Fuller, Bobby,
1943–1966—Fiction. 3. Los Angeles (Calif.)—Fiction. 4, Rockabilly
music—Fiction. 5. Rock musicians—Fiction. I. Title.
 PS3561.A8857 D43 2002
 813'.54—dc21   2001056496

Design by Laura Hammond Hough

Grove Press
841 Broadway
New York, NY 10003

03 04 05 06 07   10 9 8 7 6 5 4 3 2 1

To the memory of my father

The **Dead** *Circus*

First Words

Death: The Last Visit

Police sources confirm that Eddie Cornell, the man who was found
shot to death Thursday morning inside room ten at the Tropicana
Motel, was a veteran homicide detective assigned to the Hollywood Division of the L.A.P.D. At this time there are no plans to
release the names of any suspects or a possible motive. Lieuten-
ant Richie Arquette, who is in charge of the investigation, denied rumors that Cornell's death was is in any way connected to
Charles Manson or events that took place in the summer of 1969.

L.A. *Times*

August 18, 1985

There are things you think you know about me, but you're wrong.
I'm not a madman, despite what you have heard and read. I'm
just a boy who grew up ignored, holding his breath outside a
tavern in the late hours, waiting for his mother to take his hand
and walk him home. That's right. That's all I am, just a child
with salt in his blood and cinders underneath his skin, a chooser
not a beggar, someone who travels light and knows that when
you are lost in the terrible darkness of the big city, scared by your
own footsteps, you can only trust the helpless.

I don't need my mother now. I don't need her hugs and
kisses. There is no storytime anymore, no sugar cookies on a plate
by my bed, no tree forts, no trading cards in the spokes of my
bike, no splashing home in the rain. No rain, no sky, no stars.
I'm safe here in this cellblock, as long as I've got someone to watch

my back. But you're not safe out there, because your hearts are locked against the children who cried out for help, who left you with the silence of an empty bedroom, their clothes in their closets and their schoolbooks still on the shelves, the air crackling with their anger.

They are waking up now in dead alleys or climbing out of ditches, and soon they will be loose and running, half-starved and forgotten, crossing and recrossing this fouled country, waiting until the winds calm and the flames die out before they decide to come home.

And that, my friends, is when you get to face the truth.

Charles Manson

[Unpublished prison notes, 1972]

Part
One

One

Hollywood

Nights

At about nine P.M. on an unseasonably warm Saturday night in November of 1965, Gene Burk was sitting at a ringside table inside P.J.'s, a rock-and-roll dance club on Santa Monica Boulevard in West Hollywood. Headlining that weekend was the Bobby Fuller Four, a heavily electrified rockabilly band that was rapidly becoming the act to see within L.A.'s thriving grassroots club scene. On this, their first gig at P.J.'s, they would break all existing attendance records, and club owner Carl Reese would quickly sign them to an exclusive six-month contract.

Seated at a reserved table not far from Gene was Nancy Sinatra, one of the stars of *The Ghost in the Invisible Bikini,* a schlocky horror film in which Bobby Fuller was appearing as the leader of a hard-core surf band. At first Bobby had found the script unreadable and tried to drop out of the project, but Herb Stelzner, his manager and the owner of his new record label, convinced him that the movie exposure would help promote his first album, which he was now recording.

Right now Stelzner was standing in the back of the club, trying to appear nonchalant as a small shiver of fear skipped along his spine and spread slowly through his chest. Standing next to him, his face cold and reprimanding, was Carl Reese, who had just informed Stelzner that "the boss," meaning Frank Sinatra, did not like Bobby dating his daughter. In fact, he wanted it to stop.

"They're just a couple of kids having a good time," Stelzner said, as he nervously tugged down the sleeves of his jacket. "It's nothing serious."

Carl Reese accepted a bourbon and soda from a passing waitress and raised the glass to his lips, pausing for a moment as his hazy blue eyes scanned the crowded room. He smiled when he recognized Gene Burk. He knew Gene was a cop. He'd seen him around town, in joints like The Zanzibar and Ernie's Stardust Lounge, looking slightly uncomfortable as his partner, Eddie Cornell, hassled Hollywood's growing coalition of dope pushers, pimps, and petty crooks. He also knew that Gene had grown up in Los Angeles and was basically a good guy, a music freak who was known to smoke an occasional joint when he was not on duty.

Gene turned his head. He saw Reese looking at him intently. Herb Stelzner said, "I'm going backstage."

"Talk to Bobby. Tell him what Frank said."

"I'll tell him after the first show."

Just before the houselights came down, Gene was joined by his younger brother Ray, who apologized for being late.

"Guess who's here," Gene said.

"Who?"

Gene gestured to his right. "Nancy Sinatra."

Ray was silent for a moment. Then his heart began to speed up as he turned and looked at Nancy carefully for several seconds. During his senior year at Westside High they'd gone out once, double-dating with Ricky Furlong, a bashful boy and a baseball phenom who would later have a nervous breakdown during his rookie season in the major leagues.

Gene said, "When was the last time you saw her?"

"At State Beach, the summer before my sophomore year at Cal. I said hello but she looked right through me, like I was fucking invisible."

When the Bobby Fuller Four took the stage, Ray was still staring at the back of Nancy's head, cringing inside as he recalled their one and only date. He'd taken her to a party at someone's house in Mandeville Canyon, a rich kid from Chadwick, this private high school in Palos Verdes. The rich kid's parents were in Las Vegas for the weekend, guests of comedian Buddy Hackett, and by midnight, Ray and Furlong had finished a fifth of Wild Turkey and were both passed out in the backyard. Nancy, who had no real friends at the party and no way to get home, walked the two miles into Brentwood and called a cab.

At school on Monday Ray saw her in the cafeteria and tried to apologize, but she moved her head in denial, continuing to talk to her girlfriends as if he weren't there. Then, just when he was about to give up, she turned her face toward him, and he could see the hostility in her stony eyes.

"Ray Burk," she said, her icy smile only making his anguish worse, "you have no idea how lucky you are."

"I don't?"

"No."

"Why?"

"Because I didn't tell my dad."

Now, a little over five years later, separated only by a row of tables, she was oblivious to Ray's presence, clapping along with the audience as Bobby Fuller segued into his second number, "I Fought the Law," a rocked-up version of the Crickets' song that he was performing live for the first time. "This is a fucking great tune," Gene said to Ray, who nodded but was not completely in the present. "Ray?"

"Yeah?"

"I know what you're thinking."

Ray turned and looked at his brother. "Tell me."

"You're thinking of going over there. Right?"

"Maybe. Just to say hello."

"Don't."

"It's been five years. She can't still be pissed."

"Forget about her," Gene said, starting to sound a little aggravated. "It's over."

Midway through the first set, Gene found his attention drawn to a slender teenage girl who was leaning lazily against the far wall. She had a wide crooked mouth, and her unblinking eyes seemed haunted and trance-like as she stared into the smoke that swirled around her face. The phony ID that she carried in her plastic wallet said she was born in Cedar Rapids, Iowa, which was true, but the rest of the information, including her name and date of birth, was false.

Standing behind the girl was an older guy, small and wiry, wearing flowered bell bottom pants, a bowler hat, and a raspberry-red leather car coat. He was the rhythm guitarist for Billy J. Kramer and the Dakotas, a British band that was touring the U.S. with Gerry and the Pacemakers and the Dave Clark Five. Two days ago he'd met the young runaway back-stage at a concert in Phoenix, Arizona, and he'd snuck her on the tour bus after the show. Right now she was staying in his room on the tenth floor of the Continental Hyatt House Hotel.

His name was Archie; hers, she told him, was Alice, which was her real name and not the name on her ID. They would only be together for one more night. She would then hitchhike up the coast, stopping first in Santa Barbara for a week before continuing on to Berkeley, where she would remain for one year, a girl who turned her back on her past and tried hard to keep the devil out of her heart.

After the show, Archie took Alice's hand and led her backstage to meet Bobby Fuller. Nancy Sinatra was standing a few feet away, chatting with starlet Sharon Tate and her current boyfriend, hair stylist Jay Sebring. Sharon suggested that they all meet later at The Daisy, a private disco-theque on Rodeo Drive in Beverly Hills.

"Ryan will be there," Sharon said. "And so will Natalie Wood and Peter Fonda. Jay spoke to Peter this afternoon at his shop."

Nancy shook her head. "I can't," she said, aware that The Daisy was her father's favorite after-hours hangout, the only place where Mia Far-row, his new bride, felt comfortable. "I've got an early tennis game to-morrow morning."

Alice was standing next to Archie. He was speaking rapidly in a slurred Cockney accent, explaining to Bobby how much he admired his songs, especially "Memories of You," the frantic rocker that closed his first set. Although Archie was obviously smashed, Bobby knew the praise was sincere and thanked him.

"When are you going to tour the U.K.?" Archie asked him.

"Next year."

"If he's got a hit album to support it," Herb Stelzner said, after he moved over to join the group.

Archie turned to Stelzner and regarded him with suspicion. "Who're you?"

"I'm Bobby's manager and I own his label."

"Then how about a show of confidence in your artist, mate. He'll do fucking great in Britain," Archie said. "He's got the perfect sound. Last year Gene Vincent and the Blue Caps sold out the Albert Hall."

Herb Stelzner smiled tolerantly. "Gene Vincent is a legend in the U.K. Plus the Animals headlined that tour. I know how to do my job, son," he said, making his voice a little louder and stronger. "When it's time to cross the ocean, we'll be there."

Throughout this discussion, Alice was staring at Sharon Tate, drawn deeply into her beauty. She was so irresistibly pretty that being in her presence made Alice feel suddenly, unexpectedly sad.

Bobby said to Archie, "Who's your girlfriend?"

"My name is Alice, and I'm not his girlfriend," she said with some defiance. "We hardly know each other."

Alice broke away from Archie and came up behind Sharon Tate, hesitating for a moment with her hand raised before she tapped her gently on the shoulder. Sharon Tate turned and stared into Alice's eyes, which now contained a peculiar brightness. "Yes," she said. "What is it?"

"Are you a movie star?"

"Not yet," Sharon said, glancing at Jay Sebring, who squeezed her neck affectionately.

"You will be," Alice said, her voice filled with both envy and desire. "I'd stake my life on it."

Outside P.J.'s, Gene was saying goodbye to his brother, who was swaying in his tracks. "Be careful driving, Ray."

"I'm okay. Don't worry."

"You're not okay. You're drunk."

Ray lit a cigarette and stared into the street for several seconds before he spoke again. "I should've said something."

"To who?"

"Nancy."

"Fuck Nancy. She's history. Start thinking about yourself," Gene said.

"Stop giving me advice."

"I'm your big brother. I'm supposed to give you advice."

On his way back inside the club for the second show, Gene noticed Carl Reese standing near the backstage entrance, talking to a big man, bigger than Reese, and older—maybe sixty—who was wearing a blue knit polo shirt and white linen pants. His name was Jack Havana and, along with being the money behind P.J.'s, he was a known hoodlum and the largest purveyor of pornography on the West Coast. He and Reese were also partnered in several other businesses, including a chain of dry cleaners and the Arroyo Lodge and Racquet Club, a resort in Palm Springs.

Gene had met Havana for the first time back in 1949, when he was nine years old and Havana came by his father's newsstand one Friday, offering him magazines that he could sell underneath the counter.

"I don't peddle anything I can't display," Nathan Burk told Havana.

"You can make a bundle," Havana replied.

"No thanks."

Nathan's wife Mona was standing a few feet away, listening to this conversation while she worked the register, which she did every weekday afternoon during the summer. When she caught Nate's eye, she said, "Maybe you should think it over."

"I don't need to think it over. I know what's right."

Jack Havana nodded thoughtfully, his expression calm and undisturbed. He let several seconds go by before he said, quietly, "You should listen to your pretty wife."

Nathan Burk looked over at Mona, who everyone said was a dead ringer for Hedy Lamarr. She was staring at him with almost pity in her face. "He sells dirt," he said to her. "Is that what you want?"

"I want a nice car and pretty clothes," Mona said, turning away as the color rose in her cheeks, a color that was several shades lighter than her deep, rich, red hair. "I want things that money can buy. Is that so bad?"

Gene saw Jack Havana once more that summer. He and Ray had just walked out of the Vogue Theater after attending the matinee of *Criss Cross,* a gangster film starring Burt Lancaster as an armored car driver who gets double-crossed by his ex-wife, Yvonne De Carlo. At the corner of Wilcox and Hollywood Boulevard, while they were standing immobile, waiting for the light to change, Ray said, "What's Mom doing in that car?"

"What car?"

"There."

Ray was pointing at a white Lincoln Continental convertible that was moving slowly east on the palm-lined boulevard. In the front seat a woman with wavy red hair was sitting between two men. She was wearing a white sleeveless blouse and large sunglasses with white frames. Carl Reese was riding shotgun and the driver, Jack Havana, had his arm around her bare shoulder.

Gene's heart was pounding in his chest. He shook his head. "That's not Mom."

"Yes it is."

"No, it just looks like her."

"It's her," Ray said. "What's she doing with those men? She's supposed to be helping Dad." Ray looked both confused and angry as he started sprinting up the boulevard, trying to keep pace with the Lincoln. "Mom! Hey, Mom! Stop!"

Gene saw the woman in the car look over her shoulder and smile anxiously. A moment later she said something to Jack Havana, who nodded, and the big car suddenly turned and disappeared into the traffic moving north on Vine Street.

When Gene finally caught up with his brother, Ray was standing on the corner, trying to catch his breath. "That wasn't her," Gene said, still holding on to the lie. "It was someone else."

"It was her," Ray said, and his voice broke. "You're wrong."

Gene spun Ray around and slapped him hard across the cheek. "You better not say anything to Dad," Gene warned, bringing his face forward and speaking into Ray's trembling lips. "If you do, I'll kill you."

Inside Bobby Fuller's dressing room, while Bobby and his brother Randy were reviewing the song list for their final show, Herb Stelzner stood silently in the corner, puffing on a cigarette. Slouched next to him on a folding metal chair was a scared-looking girl wearing frayed jeans and weather-cracked boots. Resting on her lap was a battered twelve-string Martin guitar.

She whispered to Stelzner, "I'm a songwriter."

Stelzner nodded. "That's good."

"And a singer. But mostly a songwriter. I was hoping I could get you to listen to my songs."

"Send them over to my office."

"I don't have anything on tape."

"Then I can't help you."

"Yes you could," she said, almost desperately. "You could listen to me sing."

Bobby Fuller glanced at the girl and smiled. "I'll listen to you, honey," he said, and turned his head toward Stelzner, who said: "I gotta talk to you after the show."

"About what?"

"It'll just take a couple of minutes."

"I'm busy after the show. Let's do it now."

Bobby gave his brother a quick nod, and the girl, looking uncomfortable, raised herself from her chair. She said, "Do you want me to leave, too?"

"Yeah. It's business," Bobby said. "Just give us five."

After Randy Fuller followed the girl outside, Bobby turned toward the full-length mirror and smiled at his reflection. Then he took out his comb and ran it twice through his shiny black hair. "Reese wants you to sign a contract," Stelzner said. He was still leaning against the wall with his arms now folded across his chest. "Three grand a week. Divide it any way you want."

"Three grand a week," Bobby said, continuing to smile as he straightened the knot in his skinny tie. "That's big time. Is that what you wanted to tell me?"

Stelzner unfolded his arms and slowly shook his head, maintaining the serious expression on his face, the same expression he'd worn since he'd entered the dressing room. "No. There's something else," he said. "Reese said some people are concerned about Nancy."

"Concerned? About what?"

"About you and her. They don't think the combination is a good idea."

"Fuck them," Bobby said with a look, and he grabbed his guitar. "We're just friends."

"Bobby, trust me on this. I—"

Bobby strummed a B-flat power chord that stopped Stelzner's voice in mid-sentence. "When it comes to my career, I'll listen," Bobby said. "But stay out of my private life."

"You fuck up your private life, you have no career. You have nothing."

Bobby's face tightened as he started out the door, then he stopped and gave Stelzner a quick sharp glance. "Don't threaten me, Herb," he said, after some hesitation. "That doesn't feel right."

"It's not me," Stelzner said. "It comes from Frank."

"We're just friends. I told you."

Stelzner just stared at him. "I'll pass that along."

"Do that," Bobby said, trying hard to contain his anger; then he brushed some lint off the front of his sportscoat and walked swiftly out the door.

Driving back to his apartment that night, Ray Burk sideswiped a parked car on the corner of Shoreham Drive and San Vicente Boulevard. Fifteen stories above the street, Diane Linkletter, the daughter of radio and TV personality Art Linkletter, was sitting on her balcony in the Shoreham Towers, tripping on a ten-milligram dose of LSD. Because she was too stoned to hear the crash—on this night her gaze was wide-ranging but inward—she never once looked down. (Two years later, however, feeling hollow and detested and drained of hope, Diane would climb over her iron balcony and—turning her back to the world and taking in a gulp of air— plunge to her death.)

In the spring of 1969, four years after he registered her uncomplicated but unmistakable beauty inside a crowded rock-and-roll nightclub, Ray Burk attended a large housewarming party for actress Sharon Tate and her husband, Polish film director Roman Polanski, at their newly leased hillside home off Benedict Canyon. At that party, along with the drug dealer who supplied Diane Linkletter with her acid, were numerous Hollywood celebrities, including Jack Nicholson, Sonny and Cher, and all the members of the Mamas and Papas, except Mama Cass.

Ray was the guest of producer Marty Fishkin, who had recently optioned his original screenplay, "Dreamsville," which Warner Brothers was eager to finance if Robert Redford or Steve McQueen agreed to play the male lead.

"Don't drink too much and try to look smart," Fishkin advised Ray. "And remember, they're the stars and you're not."

Nancy Sinatra was also at this party but left early, embarrassed by the nude swimming and the open use of marijuana and cocaine. Ray, surprisingly, escorted her off the property.

"She was fucking furious," he told Gene the following day, "especially at Polanski, who she called a 'creepy little dwarf.'"

Gene said, "You didn't bring up any of that old high school stuff?"

"No way. She didn't even recognize me with my beard and all my hair. When I finally told her who I was, she just stopped and stared at me for about ten seconds. Then she cracked up."

"Was she impressed?"

"That I was a screenwriter? Yeah," Ray said and laughed. "I guess you can say that."

As Ray and Nancy walked down the steep driveway to her car, which was parked outside the main gate on Cielo Drive, they passed a group of stoned freaks wearing tie-dyed shirts and buckskin jackets. In the deepening darkness, the secrecy and spite in their faces was invisible, and the only words spoken came from a girl named Alice who was clutching a handful of bright orange sunflowers.

She said, "I always get a funny feeling in my mouth when I'm around strangers. It's sweet and sour at the same time, like I've swallowed a piece of homemade lemon pie."

Just before Nancy drove away, she asked Ray about his older brother. "Is he still a cop?"

"No. Not anymore. He quit in '67, after he came back from Monterey Pop."

"What's he doin'?"

"He's been helping my dad at the newsstand. On the side he deals in rock-and-roll memorabilia. He's thinking about becoming a private investigator."

Nancy's eyes had a lost look, as if her mind was moving back in time. "Did he tell you we spoke after Bobby Fuller died?"

"No."

"Gene was cool, but he was looking for something that wasn't there. I think he got a little carried away."

"Sounds like Gene. He gets that way sometimes. We both do."

"Yeah, I know," Nancy said, and now she was smiling. "Tell him I said hello."

"I will."

In their conversation the next day, just before he hung up, Gene told Ray, "I may not know much, but I know that Bobby Fuller didn't kill himself. That I know for sure."

Two

Gene and Alice, 1985:

Alive Together

Dazed and not fully awake when she first heard his scream tear the silence and echo across the canyon in the ghostly gray hour before dawn, Gene Burk's neighbor on Brookfield Lane thought someone or some*thing* was being tortured to death.

"It was not a sound that rose or fell," she told the first two policemen who arrived on the scene, "but a terrible piercing wail. It sounded like someone's heart had been obliterated."

The police found Gene standing outside on his redwood deck with his shirt off, his lips barely moving, and his dark eyes open wide with unquenchable anguish. Playing over and over on the stereo inside his living room was Little Eva singing "The Locomotion," and the large-screen TV (which could be seen through the sliding glass doors that led onto the deck) was tuned to a station that was broadcasting live from Greencastle, Indiana, the town where TWA flight 232 from Los Angeles to Boston had crashed an hour earlier, killing all its passengers and crew members, including Alice Larson, a senior flight attendant and Gene's fiancée.

By the time the police entered his backyard through the side gate, Gene had stopped making the half-human sound that had so alarmed his neighbor and prompted her to dial 911. Now he was silent, and except for a single sentence that he would repeat every few minutes, he would remain that way until Ray arrived later that evening, flying down from Berkeley as soon as he heard the news.

"I must be dreaming," Gene said, his voice empty and his fists tightly closed. "I must be dreaming."

Gene had met Alice a year earlier on a TWA flight to New Orleans, a city he was visiting for the first time since he'd lived there for six months back in 1963, the year he'd flunked out of U.S.C. and decided to spend the summer hitchhiking across the country. He'd arrived in the French Quarter on a Friday night, exhausted but brain-wired behind twenty-five milligrams of Dexedrine that was sold to him by a long-haul trucker, a skinny Cajun with an enigmatic smile who picked him up on the outskirts of Morgan City.

Gene never went to sleep that night as he roamed up and down Bourbon Street in a warm soothing rain, trying to absorb the astounding variety of music that he was hearing live for the first time. At a club called The Deuce he saw Clarence "Frogman" Henry sing "Ain't Got No Home," backed by Huey "Piano" Smith and the Clowns. And next door at The Gaslight, Chris Kenner was double-billed with Bobby Marchan, whose strange top-ten tune released on the Fury label in 1960, "There Is Something on My Mind," was one of Gene's all-time favorite 45's.

Even stranger was the encounter he would have twenty-one years later with Tony Boudreau, Marchan's road drummer, who (like Gene) was on his way back to New Orleans for the Jazz and Heritage Festival, a weeklong musical celebration in which he was to reunite with Marchan on the third night, sharing the bill with two other New Orleans natives, Fats Domino and Lee Dorsey. Over the course of their drunken five-hour flight, Gene learned that Boudreau, now a high-priced studio musician living and working in L.A., had toured with Marchan for five years, the last two as part of Dick Clark's Rock and Roll Caravan of Stars. He quit in 1963, the week after J.F.K. was assassinated.

"Actually I got fired," he told Gene. "In Portland I got in a fist-fight with Jimmy Gilmer, the lead singer of the Fireballs. He had a crush on Little Peggy March, and when he found out I was screwing her, he went psycho, busting up my drum-kit. But not as bad as I busted up his face."

In the winter of '65, Boudreau drifted down to L.A. and eked out a living doing session work for Nic Venet, the producer who signed the Beach Boys to Capitol Records. On weekends he occasionally sat in with bands playing at The Rendevous, P.J.'s, The Trip, and several other nightclubs that were springing up in West Hollywood and around the Sunset Strip. He said he met Bobby Fuller one night at Ships, a coffee shop on Olympic just west of La Cienega, and he remembered seeing Fuller in El Paso in the early sixties with a band called the Embers, right before the group left Texas for Hollywood, bringing with them rough mixes of several songs Fuller recorded in a makeshift four-track studio that he built in his parents' garage.

At this point in their conversation Gene explained to Boudreau that he once worked as a cop in the mid-sixties, and that he was part of the team of detectives who investigated Bobby's "accidental" death in the summer of 1966. His body, covered with cuts and bruises and reeking of gasoline, had been discovered in his car outside his mother's apartment in Hollywood with the radio on and the motor running.

"There was always rumors of a mob hit," Gene said, as their plane approached New Orleans and slowly began to descend. "His manager, Herb Stelzner, was a heavy gambler and supposedly owed the boys fifty grand. The word on the street was that he tried to sell half of Bobby's contract to Carl Reese, this club owner who ran the gambling and loan-sharking rackets in L.A. at that time. Bobby found out and threatened to go to the police. The next day he was dead. Unfortunately, we never got anything to check out. We investigated Stelzner and came up empty."

Boudreau scratched his scalp and thought about what he'd just heard. He started to speak but was interrupted by the pilot's voice over the intercom. He said they would be landing in ten minutes. After a moment or two, a stewardess whom Gene had barely noticed moved down the aisle, picking up empty plastic cups and other trash. When she stopped at his row, their eyes met and held, and then her fine-boned face opened into a smile, not the practiced smile worn by most flight attendants, but something more gentle and knowing.

"What's so funny?" Gene asked her.

"You," she said, continuing to smile as her eyes passed over his lap, making sure his seatbelt was fastened; then she glanced across the aisle at Tony Boudreau. "You and your buddy here. You guys haven't stopped yakking since you came on board."

The intercom crackled and the pilot's depersonalized voice said, "Flight attendants prepare for landing."

Just before she walked back up the aisle, the stewardess put her hand lightly on Gene's shoulder. "Welcome to New Orleans," she said to his upturned face, and Gene felt a current of affection move between them, a feeling that was both tentative and dangerous. "They say it's the city that care forgot."

Gene took the taxi from the airport into the center of town. It was not yet eight A.M. and both the temperature and the humidity had climbed into the nineties, the worst heat wave in twenty years, according to the cab driver, a lonesome-looking black man in his early twenties. There was a half-eaten Snickers bar in a tray on the dash, and a pair of tiny gold boxing gloves swung from a chain around the rearview mirror.

"You box?" Gene asked the driver, who nodded. "Professionally?"

"Next year," the driver said. "I won the Golden Gloves in September. Welterweight class."

"My cousin was a welterweight. Aaron Levine."

"Don't know the name."

"He fought years ago. In New York City."

The two men were quiet for several seconds. Around them the rush-hour traffic was building and the radio, preset to an all-news station, reported that an accident with injuries was blocking the exit to Lake Pontchartrain. Gene closed his eyes and tuned out the rest of the newscast, letting his mind float back to the summer of 1963, the summer that he hitchhiked into New Orleans and brazenly took possession of an empty dorm room at Tulane University, passing himself off as a visiting Kappa Alpha from U.S.C. Some of the best times he had that summer took place

at Lake Pontchartrain, and one especially dark night he would never forget: the night a freckled freshman from L.S.U. stripped off her clothes
and fucked him silly on the cool grass, while the moon vanished in the
clouds and bats sliced through the air around their faces.

"Are you gonna remember me?" she asked him afterwards, staring
at him too long, her eyes brimming with tears. "Tell me the truth."

"Sure, I'll remember you."

"Then what's my name?"

"Doris Calhoun," Gene said, kissing her wet cheek, and the girl
smiled. "The prettiest girl in Baton Rouge."

Gene actually *was* a Kappa Alpha at U.S.C. for half a semester, enough
time to learn the handshake and most of the secret lore. But he quit during hell week, protesting when his entire pledge class (which included
several aggressively recruited Mormon athletes) was forced to stand naked
on tables while they watched a stag film starring two curly-headed men
and a woman with scars crosshatched on her backside. After the pledges
became sufficiently aroused, they were encouraged to perform live sex with
a black prostitute who was hired for the night.

"What's the big deal?" asked Max Dixon, the belligerently drunk
president of the fraternity, as Gene stormed out. "It weeds out the fags."

The following day Gene found a studio apartment a few blocks away,
just off 37th and Hoover, not far from the corner where this same prostitute regularly plied her trade. One morning on his way to class he saw her
walking hand-in-hand with a little girl of six or seven. As they passed by,
Gene heard the little girl say, "Will you buy me a record after school?"

"We'll see."

"That's what you always say, Momma. And then you never do."

"You don't need no record when you got a momma that sings so
nice."

"You always say that, too."

And that's when Gene heard the prostitute begin to sing "Back in
My Arms Again," the latest hit by the Supremes. Her daughter joined in

after the first verse, their voices now in perfect harmony, and fo
sweet, luminous moment the world was theirs.

The Jazz and Heritage Festival was not the only reason that Gene had
decided to travel back to New Orleans, nor was it the most important
one. Since February he'd been conferring by phone with a man named
Hugo Porter, a collector of rare and bizarre guitars who lived in Ridley
Park, an upscale suburb of Philadelphia. Through a variety of sources, Gene
learned that Porter had traded a mint condition Les Paul 600X twelve-
string to Dexter Leeds, the rhythm guitarist for the legendary but now
defunct rock-and-roll band Nocturnal Vaudeville. In return Leeds gave
Porter a copy of "Big Boy Pants," a 45 by Danny and the Juniors, which
they recorded in high school when they were known as the Juvenairs. This
hilarious do-wop tune—the story of a fat Italian boy's humiliating shopping adventure with his mother—had been in the stores for only a week
when its local label, Dynamo Sounds, went bankrupt.

It took Gene several days of negotiations before Porter finally agreed
to sell him the record for five thousand dollars cash. They arranged to meet
at the bar in the old Roosevelt Hotel on Saturday night at six o'clock,
where they would finalize the deal over a glass of Dom Pérignon. Afterwards they had tickets to a late-night concert by the legendary blues singer
Johnny Moore.

When he arrived at the Roosevelt, Gene was surprised to see his TWA
flight crew standing by the front desk, surrounded by their luggage. Alice
was off to the side waiting to be checked in, smoking and nervously tapping her fingernails on the marble counter. Twice she turned and looked
in Gene's direction. The second time he nodded shyly but her eyes passed
quickly over his face.

Off the lobby and down some steps was a bar called The Grotto.
Inside a live quartet was playing a jazz version of "Luck Be a Lady," a song
from the Broadway musical *Guys and Dolls*. Over the music Gene heard a
woman laugh loudly, a shrill sound like the whoop of a car alarm, and he

glanced down at his watch. Smiling to himself, he thought: It's barely noon and people are already getting bombed out of their minds. That means the familiar borderline between night and day has been erased.

He heard the elevator ding, and when he looked up he saw Alice step inside, followed by the pilot and the rest of the flight crew. A bellman held the door open for a bald, red-faced man who staggered out of The Grotto holding a tall glass filled with straight scotch. Trailing behind him, panting, was a woman strapped with cameras. Once they were both safely inside the elevator, a man said, "Better check their boarding passes," and everyone laughed. And right before the door closed another man said, "Jesus, I could really use a drink."

Gene had stripped off his wrinkled traveling clothes and was lying naked on the bed when the phone next to him rang loudly, making him jump. It was his brother Ray, cold sober for a change, calling him from Los Angeles.

"Guess where I'm staying?" he asked Gene with a little giggle, clearly pleased with himself. "The Chateau Marmont. De Niro's here, too. I saw him check in."

"What're you doin' in town?"

"I'm meeting with Columbia," Ray said, and he went on to explain that he'd been hired to adapt *The Last Hope,* a darkly compelling novel that took place on the children's ward of a private New England hospital. Derek Ralston, a hot young Brit, was slated to direct, and Ray was going to be paid $100,000 for a first draft and two sets of revisions.

"That's fucking great," Gene told him, using a tiny pause to cover the quick charge of envy that made him wince. "We'll celebrate when I get back."

"Can't. I'm flying out tomorrow."

"Next time then."

"It's a deal."

Before they hung up (and mostly as an afterthought because they had run out of things to say), Ray got around to asking Gene about his trip. "Meet anyone interesting on the plane?"

"Not really. Just a couple of music freaks like me," Gene said, purposely not mentioning Tony Boudreau and their conversation about Bobby Fuller.

Back in the 1970s, Gene had tried to entice his brother into writing a script about Fuller's life and strange death, a rock-and-roll thriller along the lines of *Chinatown*. But Ray had declined the offer after keeping Gene up in the air for a month, saying only that he'd decided to develop one of his own ideas instead. Gene was furious. He took his brother's rejection personally, and for almost two years they didn't speak. Finally, around Thanksgiving in 1980, their father called Gene. He said, "Stop acting like a couple of two-year-olds and shake hands, or I'll write you both out of the will." That Sunday they met for dinner at Musso-Frank and patched things up.

"You meet any chicks?" Ray asked, and Gene told him about the stewardess who was staying at his hotel. He said he was drawn to her in a way that confused him and left him feeling slightly vulnerable.

Ray said, "You're always drawn to women for reasons you don't understand. We both are. That's what happens when your mother leaves home when you're just a little kid."

Gene was instantly sorry that he'd confided in his brother, and now he wanted to find a way to gracefully end the conversation.

"Why do you think I married Sandra?" Ray continued, trying to sound reasonable. "Huh? Think about it. She was fucking nuts, but I was obsessed with her the moment we met."

"Ray?"

"Yeah?"

"You loved her, too."

Ray went silent. Gene waited.

"Right?"

"Yeah, you're right, Gene. I loved her."

Around five o'clock, Gene left his room and took the elevator down to the main lobby. He was wearing a lightweight off-white linen suit over a dark green silk shirt that was open at the neck. As he strolled into The Grotto he felt rested and refreshed, but he kept his face blank, inaccessible, hiding the giddy buzz of anticipation that made him feel both strangely alert and slightly dizzy.

The jazz quartet was on a break and the stools around the circular bar were filled, so Gene remained standing and ordered a double Rum Collins from a cocktail waitress, a dark-complected woman, thirtyish, with pretty eyes and a voice that was almost too low to come from a female. Gene was on his third drink when he saw Alice sitting alone at a small table in a dark corner of the bar, staring into space, her face morose yet her skin beautifully brightened by the crimson wall lamp shining through her hair.

"I'd like to send a drink over to that lady in the corner," Gene told the cocktail waitress the next time she cruised by.

The waitress followed Gene's gaze. "That one's not drinking alcohol," she said, shaking her head.

"What's she drinking?"

"Diet Pepsi."

"I'll buy her one of those."

The waitress rested the serving tray on her cocked hip and gave Gene a look that held just a hint of reproof. "Are you sure?" she said, her dark eyebrows rising while she dropped her voice even a notch lower. "She's already turned down a couple of guys."

"That's okay," Gene said, lifting up his glass. "I'll take a shot."

The waitress just shook her head as she made her way across the room, stopping once to empty an ashtray before she arrived in front of Alice's table. A brief conversation ensued, in which Alice came forward in her chair in a way that seemed to indicate she was either curious or affronted. She then turned and looked over at Gene, and her face crinkled into a smile. Gene smiled back, but a few moments later, as he approached her table with his arms swinging loosely, confidently, he saw her blink, and two silvery tears, evidence of anguish or sorrow, rolled slowly down her cheeks.

The musicians walked back on stage to scattered applause, joined now by an alto saxophonist and a hugely obese black vocalist in her early fifties. Her name was Big Eileen, she announced jovially, then went on to say that she was from Colt, Arkansas, "a little bitty town just across the river from Memphis, the same town where Charlie Rich was born." Then, smiling meaningfully into the crowd, she took out her harmonica and launched into the opening of "Goin' Down Slow," a country-blues number made famous by Muddy Waters.

"Are you alright?" Gene asked Alice, who was dabbing her eyes with the corner of a cocktail napkin.

Alice nodded without looking up. "I'm okay."

"You mind if I sit down?" Gene said, and when she shrugged her shoulders, he slipped into the chair across from her. The band came in behind Big Eileen, who had put away her harmonica and was now singing into the mike with her eyes shut tight.

After the first verse Gene said, "I've got this at home."

"This what?"

"The song they're playing. I've got the original 45," he said, looking pleased with himself. "It came out on the Galaxy label in 1956."

Alice's face was dry, and her fingers were deftly folding the cocktail napkin into a small square. "Is that what you do?" she said, glancing up at him. "Are you a collector?"

"Among other things."

"Oh yeah?" Alice said, and Gene could hear something flirty in her voice. "What other things?"

"Well, I used to be a cop. Now I'm a private investigator."

"A snoop?"

"I own the company," Gene said, "so my employees do most of the snooping. What about you?"

Alice smiled and reached for her drink. "Me?" she said, studying him over the rim of the glass. "You already know all about me."

"I just know you're a stewardess. But I don't know why you were crying."

"I was crying," Alice said and paused for a moment, still staring at Gene, "because I don't want to die."

There was a long silence. Gene gazed back at her with an uncomprehending frown. "I don't get it."

Alice lowered her eyes, retreating into herself for several seconds. Then, speaking in a controlled voice, a voice that was authoritative and cool but that was unable to hide her acute distress, she explained that Ted Stewart, the pilot who flew them from L.A. to New Orleans, had a serious drinking problem. "He's probably an alcoholic."

"And nobody turns him in?"

Alice shook her head.

"That's crazy."

"I know."

After finishing their drinks, they left the hotel (at Alice's suggestion) and walked slowly east on St. Phillip Street, into the spiraling wind blowing off the Mississippi in warm gusts. Ahead of them dark clouds— huge misshapen floating bodies—moved slowly across the horizon, demolishing the light. They passed a cut-rate diner and a saloon with sheets of tin foil covering the windows. Through the open door Gene could see a row of young black men sitting at the bar, wearing snap brim hats and brightly colored shirts and pants. On the jukebox, Howlin' Wolf was singing "Moanin' at Midnight," a top-ten rhythm and blues hit from 1951, and one of Gene's favorite records.

Gene turned away from the veined eyes staring at him suspiciously from inside the bar, and he exchanged a look with Alice, taking in her exquisite face while he followed the curve of his mind back to June of 1964, the year Howlin' Wolf performed live on the TV Show *Hullabaloo* with the Rolling Stones. Gene was in the audience that night and later that week at the Ash Grove, a folk/blues club on Melrose, when Howlin' Wolf took the stage and proceeded to give a performance of such frightening intensity that Gene would talk about it for years.

"I'm not flying back with him tomorrow," Alice said to Gene, clinging to his arm with both hands as they continued up the street. "I just decided right this second. I'm going to call my supervisor when we get back to the hotel. They can find someone to fill in." Gene felt Alice move against him and her fingers tighten on his bicep. "And I'm going to move out of my room and spend the night with you."

*   *   *

"We have secrets," Alice told Gene in bed later that night. She had said it with a smile, simply and playfully, as if it were a postcoital insight that would certify their closeness. "Big ones and little ones. And some that are even the same."

"Like what? Tell me."

"Do you really want to know?" Alice asked him quietly, more serious now.

"Yes," he said, and like her his voice was solemn. "Tell me."

"Neither of us is happy with our lives."

They were lying next to each other, face to face. Alice's expression was detached, impersonal, her blond hair loose on the pillow. Without meeting her eyes, Gene said, a bit challengingly, "But you don't know what my life is all about."

"I can tell you feel the same longing. Making love is just a start for us. We're both trying to push through."

Alice smiled and their lips touched, then their tongues. Gene spoke into her mouth: "All the women I have been with were wrong."

"And all the men."

"Up until now, Alice."

"That's the first time you said my name out loud."

"I know," Gene said.

"That's how you get out of prison," she said, her eyes moving everywhere, and then she smiled as Gene rolled on top of her. "You just say my name."

The following day Gene and Alice got up late and made love deliberately before they ordered a room-service breakfast of Belgian waffles and Cajun sausages. While they were still eating, Gene called Hugo Porter to confirm their appointment later that evening. Porter had not yet checked in, so Gene left a brief message at the front desk, saying he would meet him downstairs in the bar around seven.

"If there's a problem, have him call me," Gene told the clerk on duty.

It was close to four P.M. and the air outside was warm and still when Gene and Alice walked out of the hotel. Although it was their intention to spend an hour or two sightseeing in the French Quarter, they never made it past Clifton's, a blues bar on Decatur Street with a small stage and booths upholstered in black leatherette.

"Why go to a bar if you can't drink?" Alice said to Gene, her eyes a little glassy from the booze. "That's why none of us would ever think of coming in a place like this when we were on a layover. Except Ted, of course." At least twice Alice remembered seeing him hunched over the bar as she walked by the glass window in front of Clifton's on her way back from dinner with the rest of her flight crew. "All of us saw him," she said, raising her voice over the drunken laughter that rang through the bar. "But none of us ever said a word."

"Turn him in when you get back," Gene said, and when she didn't respond he said: "It's the right thing to do."

"You need proof. You can't just accuse someone of something like that."

"But—"

"No, Gene. I don't want to talk about it," Alice said, looking at him steadily until he lowered his eyes. "Let's just have fun."

When Gene and Alice walked into The Grotto at seven sharp, a small black man was seated at the piano with a look of indifference that was way beyond cool. He was dressed immaculately in a gray sharkskin suit, and thick gold rings sparkled on his fingers as they glided across the keys. The song he was playing Alice recognized from a Broadway musical, but she couldn't remember the title.

"That must be Porter," Gene said, nodding toward a portly man with a pink face who was seated at a table against the far wall. In front of him was a small silver bowl filled with mixed nuts and a bottle of champagne. As they moved across the room, Alice said, "How long do you think this will take?"

"I don't know. Depends. Collectors are like dope dealers. They know you want what they have, so they tend to fuck with your mind."

Just before they reached Porter's table, he stood up and smiled. He was wearing white buck shoes and a wrinkled blue-and-white striped seersucker suit. Letting go of Gene's arm, Alice extended her hand and introduced herself first. "Hello," she said, smiling sweetly. "My name is Alice Larson."

"My pleasure," Porter said, kissing the back of her hand, and then he shifted his eyes over to Gene. "Finally, we meet, Mr. Burk."

After the introductions were complete, there was a momentary but awkward silence before they sat down and Porter popped the cork and poured the champagne. "To the music," he said, raising his glass in the air with great dignity. "May it always bring us joy."

For the next hour, Gene and Alice listened politely, trying not to look bored or impatient as Porter steadily filled their glasses and told them the story of his life. An only child who was brought up by his mother in Greenwich, Connecticut, during the 1950s, he mentioned his father almost as an afterthought. "He was a novelist. A fine writer. But painfully slow," Porter said and his droning voice now seemed almost apologetic. "He hung himself when a book that he'd worked on for seven years was rejected by his publisher. I was nine years old at the time."

"Dylan Porter," Alice said.

Porter turned to her in surprise. "You've read him?"

"I read *The Hottest Night of the Year*. It made me want to move to New York."

"I never read any of his novels until I was thirty. Then I read all four in one weekend. To tell you the truth, I remember very little about them."

Around nine Porter glanced at his watch and invited Gene and Alice up to his room, a large two bedroom, high-ceilinged suite on the top floor of the hotel. Once inside, Porter took off his coat and mixed them drinks from a portable bar that was set up on a collapsible card table in the center of the living room. Then, excusing himself, he disappeared into one of the darkened bedrooms, and for thirty seconds Gene and Alice traded quizzical glances while they listened to Porter whispering to someone, possibly a woman, although they were not sure at the time. He returned to the living room with a broad smile on his mouth, carrying a manilla envelope, and Gene quickly started to breathe easier when he saw the outline of the record inside.

"'Big Boy Pants,' a true classic," Porter said as he took a seat next to Alice on the couch. "I was a fatty when I was younger," he said, talking to Alice as if Gene were not in the room, "just like the boy in the song. Well, maybe not fat, roly-poly. Until I was fourteen, that is, when I started to become interested in sex. You look like you're in good shape, Alice. Both of you do."

Gene, who was still standing, now moved over and dropped into an armchair that was diagonally across from Alice. The blank, almost detached expression on his face did not betray his concern or the worried look he saw in her eyes. "It's almost ten," Gene said, after they sat silently for nearly a minute. "We should get out to the festival. Why don't we get the business done and call a cab?"

"Business?" Porter's voice sounded slightly irritated. "I'm not sure what you mean."

"Why do you think we're here?" Gene said, and Alice noticed a new hardness in his voice. "I'm paying you five grand for that record in your lap."

"Oh this," Porter said vaguely, and he tossed the record on the coffee table that sat between them. "You're right. I do recall we made a deal."

Gene reached into the side pocket of his linen jacket, removing a thick roll of one-hundred-dollar bills. He placed the money on top of the manilla envelope. "Deal's done," he said; then he heard a chuckle behind him—a mocking sound—and he felt a spasm of fear in the pit of his stomach. Snapping his head around, he saw a tall, sultry-looking black woman leaning in the doorway of the living room, licking her tangerine-shaded lips. Her head was shaved, and she wore kelly-green silk pajamas that were nearly transparent.

"This is Audrey," Porter said, as she came slowly into the room and sat down on the arm of Gene's chair. "Audrey's my wife."

"I am Hugo's wife. Yes, I am," Audrey said dryly. "Hugo and the Negro. We *are* a pair. But—"

"—a fun pair," Hugo finished for her, and Alice was beginning to smile, although Gene didn't know why.

"Because I knew what was coming," Alice told him later, after they left the Roosevelt and were in a taxi, speeding toward the fairgrounds. "I could tell he was a pervert the second I laid eyes on him in the bar."

"Oh yeah?" Gene said, laughing. "You knew he was gonna offer us a thousand dollars to watch us screw?"

"I knew he was up to something weird. I could just tell."

"You think that was really his wife?"

"No way. She was a hooker. He hired her," Alice said, and Gene was looking at her curiously until she said, "What?"

"If he would've offered us five, would you have done it?"

Alice stared at Gene for several seconds. Then she opened her purse and pulled a cigarette out of a fresh pack of Pall Malls. Lighting it casually, she said, "I hope you're kidding, Gene. I mean I really do."

Gene turned around and looked at the landscape flashing by outside the taxi. They had left the freeway and were driving through a small parish just west of New Orleans that was almost one hundred percent black. They passed a church and Gene cracked the window so he could feel the wind and smell the night air. Very faintly he could hear a choir singing a Christian hymn. Later, when he got back to L.A., he told his brother it was "Rock of Ages," but the truth was he didn't know the name of the song.

What he *did* know was that he turned away from the window and looked into Alice's waiting face. "I love you," he told her, and she released a breath and rested her head back on the seat, obviously taken by surprise.

She kept her eyes shut for several seconds, and when she opened them she saw an airplane cross the sky beyond the windshield. A car behind them whipped past and she said, "You just met me, Gene. You don't know me."

"I know I love you," Gene said, and there was an immense hole of silence. "I know that for sure."

When they arrived at the fairgrounds, Irma Thomas was on stage, backed by the Showmen, the house band for the New Orleans–based label Minit Records. She sang three songs, including her regional hit, the gentle ballad "Ruler of My Heart." She was followed by Memphis harmonica player Buster Brown and a gospel quartet called the Delta Boys. At the stroke of midnight, Johnny Moore came on the main stage with a piano player and two guitarists, all of them dressed alike in bright red suits and shoes.

For what seemed like forever they passed around a bottle while they cross-tuned their instruments, laughing and talking in a good-natured way. Finally, Johnny Moore cleared his throat and sauntered slowly up to the mike. With a sense of gratitude (and high drama) in his voice he said, "It's a great privilege to be here in New Orleans and perform for you folks. Back some years I was in prison not far from where we are now. Angola. That was a bad place. Treated me real bad. Yessir. Worse than any woman I ever been with. I wrote this tune after I got paroled. It's called, 'Devil Woman Blues.'"

Gene felt Alice's fingers clutch his when Johnny Moore threw open his mouth and his eerie falsetto floated over the crowd, holding them spellbound. "I'd give anything to sing like that," Alice said, as the audience exploded with screams and applause. "Just about anything."

In bed that night, after he and Alice made love, Gene felt a swell of loneliness open a secret wound inside his chest. In the half-dark Alice put her hand on his face and stared at him, unable to comprehend why his eyes were suddenly filled with such sorrow and desperation. When she asked him, all he could do was pull her to him and say, "Hold me."

But what he wanted to say and what he *did* say the following morning, while they were intertwined and once again desire streamed between them, was: "I'm afraid."

"Of what?" Alice asked, and when he hesitated, her voice became hard. "Tell me."

Holding her even tighter, Gene tried to explain that he was worried about the unnaturally intense feelings he had for her. And he was frightened that some reckless and irrational part of himself would spin out of control and cause her great harm, driving her away forever.

"Do you want to hurt me?" Alice asked him, as her body went still and she sat up. Gene's eyes were shut and he shook his head slowly from side to side. "Then don't worry so much. Because I'm not going anywhere."

Alice rose quickly out of bed and slipped on her robe. Then she stopped and began to hum along with the song playing on the radio in the room next door. "That was the song he was playing."

Gene looked confused. "Who was playing?"

"The piano player downstairs. It's from the show *Carousel*. It's called 'If I Loved You,'" Alice said. She was still smiling as she walked into the bathroom. "We'll rent the movie sometime and you'll see."

The song "June Is Busting Out All Over" came on while Alice was in the shower and Gene was standing naked in front of the open curtain, letting the sun kiss his face. To himself he said, very softly, almost as a prayer: "To be alive together. This is all I want."

Three

Not Fade Away

Alice's funeral in Cedar Rapids, Iowa, took place on the Sunday following the crash of TWA flight 232. Gene flew in on Saturday, arriving around noon after a brief stopover in Dallas, where he was joined by Marcia Horn, Alice's former roommate and a frequent member of her flight crew. A tall, elegant, light-skinned black woman with prominent eyebrows and a business degree from Southern Methodist University, Marcia had recently married her college sweetheart and moved back to Fort Worth, her hometown.

"I loved Alice dearly. She was the best friend anyone could have," Marcia told Gene, reaching for his hand once they were in the air. "She was kind and never gossiped or talked behind your back like the other girls. And as far as work, she was always willing to do more than her share. But she wouldn't let you take advantage of her; no way. If you tried, she let you know about it. She had a temper, didn't she?"

Gene nodded slowly. Marcia squeezed his hand, and when he looked over he was surprised by the tears that filled her soulful green eyes. "She talked about you all the time," Gene said.

"We were like sisters. We traded clothes and liked the same kind of food. The hotter the better," Marcia said, and there was a pause while she opened her purse and took out an envelope. Inside were Polaroids of her and Alice posed on the beach, their arms around each other's waists, both of them wearing poised smiles and identical white bikinis. Behind them, long clouds shaped like white feathers spanned the perfect blue sky. "These were taken in Key West, the Christmas before last."

"Before we met."

"Yeah."

"I bet you drove the boys crazy," Gene said, smiling, still staring at the picture, his face full of interest. Marcia looked at Gene, but she wasn't smiling back. Instead there was something uncertain in her eyes, a thought withheld. "What's wrong?"

Marcia turned away and looked out the window of the aircraft. Below them, herds of ant-sized cattle grazed in immense, unpenned pastures that were dominated by grain silos and bright red barns.

"I'm gonna miss her. I'm gonna miss her same as you," Marcia said. Then she said something that Gene had trouble grasping right away. "We were lovers, too," she said quickly, stealing a look at Gene. "It only lasted a few months. It started on that trip to Key West."

Gene was silent for a moment. Then he spoke softly, asking her why she was telling him this now.

"I don't know. I guess I wanted you to know. It was a mistake," she said, bowing her head slightly. "I'm sorry."

Gene nodded, but his face didn't change. "It's alright," he said. "It doesn't make any difference."

"Once she started seeing you it was over."

Gene looked a little to the side, keeping his expression neutral while his mind suddenly filled with images of Alice and Marcia lying naked in each other's arms, kissing and making love.

"You look jealous."

"I'm not," Gene said, and the sequence of pictures running inside his head abruptly stopped, leaving him with a feeling of shame and an erection growing against his thigh.

A few minutes later, as they entered the airspace above Cedar Rapids, the "no smoking" light came on and Gene took a final deep drag before he crushed out his cigarette. Then, turning to Marcia, he asked her how well she had known Ted Stewart, the pilot at the controls of Alice's plane when it crashed into the dense woods outside Greencastle, Indiana. She said she knew he was married, a father with three kids, and that he'd served in the Air Force during the Vietnam War.

"He was a P.O.W.," Marcia said right before they touched down. "He spent four years in a camp outside Hanoi. I read where he's going to be buried with full military honors."

Gene was surprised and upset by these revelations, but he waited until they were safely on the ground and the airplane had taxied to a stop before he spoke again. "You know he was a drunk, right?"

Marcia pulled a brush out of her purse and ran it quickly through her red tinted hair. Then she undid her seatbelt and sighed miserably. "I don't want to discuss that," she said, as she stood up to retrieve her raincoat from the overhead compartment.

"It's going to come out in the investigation."

"Maybe."

"Of course it will," Gene said. He was standing in the aisle behind Marcia, waiting for the passengers in front of them to advance toward the exit. "We have to know what happened."

"You already know what happened. The plane crashed and everyone died."

"But—"

"Pilot error, mechanical failure, act of God, don't make no difference. They're all gone," Marcia said, and Gene was momentarily surprised by the hardness in her voice. "Keep your memories and get on with your life."

"Alice was scared to fly with him, especially at night. Twice she called in sick when she was supposed to take the red-eye to Miami."

"The man was a war hero. He had a spotless record."

"Because no one had the guts to say anything," Gene said, as he followed her off the airplane. "You, Alice, no one."

"I don't want to hear no more of this," Marcia said to Gene, glancing over her shoulder as she walked swiftly across the tarmac. Ahead of them was a small terminal that looked almost deserted. "Let the poor child rest in peace."

Gene rented a car, and they drove to the Best Western Inn on Highway 157 and 40th St. On the way they passed the Sacred Heart Academy, the all-girls high school that Alice attended in the mid 1960s. Gene was surprised to see a large green-and-gold banner hanging over the red brick entrance to the main building, snapping in the breeze. It said: "The Beloved Alice Larson—May She Rest In Peace."

"Just like I said," Marcia muttered, and Gene shook his head, turning away from her stubborn face.

After they checked into the motel—Marcia requested a no-smoking room on the second floor, facing away from the highway, so they ended up in separate wings—Gene phoned Hal Larson, Alice's father. He'd spoken to Larson earlier in the week, and they'd made plans to have dinner on Saturday night, the night he arrived. Now Gene was calling to check in and set a time. But when Larson didn't answer after ten rings, he hung up.

Gene had never met her father in person, but the picture Alice kept on her dresser showed a large, spherically shaped man with thick forearms and a blocky head that was completely bald. He was a plumber and a professional locksmith, and, until he'd retired a few years back, he'd owned Larson's Hardware in Mt. Vernon, a small town just east of Cedar Rapids.

"He started losing his hair around fifteen," Alice told Gene, when she first unpacked the picture. "By the time he was married he looked like this." Gene said he looked like a strong man. "He was a wrestler in high school. When he was a senior, he won the state championship in Iowa City. After he sold his store, he started coaching part time over at Benjamin McKinley. Between that, his garden, and goofin' around with his buddies, he keeps plenty busy."

Next door to the Best Western was a shopping plaza that was anchored by a JCPenney and a multiplex theater. To kill time Gene went to a matinee of *The Little Drummer Girl*, the film adaptation of the John Le Carré novel, starring Diane Keaton playing a vengeful pro-Palestinian British actress, a character that was obviously inspired by Vanessa Redgrave. Although he had not read the novel, the film was so flat and predictable that Gene left before it was half over. On his way back to the motel he noticed Marcia Horn sitting at a table in the window of the coffee shop. When she looked over, he waved and smiled, and she held up a copy of the local newspaper. On the front page was a picture of Alice. She was dressed in her TWA uniform, smiling underneath a headline that read: *Air Tragedy Claims One of Our Own.*

Gene bought a newspaper from the rack outside the coffee shop. Reading the obituary as he walked across the gravel parking lot with his back to the high sun, he heard a woman's insolent laughter coming from inside one of the nearby rooms. Suddenly, his legs became unsteady and his heartbeat seemed to speed up. "My God, she's gone," he whispered in desolation, holding back a terrible need to scream, and once more he let the tears come.

Hal Larson called Gene's room around six. He said he'd spent the afternoon playing golf. "It's my regular Saturday game. I thought about canceling but I guess it's better to keep busy. Too much time to think is bad for me," he said, and then he apologized for not switching on his answering machine. "I'm starting to forget a lot of things these days. Drives me crazy."

Gene was silent. On the other end of the line he could hear Dan Rather's voice on the evening news. The television in the motel room was off, and so were the lights.

"You like steak, Gene?"

"Sure."

"I'll take you to Smokey's. They got the best beef in the state. I'll pick you up around seven-thirty."

"How did you know where I was staying?"

"Called around. Only so many motels in town."

Before they hung up, Gene told Larson that he'd read Alice's obituary in the *Cedar Rapids Gazette.* Trying not to sound angry or hurt, he asked why his name was not mentioned anywhere in the story.

"I don't know," Larson said, a little confused.

"I was her fiancé."

"Yes. That's true. When the paper called I was pretty upset. I guess I left it out. I'm sorry," Larson said in a quiet voice.

"They had quotes from a lot of people I never heard of, like her high school soccer coach."

"Tell you the truth, Gene, I didn't read it."

"Did you know she could body-surf?" Gene said. "You probably didn't."

"You're right. I didn't know that."

"I taught her. I even bought her a wetsuit for her birthday, so she could practice in the winter."

"Alice was a darn good swimmer," Larson muttered. "I remember that."

"She was good with tools, too. She could fix stuff around the house. And she never complained when she got sick. None of that was in the story."

"I don't know what to tell you, except I'm sorry," Larson said, his tone reasonable and restrained. "But I do know God is holding her close."

Throughout dinner Hal Larson was achingly shy and spoke very little, sometimes staying silent for minutes at a time. But as they sipped their coffee and waited for the check, he suddenly straightened up in his chair and began to talk about his wife for the first time. Her name was Margaret, and they'd met and started going steady while they were still in junior high.

"None of my friends thought the marriage would last. They said she was too good for me. They meant too good-looking. She was beautiful— like Alice," Larson said, and Gene smiled. "We had some good years, and I'm grateful for them. All the time I was with her I never once thought of another woman."

Alice's mother, who was later diagnosed as a schizophrenic, left Cedar Rapids in the summer of 1964, the summer Alice turned thirteen. For the next four months, Margaret Larson proceeded on a weird, almost demented series of wanderings from coast to coast, back and forth from Myrtle Beach to Seattle, Newark to Los Angeles. She only called home once, on Alice's birthday, from the Greyhound bus station in Odessa, Texas.

"Don't worry about me," she told Alice in a fear-choked voice. "I'm just searching for a friendly place, a place where I can put my head down and pain won't give me the time of day."

Exhausted and viewing the world through a haze of unreality, Margaret Larson filed for divorce on November 7, 1964, in Los Angeles, while she was living in a welfare hotel behind the Salvation Army mission. For the next six solid weeks, all she did was listen to country music and read true-crime paperbacks that she stole from the downtown branch of the L.A. Public Library. When her money finally ran out, she found a job working nights at a steakhouse in Inglewood, across from the Hollywood Park racetrack.

"She was a hostess at this place called the Buggy Whip. Looked a little like Smokey's," Larson said. "Lots of wood, and the booths had the same color leather. But the beef couldn't hold a candle. How was your porterhouse by the way?"

"Great," Gene said, and he meant it: It was probably the tenderest piece of meat he'd ever eaten.

"Prime, corn-fed, Iowa beef. The absolute best."

Throughout the fall and winter of 1964, Hal Larson regularly telephoned his wife in Los Angeles, shamelessly pouring out his love and begging her to return home. But shortly after the new year, when she declined to take his calls at work and unlisted her home phone number, he flew out to confront her in person.

"I didn't know what else to do," Larson said. "I couldn't believe she was throwing everything away, just starting over without me and Alice."

The Buggy Whip was located on La Tijera Boulevard, just a few miles north of the airport. Reputedly owned by Tony (Two Speed) Carnera, a made member of an East Coast crime family and an associate of Carl Reese, the restaurant had become, since the early 1950s, a popular hangout for those semistraight gamblers and sports freaks who liked to rub shoulders with powerful underworld types. During racing season or when the Lakers played at home, the bar was always sprinkled with Hollywood celebrities and the best-looking hookers in the city; and there was a persistent rumor that a high-stakes poker game convened after hours in a private room upstairs, where regulars like Frank Sinatra and Tony Curtis sometimes lost up to $50,000 in one night.

"When I walked in the front door I didn't see Margaret right away," Larson said, and his face tightened into a frown. "Her hair was dyed blond, and she was wearing this spangly green dress that was cut so low you could almost see her nipples. When she saw me, her mouth dropped open, and I thought she was going to scream. I told her we needed to talk. She said there was nothing to say, and that coming to Los Angeles was a bad idea. I told her I loved her too much to let her just walk away from me without putting up a fight. I think I might've grabbed her arm, and when I did someone spun me around and smashed his fist into my face. I'm a strong man, and I know how to take care of myself in a fair fight, but this was different. Four or five men—big men—came out of nowhere and dragged me outside, where they proceeded to beat me senseless with their fists. If Margaret hadn't screamed for them to stop, I probably would be dead right now."

A taxi was called and Hal Larson's inert body was transported to the emergency room at Centinela Hospital. There the resident physician on duty did his best to reset Larson's broken nose and close the deep gashes above his eyes. By noon the following day, he was on a flight back to Cedar Rapids.

"Three years later she came back home. Three years to the day," Larson said. They were now through with dinner, and Alice's father was driving Gene back to his motel. "But she wasn't the same. Maybe it was the liquor or the drugs, I don't know, but something inside her mind was gone. It was terrible for Alice, those years. It was the sixties, remember, and you saw the youngsters running away from home—and you came to expect it—but not the mothers."

Twice more over the next eighteen months Margaret Larson left Cedar Rapids, and each time she returned her mental decline was more obvious. Then one morning Hal Larson opened his newspaper and saw that Margaret had married a county commissioner from Davenport, an older man named Forrest Odom. And there was a picture—Margaret wore a flowered blouse and a bewildered stare—the same picture that made the front page a year later.

"When she was arrested for attempted murder. She tried to stab him," Larson told Gene, as they sat in front of the Best Western with the engine still running in his Chevy pick-up. "Alice probably told you the story."

"She said she went off to college, and you went down to Davenport for the trial."

"Old man Odom refused to testify against her, and Margaret got off. Not long afterwards, maybe three weeks, some teenagers found her walking naked in the woods up near Marshalltown. She ended up in the State Hospital in Westhaven. And she's been there ever since."

"Does she know Alice is dead?"

"If she does, she didn't get the news from me."

The morning of Alice's funeral was cold and overcast, and a ragged wind intermittently shook the bare branches of the tall poplars that ringed the Cedar Memorial Cemetery. Standing around the gravesite, besides Hal Larson and Gene and Alice's TWA colleagues, were several relatives from both sides of the family; nephews and nieces; friends from high school, about forty altogether, many who were now married, with their children; another seventy-five Cedar Rapids people, ordinary men and women who knew Alice and her family only casually but came to pay their respects.

Alice's mother, dressed in a soiled green trench coat over hospital pajamas, stood in the front row with a dazed look in her eyes, displaying none of the grief one associates with a mother who has lost her child. Standing beside her like bowling pins were two pear-shaped orderlies, one black and one white.

Marcia and a woman Gene did not recognize sang "Amazing Grace" and "Blessed Be the Tie That Binds." Afterwards the Methodist minister, a very handsome man with strong features and pale blue eyes, spoke for several minutes, emphasizing how loved Alice had been, and how her giving spirit touched the lives of everyone she met.

"But the lord giveth and the lord taketh away," he said, as the casket was lowered into the ground. Then his voice suddenly became fierce.

"Remember only thy last things—death, judgment, hell, heaven—and thou shalt not sin forever!"

After the funeral, Gene approached Alice's mother as the orderlies maneuvered her haltingly up a narrow pathway, past the headstones and concrete markers, toward the parking lot. When he drew alongside and tried to introduce himself, the black orderly interrupted him: "Can't be talkin' to Miss Margaret now. You want to visit, you come out to the hospital during visiting hours."

"I was engaged to her daughter," Gene said. "I just wanted to say hello."

Margaret Larson stopped walking and turned and squinted into Gene's face. At first she seemed repelled by what she saw, then she started to giggle. After a few seconds she stopped.

"Dust to dust," she whispered. Then she puckered her lips and shimmied her shoulders in a way that was almost obscene. "Dust to fucking dust."

Gene followed a caravan of cars back to Hal Larson's small white frame house, which held a corner lot on the northwest edge of town. The house, shaded by maples and surrounded by plots of zinnias and marigolds, looked well manicured on the outside; but inside there were damp spots on the walls and the curtains and window shades were covered with a thin layer of dust. In the kitchen there were bags of newspapers and garbage stacked in the corners, and the sink was overflowing with foul-smelling dishes.

The mourners were congregated on the big open back porch, where there was a table piled with church-made sandwiches and bowls of fruit salad and punch. Gene remained standing in the living room for a minute or two, admiring the waist-high, antique wooden radio that sat against a wall underneath a painting of a sailing ship. Next to the radio was a book-case, which contained the *King James Bible*, *Alice in Wonderland*, *Heidi*, a set of *Wonder Books*, several dozen paperback mysteries, and a stack of old magazines. On a bottom shelf was a chess set, a Monopoly game, and some jigsaw puzzles.

Alice's bedroom was at the end of a short hallway off the dining area. The room was empty except for an oak dresser and a small single bed that was covered with light blue flannel sheets and a navy-blue blanket. The closet was, surprisingly, crammed with winter and summer clothing. On the floor was a regulation-size basketball, a tennis racquet, skates, a dollhouse, and a large cardboard box.

"Any of this stuff is yours," Hal Larson said, and Gene spun around, startled, and they stared at each other in silence. "Go on," Larson said, looking miserable. "Take what you want. Her old skates, tennis racquet, whatever." He stopped speaking for a moment, then pointed at the cardboard box. "That box is hers, too."

Gene looked weakly out the dusty window, then back to Larson. "I'm sorry. I shouldn't have come in here."

"Don't apologize. Nothing wrong with looking at her things. She was precious to you. You loved her."

"So did you," Gene said softly.

"Yes," Hal said, blinking back tears. "I did."

Along with an armload of clothing, Gene took the cardboard box out to his rental car. It was filled with school papers (and a five-year diary that was stuffed with photographs and letters that he would not find until he arrived back in Los Angeles). After locking everything in the trunk, he stood in the street beside the driver's side door, debating whether to leave now, which he was inclined to do, or go back inside and say goodbye. When he glanced over at the house, he saw Marcia Horn standing on the front steps, holding a piece of angel food cake in a paper napkin.

"What's up?" she said, and Gene just shrugged. Marcia took a bite out of the cake and chewed it slowly while she moved down the white gravel driveway that bordered the leafless lawn. Feeling tired and strangely ill at ease, Gene walked around the car and joined her on the sidewalk.

"What time's your flight?" Marcia asked him.

"Tomorrow morning. What about you?"

"Tonight."

Gene felt rain begin to fall in a slow drizzle. Above them the power lines waved in the wind, and, across the street, a woman with a gaunt face was kneeling on the lawn, clipping her ragged hedge with heavy shears. Marcia broke off a piece of white cake and held it in front of Gene's lips.

"Open," she said, and Gene loosened his mouth, swallowing the cake in one bite. Marcia smiled. "Come on," she said, "let's go back inside."

Gene shook his head.

"Why?"

"I'm leaving."

Marcia reached out and put a hand on his wet wrist. "Where you off to, Gene?"

"I have to see something."

"What?"

"This place. This farm up in Clear Lake," Gene said, closing his eyes. After a moment or two, he felt a shooting pain in his lower spine, and inside his head a muffled scream faded into an echoing silence. When he blinked open his eyes, he saw a bolt of lightning crack the skyline like a pane of glass, causing the clouds to glitter like polished silver coins. "He was there."

"Who?"

"Hal Larson. He was in Clear Lake that night," Gene said, speaking slowly, hypnotically. "He was at the show."

"What show?"

"At the Surf Ballroom."

"I don't know what the hell you're talking about," Marcia said, staring at Gene for a moment, expressionless, before she turned and started across the lawn. At the front door she stopped and spun around. "You best be careful, Gene Burk. You hear?"

Gene raised his hand and waved goodbye. "Yeah. You too."

Before he drove away, Gene noticed a woman behind the wheel of an ancient green Volvo parked across the street. The window was down and she was staring at him and past him, at Alice's house, with a subdued recognition. When her gaze swung back to Gene's face, she said, "I knew Alice. We grew up together. We weren't friends, but I knew who she was. I cared about her."

"Then you should go inside," Gene said, "and pay your respects."

The woman's eyes went back to the house and she let out a little laugh.

"No. I don't think I need to go inside," she said, starting the engine. "Nobody would be happy with that."

"Why is that?"

"Why?" the woman asked, and Gene saw her face quickly go from irritation to acceptance. "Because that's the way it is."

Clear Lake was one hundred and fifty miles northwest of Cedar Rapids. Driving into a steady downpour, Gene kept the speedometer at an even seventy until the moon disappeared and the sky exploded, raining down hail with such force that it felt like someone was dropping rocks on the roof of his car. Twice he nearly ran off the road, before he finally stopped at an empty, nondescript diner on the outskirts of Waterloo.

He drank three cups of coffee at the counter while he hummed along with the country jukebox and stared out the long dark windows, waiting for the intensity of the storm to subside. The waitress, a shrewd but cheap-looking woman with a flat chest and uncombed red hair, gazed at him blankly when he told her he was visiting from Los Angeles.

"My fiancée was from Cedar Rapids. She died a week ago," Gene said and grimaced. "I came back for her funeral."

"I'm terribly sorry," the waitress said, her voice toneless and her expression as empty as a clock without hands. "I don't know what to say."

"I got some of her clothes in my car," Gene said. "Stuff she wore growin' up. I'm not sure why I took them," he said, still looking pained. "I just did. They're yours if you want them."

The waitress glanced at Gene while she lit a cigarette with a square silver lighter that she found in her apron. "I got enough clothes," she said warily. "But thanks anyway."

"You probably know someone who could use them. Or you can give them away if you want. I'll be right back," Gene said, and he quickly stood up and walked outside.

Seconds later he reentered the diner a little off balance, carrying several coats and dresses on heavy wooden hangers. After he dropped everything on an empty table and wiped the rain off his face, he said, "Take your pick. There's a lot of nice stuff here."

"I don't want to be responsible for any of this," the waitress said, sounding more aloof than annoyed. "I already told you that."

"Then burn them," Gene said.

The waitress gazed into Gene's face while she tried to think of something to say. Then she came around the counter and walked over to the window facing the highway. "Rain's slacked up," she said. "Maybe you better get going."

When she turned and looked at him, they were standing together in a chilly silence. Finally Gene said, "I'm not dangerous."

"I didn't say you were."

"I'm just sad and a little bit confused."

The waitress nodded. "If you leave now," she said, "I'll take care of her clothes."

"I'd appreciate that," Gene said, sounding both grateful and sad. "Thanks."

Gene drove the next seventy miles with the radio tuned to KOMA, a 250,000-watt classic rock station that was broadcasting out of Oklahoma City. The disc jockey—he called himself Cherry Terry the Rockin' Robin—played ten straight hits from 1957, including "Long, Lonely Nights" by Clyde McPhatter and "Party Doll" by Buddy Knox, two of Gene's favorite oldies.

Toward the end of the hour, Cherry Terry mentioned that Buddy Knox was produced by Norman Petty, the same man who discovered and recorded Buddy Holly and the Crickets. "Petty had this studio in Clovis, New Mexico," Cherry Terry said, "which was about a hundred miles from El Paso, where I worked for a year back in the early 1960s, when I was just starting out. Our next tune is by a fella from Goose Neck, Texas, a little bitty town right next door. His name is Bobby Fuller, and he fought the law and the law won."

By the time the record ended, the rain had stopped and Gene was parked on the shoulder of a two-lane highway, idling next to a grain elevator. If his map was correct, he was exactly eight-and-a-half miles southwest of Mason City. Back in 1969, Buddy Holly headlined a twenty-four-date Winter Dance Party Tour that included a one-night performance at the Surf Ballroom in the nearby community of Clear Lake. On the bill with Holly were Richie Valens, The Big Bopper, Waylon Jennings, and Dion and the Belmonts.

The show in Clear Lake—it was the eleventh on the tour—was played before an estimated crowd of fifteen hundred screaming fans. The concert ended around eleven, and the performers signed autographs for another hour outside the ballroom in the freezing rain. When it came time to leave, Buddy and The Big Bopper decided to rent a Beechcraft Bonanza to fly them to their next date in Fargo, North Dakota.

"Fuck the bus," Buddy supposedly said to Richie Valens, who had won a coin toss with Tommy Allsup, Buddy's guitar player, for the third seat on the plane. "We're stars. From now on we're gonna travel in style."

But that didn't sound like Buddy, Gene thought, as he looked away from the headlights of a passing car. Buddy was a humble, down-to-earth kid with heavy-rimmed black glasses and a friendly smile. Certainly he was confident, but he was also a young man who was deeply thankful for his sudden success.

Gene killed the engine. In the distance he heard a lone dog howl, and off to his left he saw a flock of ducks settle, then disappear into a muddy field of ripe corn. In the clearing sky, clouds shaped like long black fingers were circled around the bright yellow moon, caressing it like a crystal ball.

Gene lowered the window, and the breeze that spilled down and stirred his hair was warmer than he expected. Then, after a moment, he clicked off the radio and closed his eyes, allowing his imagination to find the three young rockers inside that small aircraft:

Before taking off into the bitterly cold rainy night, Buddy and Richie are talking fast and smoking cigarettes, still high from the show. Buddy misses his fiancée, Maria Elena Santiago, and he tells Richie that he can't wait until he gets back to New York City, where they now live. Richie talks about *his* sweetheart, Donna Ludwig, and how she's pushing him to get married and have kids.

"But I'm not ready to settle down," Richie says.

"Do you love her?"

"Yeah, a lot."

"That's the only thing that matters. If she knows that," Buddy says, "then she'll wait."

The Big Bopper—his real name is Jape Richardson—is dozing when the pilot starts the single engine. Only twenty-four, Richardson had already worked as a DJ for five years when "Chantilly Lace," his self-penned novelty tune, sold a million records and made him a star. The station where he's now on the air—KTRM in Beaumont, Texas—has given him a leave of absence to go on this tour.

The Big Bopper will come awake while the plane is going down, spinning crazily toward the earth. Although he knows he is going to die, he won't curse or cry out, and the last thing he will see is a white flame that is so bright that he knows it must be the hand of God.

Roger Peterson piloted the Beechcraft Bonanza that crashed in bad weather over Clear Lake, Iowa, on February 2, 1959, killing Buddy Holly, Richie Valens, and The Big Bopper. The light aircraft was owned by the Dwyer Flying Service, and both Jim Dwyer and Peterson were on Hal Larson's high school wrestling team.

Alice had told Gene this fact one night shortly after she'd moved into his house in Topanga Canyon. "That's very bizarre," Gene said. "Your dad was friends with the pilot who went down with Buddy Holly."

"He was there that night at the concert. All three of them were there."

"You sure you're not making this up?"

"Why would I make up something like that."

* * *

Right before he started the engine and pulled back on the highway, Gene felt the darkness thicken, and a melody began to play inside his head. The words, when they came, were both dark and innocent, backed by a harsh guitar and an obsessive, rhythmic drumbeat.

> *You say you're gonna leave me*
> *You know it's a lie*
> *'Cause that'll be the day*
> *When I die.*

Four

Ten Miles

from Tulsa

After he flew back to Los Angeles and walked inside his silent house, Gene was plunged into a cycle of depression and anxiety that he couldn't shut off. For two weeks he swam in this sea of suffering, keeping the curtains closed and refusing to answer his phone; and when he was not lost in grief, gasping from pain that was beyond his comprehension, he padded slowly from room to room in his robe and slippers, fighting the nearly overwhelming urge to let go, to kill himself.

On the Sunday morning of the second week, Gene took a long hot shower and brewed a pot of fresh coffee. Then, in a dazed yet matter-of-fact way, he picked up the phone and called Eddie Cornell. After four rings the machine answered, and Gene hung up without listening to the outgoing message. Next he tried dialing his brother, but Barbara, Ray's girlfriend for the past two years, said that he'd just walked out the door.

"He went for a run. He'll be back in an hour," she said, sounding both excited and relieved to hear Gene's voice. "He's been trying to reach you for days."

"Yeah, I know."

The phone went silent for a moment. Then Barbara said quietly, "How are you, Gene?"

"I'm okay. How's Ray?"

"Good. He's doing a polish on *The Last Hope*. They're supposed to go into production in May. And it looks like Louie got the lead in an off-Broadway play."

"That's great," Gene said absently, as if she'd lost his attention. "Look, I gotta go."

"Gene?"

"Yeah?"

"Ray knows what it's like to lose someone he loves. We both do."

Gene shook his head but said nothing. He wanted this conversation to end. "Tell him I called," he said, and he put down the receiver without saying goodbye.

Gene poured a second cup of coffee, turned on the stereo, and began to play *With a Little Help from My Friends,* the debut album by Joe Cocker. After the third cut, he lost interest and switched it off, sulking a moment before he wandered into his den, where he stood sideways in the doorway for at least a minute, listening to the wind chimes on the deck. Finally, almost mechanically, he took a seat behind his desk and opened the bottom right-hand drawer.

Stacked almost to the top were back issues of teen magazines from the fifties and sixties (*Flip, Teenset, Go,* etc.), slick monthlies that were part of a memorabilia collection he'd purchased from a dealer in Racine, Wisconsin. He found an issue of *Tiger Beat* from September 1967. The cover photo, taken backstage at the Monterey Pop Festival, showed Jimi Hendrix standing alongside Brian Jones of the Rolling Stones. Janis Joplin was sitting on a folding chair in the corner of the frame, wearing a silver see-through net top and a fur pillbox hat.

Inside the magazine was an article about the Lovin' Spoonful and an interview with Chris Hillman and Jim McGuinn of the Byrds. There were also more pictures from Monterey Pop, including a candid shot of Monkee Micky Dolenz dressed as an American Indian, clearly stoned out of his mind, dancing with an unquestionably pretty but not too innocent-looking girl who was smiling unattractively. In another photo on the same page, Mama Cass clowned for the camera, holding up a hot dog while she puffed on a huge joint.

Gene's hands seemed to be shaking a little as he continued to page through *Tiger Beat,* stopping to stare at a picture of Bobby Fuller posed outside the Hollywood Brown Derby with his arm around the shoulder of a plump teenage girl. The accompanying article, written by Lenore

McGowan, the president of the Bobby Fuller Fan Club and the girl in the picture, told of the "dream day" she and Bobby spent together on June 17, 1966, just a month before he died.

According to Lenore, "We met for lunch at the Brown Derby on Vine Street. I had one of their famous chopped salads, and Bobby had a cheeseburger cooked extra rare with a double order of fries. For dessert we both had hot fudge sundaes at C.C. Brown's, this really cute ice cream parlor up on the boulevard next to the Grauman's Chinese Theatre.

"Later that afternoon we went to Gold Star, this famous recording studio on Santa Monica Boulevard, and there Bobby played me the single, 'A Magic Touch,' from his new album. Afterwards, he took me down the hall to watch producer Phil Spector record the Righteous Brothers. There was this huge orchestra with a full horn section, strings, and two drummers. Tina Turner and Ronnie Bennett, the lead singer from the Ronettes, were also in the studio, singing background vocals. What an amazing experience—to watch a record actually being made! Bobby thinks Phil is a genius.

"Before we left the studio, Bobby got a phone call that he took in a private office. He was gone for about twenty minutes, and when he drove me back to my motel on La Brea, he seemed kind of preoccupied. Even so, he came up to my room and recorded an interview that I gave to KWSC, the local rock station in Springfield, Missouri, my hometown. Then he was nice enough to sign fifty of his 8 x 10's. When he was finished, he called Melanie Novack, this woman who lived in his building and typed up his song lyrics. She and Bobby were close, and the three of us were supposed to have dinner that evening, but Melanie had a cold. I could tell Bobby was really tired, so I said he could take a rain check, too. Then I walked him down to his car, where he said goodbye, kissed me on the cheek, then drove away.

"And that, readers, was my 'dream day' with Bobby Fuller."

Gene put the magazine aside and sat feeling the anguish of loneliness while he doodled on a yellow Post-it with a red felt tip pen. He wrote down Eddie Cornell's number, circled it twice, and then picked up the phone. This time Eddie answered in the middle of the second ring.

"Cornell here."

"Eddie, what's up?"

"Gene! When did you get back?"

"Couple of weeks ago."

"You alright?"

"Fair."

Eddie made a commiserating sound. "I was gonna check in. But then I figured I'd give you some space," he said, and there was a long silence. "What can I do for you?"

"I want to look over the Fuller files."

"Fuller?"

"Bobby Fuller, the rock and roller who died back in '66. It was ruled a suicide, but we were never sure."

"I was sure. I thought he killed himself."

"You didn't work the case, Eddie."

"I read all the reports."

Gene could feel himself getting irritated. He rested his forehead on his hand, taking a moment to get his thoughts together. "Eddie, listen to me—"

"I can't give you the files," Eddie said, interrupting Gene with considerable force. "You know the regulations."

"Fuck the regulations." Gene slammed his fist down on the top of the desk. "I need something to do. I need to take my mind off her."

"Can't do it, Gene."

"Two days. That's all I need," Gene said. His voice was weak, almost frightened. "Help me out, Eddie. Please."

"Jesus-fucking-Christ! You get twenty-four hours!" Eddie roared, giving in unwillingly. "That's it, amigo. That's all you get."

"Twenty-four hours. That's fine," Gene said, his expression satisfied as he picked up the magazine and rolled it into a tight cylinder. "I'll take it."

"Revells. Monday at four."

"I'll be there, Eddie."

"Gene?"

"Yeah?"

"I'm sorry about Alice." Eddie's voice was softer and unexpectedly sad. "I know how much you loved her."

Gene nodded without speaking. "Monday four P.M. sharp," he said. "I'll see you then."

Revells, which was located on the corner of Las Palmas and Selma, one block south of Hollywood Boulevard, had played a minor but distinctive part in L.A.'s most famous unsolved murder. Back in February of 1947, Elizabeth Short, the victim in the brutal Black Dahlia slaying, was observed drinking at the bar several hours before her naked body was found surgically bisected, the two halves placed side by side in a nearby vacant lot.

According to Clyde Phoebe, a Hollywood stuntman quoted in the *Los Angeles Examiner,* "She came in alone, but she left with this Spanish looking fella around midnight." And that, the article concluded, was the last time anyone saw her alive.

Clyde Phoebe was from Claremore, Oklahoma, the same town where singer Patti Page was born. In fact, he and Patti were childhood sweethearts and just about ready to be engaged when he was drafted into the U.S. Army on his eighteenth birthday. Patti abruptly stopped writing to him after basic training, and by the time Clyde was discharged in 1945, she had left Claremore and was already on her way to stardom, singing nightly on the radio in Tulsa. She had also become romantically involved with Leon McCaullife, the guitarist for Bob Wills and the Texas Playboys.

After a three-day drunk that did little to mend his broken heart, Clyde woke up on a Greyhound bus headed down to Los Angeles. Within a week he got a job wrangling livestock on *Red River,* Howard Hawks's masterful portrayal of the early west and the cattle drive that opened the Chisholm Trail; and by 1965, the year Sam Peckinpah hired him to coordinate the action sequences and play a U.S. Cavalry trooper in his production of *Major Dundee,* Clyde was the most sought-after stuntman in Hollywood. But his career ended on that location in Durango, Mexico, when his horse spooked and fell while jumping a ravine, throwing him hard, shattering several vertebrae in his back and damaging his spinal cord.

When Gene first got to know him in 1967, Clyde was collecting disability and filling in behind the bar at Revells when one of the regular bartenders was sick or on vacation. Now he worked a steady shift from three till midnight and—surprise!—there were twenty-one songs by Patti Page on the jukebox.

"Peckinpah was a helluva guy. A real man's man," Clyde told Gene on Monday afternoon, while he was waiting for Eddie Cornell. "But when he got drunk, he went totally off the rails. On *Dundee* he and Chuck Heston couldn't stand each other, always arguing about politics. One night Sam nearly shot him outside this local cantina."

"Heston wasn't a bad actor."

"He was okay in *Ben-Hur*. And I liked him in that Orson Welles picture. Played a Mexican."

"*Touch of Evil.*"

"That's the one."

Gene drained his beer and Clyde poured him one more, saying it was on the house. In a few moments a girl stepped inside Revells wearing a black T-shirt and tight black jeans. She had an unhappy, slightly beat-up face and blond hair that was combed in bangs to hide the acne scars on her forehead.

She ordered a shot of Jack Daniel's, paying for her drink with a twenty-dollar bill that she slapped on the bar. When Clyde came back with the change, she scooped up some quarters and swaggered over to the jukebox.

"What do you want to hear?" she asked Gene, as she passed by his shoulder.

"Something by Patti Page."

The girl reacted with a laugh. "Like we have some choice. Hey!" she yelled over to Clyde, putting some sarcasm into her voice. "Don't you think it's time you got over her? Talk about carrying a fucking torch."

Clyde glanced at the girl while he rinsed a glass, then warned: "Don't push it, Claudia. I'm not in the mood."

The girl gave Gene a wink while she fed the change into the machine. "Okay, let's see," she said, sticking out her ass as she leaned into the glass. "What shall it be? 'Old Cape Cod'? 'Mockingbird Hill'?"

"Play D-6," Clyde said.

"'Broken Hearts and a Pillow Filled with Tears.' That sounds upbeat."

"Just play the song."

"My quarter," the girl said, glancing over her shoulder, and Clyde gave her an unsmiling look. A few seconds later the introduction came on to "Dear Hearts and Gentle People."

When the girl came back to the bar, Clyde said to Gene, "Comes in every day just to fuck with me."

"Oh stop it, Clyde," the girl said, smiling quickly. "You know I think you're the best."

Gene took a swallow of beer and looked down at his watch. When he saw that it was already four-fifteen, he felt a rush of anxiety, wondering if Eddie was going to show.

"Did I tell you about the last time I saw Patti?" Clyde said. He was standing in front of the girl while she hummed along with the jukebox. "Stop me if I did."

"Go ahead," the girl said, closing her eyes but keeping her face attentive. "Tell me."

"It was in Vegas," Clyde said, his deep voice filled with longing, "in the summer of 1959. She was playing the Sands, opening for Sinatra and Sammy Davis, Jr. When she saw me in the audience, she made me stand up. She said, 'Ladies and gentlemen, I'd like to introduce Clyde Phoebe. He's from my hometown, Claremore, Oklahoma, which is ten miles from Tulsa and the birthplace of Will Rogers. Clyde took me to my senior prom way back in 1943. Let's give him a nice hand.' Then everyone stood up and clapped like I was some big-shot high roller, and Patti dedicated her next song to me."

The girl opened her eyes. She said gently, "'Come What May'?"

"Nope. 'My First Formal Gown.'"

"That is so perfect, Clyde."

"She brought the microphone into the audience and sang it right into my eyes. Just me and her in the dark with the spotlight shining on our faces. God, she was just as gorgeous as ever."

At four-thirty Eddie Cornell entered Revells through the rear door, carrying four rust-colored accordion files that bulged with papers. He was wearing off-brand blue jeans, worn sneakers, and a wrinkled white polo shirt that fit him tight across his burly chest.

"Let's sit over here," Eddie said to Gene, pointing at a table in the corner of the bar. Then he peeled open a pack of cigarettes and signaled Clyde for a drink. "Double Jack Daniel's with a beer chaser. And another for my partner."

"He's kind of cute," the girl said, as she watched Gene cross the room.

Clyde shook his head. "Forget it. He's not for you."

"How would you know?"

"Trust me."

Gene took a seat across from Eddie. Neither spoke for several seconds. "I Confess" came on the jukebox and Eddie pointed at the files, which were stacked in the center of the table. With a motion of his hand, he indicated they were now Gene's property. "But keep in mind," he said, "I need them back tomorrow by five."

"Got it."

Clyde limped over to the table with their drinks on a small tray. Eddie reached for his wallet and Clyde said, "Claudia wants to buy this round."

Eddie turned his head and glanced at the girl, who smiled nervously before she lowered her eyes.

"Tell her no thanks."

The girl heard Eddie but showed no irritation or surprise. She almost seemed pleased. As Clyde moved away, Gene said, "I appreciate you doin' this."

"No big deal. I just wish you'd get involved in something more . . ."

"What?"

"I don't know. Productive."

"How do you know I'm not gonna solve this thing."

"You're not gonna solve shit," Eddie said, staring hard at him. "And who cares anyway?"

"I care."

"I don't get it. If it was Elvis, I could understand. But this guy, he's just some footnote, a one-hit wonder."

Gene was quiet a moment, ignoring Eddie's deep-sunk eyes. Then he finished his beer and stood up. "I'll get this one."

When he got back to the table, Eddie was standing by the pay phone, glancing at a notepad while he punched in a number. After a quick, whispered conversation, he hung up and moved languidly back to his seat.

"We caught a triple homicide last night up in Laurel Canyon," he said. "Two chicks and a guy. Early twenties. No bullets. Just club and knives. Blood fucking everywhere. Even on the ceiling."

"Drugs."

"Most likely. But who knows," Eddie said and shrugged. He took a long pull on his beer. Then he leaned forward and his face seemed to darken and grow serious. "I got something I have to tell you, Gene. You may not like it, and part you're not gonna believe." Eddie stopped and looked down at the table, embarrassed. "I got it on with your brother's ex-wife before she died."

Gene looked at Eddie with curiosity while he processed this information. "Sandra? You're talking about Sandra? You fucked her?"

Eddie nodded. "After you got her the apartment in my building, we kinda became buddies."

"Does Ray know about this?"

"No. It just went on for a couple of months."

Gene and Eddie were silent a long time. The tune ended on the jukebox, and the girl turned on her stool and smiled in their direction. Then she lit a fresh cigarette and stood up, saying, "I think I'll play something by Patti Page."

"Play 'Left Right Out of Your Heart,'" said Clyde.

Gene said to Eddie, "Okay, you fucked her. You're right. I'm not thrilled. Now what's the part I'm not gonna believe?"

Eddie waited until the music came back on before he spoke. "One night after we had sex, we were just layin' back, watching Carson, and Sandra starts telling me about doin' her time up at Frontera. She told me she became friendly with Susan Atkins."

"Susan Atkins. You mean—"

"The Manson chick. And they got involved romantically," Eddie said, looking at Gene unsurely, measuring his reaction: Gene returned his stare coldly, distantly. "I don't know why I'm telling you this. I guess that crazy shit up in Laurel Canyon brought everything back." Eddie smiled and shrugged, trying to find a sincere expression, an expression that wasn't in his repertoire. "Anyway, Susan Atkins told Sandra that she and the rest of the girls fucked everyone in Hollywood. Actors, musicians, directors, people that were really famous, like Dennis Hopper and Neil Young. She said Charlie filmed everything."

"Bullshit."

"That's what she said. And she said something else. She said that one of the girls brought a camera inside the house during the Tate murders."

Drunk talk, Gene thought. Sandra was drunk and decided to make up a story. "We would've heard something," Gene said, after he sat without speaking for a while. "Those murders were the most investigated crime in the history of this city. If there was any chance that—"

"There *were* rumors, Gene."

"And they were checked out."

Eddie nodded. "I know. I didn't believe her either. And I still don't," Eddie assured Gene, as he finished his drink. "The only reason I brought it up is I felt guilty about screwing her. I just wanted to get it off my chest."

Gene's eyes drifted toward the bar. Clyde was leaning back against the cash register, rubbing the gray stubble on his chin. Across from him, the girl was chattering away about a summer she spent bumming around Europe in the late 1960s. "When I came back," the girl was saying, "I moved into this apartment on Shoreham Drive, just south of Sunset. The girl who was in there before me killed herself. I think she was the daughter of someone famous. Anyway, a few weeks later I was waiting tables at the Whiskey a Go Go and hanging out at the Rainbow Bar and Grill up the street. That's where I met David Carradine, Mr. Kung Fu. He said he'd taken five hundred acid trips."

Gene picked up the files and got to his feet. "Sandra was bullshitting you," he said in a mild voice, a voice without judgment, "or Susan Atkins was bullshitting her."

"I didn't believe her. I already told you that," Eddie said, but when he lifted up his drink his fingers were shaking, something they were not prone to do. "What do you think I am—a fucking idiot?"

Claudia followed Gene outside. She was smiling whimsically. "I'm more attractive in the light," she said. "You agree?"

"You're very pretty."

"But not pretty enough for you?"

Gene turned away and started walking north, looking slightly put upon when Claudia fell into step beside him. "Look, I'm not a whore, if that's what you're thinking. I'm a free fuck," she said, inclining toward him so her breast touched his arm. Gene turned his head and she shot him a challenging look. "Still not interested?"

"Not today."

They were standing on the corner of Hollywood Boulevard and Las Palmas, the former site of Nate's News, the newspaper and magazine stand that Gene's father had owned for twenty-five years. Now it was a sex emporium called the House of Love. Loitering near the entrance was a black teenage hooker wearing silver lamé pants and shiny mirrored sunglasses. Although her body was absolutely perfect, her complexion was marred by vitiligo, a pigmentation disorder that left large, irregular pink and white spots on her face and neck.

"This is mine," Gene said to Claudia, indicating the dark green Rabbit convertible that was parked by a meter. "I gotta go. I'm sorry I can't help you out."

Claudia shrugged. She was using a store window as a mirror to apply lipstick and to fix her hair. "Help? I don't need help," she said, "especially from an asshole like you."

"Look, if I hurt your feelings—"

"You didn't," the girl said, staring sullenly at her reflection. "So don't worry about it."

Driving home in the thick traffic on the Ventura Freeway, Gene left the radio off while he replayed his conversation with Eddie Cornell. Did it surprise him that Eddie had ended up in bed with Sandra? Not really. Just the opposite. It would've been out of character for him *not* to have slept with her. But his story about the Manson family was much too bizarre to take seriously.

There was, however, something else that *did* trouble Gene as he left the freeway and took the winding road through the eerie darkness of Topanga Canyon. What bewildered him and yet, strangely, filled him with wonder, were the items he found inside the cardboard carton that he'd brought back from Alice's funeral in Cedar Rapids.

He read quickly through Alice's diaries, finding very little that he didn't already know. Her schoolgirl crushes, her parents' troubled marriage, the divorce, the drive cross-country, her mom's subsequent breakdown, it was all here, written unsentimentally and honestly.

Alice had also told Gene about Nick, her first love, a photojournalist who had died in Vietnam during the Tet Offensive; and she had even shown him Nick's obituary, which she still carried in her wallet. Gene was jealous (and unwilling to believe she once hungered sexually for someone else), but he decided, wisely, not to push it. After all the guy, being dead, was hardly a serious rival.

Still, he was shocked by the photos he found stuffed in the diary, all shot by Nick: eight black-and-white nudes taken outside, in a grove of trees. In each picture she is standing next to or leaning against the same ancient black oak, holding a flower—cherry or apple blossom— between her smallish breasts. Her body looks relaxed, but there is something askew about her expression, imperfect, like the clouds on the horizon, stormy clouds that were different shades of gray and separated by the sky.

* * *

And now there were these eight mysterious letters. Letters written to Alice by someone with the same first name, the earliest postmarked from Berkeley in August of 1967. Then: San Francisco in March of 1968; Carefree, Arizona in November of 1969; Amarillo, Texas, February 1971; Springfield, Missouri, August 1971; Moline, Illinois, April 1972; Flagstaff, New Mexico, December 1972; and then back to San Francisco.

Only eight. In plain white envelopes with no return address. Just these three words in the upper left-hand corner: *Here and There.*

That night Gene woke up and saw the moon outside his bedroom window, baited by a cloud shaped like a barbed fish hook. To himself he said: Don't dig any deeper. You're in over your head. Consider getting out, because when you do there will be no evidence that your shoes marked the ground.

Five

The Other Alice: Letter #1

Dear Alice,

You're not going to know who this is until you see my signature at the end of this letter. Don't look! Please! Just try to guess as you read along.

Clue #1: I was born and raised in Cedar Rapids on the west side of town, near the waterworks and the Little League field. No, this is not Cathy Glendenning. Cathy lived close by on Waverly Street, but she had an older brother, and I was an only child.

Clue #2: I'm a girl. I'm 5'6" and I weigh about 125 lbs, and people in my family always said I was pleasant to look at. Not pretty (like you) but just pleasant, like I had a face that was easy to forget; a face with no magic powers, not a face you could die for, or a face that could give you back your life.

Clue #3: Until I left home my shoulders were always slouched and, whenever I went outside, I would act like I was ready to apologize for something I was about to do, usually something stupid. Once, when we were about thirteen, your mother and my mother chatted by the frozen food lockers in the Krogers Market on West 7th. Your mom told mine that she was taking a trip across the United States. She was talking real fast, like she was cranked up on speed, and you could see her black bra through her blouse. To tell you the truth, I thought she looked cheap.

I remember she told you to get some Kellogg's Raisin Bran, and I followed you up and down the aisles until you found the section where the cereals were stacked. We didn't speak at all, not a word, but I remember feeling happy inside, proud that people saw us together, even though you were beautiful and my face felt like a mistake.

Clue #4: *I was in my junior year at Benjamin McKinley when I saw you for the last time. It was a Saturday morning in the beginning of August. We were at the movies. You were sitting three rows in front of me, two seats in from the aisle. The movie was* Baby, the Rain Must Fall *starring Steve McQueen, who I met later in Los Angeles, but that's another story, a story you wouldn't believe.*

Anyway, after the show I walked over to Keegan's Wash and Dry. I was going to visit my cousin, Viv, who managed the laundry on the weekend. But when I knocked on the office in back, I was surprised to hear Mr. Keegan's voice. When he opened the door, he looked all sweaty and red in the face. He said Viv was out running an errand and would be back later. I knew right away he was lying. Behind him I could hear someone making breathing sounds that were just short of words, and right before he closed the door I looked down and saw his penis peeking out of his open fly.

Clue #5: *Two weeks later, when I came back, Mr. Keegan offered me money to be "sexual" with him. I said okay. We used the beat-up couch in his office, the one with the plaid cushions. He said he would give me twenty dollars if I played with my breasts while I watched him masturbate. He kept the radio on real low, tuned to a station that broadcast readings from the Bible and gave crop reports every half hour.*

When he came the first time, he snapped his head back and semen flew all over my face and hair. For about a minute I could hear my pulse pounding in both my temple and my wrists. The next time he looked at me, I saw Christ's face in the cloud of blood floating across the iris of his right eye.

Clue #6: *Inside his desk Mr. Keegan kept pictures of other girls who were "sexual" with him, all of them naked, their faces looking baffled or just plain irritated. The two girls I recognized had already graduated the year before. I'm not going to tell you their names.*

There are no more clues, Alice. Okay? I think you know who I am. If you do, keep in mind I'm no longer the person you remember, that homely girl with the greasy complexion; a girl with no sense of direction who was always swimming upstream; a girl who would have traded places with anyone raised on love.

Now I have lots of friends. The streets of San Francisco are filled with girls like me, girls who are not quite pretty. But now I stand up straight and my posture reflects my new health and enthusiasm. The people around me are happy and wise. My old life is over, smashed to bits. I'm creating my future and yours too. Just you wait and see.

Two more things I want to mention before I end this letter.

(1) *Remember Julie, fat Julie whose father was Reverend Wellsworth, the pastor at St.Paul's Methodist church on 14th Street? Well, get this, Julie is not so fat anymore. Last Sunday I saw her at a "love-in" over in Berkeley. She was wearing a T-shirt without a bra and a denim skirt cut so short that you could see her butt cheeks. She was dancing by herself to the live band, whirling all over the place with her hands stretched above her head. She was pretty now—not beautiful, but certainly someone with beauty inside her—and she moved her body in a way that was bouncy and good natured. Now men looked at her and smiled instead of looking away from her fat face.*

She was changed: You could see it in her eyes, which were clear and filled with wonder.

(2) *I took LSD later that day with a guy I met on Telegraph Avenue, an older dude named Charlie, and we stayed up all night talking and making love. I told Charlie about my hometown, about Mr. Keegan, and about all the girls he smeared with his lust. Charlie said that Mr. Keegan should die. I agreed. And now that you've read this letter, I know you do too. Good luck in college. I'm sorry we were never able to become friends. Maybe someday we will.*

Love and XXX,
Alice

Six

All That Aches

Shortly after noon on July 18, 1966, approximately twelve hours before he was found dead outside the apartment he shared with his mother, Bobby Fuller made a quick stop at Mister Fabulous, an upscale dry cleaners on Sunset and Gardner in West Hollywood. A paid receipt was later found in the right front pocket of his jeans, and, following every lead, two homicide detectives interviewed Carl Reese, the owner of the cleaners, three days later on July 21st.

According to the transcript of this interview, which Gene had read over several times, Bobby and the members of his band frequently had their clothes cleaned at Mister Fabulous.

"They each had four or five matching outfits," Carl Reese told the detectives, neither of whom were aware that Bobby had performed regularly at P.J.'s, the club Reese co-owned with Jack Havana. "Jackets and pants in bright colors, and shirts with ruffles down the front. Every Saturday, Bobby or his brother Randy would pick up the clothes and pay the bill. They were nice boys," he added. "Polite. Respectful. Not like all this hippie trash you see everywhere."

When asked if he noticed anything unusual about Bobby's behavior on that Saturday, the Saturday he died, Carl Reese said no, but he was lying, because this short, square-shouldered man with the saturnine expression was not working behind the counter on July 18th, from twelve to three. He was down the street knocking down boilermakers at the Body Shop, a topless joint he owned on La Cienega, just north of Melrose.

"Why did he bullshit the cops? Who the fuck knows. My dad had his own reasons. He probably didn't want me involved," said Jacob Reese, Carl's son, nineteen years later, when Gene met with him at Mirabelle, an outdoor café on the western edge of the Sunset Strip.

Gene said, "I take it you were the one working that day."

"Every Saturday. Ten till six. For three straight summers," Jacob Reese said, fingering the silver Jewish star that he wore around his neck. "Used to really piss me off when the surf was up."

"So you waited on Bobby?"

"Yeah."

"What do you remember?"

"Very little. It was a long time ago."

Gene, after hesitating a moment, said, "Do you remember anything?"

"Yeah, I remember a couple of things," Jacob Reese said, glancing down as he flexed the muscle in his right bicep. "He had a chick with him. She stayed in the car while he was inside."

"You remember what she looked like?"

"She was hot-looking. And she had dark skin."

"Dark? You mean she was black?"

"No. She wasn't black," Jacob Reese said, thinking it out. "She was dark. She had a suntan.'"

"What else do you remember?"

Jacob Reese stared at Gene impassively for several seconds with his eyes slightly squinted. Then, shaking his head, he said, "This is fuckin' weird."

"What?"

"Trying to remember shit from the sixties."

"You're doin' pretty good."

"The guy was halfway famous, that's the only reason. And don't get me wrong, because I know you're a big fan and all that, but I could never get into that rockabilly shit. Back then I was groovin' on the Byrds and the Rolling Stones. You know what I mean?"

"Absolutely. I loved the Stones," Gene said, with an air of agreement, and a low wind blew over a page in the small spiral binder he was using to take notes. "So back to Bobby. He picks up his laundry and splits. That was it?"

Jacob Reese shook his head and leaned forward in his chair, so he didn't have to raise his voice over the noise of the traffic. "First the chick got out and opened the trunk. That's where he put the cleaning, so he could lay it out flat. That way it wouldn't get wrinkled."

"Then the girl wasn't in the car the whole time."

"Man, I just told you—"

"Take it easy," Gene said, with authority, and motioned to the waitress for the check. "I'm just trying to get all this info down right. Okay?"

Jacob Reese lapsed into a sullen silence while his knee jiggled nervously underneath the table. Looking away, he said, "He was going to get his car cleaned."

Gene glanced up from his notebook. "Who?"

"Fuller. I remember he asked me if the Santa Palm Car Wash was right or left on Santa Monica."

"Santa Palm?" After Gene wrote down the name, he raised his head. "When I was a kid, I used to go there every Sunday with my dad. Once we saw Edward G. Robinson and Natalie Wood on the same day."

"She came in the cleaners."

"Natalie Wood?"

"Not just her. Lots of stars. Sal Mineo was a regular," Jacob Reese said, seemingly unaware that Mineo costarred with Natalie Wood and James Dean in *Rebel Without a Cause*. "And so was the guy who played Marcus Welby. Dude was always sloshed. I forget his name."

"My father knew the Rifleman," Gene said, and Jacob Reese looked at him oddly. "Chuck Connors. The guy who starred in the series."

The Rifleman. Reese burped quietly as he narrowed his eyes, thinking. "Never heard of it."

"It was on in the late fifties, early sixties. Connors played this guy, Lucas McCain, a homesteader in the old west. He lived with his son, just the two of them."

"Wait!" Reese suddenly sat up and slammed his palm on the table, making the silverware bounce. "I remember now. The guy had this trick rifle, a modified Winchester with this big-ass ring which cocked it as he drew." He brought his arm up fast, demonstrating the action. "Ka-boom!"

Gene was smiling. "That's the guy."

"He and your dad were friends?"

"Not friends. Connors used to come by the newsstand he owned in Hollywood. This was back in the late forties, before Connors was an actor, when he played pro baseball for the L.A. Angels in the Pacific Coast League. In those days he had a gambling problem, a big one. After he got in deep with a couple of bookies, my dad offered to bail him out. In return, Connors agreed to coach me for a month, so I had a shot at making Little League. We were supposed to meet at Rancho Park on Sunday mornings, but he never showed up once."

Jacob Reese thought about this for a moment. "Guy sounds like a dick. What'd your dad do?"

"Nothing. Connors just stopped coming by the newsstand."

"Never paid him back?"

"Nope."

"You make the team?"

Gene shook his head, looked away. "I was the last kid cut."

"Fucker ripped you off," Reese said. His voice was harsh, disapproving. "That shit would've never happened to my dad. He would've found a way to get even."

"I did get even," Gene said, trying to suppress a smile. "When I was a cop, I pulled him over for speeding. Turns out he was drunk. This was back in '66. His show was off the air, but he still worked a lot. He asked me if I'd give him a break. I said sure. Then I told him it would cost five grand. He thought I was bullshitting him until I explained who I was. Fucker started to get nervous right about then."

"He pay you?"

"He wanted to write me a check."

Reese started to laugh. "A check? No way."

"I told him cash or I was taking him to jail. It was around three A.M. Guess who he calls?"

"No idea."

"Ronald Reagan."

"Bullshit."

"Swear to God," Gene said, raising his right hand and placing it over his heart. "Turns out he and Ronnie are both lifelong Republicans and asshole buddies. So I drive up to Bel-Air, drop him off in front of Reagan's house, and he goes inside. Ten minutes later he comes back out with an envelope filled with hundred-dollar bills. Then I drive him back to his car and that's it."

"The Rifleman bailed out by Ronald Reagan. That's a great story," Jacob Reese said, "if it's true."

"It is. Every word," Gene said. "And what was really great about it was this: I had forgotten about everything—Little League, the money he owed my dad, all of it. Then, bingo! There he is on Sunset, shooting past Doheny in a brand-new bright red Bonneville, going sixty in a forty; and there I am with just an hour left on my shift, waiting for the light to change. Weird, huh? No way to explain it."

"Yeah, there is."

"How?"

"Karma," Reese said simply and seriously, rubbing the side of his face as he shifted in his chair. "The dude had bad fuckin' karma."

After he paid the check and tipped the waitress, Gene walked Reese up the street to Tower Records, next to the lot where Reese's car was parked. He was driving a freshly painted 1976 navy-blue Eldorado convertible with the top down.

Gene took in the Caddy with a long slow look. "Cool ride."

"My old man's," Jacob Reese said. "I inherited it when he died."

"Bobby Fuller drove a Mustang. White, right?"

"White or blue," Reese said, then shrugged. "I'm not sure."

"I drove a fifty Olds in high school," Gene said, and the thought of it made him smile. "Guy in my class, Tony Rubaloff, souped it up for me. Dual carbs, Eski cam, the works. I even had it pinstriped by Von Dutch." Gene reached down and ran his hand over the Eldorado's shiny blue fender. "Let me ask you something," he said, turning his head so he could stare straight into Reese's face. "A kid who picks up his cleaning and gets his car washed, that doesn't sound like someone thinking about killing himself. Right? He's thinking about the future, a future that includes a beautiful girl and a record zooming up the national charts. Suicide doesn't seem to make any sense, does it?"

Jacob Reese was silent for a moment, still looking Gene in the eye. "Let me ask *you* something. You think I'm a fucking idiot?"

Gene reached for a cigarette. "What're you talking about?'

"I mean you're not doing research for your brother. This is not about some movie project. Is it?"

"Sure it is," Gene said, conscious of the new tone in Reese's voice, a roughness that wasn't there a moment earlier. "Ray Burk. That's my brother. I told you his credits."

"Something's fucked up here," Jacob Reese said, and he made a disappointed face. "Something else is going on."

"Nothing's going on. I was totally up front with you. I told you I used to be a cop. Correct?"

"But you didn't tell me you investigated Fuller's death back in 1966. You left that out," Jacob Reese said slyly, smiling over his shoulder as he climbed inside the Eldorado and slammed the door. "I found that out from Larry Havana. You remember Larry, don't you?"

Gene was silent.

"Sure you do. When you were kids, you used to push Larry around in his wheelchair. You sold maps to the movie stars' homes for his dad."

Gene still remained silent.

"Right. Burk?"

"I never worked for Jack Havana," Gene said matter-of-factly.

"Really?" Jacob Reese turned over the engine. "According to Larry—"

"Fuck Larry Havana," Gene said. "His father was the scum of the earth."

"Why? Because he bought your dad's newsstand?"

"He turned a legit business into a fucking cesspool."

Jacob Reese was still smiling energetically as he put the Caddy into gear. "My dad and Jack Havana were partners. Does that make him a scumbag, too?"

"You want an honest answer?"

"Why not?"

Gene kept silent and looked away, pretending to concentrate on the cars whizzing by on Sunset. Then calmly, softly, he said, "No point in opening old wounds. Your father's dead. I'll let him rest in peace."

"If you really wanted him to rest in peace, you wouldn't have picked up the phone," Jacob Reese said, leaning back and looking comfortable as he pulled out of the parking lot. "Thanks for lunch."

Gene remained standing at the curb for several seconds as the Eldorado merged into the traffic moving east on Sunset. Then he turned around and strolled into Tower Records. In the rhythm and blues section, he was both surprised and delighted to find a newly released compilation album by Hank Ballard and the Midnighters, one of the great up-tempo, comedy-showtime acts from the 1950s.

Gene had seen them perform live in Daytona Beach back in 1963, after he'd left New Orleans and was making his way down to Key West. It was Spring Break and they were appearing at Johnny B's, a segregated nightclub that was packed with mostly southern college kids from Georgia and Tennessee.

Hank started off his set with his newer pseudo-soul hits like "Finger-poppin' Time" and "The Twist," but the songs that really got the crowd stomping and clapping were his raunchy singles from the fifties, tunes like "Work with Me Annie" and "Sexy Ways."

After the first show ended, a drunken overweight kid wearing a Vanderbilt sweatshirt and pegged blue denim pants staggered up to the front of the stage and shouted over the din of voices: "Hank Ballard, you are one cool-ass nigger."

Hank, who was still holding the mike, struggled to appear unfazed as he let his eyes play over the boy's sweaty face.

"You gonna let him call you a nigger, Hank?" someone said, a voice deep in the crowd.

"I didn't call him a nigger," said the drunk kid over his shoulder. "I called him a 'cool-ass nigger.'"

By now the club had grown silent, and Hank was staring down at the kid with profound disappointment in his yellow-rimmed eyes. Gene remembered that Hank's gaudy outfit was identical to the one he was wearing on the cover of the album: cranberry silk shirt, green luminescent slacks, contrasting see-through socks decorated with musical notes, and patent leather shoes. Behind him, the Midnighters were dressed in shiny black suits.

After a while the rhythm guitarist in the house band—a white kid wearing a suit made out of a strange blue felted fabric and blue suede loafers—took the mike out of Hank's hand and whispered in his ear. Hank nodded, still staring at the fat boy's face, on which there was now an insipid smile, and then he turned around and walked slowly back to his dressing room.

Three months later the Midnighters found the Nation of Islam and, as Black Muslims, refused to play in front of an audience that included whites. Unable to accept their religious beliefs, Ballard left the group and began touring with James Brown, eventually becoming a full-time member of his revue.

When he got home from his meeting with Jacob Reese, Gene went straight into his living room and spent the next two hours sitting on the edge of his couch, making phone calls and chain-smoking Marlboros. On his way into the kitchen for a beer, he stopped in front of the wooden bookcase that was built into the wall next to the fireplace. On a shelf at eye level was a picture of Alice that was taken near the carousel in Griffith Park. She was sitting calmly at a redwood picnic table with a sleeping cat curled in her lap. Gene took down the picture and kissed her slightly parted lips. When he pulled his head back, he thought he detected a tiny movement in her eyelids. Now she seemed to be looking at him appraisingly.

A horn sounded outside, and from the house next door he heard pool noises, kids laughing and splashing. In the months before she died, Alice and Gene had spoken several times about having children, but she was undecided, not convinced she was cut out to be a mom.

"I think I'm too selfish," she'd told Gene, the last time the subject came up. It was an overcast Sunday in June—a yearly weather pattern that the natives called "the June gloom"—and they were driving back from Zuma Beach, where they had spent most of the gray morning in the ocean, body surfing. "Why don't we see how we feel in a year?"

"I'm forty-three," Gene had reminded her.

"That's still young. We have lots of time," Alice had said. "First we have to get married."

Gene replaced the photograph and moved back to the couch, so mad with grief that his blood seemed to fly through his heart. And his house, once a zone of warmth and security, now felt choked and haunted, filling him with destructive urges.

That night they were running several episodes of *The Twilight Zone* on one of the local television channels. It was part of a tribute to Rod Serling, the writer who created and hosted the series. Gene's favorite episode came on around ten. It starred Inger Stevens as a troubled young woman taking a road trip by herself, followed by a strange hitchhiker, a deranged-looking man whose scourged face and eerie presence seemed to silently foretell her imminent death.

When the show ended, Gene switched off the television and remained seated on the couch, staring at the pleated folders that were spread out on the coffee table in front of him. Inside was all the written evidence pertaining to the death of Bobby Fuller: transcripts of interviews given by Fuller's mother, his brother, band members, and his manager, Herb Stelzner; bills, bank statements, and a complete inventory of Bobby's possessions, including his books and records and several small notepads that were filled with lyrics for songs that he'd yet to record.

After Bobby's death was ruled a suicide, Gene had continued to investigate the case on his own for several weeks, gathering much information that was not contained in these folders, information that Gene felt was fundamental to solving this case, that only he knew—like the growing affection between Bobby and Nancy Sinatra in the spring and summer of 1966 (following her divorce from teen idol Tommy Sands), and her father's stern disapproval.

Gene interviewed Dewey Bowen and Deborah Walley, two of the young costars in *The Ghost in the Invisible Bikini,* and they both separately confirmed that Bobby and Nancy were seeing each other away from the set.

"I used to run into them at the Seawitch, this hangout on the Sunset Strip," Bowen told Gene. "They were always in a booth in the back. They looked cozy. Were they falling in love? Who knows?"

According to Deborah Walley, one of the drivers on the film, a teamster named Benny Moretti, was one of Frank Sinatra's boyhood pals. "He told me they grew up on the same block in Hoboken, New Jersey. And it was common knowledge that Frank used his clout to have Benny hired on the movie to keep tabs on Nancy. Once while we were filming late, Nancy asked me to distract Benny so she and Bobby could sneak off the lot for dinner."

Bowen remembered Frank Sinatra coming by the studio only once. "We were shooting a rock-and-roll number in this haunted mansion. After the last take, Frank yelled out, 'That was the worst fuckin' noise I ever heard!' Then he looked over at Bobby and they just stared at each other for about fifteen seconds. But it seemed more like an hour," said Bowen. "And no one—cast, crew, director—moved or said word one. Even Boris Karloff just stood there frozen like a goddamn statue. Finally, Bobby just put down his guitar and walked off the set."

And now, as Gene reviewed the notes he'd made earlier that day, after his conversation with Jacob Reese, he recalled that odd link between Carl Reese and Frank Sinatra—two men with unpredictable impulses and moods that were hard to comprehend—who had a friendship (that was never carefully concealed), dating back to the early 1950s, 1953 to be exact, the year that Sinatra starred in his comeback film, *From Here to Eternity.*

"They used to go to the fights together," Reese had told Gene. "Frank, my dad, Jack Havana, and this producer, Max Rheingold. Afterwards they'd hit Ciro's or the Melody Room. Or sometimes they'd have a late dinner at this joint in Inglewood called the Buggy Whip."

The Buggy Whip, the steakhouse where Alice's mother worked back in 1964. How strangely coincidental was that? Without showing his surprise, Gene had asked Jacob Reese if Nancy Sinatra could've been the girl with Bobby on the day he came by Mister Fabulous.

Jacob Reese had shrugged. "Could've been."

"But you're not sure?"

"What difference does it make?" Jacob Reese had said, making it clear with his attitude that he knew far more than he was telling. "It's a fucking movie. Make up anything you want."

Gene said nothing.

"Right?"

Gene did not answer right away. His mouth had gone dry, and a thin trickle of perspiration slid slowly down his neck. Finally, he nodded his head. "You're right, Reese. It's just a fucking movie."

Before he went to sleep, Gene reread the taped transcript of the phone conversation he'd had with Lenore McGowan, a few weeks after her article appeared in *Tiger Beat*. When he told her that he was a detective investigating Bobby Fuller's death, she seemed startled and her voice became frightened. With a little professional prompting, she quickly admitted that she did not disclose everything that happened on her "dream day" in Los Angeles, leaving out Herb Stelzner's unexpected appearance at Gold Star Studios.

"Bobby did play me his new single. That was true," Lenore said. "But then he and Stelzner got into a loud argument over the B-side choice. Stelzner said that he owned the record company, which gave him the right to make the final decision. He also said he didn't want to record a live album at P.J.'s, that it was way too expensive, and he was thinking about canceling the U.K. tour that had been planned for the fall. Bobby was furious. For a minute I thought they were going to come to blows, but then the engineer quickly jumped between them and walked Bobby outside."

"Then what happened?"

"Stelzner just laughed everything off. He told me that he and Bobby fought all the time, that it was no big deal."

"Did you believe him?" Gene asked her.

"No."

"Did he know you were going to write an article about your trip?"

"I said I might."

"And what was his response?"

"He said that as president of the fan club I was part of Bobby's team, and that I shouldn't write about anything that could harm his reputation."

"But he never threatened you?"

"No. But . . ."

"But what?"

"He scared me."

"Why?"

"Because he was scary."

Gene said, "What about the phone call Bobby received before he left?"

"That was true."

"Did he tell you who it was from?"

"Yes. He said it was from a girl, but he couldn't tell me her name. He said it was a secret."

"Did he give you a hint?"

"No."

"Are you sure?"

"Yes."

"Try to remember. This is important."

"Mister Burk, I told you everything. Okay? I swear."

"I believe you."

"Then can I get off the phone?"

"Sure, Lenore. You've been a big help. Thanks."

* * *

That night Gene had a dream in which his mother appeared for the first
time:

She was in her early twenties, no older, and she was sitting
at the end of a long bar inside a crowded gambling club. Counting money behind the bar was actor Steve Cochran, who Gene
had recently seen on the late show in *White Heat*, a brutal crime
drama that starred James Cagney as a mother-fixated gangster.

Nathan Burk was dealing blackjack at a table in the center
of the casino, keeping one eye on the cards and the other on his
wife. Among the gamblers at his table was a female impersona-
tor who was seated in a wheelchair. In front of her was a glass of
champagne and a dwindling supply of one-hundred-dollar chips.

Carl Reese entered the club wearing a dark blue suit with a
gold handkerchief in his breast pocket. After he winked at the silent, big-fisted doorman, he crossed the room and took a seat at
the bar alongside Gene's mother. She greeted him with a kiss next
to his lips, while he reached around her to shake Cochran's hand.

Jack Havana came into the club through a private entrance,
accompanied by two gym-toned bodyguards wearing matching
gray double-breasted suits that shone like polished armor. At the
same time, a band led by Bobby Fuller took the stage in the
lounge. His hair was greased into a king-sized pompadour, and
his face showed the signs of anxiety and fatigue.

The music started and Carl Reese tapped Gene's mother
lightly on the knee, keeping time. Steve Cochran transferred
money from the register into the strongbox below the sink, and
then he was joined behind the bar by Bobby's manager, Herb
Stelzner. Nathan Burk dealt himself a blackjack and raked all the
money off the table with a quick swipe of his hand. A man with
an Irish face muttered a curse and stormed off, and the drag queen,
who was Larry Havana, Jack's son, began to weep silently while
Nathan reshuffled the deck.

Jack Havana moved slowly into the bar and sat down heavily
next to Gene's mom. When Carl Reese offered Havana his right

hand, his sleeve brushed against Mona Burk's nipple and his coat fell open, revealing a pearl-handled revolver that was holstered underneath his arm. Gene's mother lit a cigarette and smiled when Carl Reese pushed a stray hair away from her face. Under his breath, Nathan Burk called his wife a dirty little whore. He said it three more times before he flipped over his hole card—a queen of diamonds to go with the five of clubs that was already showing. He hit himself with a winning six, and the only player left at the table, a hostile-looking black man, pushed his money forward and mock-backhanded Nathan across the face.

Bobby Fuller finished his second song, a punch-out version of "C'mon Everybody," by one of his idols, singer-songwriter Eddie Cochran. The applause was scattered, nothing like the standing ovations he used to get every weekend at P.J.'s. Gene's mother was smiling at Carl Reese, her eyes beaming approval as she took a small sip from her brandy glass. Nathan Burk stopped dealing cards. He discarded his apron and started into the bar, but the doorman was blocking the entrance.

Herb Stelzner was standing by the register quartering limes and lemons, using a serrated knife that was as sharp as a razor. Steve Cochran and his scowling eyes were no longer in the dream. He'd disappeared. Jack Havana turned on his stool and stared at his crippled son with a look of utter contempt. Nathan Burk slipped through the doorway while the doorman's head was turned. Right away he noticed a mole on his wife's cheek that wasn't there when they were together. At the same time he saw the knife in Herb Stelzner's hand, the silver blade glimmering in the smoky blue light.

Carl Reese whispered something to Jack Havana, their uneasiness growing as they watched Nathan Burk move forward, glowering at his wife, ready to split her lips with his fist. When he pulled her off her bar stool, Carl Reese reached for his pistol. The moment his fingers curled around the grip, his eyelids jumped and the knife of his assassin, Herb Stelzner, walked a pathway up the center of his back. Reese took one step to the side, as if he were letting someone pass, then pitched forward on his face.

For the first time in his life Jack Havana looked worried, even though he was flanked by both of his bodyguards. He was staring down at the bloody trench in Carl Reese's back. His face was as white as a cloud. Gene's mother told Nathan Burk that she'd learned her lesson. She said she wanted to come home. Fast tears of remorse fell from her eyes and, simultaneously, their hands came together and they walked out of the bar.

Actor Steve Cochran reappeared in the dream. Now he was in the lounge, sitting ringside, singing along with Bobby Fuller and the house band. Larry Havana was there too, in a back booth, now dressed like a man, surrounded by a collection of long-legged, tight-skirted women with devious mouths and secret names that only the waiters knew. In the booth next to them, a bug-eyed Gypsy woman was reading Gene's palm. She told him that "one's deepest emotions are always shown in silence."

And that's when the song ended in the dream, and Gene woke up.

Feeling restless but not quite panicky, he went into the kitchen and washed the dishes that were piled in his sink. Afterwards he took a hot shower and came back into the living room and switched on the TV. Barbara Hershey was appearing in a late-night rerun of the television series *Run for Your Life*. In this episode, which was titled, "Saro-Jane, You Never Whispered Again," Ben Gazzara, who starred as Paul Bryan, a man with only two years to live, searches throughout Los Angeles for a missing teenage girl. He finds her finally in Topanga Canyon, living in a teepee with a bunch of hippies.

Several residents of Topanga—authentic freaks, most of them zonked on psychedelics—were used as extras in this show. Among them was Rachel Cooper, a thirty-two-year-old ex-prostitute who lived on Sandpiper Lane, just down the hill from Gene, in a house that was once rented by Gary Hinman, a musician who was brutally murdered by Susan Atkins and three other members of the Manson family.

At a Fourth of July party that Gene threw in 1985—actually it was more of a housewarming for Alice, who had moved in a few weeks earlier—Rachel told Gene that she knew and occasionally "worked for" Charles Manson back in the late 1950s, when he first came to L.A. with his seventeen-year-old pregnant wife, Rosalie.

"When I first met him," Cooper said, "he was running chicks out of The Wipeout, this thieves' bar on South Western that was owned by the mob. I was Charlie's main lady for six months, until he found Judy, this rich-bitch, Jewish college girl he met one day in Westwood Village. She owned a white T-Bird convertible that she put into his name and bought him a whole new wardrobe. When her dad found out Charlie was turning her out, he went nuts and tracked him down, and Charlie went back to jail. In the two years I knew him, he got popped at least five times. Of course, that's what he learned in the slam: how to turn out chicks."

In a later conversation at his house, Rachel Cooper told Gene that Charlie's mother Kathleen was living in Los Angeles at this time. And that she (Rachel) and Charlie had visited her in 1957, on Christmas eve.

"Her apartment was on Mariposa, just west of the Hollywood Freeway and one block south of Sunset. We got there around nine," Cooper said. "Charlie brought her a couple of presents—pocket books he got cheap at this secondhand bookstore over on Cherokee. They were westerns, I think, and one had a picture on the front cover of a woman holding a knife to a man's throat. I wrapped them up in pretty paper that I stole from the Rexall on Gower."

Cooper said there was a man visiting Kathleen Manson when she and Charles arrived. He was sitting in the center of the couch with his shirt off, drinking beer out of a can. Charlie's mother, who answered the door in her slip, said hello fast and rushed into the bathroom, where she changed into a skirt and blouse. Charlie put the gift-wrapped books on top of the TV and walked into the tiny kitchenette. He found a beer in the fridge, opened it, and remained out of sight until his mother came back into the living room and sat down on the couch next to the shirtless man. That's when Charlie reappeared in the living room with a Budweiser in one hand and a steak knife hidden in his pants.

Cooper said, "Charlie told his mom I was a whore, just like she was, the only difference being that I was younger and prettier, and my pussy was tighter. Mind you, these were the first words out of his mouth. Nobody said a thing for about ten seconds. Then the skinny guy put down his beer can and tilted his head to the side, looking at Charlie like he was stone-crazy. He told Charlie it was wrong to say these things about his mother. And Charlie said he would talk about his mama anyway he wanted, that he'd been watching her fuck men since he was five years old. He also told the man that he could fuck me for free, a two-for-one deal since it was Christmas eve. Then he brought the knife out from behind his back and smiled.

"Charlie's mom put her hand on the man's jumpy knee and told him to keep still. She said, 'He ain't gonna hurt you none. He's my son.' Charlie ordered his mother off the couch and told me to take her place next to the bony man. Then he told us to start having sex.

"The man crossed his arms over his chest and told Charlie he was not prepared to do what he said. Charlie said if he didn't, he would cut him with his knife. His mother began to get upset, saying Charlie had a sick mind. She was talkin' real loud. When she wouldn't be quiet, Charlie reached over and slugged her in the forehead with his fist, knocking her to the floor.

"By this time I was out of my clothes, and 'Mr. No-Sex' on the couch was staring at me with a little more interest, paying special attention to my seventeen-year-old boobs. I told him I liked people watching me fuck, that it turned me on, and I reached over to unbuckle his pants. Afterwards all four of us went up to Revells and drank and played shuffle pool until the bar closed. On the way home Charlie told me a little bit about his childhood. He never knew his dad but said his last name was Scott. Manson came from one of his stepfathers. He said this Mr. Scott worked as a fry cook at a luncheonette near the bus depot in Louisville. Then he said something really weird. He said that he was black.

"That's the only thing he told me I didn't believe."

Seven

Another Letter

from Alice

Dear Alice:

    Well, a lot has happened since I last wrote you. Remember that guy Charlie I told you about, the older guy who did a bunch of time in prison? Did I mention the prison thing? I'm not sure. Anyway, he and I have become lovers and soul-mates, and I have never felt this happy in my life. He is the first man who has ever made me feel safe, with or without my clothes. When we have sex, all I see is rainbows.

    Right now I'm sharing him with a girl named Mary. Mary worked at the university library until the day she saw Charlie hunched over his guitar outside the student center, singing in the rain. Before she knew him for even five minutes, she knew "he'd love me for the parts that were missing inside." And when he said that one day she would live in paradise, she knew that was true, too.

    For both of us, Charlie was the first man to notice and care. He taught us to forget, to forgive, and to dream.

    The summer of love is over, Alice. The streets of the city used to be filled with love and good vibes, and all the dope and food you wanted was free. Now the only thing you get free these days is the clap.

    Charlie knew the end was coming long before me and Mary. He said everyone got too busy selling love to give away any more free samples. So we've decided to leave San Francisco and hit the road. Charlie bought a school bus that we're fixing up like a home. When I asked him where we were going, he said, "Someplace where no one's got their hands in our soulpockets."

All my life I wanted to take it all back and start over. That's where I am right now, standing at the edge of a cliff, ready to fling my body into the sun, with nothing to break my fall. Charlie said if I step back I'm moving toward the exit, away from the light. He said I owe my life to letting go.

Love,
Alice

Eight

Looking for
the Enemy

Gene exited the Hollywood Freeway at Vine, drove south for two blocks, and parked on Gower, between Selma and Sunset. Across the street was My Friend's Place, a free medical clinic and drop-in center for homeless teens. Herb Stelzner had an office next door in the oldest building on the block, a squat, two-story cement structure that looked barely respectable in the harsh midday light.

For the last two weeks Gene had tried unsuccessfully to contact Stelzner over the phone. He was always in a meeting, out of town, out to lunch, or otherwise unavailable. Yesterday, when Gene called his office, Stelzner's secretary very pleasantly told him, "Mr. Stelzner is not interested in speaking to anyone regarding Bobby Fuller or any of his former clients."

"Gimme a break," Gene said in a raised voice that was just short of anger. "Just tell him I need a half-hour of his time. That's all."

"I'm sorry, I can't help you," said the secretary, and right before she hung up Gene heard a man's voice gruffly shout out, "Tell him to go fuck himself."

A fragile-looking girl with bad skin walked out of My Friend's Place carrying a baby wrapped in a blue blanket. Trailing a few steps behind her, smiling maliciously, was a skinny shirtless boy wearing camouflage pants and big heavy boots. When they passed Gene on the sidewalk, the boy cut his eyes away and hocked a load of spit on a parked car. Then he reached out and yanked the girl's scraggly ponytail, calling her a "stupid bitch."

The girl spun around and tried to kick the boy, but he danced out of reach, laughing. "Don't you call me names," she screamed.

"Fucking spider bite. I told you it wasn't serious," the boy said.

"You didn't know. It could've been a black widow. Jamie could've died," the girl said and stopped walking. Tears were now streaming down her scarred cheeks. "We have to be careful."

The boy stepped forward and put his arm around the girl, pulling her close. Still a little ashamed but too proud to show it, he leaned over and sloppy-kissed the pocked skin next to her eye, making a loud smacking sound with his lips. The girl grimaced in mock-discomfort, and, when the boy grabbed her wrist and tried to tickle her, she roughly pushed him away.

"I want you to be nice to me," she said, and the boy froze, throwing up his hands as though she were placing him under arrest. "This is not a joke. I want you to show me some respect. Okay?"

The boy nodded, still keeping his hands in the air. "Okay."

"Promise?"

"Promise."

"Then put your hands down and start acting your age for a change." The boy lowered his hands and the girl put the baby into his arms. "You're a dad, Billy. Act like one."

Gene entered the office building and stood in the small lobby for a moment, looking hesitant and confused, until he saw the building's registry on the wall next to the elevator. Herb Stelzner was not listed, but his company, Big City Music, had an office on the second floor. On the same floor was the Sad Sack Society, a self-help organization for retired circus clowns, and a magazine called *The Orphan Digest*. There was also, in room 208, a Dr. Milton Chong, who listed himself as "Forensic Dentist and Judo Instructor."

Stelzner's office was located at the end of an unlighted hallway. Gene passed an open door and saw a tall man with a petulant face standing in front of a large aquarium, speaking into a white Princess phone. On the fingers of his free hand was a puppet with an owl's face. A black woman with a spectacular body walked out of the ladies room and opened the office across the hall, using a large ring of keys. Before she closed the door, Gene caught a glimpse of a man, also black, stretched out on a couch in his Jockey shorts, his face and chest beaded with sweat.

Gene walked into the office of Big City Music without knocking. In the waiting area, a receptionist with grayish-blond hair was sitting behind a large wooden desk, reading the latest issue of *Billboard.* When she looked up, Gene noticed right away that her rosy red lipstick matched the broken capillaries on the pale skin next to her nose.

She said, staring at him with unblinking interest, "I take it you have an appointment?"

Gene shook his head. "I've tried to get one," he said, his secret seriousness hidden behind an easygoing smile, "but I don't seem to get anywhere."

The woman put down her magazine but continued to stare at Gene with polite reserve. "I recognize your voice," she said. "You're the one writing the book."

"My brother. It's a movie. I'm helping with the research."

"It's not gonna happen."

"Nothing's a sure thing in Hollywood, but—"

"Mr. Stelzner, I mean. He's not going to see you," the woman said, her eyes still focused on Gene's face. Before he could respond, the door behind her opened and a thin, restless-looking man entered the waiting room. He was wearing heavy glasses with light blue lenses and a blue velvet suit.

Glancing at the woman, he said, "What's the problem, Dee?"

"He doesn't have an appointment."

"Then he's got to leave."

"I just need a few minutes. Ten at the most," Gene said, but the man shook his head. "Look, just ask Herb if—"

"Forget it," the man said to Gene, blinking rapidly as he stepped behind the woman and slowly massaged the muscles in her shoulders. "Herb's in the studio with Steel Mouse. He's making records. He ain't got time to bullshit with guys off the street."

Gene was opening his mouth to speak when the phone rang and the woman picked it up, saying, "Big City Music."

"Gonna have to ask you to leave," the man said to Gene. "That's twice. I don't want to ask you a third time."

The woman put her hand over the mouthpiece. "Jake Reese," she said to the man standing behind her, his skinny fingers still digging into her neck. "He wants to talk to Herb."

"Everybody wants to talk to Herb," the man said with a trace of a smile, a smile that faded the moment his eyes came back to Gene's face. "Don't make me do something I don't want to do, pal."

Gene addressed the man with an expression of innocence. "And what would that be?"

"Hurt you."

The man started around the desk, but the woman suddenly reached out and grabbed him by the sleeve. "Don't, Nick. He's gonna leave."

Gene took a step backward. He seemed more amused than frightened. "My name's Gene Burk," he said to the woman. "Tell Stelzner I dropped by."

"I certainly will," the woman said, avoiding eye contact as she picked up the *Billboard* and resumed reading. "I'll tell him as soon as he calls in."

Gene was almost smiling as he turned around and opened the door. On the way out he heard the woman say, "What do you want me to tell Reese?"

"Tell him Herb will call him back."

After changing a five-dollar bill into quarters at the Astro Car Wash on Gower and Melrose, Gene walked next door to use the pay phone behind the 7–Eleven. He spent the next thirty minutes bent over the yellow pages, intently dialing all the recording studios in Hollywood and the West San Fernando Valley. Not one person he spoke to recalled booking time for Herb Stelzner, and the name Steel Mouse also drew a blank.

Using his final quarter, Gene called Lenny Deluca, a senior publicist at A & M records and, like Gene, an avid collector of rock-and-roll records and memorabilia. Lenny grew up in New York City, in the South Bronx, and his father, Lenny Sr., also known as "Lenny the Schmooze," was a legendary promotion man in the 1950s, working first for Morris

Levy at the Brunswick label, where he broke Jackie Wilson and the Orlons, then later at Atlantic under Jerry Wexler. He committed suicide in 1963, after he was indicted during the payola scandals along with DJ Alan Freed.

Gene and Deluca had traded 45's through the mail but had met in person only once, in September of 1973, at the funeral of country-rock singer Gram Parsons, a founding member of the Flying Burrito Brothers.

"I need some information," Gene told Deluca when he came on the line. "What do you know about a group called Steel Mouse?"

'Not a thing. Should I?"

"They're being produced by Herb Stelzner."

"Herb Stelzner?" Deluca's voice became slightly more interested. "Big City Music?"

"Right."

"Used to manage Bobby Fuller."

"I need to talk to him."

"Bad idea."

"Look, Lenny—"

Deluca cut him off. His voice was low, almost a whisper. "I said, leave it alone."

"Then you can't help me?"

"No. But I have something else that might interest you."

"If it's about records, forget it."

"No records. Pictures."

"Pictures of what?"

"Publicity stills of Linda Ronstadt," Deluca stated with some pride. "They were taken in 1968, while she was in the studio recording her first album."

Gene laughed sarcastically. "Is this some kind of a joke?"

"Cathy Share sang background. She's in all the pictures," Deluca said, sounding calm, innocent-seeming, but there was something in his voice that he was trying to control. "Remember her?"

"Cathy Share?"

"Her nickname was Gypsy. She was one of the Manson girls. Mansonabilia is gonna be the next big thing."

Gene felt his hand tighten on the receiver. Out of his side vision, he saw a middle-aged black man standing in the bright yellow sunlight, patiently waiting for his turn to use the phone. Gene held up one finger to indicate he was almost through.

"That's pretty far-out," he told Deluca. "What gave you the idea I might be interested?"

"Wild guess."

"Who else is in the picture?"

"Linda. Session players. Ricky Nelson."

"Ricky Nelson? No way."

"He was singing background, too. I'm staring at his face as we speak."

"Ozzie and Harriet meet Charles Manson."

"I'll give you the whole batch for a grand."

The black man had now moved over so he was directly in Gene's line of sight. His half-closed eyes were bloodshot and he reeked of fried onions and cheap wine. "Let me think about it," Gene said.

"This stuff goes fast, Gene. I need an answer by Monday."

"You'll have one."

When Gene stepped out of the booth, he saw a beat-up old Ford truck parked at the curb with a wispy black woman sitting in the passenger seat, holding a baby in her lap. The black man moved forward and picked up the phone. Gene started to thank him for waiting, but the man just shook his head, waving him away with a complicated movement of his large, trembling hand.

Gene was not prepared to drive home and spend another night alone in voluntary solitude. It was still light outside, but he felt an aura of estrangement, of almost invisibility, as he followed the stream of shirtsleeved pedestrians down Hollywood Boulevard. When he reached Las Palmas and stood on the corner outside the House of Love, he suddenly experienced the echo of bygone twilights, of happier times, when his mother still lived at home and he and his brother Ray were part of a family, and everything (it seemed) was in perfect harmony.

A bald man with pink skin and a barrel chest was standing by the entrance to the House of Love, coldly scrutinizing the blank faces of the passing strangers. On his forearm was a faded tattoo of Jiminy Cricket holding his erect penis. Behind the man, sitting on a tall stool with her unexceptional face partly hidden by a beaded curtain, was a pregnant woman wearing stiletto heels and a short black skirt.

Gene caught the man staring at him and smiled good-naturedly. "My dad had a newsstand on this corner," Gene said. "Right where we're standing. Nate's News. He had the biggest selection of magazines in the city."

"Yeah?" The man nodded but his face showed little interest. "When was that?"

"He started up in '46, right after the war ended. He had it for twenty-five years. Never closed," Gene said, a little awed. "Open twenty-four hours, seven days a week."

The woman on the stool pushed aside the curtain to get a better look at Gene. She wore ivory earrings shaped like dice and mascara the color of pool chalk. "How come he sold it?" she asked Gene, as she batted a fly away from her face.

Gene looked thoughtful for a second before he answered. "He got old."

"We all get old," she said, giving Gene a quick smile. "Right, Manny?"

"I don't think about it," the bald man said.

"Sure you do," the woman said. "We all think about it."

"I want to talk to a woman," Gene said, and he suddenly felt his face turn hot. "What will that cost me?"

"Talk is cheap," the man said, and the woman behind him smiled for the second time. "There's a fixed price for the room. Fifty bucks. The rest is negotiable."

The woman rose to her feet. She then came forward and stood before Gene with her hands on her hips. "Do you want to talk to me?" she said, tilting her head a little to the side.

"Sure. Why not?" Gene said with a shrug. But he found himself vaguely fearful and more confused than he was just moments before. "You're fine."

The woman smiled reassuringly and touched his arm, then took his hand. "Follow me."

The House of Love offered rooms for a multitude of activities; rooms to please everyone.

Near the drafty entrance was a row of small cubicles where customers could watch X-rated videos alone or with friends of either sex. These came with a sink, towels, and two folding metal chairs that were bolted to the floor. In other more spacious rooms, women alone or with men or other women would disrobe and do whatever they were asked to do by the customers, for the right price.

At the end of a long twisting hallway there was a room with a trap door that led to a prison cell bathed in red light. Next door was a room with a sharply slanted ceiling that could be entered only on your knees. There were rooms that came with aerobic equipment or with an array of medical devices, including an x-ray machine, scalpels, and even a bone saw. In one room—"the chamber of the missing"—a young woman with a tormented face pushed an empty stroller in circles, while recorded nursery rhymes and the playground laughter of children were piped through the speakers in the walls. Across the hall was a splendid re-creation of Anne Frank's bedroom, as picture perfect as a stage set. In this room there was a television that played a continuous loop of *Shoah,* the nine-hour documentary on the holocaust.

Gene was escorted into a good-sized room with shuttered windows, a single bed, a leather armchair, and a ceiling fan that turned slowly, barely moving the spiderwebs strung high in the corners. On the cherrywood table by the bed was a vase filled with blue tulips and a large silver ashtray. Placed inside the ashtray was a matchbox with a picture of Elvis kneeling in front of St. Peter.

Gene went to the window that looked out at the intersection of Hollywood Boulevard and Las Palmas. A drunk couple in their forties turned the corner, followed by a nurse carrying a large bag of groceries. Walking beside the nurse was a boy of ten or eleven who looked mildly retarded, holding a red balloon in the shape of a heart. When he saw Gene framed in the window, he quickly ducked his head behind the nurse's hips, hiding his eyes.

"Why don't you sit down. Then we can talk."

Gene spun around at the sound of the woman's voice. She was now reclining on the bed with her unmanicured fingers clasped tightly over her pregnant belly. There was something about her that was different, something in her face, an undefined softness that had not revealed itself earlier on the street.

After several moments, Gene sat down in the armchair and leaned forward, looking precisely into the woman's tired, nearly colorless eyes. With little attempt at secretiveness, in a voice that was peculiarly detached, he talked about his childhood, which seemed so impossibly far away and unbearably near, like yesterday.

He said, "There were so many happy times I spent up here helping my dad. Me, my brother, my mom, we all pitched in. Fridays were the best, when the trucks came by to deliver the new magazines and comic books. Dad let us take home whatever we wanted, as long as we put everything away in the racks first. Ray's favorite comics were *Archie* and *Little Lulu.* He was younger. I liked reading the *Baseball Digest* and *Ring Magazine.*"

"I don't read much anymore," the woman said, breaking in softly, "but in high school I was a regular bookworm."

"Yeah?"

"*The Sea Wolf* by Jack London. I remember reading that."

"My mom read the movie magazines and *True Detective,*" Gene said, looking away from the woman for the first time. "And she liked the crossword puzzle books, too. My brother remembers sitting with her up at Coffee Dan's, eating lunch together, while she used a pen to fill in the squares. I don't remember that."

"My mom read a lot from the Bible."

"During the summer she wore saddle shoes and Levi's with the cuffs rolled up to her calves, like a schoolgirl. On top she wore a stitched cowboy shirt with the top two buttons undone."

"Was she pretty?"

"Very."

Gene closed his eyes and breathed in the woman's scent and tried to hold it. It was a scent he recognized: cinnamon mixed with honeysuckle.

"You smell like someone I know," he told her.

"Who?"

"Someone who died."

"Is that who you want to talk about?"

No. He did not want to talk about Alice. Even thinking about her now made him sad beyond all reason. But the scent, her scent, was it just coincidental, or was it a sign of some kind, a reunion with her spirit, a reminder or maybe a simple promise that he would never be abandoned or need someone else to replace her, that what they had was sacred and would last beyond his lifetime?

"She died in a plane crash," Gene said, and the woman's face showed distress for a moment. "It happened a few months ago. She wore your perfume. I was reminded of her."

The woman smoothed her hair back while she looked at Gene with a sympathetic expression. "I'm sorry," she said. Her voice was tender, and the sadness she felt came into her eyes, making them look wet. "I really am."

Gene managed a smile that barely concealed his pain. He took a long breath in the silence and a memory, like a day torn off a calendar, suddenly floated out of the wings of his mind.

He and Alice have decided to drive down the coast on a Saturday morning. It's three weeks after they've met, and Gene wants to teach her to body-surf in the long rolling swells off the beach at San Onofre. They stop at the Coral Reef Motel, a dump that faces the open sea, with a broken neon sign and a $19 room rate, double occupancy.

They love the tackiness of this place: the amber-colored carpet, the water stains on the wallpaper, the *Bible* on the bureau, the TV with only one cable channel, and the quarreling voices from the couple next door, the woman screaming, "You owe it to me, Paul."

They are inside only for a moment when their bodies come together and they start to tear off each other's clothes. Alice's voice, when she comes, cries out his name twice, and in her eyes he sees a shocking happiness for which he is unprepared.

"Boy, that was delicious," she says, a few minutes later, after her skin has cooled and her body stops shaking. "Maybe the best ever. We are fabulously lucky, Gene. You know that?"

"Yeah," Gene says, a little spooked by the intensity of her stare. "I do."

"Would you like to hold me?" the woman asked Gene, who was once again standing by the window, staring out. He shook his head. "You sure? No extra charge."

"No thanks."

"What do you want to do?"

Gene didn't answer. He was distracted by a young woman who rushed out of a bar across the street, screaming at her boyfriend, a pint-sized man with a big belly and long greasy black hair that was tied in a ponytail. When he shouted back and slapped her face, she took off running down the boulevard. On the corner she passed a beat cop who was watching the scene with wordless amusement, the sharply angled sunlight bouncing off his blue baton and his silver shades.

In the white silence of the room, Gene heard the woman's voice. She was speaking about Rod Cameron, the tall, handsome B-movie actor who had died earlier that week of natural causes. She'd met him down the street at Revells a few months back, and he'd dropped by to see her occasionally at the House of Love. They had two things in common, she said. They both liked guns and roasted garlic.

"He-man. That's the only way to describe him," she told Gene with a little snicker. "And he was hung like the horse he rode in *Stampede.* You ever see that one?" Gene shook his head. "Rod couldn't act for shit, but if you put a gun in his hand he could carry a picture—just as easily as I'm carrying this baby."

Gene turned and gazed at the woman, who smiled at him with a new intimacy. The perfume she wore still lingered in the air around his face, haunting him, and he started to feel a sense of panic that made his heart beat wildly, almost violently. Without quite knowing why, he asked the woman if Clyde Phoebe ever visited the House of Love.

"Clyde, sure. Clyde's a regular," the woman said. "Got a special room for him down the hall that we decorate to look just like his bedroom back in Claremore, Oklahoma, when he was a youngster."

Gene said, "I bet there are lots of pictures of Patti Page."

The woman winked at Gene, then smiled in a way that pretended shyness. "And a girl dolled up to look just like her."

"But not the real thing."

"Something close."

"No." Gene was standing motionless. Alice's grinning face had suddenly flashed into his mind. Just for an instant he remembered her fine features and the terrifying delicacy of her touch. "No. If it's not real, it's not anything."

The woman came to her feet so quickly that Gene was startled. A bar of sunlight bisected the wall behind the bed, and from somewhere inside her skirt she produced a photo that was ripped in half. She held the pieces together in front of Gene's face. It was a black-and-white picture of a girl around fourteen, sitting alone on a sandy beach.

"This is me," the woman said. "Is that real enough for you?" Gene started for the door, but the woman moved sideways, blocking his exit. "This is me on Myrtle Beach after I ran away from home twenty years ago. I'm pregnant like I am now, but you can't tell from the photo."

Gene said, "Why are you telling me this?"

"Twenty years ago I gave up my child for adoption," the woman said, ignoring his question. "Last year I hired a private detective to find her. She lives in Denton, Florida, a little town outside of Jacksonville. I sent her a long letter and included this picture. An envelope came back two weeks later with it torn in two. No note. Nothing."

For a long time Gene just stared down at the floor, keeping his body and face perfectly still. Then he looked up and brushed away a plump tear that moved slowly down the side of the woman's face. He told her he was sorry.

"I'm gonna keep this child," the woman said, nodding as she tried to compose her distorted face, but moments after she resumed speaking, a man's agonized cries suddenly reverberated throughout the building, interrupting her voice and leaving Gene frozen in place. Abruptly the screaming stopped, and they stood together in silence for several seconds, listening to the diminishing echo.

"Jesus Christ," Gene said. "What the fuck was that?"

"It's nothing," the woman said, with a look of disinterest. "Just the Manson suite."

Gene stood staring at the woman's face searchingly, almost querulously. "The *what*?"

"The Manson suite," the woman repeated.

"What goes on in there?"

"They re-create the murders," the woman said, taking a small step backward. "It's like a show. I'd be in it today, but I'm not big enough to play Sharon Tate. You need to be at least six months." The woman pulled down the straps of her dress, exposing her pregnant belly and her large womanly breasts. "See?"

Gene did not believe what he was hearing. His eyes were all over the room. When they came back to the woman, he said, "Is that why you got pregnant, so you can be in this . . . show?"

"Sure." A siren sounded outside, and the woman glanced away from Gene as she pulled up the straps of her dress. "All the girls take their turn."

"Who pays to see this?"

"Anyone who has the money. Sometimes we do it twice a day, sometimes once a week. Everything is performed according to the trial transcript. The dialogue, the floor plan, it's all exactly the way it was. Rod Cameron saw it twice back in March."

Gene shook his head in amazement, and the confusion in his face slowly gave way to anger. "This place is fucked," he said. "How much do I owe you?"

"Fifty dollars for the room."

"What about you? I have to give you something."

"Give me a hug," the woman said, smiling timidly as her body leaned toward his. "Just a hug. That's all I want."

Gene put his arms around the woman and the warmth of her body seemed as familiar as her perfume. More screams and sounds of rage erupted down the hallway, and Gene fought back the urge to scream too.

"Make me a promise," the woman said softly, when all the voices in the building stopped. "Don't ever come back to the House of Love."

Nine

New Territory

In November of 1985, Gene received in the mail his quarterly issue of *Bim Bam Boom,* a rock-and-roll fanzine and collector's guide that was published out of a dingy basement apartment in Ann Arbor, Michigan. This particular issue was devoted to rockabilly music, and slashed across the cover was a bright yellow banner asking the question "Who Killed Bobby Fuller?" in blood-red letters.

The article was written by Chris Long and consisted mainly of the interview he'd done with Melanie Novack back in 1966, when Melanie had operated a secretarial service out of her one-bedroom apartment at 1770 Sycamore Avenue, one floor below the apartment Bobby shared with his mother. At the time Long was a reporter for the *Bad Seed,* a local underground newspaper that tried and failed to compete with the *L.A. Free Press,* finally folding three days before the article was scheduled to be published.

Melanie spoke at length about Bobby's opening night at P.J.'s back in November of 1965, the same sold-out show that Gene had attended with his brother.

She said, "Usually after a show he was all pumped up and hyper, talking a mile a minute. But that night when he came upstairs he seemed depressed, almost frightened. I couldn't figure it out, because I had friends who were at the first show, and they called and told me he got a standing ovation.

"When I asked Bobby what was wrong, he looked down at the rug and shook his head. He wouldn't talk about it. We just sat and watched the late show and ate snacks. The next day I heard that Phil Spector came backstage drunk after the second show. In front of Bobby, he told Stelzner that he was a no-talent mobster. He said if he had any brains he'd let Bobby record on his label. That's when Stelzner threatened to kill Spector if he ever saw him on the street.

"Of course, Bobby never mentioned any of this. Before he left, he asked me to type up a song he'd written on a paper napkin between shows. The first verse went something like:

> *Now that we've given our hearts away*
> *We can only buy them back with our*
> *Sorrow and our songs*

"That's all I can remember. As far as I know, he never recorded this tune."

Gene read the story through twice, making notes in the margin and underscoring passages that he found significant. When he was done he dialed Billy Legend, the fanzine's editor and publisher and a former counterculture impresario who, using his real name, Myron Koplewitz, co-authored the manifesto for the White Panther Party back in 1968.

Through the years Gene had spoken to Koplewitz several times, usually to verify the authenticity of a 45 he was seeking to acquire. And it was Koplewitz who convinced him not to buy "Hollywood High," a song that was supposedly recorded by the late Eddie Cochran, when he was a member of Richard Ray and the Shamrock Boys. The record, released on the Big Top label, later turned out to be counterfeit.

"I need Chris Long's number," Gene told Koplewitz, when he came on the line.

"I can't help you."

"Why not?"

"Because I don't have it," Koplewitz said. "You can only reach him by calling certain pay phones at times that are prearranged."

"Dude sounds paranoid."

"To say the least."

"Why?"

"Don't know."

"In the editor's notes you say he used to manage some bands back in the sixties."

"That's what he told me."

"What's he doing now?"

"Don't know that either."

"Did you ask?"

"Listen," Koplewitz said, lowering his voice and speaking in a tone that was almost conspiratorial. "You sound pretty flipped out. What's the deal?"

Gene paused before answering. Although he had never before shared anything with Koplewitz about his private life, he decided to tell him the truth, admitting that he was reinvestigating the death of Bobby Fuller as a way to escape the pain that was inflicted upon him by a brutal romantic tragedy. A tragedy, Gene made clear, that he was unwilling to discuss.

"That's cool. I understand. I know about pain," Koplewitz said, and his response sounded genuine. Then he said, "I can't believe you're a cop."

"Ex-cop."

"But you're telling me the truth? You actually worked on the original Fuller investigation?"

"In '66. Yeah."

Koplewitz laughed. "Far out. You're part of rock-and-roll history. I should be doin' a piece on you," he said, continuing to laugh. "I love it, man. And all this time I thought you were some rich Hollywood asshole who thinks it's cool to collect oldies."

Gene let some time go by without speaking. Suddenly it occurred to him that he might not need Long if he could find Melanie Novack, assuming she was still alive.

"She's dead," Koplewitz said, breaking the silence.

"Who?"

"Melanie Novack. That's where you were going, right? Fuck Long, find her."

Gene smiled to himself. "Maybe you should've been a cop, too."

"Nah. It was an obvious jump. I asked Long the same thing," Koplewitz said. "I wanted to speak to her, verify the interview."

"Maybe he was lying."

"Could be. But why?"

"For her. She could be scared."

"She wasn't scared back in '66. What changed?"

"I don't know."

"She's dead, Gene. Cancer."

"When?"

"Last year."

Gene made a quick calculation. "If she was thirty in 1966, that means she wasn't even fifty."

"Heavy smoker."

"It's still too young," Gene said. "I'm gonna check around."

"Good luck."

"Myron?"

"Yeah?"

"We should stick together. We're both sixties guys."

"True. Except I was a Weatherman and you were a pig."

In the weeks that followed, this is what Gene learned about Melanie Novack. She was born and raised in L.A., attended Hollywood High School, and was nine weeks pregnant when she graduated in the fall of 1956. The day after the prom, she and the father traveled to Yuma, Arizona, where an abortion had been arranged by one of her mother's coworkers at Paramount Pictures. At the last minute Melanie changed her mind and decided to have the child, a boy, and she gave it up for adoption with the father's consent.

After attending Woodbury Business College for a year, Melanie, with her mother's help, secured a job at the studio as a script-typist. She wore flashy earrings and tight skirts and drank her lunch with the boys at Nickodell's on Melrose. It took six months before her boss noticed that her job performance went into a steep decline every afternoon around three o'clock. According to her employment records, she was warned twice for drinking on the job, then fired.

Laurie Gross, one of the women who worked in the typing pool with Melanie, told Gene: "She was a sassy gal, always cracking jokes and chewing gum. Not beautiful, but the kind of rinsed-out blonde that some men like."

Melanie moved out of her mother's house on Selma Avenue in the summer of 1958. She quickly found a job as a secretary for Holmes-Tuttle Ford, a car dealership on La Brea, and for the next year she lived in a furnished single on Gramercy Place. Over Christmas, two friends of her mother's spotted Melanie in Las Vegas, accompanied by a man they described as "rough-looking." She was so drunk, they said, she could barely stand up.

In February of 1959, she was arrested for drunk driving. Six weeks later she was arrested again, and the judge fined her $450 and suspended her driving privileges for six months. Too proud to take the bus, she quit her job and went on unemployment, spending most of her days alone, sick at heart, drinking inside her perpetually dark apartment.

Gene spoke to Lou Sloss, now retired, who managed the car dealership where Melanie had worked. Lou remembered very little about her, only that she had "bountiful breasts."

Melanie's mother died of lung cancer on May 1, 1964. She had just turned fifty-one years old. In her will, her modest savings and the proceeds from the sale of her house were given to the March of Dimes, her favorite charity. Melanie was left nothing.

Seven weeks after the funeral, Melanie was found sleeping on a bus bench at the corner of Sunset Boulevard and Gardner Avenue. Her body, clad only in a thin cotton bathrobe, was covered with bruises and lacerations. She told the police she'd been beaten and raped by a gang of teenage boys she'd befriended earlier in the evening. At the time she was working as a shampoo girl at Umberto's, a fancy hair salon in West Hollywood.

Once she was released from the hospital, she began regularly attending meetings of Alcoholics Anonymous, putting together thirty days of sobriety before she suddenly left Los Angeles on Easter Sunday. She reappeared one year later, bringing back with her a man named Dean Landry, a silent middle-aged L.L. Bean type, who was the foremost breeder of orchids in the western United States. At least that's what Melanie told her neighbors when she moved into her new apartment on 1770 Sycamore Avenue.

On the morning of August 31, 1965, while Melanie was at an A.A. meeting celebrating her sobriety birthday, Dean Landry moved out, taking with him her TV and $400 she had stashed in her jewelry box. The following day she placed an ad in both the *Daily Variety* and the *Hollywood Reporter,* announcing her new business, a secretarial service she called, simply, Melanie's Place. Word of her skills spread quickly, and within three months she'd saved enough money to buy a new television and put a down payment on a red 1955 Chevy convertible.

One of her first customers, Ted Reuben, a screenwriter Gene found through an ad he placed in the Writers Guild newsletter, said: "Melanie was not only a superb typist, but she also had an interesting mind. She was not stupid, by any means. Sometimes when I was bored, I used to go over and bullshit with her. If she was working, I'd take a nap or watch television with the sound down low."

Twice while Reuben was at her apartment, Melanie received calls from Joyce Haber, the gossip columnist for the *L.A. Times.* She also had regular conversations with Natalie Wood and George Kennedy, the rugged character actor who her mother met back in 1947, when she was the script supervisor on *She Wore a Yellow Ribbon.*

Reuben said: "From these conversations I assumed that her mother and Kennedy had had an affair. Apparently her mother had lots of affairs. According to Melanie she had been a beautiful woman, much prettier than her, she said. But she never knew her father, who abandoned her mother shortly after Melanie was born."

Reuben told Gene that he and Melanie had once made love after she'd completed the draft of one of his screenplays. She told Reuben: "I'm just one of those people who needs love, and I'm not afraid to give it. When I was drinking I went with liars and connivers, and over and over I was betrayed and abandoned. My life became an unbroken circle of isolation and pain. For years I detested my body. But now, more and more, I want to be touched."

On August 1, two months after Bobby Fuller's death, Melanie Novack vacated her apartment on North Sycamore Avenue. Over the next year she moved three more times, and her last known address that Gene could find was the Argyle Manor, a twelve-unit apartment building on the corner of Franklin and Argyle in East Hollywood.

The apartment manager at that time, Norman Swain, had long since died, but the building's owner, Lillian Ohrtman, now in her mid-eighties and living in a Pasadena retirement home, thought she remembered Melanie but wasn't certain.

"We used to rent to so many different girls," she told Gene when he came to visit. "Good girls, bad girls, widows, orphans, runaway teenagers, runaway moms, wannabe starlets, and just plain girls who were trying to find someplace that was endurable."

Gene said, "She ran a secretarial business out of her apartment. Melanie's Place, she called it. She mostly typed screenplays."

"My second husband wrote films. Leonard Lewis. He was blacklisted. Melanie's Place, you say." Lillian Ohrtman drummed her heavily ringed fingers on the arm of her wheelchair. "I guess I should remember but I don't."

Gene told Ohrtman that he'd spoken to her son, Mark, when he'd dropped by the Argyle Manor earlier that day. "I asked to see the records. He wasn't much help."

"Was he drunk? Of course he was," Lillian Ohrtman said quickly, giving Gene a knowing look. "He's always drunk, staying up all night with his sissy boyfriends, carousing and doing whatever they do. The whole business just turns my stomach." Lillian Ohrtman took a tired, heavy breath. "Oh, don't mind me, I'm just angry because I wanted grandchildren. Mark's a good boy. He can't help the way he is."

Before Gene left the Arcadia Arms Retirement Village, Lillian Ohrtman promised to call her son. She said she'd have Mark send him anything he needed. Then she asked Gene what made him so certain that Melanie Novack had been a tenant at the Argyle Manor.

"I tracked down one of her customers," Gene said. "A screenwriter. He told me."

Lillian Ohrtman nodded her head as she stared at Gene. She seemed exceedingly alert, her body tensed with a troubling thought. "You're a driven man, aren't you, Mr. Burk?"

"Yes, I am."

"Give me the dates again."

"July through September of 1967."

"And then where did she go?"

"I don't know. She disappeared," Gene said. "That's why I'd like the names of all the tenants who lived there during those three months. Someone may know something."

"The summer of 1967," Lillian Ohrtman said, staring ahead, her face taking on a melancholy expression. "Yes. I remember that summer. All those girls and boys acting so free, dancing in the streets and in the park. Such happy times they were."

"Not for everyone," Gene said.

"Well, that's true. But they were for me," Lillian Ohrtman said, patting his hand. "Now would you mind wheeling me into the garden. I want to feel the afternoon sun on my face."

That night Gene received a phone call from his brother, who sounded drunk. He said he'd be flying down to L.A. on Monday for a week of meetings. "I'm doing a final polish on the script," he told Gene. "Once I'm done it goes out to actors with firm offers attached."

"Sounds like they're going to make this one."

"Yeah, maybe. Who knows?" Ray said, without much excitement. "I've been through this before."

Which was true. Twice Ray had written scripts for films that were only weeks away from principal photography when they were abruptly canceled. The first time, at Paramount, the head of production was fired, and all the movies he had in the pipeline were permanently shelved.

Through his agent, Ray tried to repurchase his script, but the new studio chief, fearful that the project might become a success somewhere else, turned him down. That was back in 1977.

Two years later Ray wrote an original screenplay called *The Twilight Man,* a chilling story of a small boy, his mother, and a serial killer posing as a traveling magician. Universal optioned the script for director Hal Ashby, and Mick Jagger had agreed to star as the homicidal Houdini. Sets were already under construction in Louisiana when Ashby began to have second thoughts about the script. He suggested adding a new character and a convoluted subplot that seemed to make little sense to Ray or the studio.

Jagger, already anxious about taking on a role this large, and one that required a southern accent, decided to abandon the project, citing a clause in his contract that gave him approval over any changes in the script. The following day Universal shut down the film.

"I've told you about these cocksuckers," Ray said. "They encourage you to death. You can't believe a fuckin' word they say. If it happens, it happens."

"Where you gonna stay?"

"The Beverly Hills Hotel. I've got a two-bedroom suite. Louie's flying in."

"Louie?" Gene's voice sounded skeptical. "I thought he was doing a play."

"He is. It opened last week," Ray said. Then he explained: his son's explosive performance as "Hoss" in the off-Broadway revival of Sam Shepard's *Tooth of Crime* had received rave reviews in both the *New York Times* and the *Village Voice.* "He's hot. William Morris is bringing him out to audition for a pilot on NBC. Some futuristic cop show."

"That's exciting," Gene said.

"The three of us will have dinner."

"We'll see."

"What's this 'we'll see'? Fuck 'we'll see.' You, me, and Louie. On Thursday."

"You're drunk," Gene said.

"So what?" Ray shouted. "So-fucking-what?"

"Call me when you get in," Gene said, in a tone that was not quite sincere, and when the line clicked he stared at the receiver for several moments before replacing it gently in the cradle.

The house was suddenly silent, a silence so complete that the only sound he heard was the exhalation of his breath. Feeling jumpy and a little bit frightened, Gene lit a cigarette and opened the sliding glass doors that led out to his deck. A soothing breeze brushed against his face and he closed his eyes, breathing in the darkness. For a moment his mind floated free, and he was able to stand apart like a bystander in his own dream, amazed and mystified, observing the different strands of his life, past and present, and how they seemed to be tangled like roots beneath the weight of the earth.

First there was Alice, her death in a mangled aircraft and then his guilt, a survivor's self-punishing guilt, followed by his burning need to erase her face from his memory, to somehow replace with rage and blame the pain that never seemed to ebb; to find a cause to be consumed by, a mystery to solve, some lust for justice . . . like, perhaps, discovering who killed Bobby Fuller.

Next was Melanie Novack, a vulnerable and slightly desperate creature, he assumed, whose life was like an impenetrable maze, filled with the tawdriness of things. She was a woman who saw something murderous in the wild darkness and told her story in a voice, Gene imagined, that was hoarse from cigarettes and edged with fear.

And what about his brother's wife Sandra, dead for two years, and her purported prison friendship with the Manson girls, especially Susan Atkins. Did Sandra bullshit Eddie Cornell, or was she telling him the truth? But more important, what was Eddie holding back—about Manson and Bobby Fuller?

Then Gene thought about his mother, trying but failing to understand why she left her family in the summer of 1950. Would his father tell Gene the whole truth if he asked? Did his father even know the whole truth? And, finally, did his father know that, standing on the site of his former newsstand, the largest and most successful newsstand in Hollywood, was a building that heaved with vile desires, where the atrocious indecencies that took place inside were limited only by the customers' imaginations and whatever dark wind blew through the cellars of their souls?

Ten

More from Alice

Dear Alice,

So much has happened since I last wrote you. To set it all down would take way too long. So I'll just give you the highlights. The single most important thing to understand—and I know you won't believe me, Alice—is that we're going to change the world: Charlie and me and everyone who is living with us here in the desert.

You remember Charlie from my last two letters, right? The man I met in Berkeley, the ex-con with the scraggly hair and eyes that were unimaginably dark. Well, it turns out that this funny-looking little man in faded blue overalls is really God. That's right, Alice. G - O - D.

If you don't believe me, ask Dennis Wilson of the Beach Boys or Papa John Phillips or Warren Beatty, or any of the big-shot actors or musicians who met Charlie while we were living in Los Angeles. We even stayed in Dennis Wilson's house for a month, me and Charlie and the girls, dropping acid and playing poker in the nude; a bunch of fallen angels making love on all fours, while God himself looked on with a knife in his pocket. Boy that was a crazy month, let me tell you!

Hey, remember in high school when all the girls swooned over the latest heartthrob on American Bandstand, *guys like Bobby Rydell or Tommy Sands or the Everly Brothers? Well, guess what, Alice? They're not all that different from Jimmy Bascomb or Billy Hayes or the rest of the guys we knew in Cedar Rapids. Okay, maybe they're richer or better looking, but they cry and bleed like everyone else.*

Not too long ago I saw a rich person cry and bleed at the same time, and I saw a famous person so scared she couldn't talk. Scared of who? Charlie. Little ugly puny Charlie, barely five-foot-five on his tippy toes. God.

Four highlights so far:

(*a*) *We're going to change the world.*
(*b*) *Charlie is God.*
(*c*) *Famous people cry and bleed.*
(*d*) *Sex is good. More sex is better.*

One afternoon in July, Charlie drove me into Hollywood and left me on a street corner. He told me to make men pay to have sex with me. He made me dress like a schoolgirl, in a starched white blouse, a scotch plaid mini-skirt, bobby socks, and Mary Janes. In an hour and a half I made four hundred and fifty dollars.

When it got dark, I hitched back to Spahn Ranch, this place where we were living in L.A. It took five rides and I made another three hundred dollars. You know something, Alice, it's amazing how men can get so excited when they know you're gonna show them your pussy or your boobs. On my last ride, I pulled up my skirt and let the driver finger-fuck me while we were on the Ventura Freeway, going eighty miles per hour in the fast lane. When I came he paid me fifty dollars! Figure that out.

Now I know you think what I'm doing is wrong. Neither of us were brought up to act this way. But let me ask you something: How can it be wrong if God says it isn't? Answer: It can't be. You know what's wrong? Not giving your love away. Charley says, "Hell is where people can't give love." What's weird is, sometimes you have to hurt someone to give someone else love. And sometimes you have to kill people, too.

I guess you think it's really strange me writing you like this, since we were never that close—hardly knew each other, to be totally honest. I worry (a little) that you think I'm careless or just plain crazy, but I'm not. In fact, I'm happier now than I've ever been.

I told Charlie about you, what you looked like, how you walked, your height and weight (approx); how tan you got in the summertime, the way all the boys paraded past your towel while you were sunbathing up at the lake. Your bikini drove them crazy, you could tell by the little bulges in their trunks.

Charlie said I should ask you to join our family. I said I would, but I knew you would never come. To tell you the truth, I wouldn't want you around. You're not like the other girls who are here. You've never traveled alone or slept in the woods on wet leaves. You haven't screamed your heart out and broken all the rules like we have. And you haven't broken out of yourself. Too much has been held in. The tears you cry slide down the inside of your face.

Be honest, Alice. When was the last time you ever shared your life with someone? Really shared your life. Insisted that they find out who you were, explained that all you wanted was love, told them what you would give up to have that love, and asked for nothing more.

I have.

Love,
Alice

Eleven

In the Air

with Louie—

and the Other Alice

Even though they had been in the air for thirty minutes and were cruising silently above the clouds, Louie's eyes were still closed, and he was conscious of nothing but his thundering heartbeat, which sounded in his ears and overwhelmed the buzz of voices around him in the first-class cabin. Earlier in the week, when he'd told his therapist how frightened he was to fly, she wondered if he'd ever experienced a similar kind of fear before he went on stage.

"All the time," he told her. "But as soon as I say my first line of dialogue, it disappears."

His therapist smiled. She was a heavy-set woman in her fifties with large features and serious blue eyes that rarely blinked. "So when you become someone else, you're relaxed?"

"Yeah."

"It's easier than just being Louie."

"I'm okay with who I am."

"But you're scared," his therapist said, and she looked at him questioningly. "Not just of flying. You're scared of lots of things."

"I'm scared the fucking plane is going to crash."

"Yes. I understand that. But the plane is not going to crash."

"You don't know that," Louie said, looking away from her eyes. "It happens all the time."

"That's not true, Louie. It doesn't happen all the time."

"It happened to my uncle. That's how his fiancée died."

"Yes, I know," the therapist said. "But you're going to be fine," she reassured him. "This is an exciting moment in your life. Enjoy it."

* * *

"Can I take your order, Mr. Burk?"

Louie blinked open his eyes at the sound of his last name. A trim stewardess with a pert expression and short, reddish-blond hair was standing in the aisle by his row. She was staring down at him with her brows slightly arched.

"Sorry to wake you up."

"I wasn't really sleeping," Louie said, sitting up and reaching for the menu that was tucked into the seat pocket in front of him. "I was just trying to relax."

"I would go with the chicken piccata or the prime rib," said the man sitting next to him by the window. He was around forty and deeply tanned, dressed in jeans and a faded blue denim shirt with silver snaps instead of buttons. A pair of aviator sunglasses were balanced on the top of his head. "Skip the fish. It tastes like cardboard."

Louie said, "I'll take the prime rib."

"Good choice." The stewardess gave Louie a sly wink as she wrote down his order. "Would you like a glass of complimentary champagne with your dinner?"

"No thanks."

"Wine?"

"If you have a Diet Coke, that would be great."

"Mr. Geller?"

"Let me have another double vodka," said Louie's seatmate, and when the stewardess stepped away he held out his hand. "Ronnie Geller."

"Louie Burk."

"Louie Burk? No shit! I thought I recognized you," Geller said, and pulled back to stare at Louie's slowly reddening face. "I saw you in *Tooth of Crime* the night before last. You were awesome."

"Thanks."

"I love Shepard. I love the fucking theater, period. When I'm in New York, I see everything I can. Unless I'm banging some broad," Geller added in a voice that was a little too loud. "What're you doin' in L.A.?"

"I'm auditioning for a pilot."

"Good for you. That's terrific," Geller said, and, after an awkward moment, Louie asked him if he was in the business. "Fuck no! Are you kidding? I'm in the rag trade. I got a couple of sportswear lines. Geller Casuals. All the big stores carry them. But half the kids I knew in high school became either agents or writers."

"My dad's a writer."

"Yeah?"

"Ray Burk."

"Ray Burk. I know that name. Wait a second," Geller said, almost to himself, pausing to create a melodramatic moment. "By any chance does your dad have a brother named Gene?"

"Yeah."

"You're kidding me?" Geller looked utterly taken aback. "I went to high school with Gene. He was a cool guy. Quiet but tough. Really tough. In our senior year he went with this chick from Venice named Barbara Westbrook. Redhead with huge tits." Geller paused to gulp down his drink. "So how's he doin'?"

"Not too good," Louie said, and he suddenly looked weary, older. "He was supposed to get married, but his fiancée died a few months ago."

Geller simply stared at Louie for several seconds. "That's terrible. I'm sorry to hear that," he said somberly. "How did she die?"

"In a plane crash," Louie said, and Geller came forward in his seat, as if he were jolted by a small electric shock. "She was a stewardess. Gene thinks the pilot had a drinking problem."

By now the conversation in the rows around them had stopped. A *Time* magazine slipped off someone's lap, landing in the aisle, and a stewardess near the galley was staring at the back of Louie's head while she poured ginger ale into a plastic cup. Her hand was shaking as she tried to block her mind from imagining the unimaginable.

Louie's eyes were now closed, but he was wearing on his face an expression of wild agitation. Geller said softly, "Are you okay?"

"Yeah, I'm fine."

"You sure?"

"I'll be okay as soon as we land."

"That's in three hours."

Louie opened his eyes and forced a smile. But inwardly he was straining against some kind of primitive fear that he couldn't eradicate. "I'm sorry," he said. "Flying scares the shit out of me."

"I can see that," Geller said dryly. "But don't worry, this plane isn't going down. You know why?"

"Why?"

"Because you and I have a lot more to talk about. That's why," Geller said and checked his watch. "Right now it's two o'clock on the West Coast. I'm gonna nap for an hour. We'll continue this conversation after lunch."

Geller grabbed a pillow and a blanket from the overhead compartment, and, not long after his eyes were shut, Louie heard him snoring softly, his uneven breaths making a tiny purring sound as they left his nose.

In a while, Louie reached under his seat for the leather shoulder bag he'd bought at Bloomingdale's earlier in the week. Inside was the latest issue of *Rolling Stone,* a day-planner, a collection of plays by Tennessee Williams, and the script for *Cool Heaven,* the television pilot he was reading for the following morning. After he took out his script and leaned down to store his bag, he noticed a woman gazing at him thoughtfully through the slightly parted curtain that separated the first-class passengers from those flying in coach. She was in her late thirties, decent-looking but certainly not pretty, dressed in a Levi's jacket and corduroy pants with a light blue crew-neck sweater underneath the jacket.

Louie maintained eye contact while she took a sip from the plastic cup she held just short of her lips; then, shivering slightly in the alien air, he turned away from her intensely curious stare and began to study his lines. But twice during the next hour he glanced over his shoulder, and both times this woman's face was filled with a sadness so pure and complete that he thought it must have been drink-inspired.

"My dad was in retail. Women's wear. He had a store on Hollywood Boulevard called World Wide Fashions. He knew your grandfather," Geller told Louie, as the aircraft descended slowly through a sky that was the color of dead skin. Lunch was over and they were not quite an hour away from landing in Los Angeles. "That's where he bought all his magazines."

"It was the best newsstand in the city."

Geller nodded. "Yeah, I know. And now it's some fucking porn palace. Must make your grandfather sick, huh?"

"I don't think he cares," Louis lied, remembering his grandfather's ceaseless rants about the "perverts and other garbage" who now roamed the boulevard, frightening the tourists and driving away what little glamour was left over from Hollywood's halcyon days: the decades of the thirties, forties, and fifties. "He's retired, anyway. I don't think he's been up there in five years."

Which was another lie, because the last time they had spoken on the phone, his grandfather told Louie he'd eaten lunch at Musso-Frank earlier in the week. "And when I'm done, I walk outside and what do I see? Whores with skirts barely covering their private parts are posing on my corner. Nate's corner," he said, with a fatalistic laugh. "It makes me want to throw up."

"House of Love! That's it!" Geller said, and his voice, filled with energy, pulled Louie back to the present. "I heard it's owned by Larry Havana, Jack Havana's son."

Louie nodded his head but didn't reply, hoping his silence indicated indifference. He was getting a little tired of Geller's overhearty friendliness, which seemed unearned and was the reason he'd lied to him in the first place. But Louie's impassive face hid the tremor of apprehension that came with hearing Jack Havana's name, a name that was discreetly mentioned by his father and his uncle Gene while he was growing up, but never by his grandfather. There was a mystery surrounding this faceless person that Louie didn't understand, a secret that pertained to the disappearance of his grandmother in 1950, when his father was only eight years old.

With a certain pride, Geller continued to talk about his father and the store he owned on Hollywood Boulevard. Competing against the Broadway and other department stores in the neighborhood, Maury Geller barely scraped by until the late 1950s, when he made a bundle selling hand-painted Mexican skirts and blouses that he imported from a manufacturer in Mexico City, a company owned by a German named Luther Von Lang.

"It was common knowledge that this guy was a Nazi," Geller said. "But my dad didn't give a shit. That's how he paid for our house in Brentwood. In the sixties, when the whole Mexican fad was over, he switched to suede. Geller's House of Suede. By the seventies he had five stores, including one in San Francisco. I could've taken over the whole deal, but I needed to make it on my own, which I did." Geller smiled suddenly. "That's probably why you became an actor, not to compete with your dad, right? What about your mom? What's she do?"

"My mom's dead," Louie said, looking a little bit angry. "She killed herself two years ago. She drank herself to death."

Geller stared at Louie with such great pity that it seemed insulting. "I'm sorry," he finally said in a soothing voice.

"That's okay. You were just being friendly. Don't worry about it," Louie said, and he flipped open the script that was resting in his lap. "I think I better work on my lines."

"Yeah. Sure," Geller said, making a professional face. "When's the audition?"

"Monday."

"You got a big talent. You'll do great."

Louie shrugged. He was less concerned about the audition than the time he would be spending with his father in Los Angeles. He'd already angered Rick Hirsch, the producer of the pilot. Hirsch's secretary had booked Louie into the Burbank Hilton, which was located directly across the street from the production offices, but his father had called and insisted that he stay with him at the Beverly Hills Hotel.

"Come on. We'll have a blast," his father said, a few days before Louie's flight. "We haven't seen each other in six months."

"Dad, we talk to each other on the phone all the time."

"Look, I'm proud of you. I want to see you. Don't you get it, Louie?"

"Yeah, I get it," Louie said. "But I'm not a little kid anymore. It's not like . . ."

"Like what?"

"Forget it."

"No. Tell me what you were going to say."

Louie sighed. "I'll see you when I get in," he said, taking a moment's pause before he gently hung up the phone.

"We're almost home," Geller said, holding Louie's eye while the aircraft circled slowly over the ocean, preparing to approach their runway from the west. "I told you we'd be okay."

"We're not there yet."

Geller met this remark with silence, his face taking on an expression of relief as the wings flattened out and the landing gear dropped with a jolt. When the wheels touched down, the woman seated directly behind Louie in coach quickly stashed her magazine inside her purse and checked her ticket to make sure the baggage claim tags were still stapled to the envelope. Then she prayed silently, thanking God for letting her arrive safely and then asking him to allow her to leave the airport undetained with her suitcase, the contents of which she had hidden for the last sixteen years in the weedy backyard of her childhood home, the home she had inherited when her parents died but where she rarely stayed, until the first week of June, when she decided to come back to Cedar Rapids for good.

The woman—her name was Alice McMillan—stood to Louie's right and slightly behind him, calming down a little as the moving walkway slowly carried them from their gate to the front of the terminal. Of course neither knew that twenty years ago, back in November of 1965, the November before Louie was born, she and his father and his uncle Gene had spent an evening together inside the same nightclub, watching Bobby Fuller perform live. That was also the night Alice saw Sharon Tate for the first time, the first time Alice touched her skin.

At the end of the moving walkway, Louie was surprised to see a limousine driver holding up a cardboard sign showing his name printed in large blue letters. When their eyes met, Louie said tentatively, "I'm Louie Burk."

The driver reached for Louie's carry-on luggage. "Welcome to Los Angeles, Mr. Burk. We're parked just outside."

"I wasn't expecting a limo."

"Compliments of William Morris."

"Lucky boy," Alice McMillan said to herself, as she watched Louie walk outside, into the buttery sunlight. "So handsome and with his whole life ahead of him, unlived. Lucky, lucky boy."

■

On October 8, 1969, the night before he was arrested, Charles Manson, speaking with a half-mournful smile, told Alice McMillan a story that he'd never told anyone before. It was a story about Charlie's mother and a day they spent together after she was paroled from the West Virginia State Penitentiary in 1942, where she served two years for armed robbery. She was twenty-four years old and Charlie had just turned eight.

Kathleen Manson never had a decent job, and prior to the summer of 1942, she had spent little time with her only son—a boy who could barely read but only wanted to please—abandoning him for weeks and sometimes months at a time, while she ran around the country following her restless heart.

"Growing up, I lived in Kentucky, either with my grandmother or Betty, my maternal aunt," Charlie told Alice McMillan. It was after midnight in Death Valley, and they were sitting in a dune buggy that was parked on a small hill overlooking Barker Ranch. "When my mom got out of jail I was living with Betty. It was Sunday. Usually when she came to pick me up she was with an older man, some needle-jerk she'd introduce as my uncle, and we'd go back to a fleabag hotel, where I ended up out in the hallway, listening through the door while they drank and fucked and shot dope.

"But this time she was by herself, and she was driving a shiny new Buick convertible with spoked wheels. I knew it wasn't hers, but it didn't matter as long as we were alone. You know what I mean, Alice?"

"I do, Charlie. I know exactly."

"It was summer and we drove with the top down all the way to Panama Springs, this resort by Lake Lorraine in the Blue Ridge Mountains. At a store on the boardwalk she bought me some swimming trunks and some comic books and a deck of cards so we could play casino and gin rummy. The beach was really crowded, but we found a place by ourselves down near the shoreline."

Alice said, "I remember goin' to the beach with my mom. I remember bein' embarrassed because she was overweight. We were both fat."

"You look fine now," Charlie said.

"Thanks, Charlie."

"You know I wouldn't fuck you if you didn't."

"I know that."

"I like my girls trim. My mom had skinny legs, but she was built on top," Charlie said, shifting in his seat a little as he watched some car lights slowly wind their way down the mountain on the eastern edge of Goler Wash. "She was wearing a one-piece swimsuit that was so tight I could see her moneymaker when she opened her legs. I saw some hairs there too, curly hairs. I remember that."

"I'm surprised she didn't shave down there," Alice said.

"You forget about that stuff in prison," Charlie said. "Shaving your pussy is something you do on the outside, like dancing in the kitchen or opening a bank account. I know about prison."

"I know you do, Charlie."

"She was sweet to me that day," Charlie went on, still keeping his eyes on the approaching headlights. "She played with me in the water and, when we got out, she rubbed suntan oil on my back so I wouldn't burn. For lunch she bought me a hot dog and a sno-cone, and when some men tried to start up a conversation she shooed them away. I wanted that day to last forever, because I knew that once we left the beach we had to go back to wherever she was staying, and I knew a man would be there waiting for her."

"The man who owned the car."

Charlie nodded his head, his moist eyes looking across the valley, his blank expression only a transparant protection against his private pain. "Can you see me as a small boy on the beach?"

"Yes. I can, Charlie."

"What color are my trunks?"

"They're striped, blue and white in a slanting pattern."

"What else do you see?"

"Just a little boy with his mom, lying next to each other, both of them on their bellies with drops of water drying on their backs."

"Can you see the hair snakin' down her thigh?"

"Yes, I can."

"I get a hard-on thinkin' about it. I think that might be wrong."

"Why?"

"It's my mother."

Alice reached over and felt his crotch. "I like it when you get hard."

"I may want to feel your mouth down there when I'm done telling this story."

"Sure, Charlie. Anything you want."

Charlie remained silent for several seconds. Then Alice saw him blink twice and smile wryly, then sadly, his lips wide with pain. "We played gin rummy after we dried off. I think she let me beat her," he said, as more headlights appeared in the distance, at least five cars moving across the desert from the west in a snakelike line. "We played cards and swam and laughed and talked until the air got cool. I told her I didn't want her to leave, that I missed her when she was in prison. She said she missed me, too. I started to cry."

Alice's hand was still resting in Charlie's lap. She was surprised to see a tear slide down his cheek and disappear into his beard. She said, "You loved her. Didn't you, Charlie?"

"Yes, I did. I loved her that day very much. I didn't want it to end."

Alice leaned over and kissed the side of Charlie's face. "You can cry, Charlie. It's okay."

"Mama took me back to the hotel, the Hotel Sherman in Lexington,

Kentucky, this ugly five-story brick building in the middle of skid row. Her room was on the second floor," Charlie said with a cold stare, his tears drying and his voice powered by rage. "In the middle of the room was an iron bed where her boyfriend, Joe Charles, a black man, lay asleep. Under the bed were two suitcases, his and hers, and a bag filed with loose cash."

"Money he'd stolen."

"Him and his crime partner, Whitey, who was stayin' in the room next door. They both ended up dead, shot during a bank robbery in Akron, Ohio. But that was years later."

"How long did you stay with your mom?"

"That time, two weeks, the three of us sleepin' in the same bed. At night when Joe Charles thought I was asleep, he'd fuck my mom; and when he was done, he'd send her next door to Whitey."

Alice, gazing away, her face filled with disgust, said, "That's no way for a little boy to see his mom."

"When she left the room, Joe Charles took advantage of me. He fucked me up the ass. He said if I told my mom, he'd kill me. And I believed him," Charlie said, speaking firmly and holding back his shame. "He came in my mouth. He just used me like he used my mom. But that was the last time I sucked a man's dick. In the penitentiary a nigger tried to punk me out, but I slid a shank in between his ribs and that was that. The word got out quick that Charles Manson was no one's butt-boy."

Alice said, "I only fucked one nigger, this musician I met at Monterey Pop. I was high on LSD at the time."

"I don't want to hear about it," Charlie said.

"That's okay. I don't remember much anyway."

Charlie smiled and his hand went up to squeeze her breast. "You're a good chick, Alice."

"I know I am. I used to think I was bad, but not anymore."

"Ain't none of us bad," Charlie said, staring into the darkness. "Me, you, Joe Charles, Whitey, my mom. None of us. We're just doin' the best we can."

Alice pointed at the mysterious headlights crawling across the landscape. "Those cars are getting close, Charlie."

"I can see that."

"Are they comin' for us?"

"They might be."

"What're you gonna do?"

"Hide, I guess."

"What happens if they find us?"

"I don't know," Charlie said. His eyes were sealed, and there was a new peacefulness in his face. "It doesn't matter anyhow. In jail or not, I'm still serving a life sentence."

When Louie arrived at the Beverly Hills Hotel, there was a message at the front desk to call Jeremy Platt, his West Coast contact at William Morris. There was also a note from his father, explaining that he was at a meeting and would be back at the hotel by five o'clock.

"He arranged for a two-bedroom suite," said the desk clerk, a young woman with thin shoulders and dark-framed glasses that seemed to magnify her eyeballs. "It's on the second floor, overlooking the garden."

Louie looked disturbed by this information. "You mean I don't have my own room?"

"You did, yes. But your father thought it would be more convenient this way."

"I'd rather have my own room."

"I see," the woman said, with exaggerated dismay. "Perhaps you should discuss—"

"I don't have to discuss it with anybody," Louie said, losing his temper. "NBC is paying for my room, not my dad."

"That was not my understanding."

The desk clerk stepped away to summon the hotel's assistant manager, a tall man, fortyish, with an expression on his face of unreasonable annoyance. Speaking with a slight French accent, he told Louie that the billing had been switched and Columbia Pictures, his father's employer, was now picking up the tab.

"If you like, we can go back to the original arrangement," he said, gazing over Louie's head. "However, it could take an hour or two to get everything straightened out. It would mean calling the network and getting their okay, which I would be happy to do."

"I can't believe he did this," Louie said. Then his face broke into a forgiving smile. "All right. Screw it. I'll stay with him."

The assistant manager presented Louie with a key. "Enjoy your stay," he said, and Louie turned and crossed the lobby, while the bellman and the desk clerk exchanged glances, that were impenetrable, lacking any sign of professional kindness.

Louie had not yet finished unpacking when the phone rang inside his suite. It was his uncle Gene calling from his grandfather's house in Mar Vista.

"Welcome back," he said, his voice competing with the televised baseball game that was playing noisily in the background. "When did you get in?"

"Just a while ago. How's Grandpa?" Louie asked hopefully. "Is he feeling okay?"

"He's watching the game. You want to say hello?"

"Sure."

Two weeks earlier on a stroll to the drugstore, Nathan Burk took a false step and tripped over a curb, straining all the ligaments in his right knee. At the doctor's office his leg was put into a brace and he decided to get his yearly physical. The results that came back the following week indicated a suspicious elevation in his red blood cell count. More tests were run, including a colonoscopy and a biopsy of his prostate, the latter revealing the presence of a slow-growing cancer that his doctor recommended treating nonaggressively.

"As long as you're not in any discomfort, I don't feel surgery is necessary," the doctor told Nathan Burk. "Not for a man of your age. If it grows at its present rate, it would not be a problem until you're well into your nineties."

"And presumably dead," Nathan Burk said, without smiling, and he then informed the doctor that he was still capable of having orgasms. "Not that you asked."

"Another reason to leave things as they are," the doctor said, and he told Nathan Burk to schedule an appointment in six months.

"So how's my grandson?" Nathan Burk asked Louie. His voice sounded tired, hoarse. "I hear you're going to be a big star."

"Not quite. I'm just auditioning for a pilot."

"You're playing a pilot. That's a good role. John Wayne was a pilot in *The High and the Mighty*."

"Not that kind of pilot. It's a television pilot, a new series for next fall. I play a cop."

"I don't understand but never mind. Your father will explain it to me," Nathan Burk said. "When am I going to see you?"

"Friday. On my way to the airport."

"Good. Are you watching the game?"

"No."

"What's wrong with you? Turn on the television. The Dodgers just tied the score."

There was a short silence. The phone in the other bedroom rang, making a slightly muffled sound. Standing up, Louie said, "I met this guy on the plane. He said his father knew you. Something Geller. Marvin, I think."

"Maury Geller! World Wide Fashions. He was a putz," Nathan Burk said. "Here, your uncle wants to talk to you."

"Let me speak to your dad," Gene's voice said in his ear.

"He's not here. He's at a meeting. I have to get the other phone," Louie said. "I'll see you tonight."

Louie hung up quickly and moved into the adjacent bedroom. The ringing phone was on the floor next to the dresser, buried underneath the morning newspapers and some twisted clothing. When he reached for the receiver, a small green tinted vial fell out of a shirt pocket and rolled across the rug. It was half-filled with a white powdery substance that Louie knew was cocaine.

"Hello?"

"Louie?"

"Yeah."

"Jeremy Pratt from William Morris. You get my message?"

"I was just about to call you." Louie picked up the vial and placed it on the bedstand next to an empty pint of tequila. "I got in a few minutes ago."

"That's cool. Just touching base. You all set for tomorrow?"

"Pretty much."

"I hyped the shit out of the casting director. I told her you're the man," Jeremy Pratt said, his voice brimming with confidence. "This could be a huge break for you."

Louie took a moment, then mumbled something about doing the best he can, but his mind was really elsewhere, occupied with thoughts of his father and what the night ahead would hold if he were drinking heavily or taking drugs.

"So what about tonight," Jeremy Pratt said, as if he were dialed into Louie's mind. "You have any plans?"

"I'm going out to dinner with my dad."

"Too bad. I got this chick who's dyin' to meet you. Jessica Santee. You know who she is?"

"The name sounds familiar."

"She plays Angie on *Crooked Hearts*," Jeremy said. "She saw your picture in my office and flipped out. Let's get together for a late drink."

"I don't think so," Louie said. His voice was friendly but firm. "I appreciate the offer, but I better get eight hours tonight."

Jeremy Pratt made a humming sound. "Yeah. You're probably right. We'll be at Le Dome if you change your mind. By the way," he said. "How'd you like the limo? Surprise, huh?"

"Yeah," Louie said. "It was."

"We treat our clients right. Look, I gotta take another call," Jeremy Pratt said, his voice recapturing a more businesslike tone. "If we don't hook up tonight, I'll talk to you after the audition."

Louie replaced the receiver and sat on the edge of the bed with his elbows on his knees. His face felt hot. In the back of his head he heard his psychiatrist's voice.

"You're a talented and dynamic young man," she told him toward the end of their last session. "But you had a difficult childhood. And growing up without a mother can make you—at times—feel angry or deeply shameful. There is nothing wrong with shame," she wanted him to know. "Or sadness. And to be vulnerable and cry was not a sign of weakness but a sign of courage."

Louie, breaking out in a sweat, told her he'd visited the Museum of Modern Art earlier that day. He said he saw a painting there that frightened him.

"By who?"

"Mark Rothko."

"What did it remind you of?"

"Drowning. Going underwater and being unable to breathe."

"Have you ever been close to drowning?" the psychiatrist asked Louie.

"No. I'm a great swimmer. My mom taught me," he said. "In fact the best times I remember were the days she took me to the beach."

"Did she ever leave you by yourself while she went in the ocean?"

"I don't remember."

"Could it be you were afraid that she would drown and leave you all alone?"

"That's what happened. She did drown—in fucking booze." Louie stopped speaking and peered closely at his psychiatrist. "What are *you* afraid of?"

The psychiatrist showed Louie a brief expression of surprise. Then she smiled. "Many things. But I don't let these fears ruin my day. I know they're mostly irrational," she said, and Louie told her he was worried that his father was going to die. "What do you mean?"

"That he'll kill himself, like my mom."

"You mean die of alcoholism?"

"Maybe. Or commit suicide. I don't know."

"Do you ever feel like killing your father?"

Louie responded immediately, with almost a compulsion to confess. "Yes. Lots of times."

"Because if he was dead, you wouldn't have to worry about him. Is that true?"

Louie lifted his shoulders in what was kind of a shrug.

"Your father is fortunate to have a son like you."

"He wants to help me too much."

"Maybe you should let him."

"No. You don't understand," Louis said. "If he helps me, and I get too far ahead, he'll have to kill *me*."

"I don't think so, Louie."

"But that's the way it feels."

Louie took a long shower that started out burning hot and ended up so shockingly cold that his body felt almost numb. While he was toweling off, he heard his father using the phone in the living room. He was speaking to his agent in a harsh, grinding voice, demanding that he take his side in a script-related conflict with Derek Ralston, the director of his movie. The last words his father said before he slammed down the phone were: "Tell Ralston to kiss my ass."

Moments later Louie came out of his bedroom wearing Levi's, a clean white T-shirt, and a loosely structured black linen jacket.

"Well, look who's here," his father said, and he smiled admiringly as he pulled himself up from the couch. Unsteadily, he crossed the room and embraced his son, giving him two manly slaps on the back before he pushed him away and said, once they were at arm's length, "You look fucking great."

"You too."

His father snorted. "Yeah, right. But I can still kick your ass," he said, and faked throwing a punch. "You pissed about the room?"

Louie looked away from his father, back toward the television, which was tuned to the evening news. "A little bit. Just because we're in the same city doesn't mean we have to stay in the same hotel, let alone the same room."

"I thought it would be fun. You know, a father-son show-biz moment," his father said, seating himself again on the couch. "Come on, sit down. Let's talk about this piece of shit." His father looked amused but also strangely hostile as he held up the script for Louie's pilot. "This sucker needs a lot of work."

Louie was staring coldly at his father. "Where'd you get that, Dad?"

"Out of your bag. Where do you think I got it?"

"When I was in the shower?"

"Yeah."

"You unzipped my bag and—"

"Wait a minute. No one unzipped anything," his father said, with an excessive indignation that he knew sounded defensive. "Your bag was already open. I saw the script on top. I got curious. I'm a writer. Big fucking deal!"

Outraged, Louie said, "It *is* a big fucking deal! I don't want you going through my shit!"

Louie's father slowly stood up. His face was tight and red from alcohol. "Fuck this. Nothing I do is ever right," he said, and he moved inside his bedroom and shut the door. He came back out in less than a minute, and Louie was surprised to see him smiling strangely, almost rapturously. "Look, I'm sorry," he said. "I apologize. You're right. I shouldn't have gone through your things. Okay? Now let's see if we can get along for a couple of days."

Tears suddenly came into Louie's eyes, blurring and doubling his father's face. "This is wrong," he said, almost sobbing. "This is really wrong. You're not supposed to act this way."

"What way? What are you talking about," his father said, the cocaine he'd just snorted making him feel pleasantly excited. Then he looked around the room, as if he was searching for an ally. "Hey, I'm your dad. I love you. Don't you get it? I *love* you."

* * *

Gene was already at Musso-Frank, nursing a beer at the far end of the bar, when Louie and his father arrived thirty minutes late for the eight o'clock reservation. Ray slipped the maitre d' a ten and they were quickly shown to a spacious booth in the back room. Sitting directly across the aisle was Bruce Springsteen and a party of six which included singer Linda Ronstadt and Nils Lofgren, Bruce's new rhythm guitar player.

Keeping his eyes turned down and his voice low, Louie said, "I saw Bruce live at Madison Square Garden. He was unbelievable."

Gene nodded in a knowledgeable way. "Great act. No question about it."

"But not compared to Elvis," Ray said, taking a sip of the double martini he'd ordered before they sat down. "Maybe he's the boss, but Elvis was the *motherfucking king!*"

Louie made a face at his father, a warning face, and Gene said, "Keep your voice down, Ray."

"What did I say that's wrong? I was just telling the truth. Gene and I saw Elvis in person," Ray said to Louie, ignoring the rage and frustration he saw in his son's eyes. "We saw all the great ones. Right, Gene? Elvis, Buddy Holly, the Drifters, Bobby Fuller. Now *that* was a great show. Gene's a Bobby Fuller fanatic. He's convinced he was murdered but he's wrong."

Gene's hand found his brother's wrist. "Take it easy, Ray."

"He's drunk," Louie said.

"That's right. I'm drunk," Ray said in a vicious tone. "Too fucking bad. If it bothers you, leave. You too, Gene—split."

"You're on probation," Gene said. "You get popped again and you're going to jail."

Ray stared at his brother. His mouth began to twitch. "Let go of my arm, Gene."

Gene relaxed his grip and Ray flexed his fingers a few times; then he lifted his head and glanced around the restaurant. He didn't move when Louie tried to slide out of the booth.

"Let me out. I'm leaving," Louie said, and his father stubbornly shook his head. "Dad, don't be an asshole."

"Stick around. Come on."

"No."

"Please. I had a bad day," Ray said, in a voice that was distraught. "I'm sorry."

There was a long chord of silence. Then Louie, trying not to sound concerned, said, "What happened?"

"They want to get rid of me, hire another writer."

"Who's they?" Gene asked.

"Ralston, the producer, the studio, everyone." Ray chugged down the rest of his drink. He looked angry now, almost dangerous. "They want me to change the ending. They don't want to see any kids die. That's missing the whole point of the book. Fuck them. I'm not changing a word."

The table fell silent. Across the aisle, Nils Lofgren had a quiet smile on his face. Then he glanced at Gene and exchanged a friendly nod. Gene and Nils had known each other since the late seventies, when they both lived in Topanga and Nils played regularly with Crazy Horse, the band that backed up Neil Young on his album *After the Gold Rush*.

Nils was still smiling as he lifted up his glass of wine and saluted Gene. "To the good old days."

"Yeah," Gene said, smiling back. "It's been a while."

"The party last year on the Fourth of July. You broke out all those killer oldies. You still have them?"

"Every one."

"What about the blond?" Nils said. "You still have her?"

Gene slowly answered. "No," he said softly. "She's gone."

While the waiter was taking their order, Louie watched heads turn as Steve Martin was seated in a booth on the other side of the room. He was wearing a smirking grin and a loud peppermint striped shirt that was tucked into white duck pants. With him was a smaller man with carefully parted hair and two women, both blonds with skinny waists and large breasts, and all four were laughing playfully, delighting in some secret joke.

Bruce Springsteen wrote a note on a napkin and Nils passed it over to Louie. It said: "*Pledging My Love* was a great movie. Your dad's an artist. Stop breaking his balls."

Louie smiled. The next time Ray made eye contact with Springsteen, he said, "That was cool. Thanks."

"I meant it."

Gene said to Nils, "Alice is dead. She died in a plane crash."

Conversation stopped at both tables. Linda Ronstadt looked frightened as she stared at Gene with her round, doll-like eyes. "Why did you bring that up?" Ray said to Gene.

"Nils met her. I remember on the Fourth they talked about books. They both liked Kurt Vonnegut and Flannery O'Connor. And Alice used to fly out of D.C.," Gene said. "That's where he's from. Right, Nils?"

"Baltimore."

"Close," Gene said. Then, without expression, he revealed that Leon Russell, the legendary Tulsa-born piano player, was also at the party. "I remember talking to him about Bobby Fuller. He was a real fan."

Ray gave Gene a dreary look. "Why don't you let these guys finish their dinner?"

"We're cool here," Nils said.

"Maybe too cool," Linda Ronstadt said, with a hesitant laugh.

Bruce Springsteen was chewing a piece of steak. After reflecting for a moment, he said, "Bobby Fuller could write some tunes," and no one disagreed.

Ray excused himself to use the restroom. Once inside he locked the stall and broke out the vial of cocaine that he always carried in the right front pocket of his jeans. Four quick toots and he was standing in front of the sink, feeling light and graceful as he splashed water on his frozen face. On his way back to his table he saw Steve Martin glance in his direction with a stiff smile, as though a disagreeable and long-dormant memory had suddenly surfaced in his consciousness. After a moment, he put down his fork and said something to the busty blond companion on his right.

Ray, his face tingling and his heart beating hard, crossed the room and stood in front of Steve Martin and stared down at him with some dislike. Several seconds passed before the man with Martin, the weak-looking but well-groomed man, turned toward Ray and said impatiently, "Can I help you with something?"

"Do you remember me?" Ray asked Steve Martin.

"Should I?"

"I worked at CBS back in the sixties. I was the censor on the *Smothers Brothers' Show* during their second season."

Steve Martin grimaced. He avoided looking at Ray's face. "Burk?"

"Yeah. I'm not a censor anymore. I write movies now," Ray said, not quite smiling as he recited his credits.

"That's good, Burk. Good for you. Maybe you'll write something for me."

"I don't think so, Steve."

The blond sitting next to Martin turned and looked at Ray with a kind of cruel sweetness. "Why don't you go back to your table," she said.

"He's drunk," said Steve Martin's male companion.

"He treated me like shit," Ray said to everyone at the table, and Steve Martin, helpless in the face of Ray's anger, just shook his head and stared down at his plate. "Tommy, Dicky, the writers, everyone. They all treated me like shit." Ray spun around and pointed across the room. "See over there? That's my son, Louie. He's an actor. The guy sitting next to him is my brother, Gene. Gene Burk. The Burk brothers say fuck the Smothers brothers, and I say fuck Steve Martin."

The man with Steve Martin made a move to stand up, but the blond on his left said, "Don't, Lee. It's not worth it."

"What an asshole," the other blond said under her breath.

Ray turned around with excessive care, trying to maintain his balance while he ignored the diners who were staring at him with faces that were quietly appalled. Gene stood up quickly and, using both hands, he maneuvered Ray back to their booth. Louie was already gone and so were the rock and rollers across the aisle.

Before Ray could order another martini, the maitre d' appeared at their table. "I'm sorry," he said to Gene, "but I must ask your friend to leave."

Gene said, "He's not my friend. He's my brother."

"Nevertheless he—"

Gene waved the whole thing away. "I'll take care of him. Don't worry. He just had too much to drink."

The maitre d' shook his head. He made a signal and a waiter materialized at his side with the bill. "He insulted my customers. He must leave now," the maitre d' said, "or I will call the police."

"Go ahead. Be my guest," Gene said, as Ray pretended to be absorbed in chewing on a breadstick. "And I'll point out the six customers I saw snorting coke at their tables. This place will be closed down in thirty minutes."

The maitre d' was silent for several seconds. Then, with a proud face, he held up their bill and slowly tore it in half. "You are not welcome here anymore," he said in a firm voice, dismissing the waiter with a brisk nod, before he returned to his station at the front of the restaurant.

Ray looked at his brother. "I guess I fucked up."

"Yeah, you did," Gene said, and Ray laughed softly. "You might think about going back to A.A."

"You're probably right," Ray said. His voice was steady, but he looked a trifle uncertain. "What about you?"

"What do you mean? I'm not the one with the drinking problem."

Ray shrugged him off. "You got other problems, Gene."

Gene leaned across the table. "Did you see Springsteen's face when I mentioned Bobby Fuller? Did you see it light up?" he said. He was staring into his brother's red floating eyes with a new intensity. "He was a fan, big time. You could tell. And Ronstadt and Nils, they all knew his story."

"So what, Gene?"

"So what?" Gene slumped back against the booth with a righteous expression. "I can't believe you said that. You were with me, Ray. We saw him together. You were fucking *there*. How could you not want to know who killed him?"

"Nobody killed him, Gene."

"You're wrong. And if you had any brains, this would be your next screenplay."

"You mean after I sober up," Ray said, and stood up. "Fuck this place. I need another drink."

* * *

The air was muggy and Gene felt woozy and kind of sad as he silently watched Ray's rented red Mustang pull up to the curb. After his brother tipped the valet and slid behind the wheel, Gene crouched down so he could speak through the open window on the passenger side. "Let me drive you home," he said, quickly reaching in to stop Ray's hand before he could turn over the engine. "You're fucked up."

"Don't worry about me, Gene."

"I do worry about you. So does Louie."

"And if Alice were alive, Gene, she'd be worried about you."

Gene slowly let his hand fall away from the ignition. When he stood up and glanced around, his face looked lost, and he was barely conscious of the cluster of diners who had walked outside and were now chatting loudly as they waited for their cars.

"Gene?"

"Yeah."

"I'm okay now."

The Mustang's lights came on and Gene looked with concern at his brother's face through the windshield. He was smiling feebly.

"Really," Ray said. "I am. I'll be fine."

"Yeah," Gene said brusquely, and then he smiled back. "So will I."

Gene remained standing by the curb with his head bent, looking slightly puzzled, watching Ray pull into the light traffic moving west on Santa Monica Boulevard. When he could no longer see the red taillights in the blue darkness, he pulled out the letter he had neglected to show his brother, the letter from Alice McMillan, the other Alice who later joined the Manson family back in 1967, becoming one of its earliest members.

Gene had read through all the letters several times since returning from Cedar Rapids, all eight, but he still remained mystified by their sheer strangeness. Although he knew it was not possible—the prose was too flat and cool, and the impressions and memories, no matter how loathsome or weird, were too precise—there were moments in the middle of the night when he'd come awake thinking that he was the victim of some elaboraate hoax, that it was all an illusion, something he'd created out of his abysmal despair, and that (in fact) he had written the letters himself.

The letter he carried with him tonight was a long letter, almost seven legal-sized pages with writing on both sides. Toward the end, Alice McMillan mentions a night she spent in a town near Springfield, Missouri. She writes:

A man named Dan picked me up in a white Chevrolet on Highway 30, just outside Camden, Ohio. It was dusk, my favorite time of day. Dan was driving straight through to Omaha. He was wearing pressed jeans and a clean white button-up shirt with the sleeves folded back twice, so you could see the dark hair on his forearms. Talk about sexy! Wow!

He was coming home from college in Santa Barbara, California. I wanted to tell him I was in Santa Barbara once with Charlie, living in a school bus that was painted black, but I decided to keep my mouth shut. That would be the last thing he would need to know. Right? After an hour or so we stopped for cigarettes at this little store off the interstate. Dan bought a pint of dark rum and a bottle of Coca-Cola, which he mixed together, and we passed it back and forth until it was all gone.

Around midnight he pulled off the road near Thurman. We found a motel and fucked like bunnies, telling stories in between. He told me he had a girlfriend back at college, a sorority girl, and I told him I once fucked Charles Manson. He said I was a liar and I said "you're right," but I could tell he wasn't quite sure.

Just before he passed out, a car pulled up outside blasting the radio, playing "I Fought the Law," an oldie by Bobby Fuller. I was gonna tell Dan that years ago I met Bobby Fuller, but I was pretty sure he wouldn't believe that either. When he was asleep, I put on his white shirt and walked outside and danced backward in the parking lot, the taps from my boots throwing red sparks around my shins. The sky was clear and as dark as the sea. A cool breeze opened my shirt and stroked my breasts. My lips were smiling, mostly from the sex I just had. I felt good about my life.

And it was not over yet.

Love,
Alice

Twelve

No End

in Sight

"The audition was fucked. I was terrible."

That's how Louie, speaking slowly and spacing his words, started the session with his therapist on the Monday after he flew back from Los Angeles. Saving the details for later in the hour, he told her first about the dinner with his father on Thursday, the endless martinis, the cocaine, the incident with Steve Martin, then his early exit and the phone call around midnight from the emergency room at Cedars-Sinai.

"He got into a fight at The Palm. His nose was broken and he needed ten stitches above his eye. They wouldn't let him drive so they called me."

"And you went to get him."

"What was I supposed to do, just leave him there?"

"Why not? He could've called a taxi."

"He was broke."

'I'm sure he—"

"Don't you get it? He's my dad!" Louie said quickly, and there was such a wild note in his voice that the therapist looked slightly intimidated. They sat without speaking for over a minute, while the rush of red faded from Louie's neck, and when he lifted his eyes from the rug, she looked at him and nodded silently, smiling a warming smile, as though something had passed between them, something of importance. It seemed that she fully understood the complex and punishing feelings of pain and guilt he was now experiencing in her office.

After they tolerated this silence for a while, she said, "So you picked him up. Then what happened?"

"We got back to the hotel and I tried to go to sleep. But there was no way. My mind was racing and I could hear my dad crying in the living room."

"You must have felt helpless."

"Yeah, I did. It was terrible hearing him like that. Maybe I got an hour of sleep," Louie said. "I had a wake-up call at eight. That gave me enough time to shower and shave and grab some coffee before the limo arrived. The living room was empty, so I assumed my dad had crashed in the other bedroom. But when I came downstairs I learned that he'd checked out without leaving a note or saying goodbye, wishing me luck, anything."

Louie was staring at his therapist. There was a coldness in his expression that she had not seen before. Then his gaze veered sideways, away from her face, and he closed his eyes for a moment, as if he was organizing his thoughts.

"Have you spoken to him since?" she asked.

"No. But I spoke to my uncle. I told him what happened."

"What did he say?"

"Nothing really. He just listened. He didn't act surprised."

"Would you like to talk about the audition?" the therapist asked Louie, after she glanced at the clock. "We still have a few minutes."

"I was too intense. That's what they told my agent," Louie said, still sounding a little bit angry. "I could tell as soon as I walked into the room that something was off. The producers, the casting director, the suits from the network, they all looked at me with these disappointed expressions."

"But they had not heard you read yet," the therapist said. "Why would they look disappointed?"

"I don't know. That's the way it seemed. It pissed me off."

"Maybe you were angry when you walked in. Angry that your father—"

"*Not even a fucking note!*" Louie screamed, looking at her square in the face. "I couldn't believe it."

The scene that Louie read was supposedly set in an underground prison on the planet Zorlon, a lunar-lit Sodom and Gomorrah that was colonized by teenage drug addicts and a species of highly intelligent monster dogs with transparent blue fur. His character, an intergalactic cop, was to question a young woman suspected of poisoning her boyfriend, chopping up his body, then burying the pieces underneath an ice field where giant fish slept like mummies.

"I rehearsed the pages on the way over in the limo," Louie told his therapist, after he regained his composure. "The way it was written, the girl was a real bitch. At one point she's supposed to slap me across the face open-handed, knocking my cigarette out of my mouth. But in the office, when the casting director read the girl's part, she sounded flat and tired, as if she were purposely trying not to act. I was totally thrown off. She was sucking all the energy out of my performance, so I overcompensated by making bigger choices. I sort of went crazy."

"Oh?" The therapist leaned back in her chair. "How?"

"I ignored the casting director and started playing to the producers and the network guys, improvising, using the whole room as a stage. I think I kicked over a coffee table and ate someone's tuna sandwich before one of the producers stood up and stopped the audition. At least that's what my agent said."

"You don't remember?"

"Not really," Louie said. His answer was easy but unexpected. "I was in kind of a blackout."

"How did you feel when you left?"

"Actually, I felt pretty good. I mean I knew what I did was over the top, but at least I took some risks. I was proud of that."

"Did you think there was any chance you might get the part?"

"I didn't care. I just wanted to get back to the hotel and pack."

"You must have been exhausted," the therapist said, and on her lead they both stood up. "What time was your flight?"

"Five. But I almost missed it."

"Why is that?"

"I was at my grandfather's house," Louie said, and the therapist stood waiting, watching his changing expression. "He was telling me stories."

■

Nathan Burk was stretched out on his sofa with the blinds closed, dozing peacefully, when the sound of the ringing doorbell lifted him slowly out of the warm excitement of his dream. But even sitting upright, he needed nearly a minute to grope through the fog of sleep before he recognized Louie's voice calling out his name: "Grandpa, Grandpa. It's me. Open up."

Nathan Burk yawned. "Okay, okay. I hear you," he muttered, pushing himself up with his cane. When he opened the blinds he saw Louie standing on the porch in his elongated shadow, his body shifting impatiently, dressed in a blue polo shirt and clean khaki trousers. Behind him was a black stretch limo that was parked in the driveway with the motor running.

Louie released the doorbell when he saw Nathan Burk's drowsy face. "Come on, Grandpa. Open up."

"I'm coming. I'm coming," Nathan Burk said, grimacing with each step as he shuffled across the living room and unlocked the front door. "You should call first. That way I would be ready."

Louie gave his grandfather a gentle hug and stepped inside. "I told you last night I'd be by around noon," he said, feeling a sort of nervous sadness as he discreetly took in the piles of old newspapers, plates of stale food, crumpled tissues, and other miscellaneous debris that lay scattered around the room. "What were you doing?"

"I was giving it to Kim Novak."

"You were what?"

"I was dreaming," Nathan Burk said, making a little grunting sound as he resettled himself on the sofa. "You heard of Kim Novak?"

"Sure. The actress," Louie said, sitting down next to his grandfather. "She was in *Vertigo* with James Stewart."

"That's correct," Nathan Burk said. "And she used to be a regular customer at my newsstand. She came by first with Sinatra, while they were making *The Man with the Golden Arm* over at Columbia. On screen she was cold and mysterious, but in person she was just a nice sweet girl. But what a body." Nathan Burk smiled at the memory, his features suddenly those of a young man. Then he saw Louie studying him and his dry lips parted. "So what about you, mister big shot with the fancy car. How did your audition go?"

"Not good."

"Yeah."

"I don't think I got the part."

"So maybe you'll get the next one. This is a rough town," Nathan Burk said. "But you can't let it eat you up."

"It eats up my dad."

"This I know."

"He got into a fight last night."

"I know that too. He came by this morning. He needed to borrow some money," Nathan Burk said, and Louie made no reply to this. "You want something to eat?"

"No thanks."

"There's some cold chicken in the fridge. Or you can make yourself some cheese and crackers."

"That's okay," Louie said. "I'm fine."

Nathan Burk shrugged. After a moment or two he switched on the television and flipped through the channels until he found a black-and-white cowboy movie from the forties. "Your father loved westerns. And so did your uncle," he said, speaking brightly, his eyes following the action on the screen. "Every Saturday morning they would put on their holsters and go up to the Pantages for the special matinee. Hoot Gibson and Tim McCoy were their favorites. Afterwards, they would hang around the newsstand reading comics or sneaking peeks at the nudie mags when I had my back turned. Their mother worked on Saturdays, and later we would all go to dinner at the Farmer's Market."

"What was Grandma like?" Louie asked in a low voice, and Nathan Burk seemed surprised by the question, his mouth slightly open as he pulled his eyes away from the screen. "How come you never talk about her?"

"Your grandmother? You want to talk about your grandmother," Nathan Burk said. "What do you want to know? What she looked like? Was she pretty? Yes, she was pretty. No, she was beautiful. Red hair. Eyes that were silver and green." Nathan Burk reached in his wallet and took out a faded five-dollar bill. "This color. And her skin? Her skin was flawless," he said, and gave Louie a meaningful glance. "Go out to the garage. You'll see some cardboard boxes on the shelves against the back wall. Bring the one on the far left."

Growing up, Louie had seen only one black-and-white photograph of his grandmother. It was taken at the pony rides in the north end of Griffith Park, when his father was eight and his uncle was ten. In this picture her hair was loose and she was wearing tight, white capri pants and a white T-shirt that clung to her breasts. On her face was a smile that looked tense.

"My dad said she left a week after that picture was taken. On a Sunday morning," Louie told his grandfather later that afternoon. He was sitting on the floor in the bad light, surrounded by photographs and news clippings that dated back to 1946. "He said she walked out while you were watching a football game on television. She didn't say goodbye or anything. She went to Miami, my dad said."

Louie picked up a photograph that had been neatly scissored out of a movie magazine called *Hollywood Nights.* It showed the interior of the Mocambo, a plush nightclub on the Sunset Strip that was popular in the forties and fifties. Sitting around a table that was close to the stage were three men and three women, all dressed in evening clothes, their faces glazed with alcohol and anticipation.

"Do you see anyone you recognize?" Nathan Burk asked his grandson.

"No."

"Of course you don't. You're too young." Nathan Burk pointed at a man's face. "Robert Walker, this pretty boy with the pomaded hair. He was married to Jennifer Jones. I bet you've never heard of her either."

"I've heard of Jennifer Jones," Louie said, lifting up his chin but still keeping his eyes on the photograph.

"They did one picture together, *Since You Went Away,* a real flag-waver that came out in 1944, the year they separated. That photograph was taken in 1950, a couple of years before Walker died. He was terrfic in that Hitchcock picture, *Strangers on a Train.* The blond sitting next to him is Betty Asher, his publicist. She was always getting him out of scrapes. That night they got arrested for drunk driving. The man on his left is Jack Kaufman, Dr. Jack, the doctor to the stars. He supplied Walker with his dope."

"Who's this?" Louie said, pointing at a dark-haired woman with her back to the camera. In her hand she was holding a stemmed glass filled with either white wine or champagne.

"That's Mona, your grandmother," Nathan Burk said, and the smile on his face when Louie looked up, surprised, was unfeigned. "The guy next to her with the five o'clock shadow is Carl Reese. He was a hoodlum. The girl on the other side, looking over his shoulder? She was a whore." Nathan Burk stabbed his finger at the photograph. "A drunk, a whore, a quack, a hoodlum, and Mona, your grandmother."

Louie was silent a minute, aware that the house seemed unnaturally quiet. He said finally, "What was she doing with those people?"

"Walker came by the newsstand. So did Reese. They all came by," Nathan Burk said, reaching for the photograph. "Martin and Lewis were headlining that night, their first local appearance in two years. It was the hottest ticket in town. Reese invited Mona and me, plus the boys, but I couldn't go. I had to work. Ray and Gene had the flu, so she went by herself." Nathan Burk sighed deeply, and then he put aside the picture and curled up on the couch, letting one sockless foot dangle over the side. "You know who else was there that night?"

"Who?"

"Mr. Suede. Maury Geller. He came by the next day. He said he saw Mona and Carl Reese playing kissy-face in the parking lot after the show. I confronted her that evening and she denied it, of course. We had a screaming fight that ended when she kicked me in the balls and I punched her face, chipping one of her teeth. It was terrible."

"Is that why she left, because you hit her?"

Nathan Burk shook his head. "No. That's not why she left. She left because she was tired of her life with me. She was tired of her life, period," he said. "I sensed she wanted something else, something I couldn't understand."

"My dad said she came back a few times."

"Once or twice a year, usually when I was at work. She'd pick up Ray and his brother after school and drive to the zoo or to the pony rides. She'd spend two, maybe three hours with them, at the most. On Gene's thirteenth birthday she called up drunk and he gave me the phone. I told her not to bother calling when she was drinking, that we were doing fine without her. I had not spoken to her in three years. When she hung up, I started to cry and couldn't stop. She broke my heart, Louie."

"Did you ever see her again?"

"Only once," Nathan Burk said, and paused importantly. "In 1961. She was in Los Angeles for a reason that I can't recall. She called and asked to borrow some money."

"Did you give it to her?"

"Yes. Yes, I did," Nathan Burk said. "I was a fool. I always gave her what she wanted."

Nathan Burk suddenly turned away from his grandson and looked furtively around the room, as if he were distracted by the sound of someone's voice.

Louie said, "What's wrong, Grandpa?"

Nathan Burk was silent for a moment. "Nothing. Nothing's wrong," he said, still looking away, and then he closed his eyes and smiled secretly to himself, letting his mind slip back to the last time he saw his ex-wife.

It was at the very end of a hot September. For the previous six months Mona had been traveling with Izzy Martin, a runty, feminine-looking man who moved from city to city, wagering only on horse races that were fixed, either by himself or one of his "associates," members of a loosely knit but shadowy underworld organization that had branches in every state. But not only was Izzy a compulsive gambler, he also had a serious problem with narcotics, mainly heroin, and whatever money he won on the ponies quickly disappeared into his veins.

He died of an overdose in room ten at the Tropicana Motel in West Hollywood. Mona, who was sunning herself by the pool, drinking beer and chain-smoking Chesterfields, discovered his hairy naked body when she came in to take a shower. She called Nathan Burk later that afternoon from the Hollywood Police Station on Wilcox, where she'd been interrogated in a featureless room by detectives from both homicide and vice. In a stunned but quiet voice she told them everything she knew, naming names and disclosing all the crimes and petty scams in which Izzy was a participant. When she was finally done, her lips were parched and white at the corners, and the information she provided led to the arrests of nineteen men.

Later that evening Mona told Nathan Burk how much Izzy loathed his body, his enormous head and his sawed-off stubby legs. He also had a mysterious but compelling need to scratch his arms and legs until they oozed with blood and pus. "He was a disturbed man," Mona said, as she watched her ex-husband remove his pants and, with a stiff dignity, fold them carefully over the chair in front of the desk. "God knows what I saw in him."

Traffic noises drifted up from the street and a door down the hallway was slammed hard. On the nightstand by the phone was a matchbook with the hotel's name embossed on the cover in raised gold letters: the Hollywood Knickerbocker, the same hotel where Mona and Nathan stayed back in 1946, the year they arrived in Los Angeles.

"Izzy had a big dick," Mona said, smiling as Nathan Burk stepped out of his Jockey shorts. "Not as big as yours, Nate. But big." Mona pushed her hair back as she lit a cigarette and took a quick puff, trying to act uninterested as she pulled off her sweater and leaned forward to unhook her bra. "So what do you think?"

"About what?"

"My tits."

"Take off your pants."

"Mr. Romance," Mona said, laughing slyly, ignoring the cold fury in Nathan Burk's face. "You used to love to come on my tits. Remember, Nate. You would sit on my stomach and fuck my face until you were ready to burst. Then—whammo—all over my chest." Mona kicked off her shoes. Then she took a step backward and sat down on the edge of the bed, making it easier to slide off her pants. "You want to fuck my face, Nate? Come here."

"Take everything off."

Mona rolled her eyes upward in pretend exasperation. "Sure, Nate. Whatever you say." She stood up and, facing him resolutely, she stepped out of her underwear and dropped them by her feet. They were a few paces apart, staring into each other's eyes.

Nathan Burk reached for Mona's hand. His eyes were still fixed on her face. "So here we are again," he said, stepping forward to take her into his arms. "Fifteen years later."

Mona's shoulders trembled. She felt Nathan Burk's breath in her neck and his cock pushing into her thigh. "How're the boys, Nate?"

"The boys are fine."

"I miss them."

"I'm sure you do."

"You don't believe me. I can tell."

"What difference does it make?" Nathan Burk said. He kissed her ear, then moved his mouth down to the hollow of her throat. "We're not here to talk about our boys."

"I'm their mother."

"Not today. Not this afternoon."

Mona flinched when she felt Nathan Burk's teeth on her nipple. "Don't hurt me, Nate."

"Hurt you? Why would I do that?"

In a moment Nathan Burk was on his knees, licking Mona's pubic hair and separating her thighs with his tongue. When he tasted her, she gasped and lost her balance, nearly tumbling backward until his hands came up to grab her round hips and hold her steady.

Feeling her body begin to shudder, Mona said, "If I'm not a mother today, who am I?"

"Who are you?" Nathan Burk slowly got to his feet before he answered this question. "Just someone I used to love."

*   *   *

Before Louie left for the airport, Nathan Burk went into his bedroom and came out holding a black-and-white snapshot that he kept hidden underneath the shirts in his dresser. It showed Mona in a tight-fitting one-piece bathing suit, standing on the shoreline of a lake that sparkled in the summer sunlight. She was smiling but looked slightly anxious, too. Behind her a boy of nine or ten stood at the end of a long dock holding a fishing pole. In the clear sky overhead a streaking swallow was caught in mid-flight, its wings extended outward, following the wind.

"This is where we met," Nathan Burk told Louie. The front door was open and they were both standing on the porch, blinking in the sunshine. "Blue Bay Ranch. It was a summer camp in Pennsylvania, in the Pocono Mountains. I worked in the kitchen and she taught swimming and other water activities." Nathan Burk pointed at a grove of trees on the far shore. "Once late at night we took a canoe over to the other side of the lake. We found a private spot, cozy and dark, and that's where we made love for the first time. I was a virgin. She wasn't."

Louie blushed as he looked down at his wristwatch. "I think I better get goin' or I'll miss my plane."

"You want to leave? In the middle of my story?"

"Grandpa—"

"So go," Nathan Burk said. He was smiling now as he handed Louie the photograph. "And take this with you."

"But Grandpa—"

"It's your grandmother. Now take it and go. You're late," Nathan Burk said, playfully pushing him toward the limousine. "Call me when you get home. Call your father too. And stop being so hard on him."

At the exact moment that Louie's flight lifted off the runway at LAX, moving away from the sun, Alice McMillan was sitting in her room at the Tropicana Motel. The door was double-locked and she was staring at the phone, growing more anxious and tense with each moment. Outside she could hear loud curses and shrieks of laughter coming from the pool, where a British rock band and their underage groupies had been partying since she'd arrived. A Four Tops tune blasted from a portable radio and burgers sizzled on a nearby barbecue, tended by a girl wearing orange tights and nothing on top.

Alice had been to the Tropicana once before, in October of 1969, on a starless autumn night. Charlie had sent her and Tex Watson on a mission to buy an ounce of speed from a biker who was staying at the motel. But the deal never went down.

"The dude was paranoid. He thought we were narcs," she told Charlie later, when they got back to Spahn Ranch. But instead of showing anger, which she expected, he just twisted his mouth into a goofy grin and shrugged it off.

Charlie was drunk that night, the only time Alice ever saw him even slightly out of control, and for some reason he seemed smaller than usual, almost puny, a tiny animal with a fine scent for fear and blood.

She and Tex went to sleep separately in the back bunkhouse, in the same room with Clem Grogan and a new girl who had arrived that afternoon high on LSD. In the morning Alice woke up and saw the girl, naked from the waist up, still sleeping with her mouth half-open, showing her teeth. Her toenails were painted purple and she wore dimestore rings on every finger.

Clem and Tex were outside on the wooden porch, smoking cigarettes and talking in low voices. The only words she remembered hearing were: "I don't know nothing anymore except . . ."

". . . what I'm doing is wrong," Alice said out loud inside her motel room, while she continued to stare at the phone. "I don't need to do this. I can stop right now. If I don't, I know I will die."

Suddenly Alice's hand shot out and seized the receiver, and seconds later the phone rang on the nightstand next to Gene's empty bed.

Part
Two

Thirteen

Las Vegas

Melanie noticed Gene first in the noon meeting at the Turning Point, the Alcoholics Anonymous clubhouse on Marion Street in North Las Vegas. They were seated in folding metal chairs on opposite sides of the room, and several times during the speaker's story—a story filled with gratitude and grace—she caught him gazing at her with an expression that was calm but uninviting. Right away she was attracted to his thick wrists and worn-out face; and the way he dressed—faded blue jeans, white T-shirt, sneakers and no socks—reminded her of the boys she went out with in the early sixties, college boys she'd fucked on the first date, usually when she was drunk or in a blackout.

Because she didn't recognize Gene from any of her regular A.A. meetings, Melanie assumed that he was either visiting from out of town or newly sober. And, as the minutes ticked by, she closed her eyes and tuned out the speaker, concentrating instead on the fantasy that was coming alive in her mind—a reverie of erotic yearning:

> Gene slowly rises to his feet and Melanie, being careful not to draw attention to herself, waits a moment before she follows him outside, into the parking lot and the hard cold light. While he wordlessly smokes a cigarette, she wraps her arms around his waist and presses her face into his back. They stand like this in the dark for several seconds, her attention concentrated on his breathing, which is deep but almost inaudible. Then Gene drops his cigarette on the ground, turns around slowly, and puts his hands on her hips. When Melanie lifts her head to look up at him, he says,

"I don't think I know you."

"That's true. You don't."

"But I know what you want."

"Oh? Tell me."

Gene leans down to kiss her lightly on the lips. "You want me to fuck you."

"That's not all I want," Melanie says, grinning foolishly but feeling wonderfully alive. "But it certainly would be a good place to start."

Melanie was jolted out of this imaginary encounter by the woman sitting next to her in the meeting—Brenda, a cocktail waitress at The Dunes with eight years of sobriety. "That man is staring at you," she told Melanie, poking her in the ribs with her elbow.

Melanie's eyes snapped open, her head dizzy with unfulfilled desires. "Really. Which one?"

"The new guy with the big shoulders who just walked outside."

That evening Melanie was halfway through her shift when she noticed Gene playing blackjack at the table next to hers. Resting by his elbow was a drink that looked like ginger ale, and, judging by the row of chips stacked in front of him, he was winning big. Although they were once again in each other's line of sight, the only time their eyes met Gene reached for a cigarette and self-consciously turned away. A disagreeable sadness radiated from Melanie's eyes as she opened a new deck of cards and fanned them across the green felt table. The next time she glanced over, Gene was already out of his chair and striding briskly toward the cashier.

The following day, Melanie woke up around six A.M. with an electric current of energy surging through her shapely body. After saying her morning prayers, thanking God for her twenty years of sobriety, she quickly threw on her sweats and drove crosstown to the Westlake Academy, a private parochial school that was newly built on the east side of this ever-expanding city. Using a stopwatch to time herself around the quarter-mile dirt track, she ran six miles in just under forty-eight minutes.

She usually stretched and then walked a mile to cool down, but midway through her second lap she slowly became aware of a man sitting high in the bright yellow bleachers watching her—the same man she saw the day before at the A.A. meeting and later playing blackjack at the Desert Inn.

"I wonder if I could speak to you," Gene said. He was on his feet now and moving down the bleachers.

Melanie picked up her towel and reached inside her gym bag for her car keys. "Speak to me about what?" she asked, not making eye contact as she angled toward the student parking lot behind the grandstand. "I don't even know you."

"You're Melanie Novack. Correct?" Gene was standing a few paces away, smiling a little as Melanie got inside her sporty blue Datsun Z-200. Rolled up in his fist was the latest issue of *Bim Bam Boom*, the fanzine in which her twenty-year-old interview had appeared. "This Melanie Novack."

When Gene passed the magazine through the driver's side window, Melanie kept a detached expression on her face, trying not to show her surprise as she glanced at the cover. "Are you a cop?"

"No."

"You look like a cop."

"I'm not."

"You sure?"

"Okay, I used to be a cop," Gene said. "Now I'm a private investigator."

"Investigating me."

"No. I'm investigating the murder of Bobby Fuller."

Melanie handed back the magazine. Then she turned the key and the Datsun kicked over. "Sorry," she said curtly. "I can't help you."

Gene said, "My brother's an alcoholic," and Melanie glanced up at Gene with a shade more interest. "I just thought I'd mention that."

"Is he in the program?"

"No. He's still drinking."

"That's too bad."

"He's a screenwriter," Gene said. "Which reminds me, I ran into one of your former clients the other day. Ted Reuben. He said if I ever found you to say hello."

"Tell him hello back," Melanie said, looking a little uncomfortable. "By the way, who's paying you?"

"No one."

"I don't believe you."

Gene shrugged.

"How'd you find me?"

"A little leg work. A few phone calls. I'm good at what I do."

Melanie shut off the engine and rested her forehead on the steering wheel. Her cheeks were flushed, and she smelled of coconut oil mixed with sweat.

Gene said, "Are you okay?"

"I'm fine."

"Are you sure?"

Melanie raised her head. Gene looked tense, shifting from one foot to the other, staring down at her with an expression that tried to minimize his uneasiness. "Okay, let's talk," Melanie finally said, her attitude now matter of fact, and she took her keys out of the ignition and opened the door.

Melanie sat next to Gene in the shaded bleachers underneath the announcer's booth, letting the tension dissipate as she slowly and carefully answered his questions until the school bell rang and the first period classes began to assemble on the wide grassy field. In that hour Melanie learned that Gene had located Joan Reynolds, her downstairs neighbor when she lived at the Argyle Manor.

"She told me you were in A.A. So I went to a few meetings in Hollywood," Gene said. "I said you and I were old friends and—"

"Basically you lied. You passed yourself off as a drunk and scammed my whereabouts."

"More or less."

"Gene, isn't that a bit sleazy? Impersonating an alcoholic?"

Gene nodded. "You're right. I'm sorry."

She shrugged off his apology. "You don't look sorry."

"No. I am. A.A. meetings should be a safe place. What I did was wrong. It's been bothering me for a while."

"Is that why yesterday you left the meeting early?"

"Yeah."

"You didn't look like anything was bothering you. In fact, you looked pretty laid back. And as long as we're being honest, I kind of liked the way you looked."

Gene crushed out his cigarette. In his side vision he caught Melanie smiling at him knowingly. She was trim, tan, much prettier than he'd imagined, but he knew that getting involved with her was absolutely out of the question. This was business, and he'd always maintained clear boundaries when it came to his work, no matter how horny he was.

"What changed your mind?" Melanie asked Gene later that morning, when he found himself naked between her flannel sheets, his arm comfortably around her shoulder, having passed easily, almost effortlessly, from acquaintance to intimacy in less than three hours. "You figure you'd get more info if you fucked me first?"

"Never crossed my mind."

"Oh, please. You've been thinking about banging me all morning."

"How do you know that?"

"Because you're a guy," Melanie whispered, as she softly pressed her lips into his neck. "That's why. Here's what happened," she said. "As soon as I invited you back for coffee, your mind went directly into fantasy mode, and your dick started to get hard, just like it is now. But since you were up here on a mission and you didn't want to blow it, you tried to put pussy—specifically *my* pussy—out of your mind. Right so far?"

"Pretty close."

Melanie was now smiling as she rolled on top of Gene and sat up, cupping her breasts. "But then driving over you started to think about these. Correct?"

"I may have entertained a thought or two about your breasts."

"Which you were just dying to squeeze, like I'm doing now," Melanie said, and when Gene's cock slipped inside her, she said, "I'm kind of a slut, huh."

"A 'sober slut.' Isn't that a contradiction?"

"You'd be surprised."

"So let me ask you something," Gene said, reaching for her nipples, then feeling them stiffen underneath his fingers. "Did you fuck Bobby Fuller?"

Melanie's eyes flinched but nothing happened to her face. "I wondered when the question-and-answer period was going to start up again."

"Didn't mean to take you by surprise."

"No, that's exactly what you meant to do. But I was hoping you'd let me come once more before you started."

"I bet you did. I bet you fucked him."

"Stop talking, Gene."

"But—"

Melanie clamped her hand over Gene's mouth. Right before she came, she thumped his chest twice with her fist and sat back on her haunches with her eyes closed. "*No,*" she screamed at the ceiling. "*I did not fuck Bobby Fuller!*"

While Melanie was splashing and singing in the shower, Gene used her phone to dial his home in Los Angeles. There were two hang-ups on his answering machine and a message from Jacob Reese, who repeated his name twice in a cautious but measured voice. Gene replaced the receiver and drifted over to the blinded window, separating the slats with his fingers. Down below, a middle-aged woman with slim long legs was sunning herself in a lounge chair by the pool. Seated next to her, rubbing baby oil into her coppery skin, was a gloomy-faced man around the same age, dressed in a pink short-sleeved linen shirt and madras shorts.

"Can't stop snooping, can you?" Melanie reentered the bedroom naked with her hair still wet and water trickling down her stomach, dampening the dark triangle between her thighs. "Who's down there—a couple of topless showgirls?"

"I wish."

"Oh, I see. You didn't get enough."

Gene dropped the blinds and took a seat in the rattan chair by the bed. Melanie seemed to be smiling as she fastened her bra and disappeared into the closet, coming out a moment later wearing a cream-colored blouse with the Desert Inn logo stitched over the pocket. She quickly pulled on her slacks and stepped over to Gene so he could zip her up from behind. When he was finished, he asked her when her shift ended that evening.

"Ten."

"Then what."

"Quick bite. Maybe I'll catch a late-night A.A. meeting downtown."

Gene got to his feet and stood behind Melanie, watching her while she brushed her hair in a full-length antique mirror that was mounted on the wall. When his arms went around her waist, she backed up into his groin and their eyes met in the glass. She was looking at him carefully.

Gene said, "We didn't really get a chance to talk."

"True. But I think screwing was way more fun."

"What if I stayed over? Would you talk some more?"

Melanie separated herself from Gene's embrace. She then put her brush in the dresser and picked up her car keys. There was an awkward moment before she turned to him with an expression that was slightly troubled. "I want to tell you a story. So pay attention," she said, staring at Gene intently until he slowly nodded his head. "When I was nineteen, I had this really cool boyfriend. Ted Babcock. He was a senior at U.C.L.A. We met at the beach one Saturday. I got drunk on warm beer and fucked him that night. I fucked him all summer. That fall Ted went to law school and we stopped going out. It was just a summer fling. Eventually he got a job downtown working for the D.A., and I began to see his name in the *L.A. Times* every once in a while. He was part of a team of lawyers who were investigating the infiltration of organized crime into the music business. Are you following me, Gene?"

Gene looked confused. "I'm not sure what this has to do—"

Melanie raised her hand like a crossing guard, and Gene stopped speaking. "You mean what does this have to do with talking to you? Well, lots. Because you see, in 1964, two years before Bobby died, I got popped for driving drunk. That's on my record, the record that you already scoped out. But what you don't know is, not only did I get a D.U.I., but in my purse I was carrying two ounces of high-grade heroin that I was dealing in clubs around Hollywood, clubs like the Melody Room and Ernie's Stardust Lounge, heroin that I copped from Carl Reese. Still with me, Gene?"

Gene's eyes wandered past Melanie's face and over to the coffee table, where several college textbooks were stacked in a neat pile next to a tray filled with sharpened pencils.

"Gene?"

"Go on. I'm listening."

"Who do you think busted me?"

"No idea."

"Your ex-partner Eddie Cornell. And guess who scored an ounce from me earlier that night at The Tally-Ho? That's right. Chris Long."

Gene's head turned and he stared at Melanie, who coldly met his eye for a moment and then looked away. "Let me get this straight. You and Long are drug buddies. And this guy Babcock, he—"

"Ted offered me a deal. Snitch off Reese and he'd drop all the charges. But I said I couldn't do that."

"Why not?"

"Too frightened. Reese, Havana, that's a very bad crowd," she said, and Gene's head went up and down. "But Ted dropped the charges, the drug charges anyway. Ask me if I let him fuck me?"

"Did you?"

"Of course I did. Just like I let you fuck me, too. And I didn't tell you shit either. And now," Melanie said, looking at her watch, "I have to go to work."

Gene said quickly, "Where does Eddie fit into all this?"

"Ask him yourself."

"What about Long?"

"You're getting close."

Melanie swung open the front door and Gene followed her outside and down the stairs to the first floor. The temperature was over 100 degrees, probably closer to 110, and, by the time they reached the parking lot, Melanie's face was already wet with sweat. There was something semi-secret in her smile as she turned away from Gene and unlocked the Datsun.

"Am I going to see you later?" Gene asked, as she slid behind the wheel.

"I don't know. I think I've told you enough."

"Who killed him, Melanie?"

"Who, Bobby?"

"Yeah."

Melanie thought for a moment. Then she looked up at Gene with her smile still in place. "No one killed him, Gene. He just fucking died."

Gene drove back to the Desert Inn and left his car with the valet in front, a Mexican kid with yellowish circles under his tranquilized eyes. When he got to his room, he cranked up the air conditioner and dialed room service, ordering a cheeseburger, fries, a Caesar salad, and a pitcher of iced tea. Then he called Jacob Reese, who picked up immediately, taking Gene by surprise.

"Hello?" His voice sounded loud, irritable.

"Reese?"

"Who's this?"

"Gene Burk."

"How's everything in Vegas, Burk?"

Gene was silent.

"Burk?"

"What's the deal, Reese? Why're you following me?"

"Why?" Gene could hear Reese light up a cigarette before he resumed speaking. "Because you're a fucking nuisance. And you're starting to aggravate the wrong people."

"And who might that be?"

"Me. Stay away from the broad."

"Are you threatening me, Reese?" Gene's voice was soft, almost thoughtful. "Is that what's going on here?"

Reese laughed abruptly, then his voice became hard. "Let's just say you've been warned."

Gene put down the receiver and lay back on the bed with his eyes closed. From his conversation that morning with Melanie he understood now that she had never been interviewed by Chris Long. What she told Long while they hung out together, and what appeared many years later in *Bim Bam Boom,* were the mood-enhanced ramblings of an alcoholic, careless and fragmented conversations that were never meant to be printed anywhere.

"And a lot of what's in there is bullshit. For instance, I never met Nancy Sinatra," Melanie had told Gene earlier that day, while they were sitting in the bleachers in the absolutely still air. "Once or twice Bobby called her from my apartment, but I got the feeling that they were no more than friends. I know he slept with a lot of girls, but he didn't brag about it like a lot of guys. He liked chicks who were smart."

Gene said, "In the article you talk about Bobby's mother. You say she was jealous."

"She was protective. She wanted Bobby to be successful."

"You said she didn't like you."

"That's true. She didn't like the way I dressed. She thought I looked cheap. I wore tight skirts and sweaters. I wanted men to stare at my tits and ass, because I was ashamed of my face."

Gene admitted that he was surprised when he saw her at the A.A. meeting. "I was expecting someone—"

"A little more used up."

"That's not what I was going to say."

Melanie gave Gene a long quiet look. "I know. You were going to say something nice."

"You're right."

"Then say it. No. I'll say it. I looked younger than you expected."

"By ten years."

"Exercise and clean living. Does it every time."

"And the way you were dressed," Gene said. "Just like a college girl."

"I am a college girl," Melanie said, and she took an extra moment, arching her back and stretching her arms luxuriously above her head, before she explained: "Two days a week, Tuesdays and Thursdays, I go to college. U.N.L.V. Ten units a semester. I've been going for five years. I'm a senior," she said with cheerful independence. "Surprised?"

"Impressed."

"Good. I like it that you're impressed. When I graduate I'm gonna work at Covenant House, this home for troubled teenagers. There's a lot of fucked-up kids in Vegas."

"There's fucked-up kids everywhere."

"You're right." Melanie was looking away from Gene now, her eyes following the trail of a jet taking off from nearby Nellis Air Force Base. "There's a never-ending supply."

"I was a pretty fucked-up kid. And so were you," Gene said, looking down as a soft breeze moved the blond hair on her arms. "But we turned out okay."

"Did we?"

"Yeah. I think we did."

Melanie got to her feet and grinned down at him. "I think you should speak for yourself."

A little before eleven Gene left the hotel and drove down to the Pony Express, a small poker club located next to a sporting goods store on Fremont Street. Playing seven-card stud, he was up close to five hundred dollars in less than an hour, but he dropped it all on one hand when the full house he was holding was trumped by four nines. As he was leaving the club, he noticed a pit boss with puffy cheeks and heavy veins in his hands, meticulously cleaning his clear-rimmed glasses. He was talking to a jittery, rat-faced man whose lips barely moved when he spoke. When his elusive eyes caught Gene staring at him, the rat-faced man flashed him a queer, twisted half-smile that quickly faded, and then he hunched his shoulders and looked away. It was not until he arrived back at the Desert Inn that Gene recalled meeting him earlier that week in the offices of Big City Music.

Gene felt a flutter of fear and even some anger as he reentered the hotel. In the elevator he realized suddenly that he had to speak with Melanie, to be rigorously honest and explain to her that he was probably being followed, and that she might be in some danger. He called her from his room, but her machine picked up after six rings. He put down the receiver without leaving a message and sat motionless on the bed for several seconds, before he bolted to his feet and grabbed his car keys off the side table nearest the door.

On the way back to Melanie's apartment, Gene's radio was tuned to *Night Forum,* a talk show broadcasting out of Logan, Utah, that was hosted by a gentleman named Gil Dean. The topic for the evening was: "Telling Lies."

"I lied to my mom when I was fourteen. It might have been the worst lie of my life," said the first and only caller that Gene heard that night, a man who didn't give his name until later in the conversation. "It was on a Saturday back in 1955. I was living in Rutledge, Indiana, where I was born. I'm a Hoosier, Gil."

"What did you lie about?" Gil Dean asked, trying to draw him out.

"I said I needed some money for the movie playing downtown, but my mom wanted me to do my chores. I said I'd do them after the show and we argued. Finally, she gave in and gave me two dollars for the show and a snack. But I never went to the movie on that Saturday. Instead, I took the bus into Indianapolis and spent the afternoon wandering around the city."

"Did you do this for any particular reason?"

"I was lookin' for my dad," the caller said. "He left me and my mom when I was ten."

"When was that?"

"In the spring of 1951. He came by my school and gave me fifty dollars and a piece of paper with his phone number written in green ink. He said, 'You ever need anything at all, Robert, you just call me.' That same night I dialed the number but it was disconnected."

Gil Dean said, a little impatiently, "Did you find him on that Saturday that you lied to your mom?"

"No, I didn't. I didn't even know where to start looking. After a couple of hours I got lost and ended up in a run-down neighborhood where only black people lived. At a stoplight two boys around my age called me names and punched me in the stomach for no reason. Then they stole my bus ticket back to Rutledge and the rest of the money I had left over, which included three weeks' worth of allowances, about nine dollars altogether."

"How did you get home?"

"I didn't go home," said the caller. "I spent the night with a man I met in the park. He was an old guy, a folksinger named Harry Keystone, but he called himself Stoney. And no, he was not what you think. He was not a homosexual. In fact, he'd just gotten divorced from his wife, a lady named Kate who taught journalism at Duke University in North Carolina. And now he was back on the road. Actually he wasn't really that old, about forty-five, the same age I am now."

Gil Dean waited for the caller to continue his story. When he didn't, Gil broke the silence. "Did this man, this folksinger—"

"Stoney."

"Did he bring you home?"

"I never went back home. Not for five years."

Gene was parked in front of Melanie's townhouse with the engine off but the radio still playing. At first he didn't believe the caller's story. It seemed overrehearsed, presented in a voice that was strangely uninflected, a neutral tone that Gene felt was designed to deceive. He reached for the dial, ready to switch off the program, when the caller stated that he and his "road buddy" hitchhiked out west to Shawnee, Oklahoma, where Stoney introduced him to legendary folksinger Del Durand.

"We sat around Del's living room, drinking whiskey and singing all his songs, classics like 'Lucinda Over the Valley' and 'Fortune's Child.'

Folks kept dropping in all night, other folksingers like Cisco Houston, Ramblin' Jack Elliott, and Jocko McPherson, this black blues guitarist from the Mississippi Delta.

"I got high on reefer for the first time that night, and later on that weekend I lost my virginity to one of Del's cousins, a girl named Polly who told me that Del had a rare form of cancer that was sure to kill him in a few years."

The caller, whose voice was now spinning out into the night with more intimacy and warmth, went on to talk about his travels with Stoney, briefly touching on their stay in Denver with a prostitute named Gail, a girlfriend of Beat legend Neal Cassady, the model for the character Dean Moriarty in Jack Kerouac's *On The Road*. The caller also claimed he met Elvis at a church barbecue in Greenwood, Mississippi.

"Eventually we made it out to California, and that's where me and Stoney went our separate ways," the caller said, and a note of real sadness slid into his voice. "He went back to North Carolina to see if he could patch up his marriage, and I stayed in L.A. Like everyone else I thought I could become an actor, and I did get a few parts, because I was a good-looking boy and I had a nice build. I appeared on a couple of episodes of *Sugarfoot,* this western series starring Will Hutchins. And I played a young killer with no name and no lines on an early *Maverick*. I'm in the movie *Invasion of the Body Snatchers,* too. I got to know the director Don Siegel, and he let me stay in his guest house for a few weeks after we wrapped."

"What about your mom?" Gil Dean said, breaking into the caller's story, which was threatening to become a monologue.

"What about her?"

"She must have been concerned. Did she know where you were?"

"More or less. I wrote her postcards now and then, and I called her on her birthday."

"But—"

"She was cool with it, Gil. Six months after I left she got married to a guy with kids of his own. All of a sudden she had a whole new family to worry about, and as long as I was safe and sound she was happy."

Gene leaned toward the radio, thinking, I was fucking wrong. No way this guy is making this up: Will Hutchins, *Sugarfoot,* Don Siegel's guest house—the details were too exact.

"Did you ever see your father again, Robert?"

"Robert?" The caller's voice tightened with suspicion. "How did you know my name?"

"You said it earlier in our conversation."

"No I didn't."

"Yes, I think you did."

"Did I say my last name?"

"No."

The caller let out a slow breath. "That's good. I'm hanging up now."

"Wait a second," Gil Dean said. "What about your father?"

"He's still alive. Did I mention that he knew Charles Manson?" the caller said, and Gene felt his body become perfectly still. A moment later the porch light came on outside Melanie's apartment.

"Charles Manson. You sure?" Gil Dean said. His voice sounded cool, somewhat disbelieving.

"Back in the forties, Manson's mother Kathleen moved to Indianapolis. She lived with a salesman from the National Shoe Company, the same place my dad worked. They used to party together. Manson was about twelve. His mom kicked him out of the house when he got caught stealing a bike, and he ended up in the juvenile center downtown. He escaped and was sent to Father Flanagan's Boys Town in Omaha. He escaped from there, too. He and another boy stole an old Plymouth and rolled it into a ditch near Johnsonville, Iowa. Along the way they committed two armed robberies—a gas station and a grocery store. Manson was still only thirteen when he got arrested."

A man around thirty with closely cropped blond hair appeared in the doorway of Melanie's apartment. He wore tight white Jockey shorts and a workshirt that was faded bluish white. "You think you could turn that radio down?" he said, glancing into the parking lot. "If you don't mind, we'd like to get some rest."

Gene's hand moved toward the radio dial, and he faded Gil Dean's voice as he was saying, "You seem to know quite a lot about Mr. Manson."

"My dad's the one with the scoop. I just get it secondhand. He and Charlie have been corresponding since he first got jailed. You should see the letters he's got. They're gonna be worth something someday."

With her hair uncombed and her athletic body covered by a plain nightgown, Melanie Novack languorously came forward from the interior of her apartment. She took up a position behind the crew-cut man and gently squeezed his hips. After a second or two Gene saw her lips drift across the man's shoulder while her hand moved around his waist and slid down his shorts.

"Cut it out," the man said, laughing as he pulled away.

"What's wrong?"

"They can see us."

Melanie cocked her head. "Who?"

"Whoever's down there."

"Fuck whoever's down there," Melanie said in a carrying voice, yawning widely as she turned and pulled the man out of the flickering shadows. Gene, experiencing a stab of jealousy that made him feel faintly embarrassed, waited until they were both inside the apartment and the porch light was off before he started his engine.

Driving back to the Desert Inn, Gene quickly felt his jealousy overtaken and smoothed away by a wave of carnal scorn: How fucking dare she spend the night with someone else only hours after screwing him? "That's just wrong," Gene said out loud, the wind lifting his angry voice into the soft desert air, and then he slammed his closed fist down hard on the steering wheel, loudly beeping the horn.

"Good talkin' to you," Gil Dean told the caller. "That was quite a story."

"And every single word was true."

"I'll let our audience be the judge of that," Gil Dean said and broke for a commercial.

In his room later, his body both alert and sleep-deprived, Gene twice raised the phone to call Melanie, stopping himself both times before he could punch in the last digit. Toward dawn, when it was not yet dark or light, his mind swerved back to the brief but confusing conversation he'd had on Wednesday with Martin Bender, the attorney representing him in a civil suit against TWA. Talking softly, almost affectionately, Bender told Gene that he'd received a partial transcript of the conversation that took place in the cockpit moments before Alice's plane crashed.

"The aircraft was destabilized by a problem with the wing," Bender said. "Both Stewart and Lee Doerr, his copilot, mention a gear assembly light that was blinking red. They were attempting to make an emergency landing in Moline when they lost power."

"They're certain it was mechanical?"

"The voice recorder seems to back up the F.A.A. report."

"Marty, the guy was a fucking lush. He was probably hungover and—"

"His copilot wasn't hungover, Gene. Even if Stewart was passed out cold in the aisle, Doerr was fully capable of landing the plane. We'll never be able to prove pilot error."

"So what you're saying is, we'll lose in court if I try to fight it."

"They've got a five hundred thousand offer on the table. Everyone else has settled."

For a while the line was silent. Then Gene took a breath. "Were there any other voices on the tape except Stewart and Doerr?"

"What do you mean?"

"In the transcript you read, was there anyone else speaking? Was Alice ever in the cockpit?" Gene asked, and when he said her name, Alice's face came alive in his mind, making him flinch.

"I don't know. It's possible," Martin Bender said. "We only received those parts that were relevant to our case."

"I want to know her last words, if they exist on that tape."

"I'm not sure I can find that out. That information is released only to family or next of kin."

Gene said, "But she was my fiancée."

"I know, but—"

"I'm not going to settle—unless I know for sure."

Fourteen

A Moment
with Charlie

Beginning in the late 1970s, the underground market for pictures and artifacts associated with the Manson murders had been growing steadily, not only in the U.S. but worldwide. This fact had not gone unnoticed by Charles Manson or those members of his family who still remained loyal to him while he was incarcerated. In 1981, for example, a welder from Traverse City, Michigan, paid $500 for a pair of soiled panties owned by Patricia Krenwinkel; and, six months later, he paid another $750 for the Kinks concert-logo T-shirt that Clem Grogan was photographed wearing outside the downtown courthouse in Los Angeles, where Charlie was on trial.

"He said he would give me a thousand if I gave him a picture of me naked," Sandra Good told Charlie, the next time she wrote him from the Federal Correctional Institution at Alderson, West Virginia, where she was serving a fifteen-year sentence for using the postal service to threaten business and government leaders. "He wants something candid from Death Valley or the days at the ranch. I don't have any stashed away, but Squeaky does," she said, referring to Lynette Fromme, who was also incarcerated at Alderson, after she tried to assassinate President Gerald Ford. "I bet if you signed them, he'd pay a lot more."

"Let me think about it," Charlie wrote back."

Then, in 1982, a magazine devoted to Mansonabilia began to appear on newsstands in Los Angeles, New York, and several other major cities. It was called *The Dead Circus,* and, in the premiere issue, there was a full-page ad offering a color photograph of Charlie sporting a full erection. The photo, which was purchased by a prominent art dealer in Philadelphia for $10,000, proved to be a fake. The picture had actually been taken at Woodstock, on that famous rain-soaked Sunday when all the hippies were rolling around naked in the mud. The Manson look-alike with the beard and the big dick turned out to be a sandal-maker from Taos, New Mexico.

When he read about this scam in the *San Francisco Chronicle*, Charlie laughed. "Well," he said, "at least I know how much my pecker is worth."

But in the wake of this news item, an idea moved slowly through the pathways of Charlie's twisted mind—an idea both cunning and malignant, and one that he'd been pondering for several years. Forget about the lewd photos of the girls, their perky breasts and their uncensored vaginas. Forget about Patricia Krenwinkel's stained panties or Tex Watson's crumpled condoms. If you really wanted to own a piece of the Manson family legend, what would be the ultimate possession?

Charlie posed this question to Victor Zimmer, the sexual psychopath who occupied the cell next to his in Vacaville.

"I don't know," Victor said, his fingers tightly gripping the bars, his expressionless face slowly descending into confusion. "Gimme a hint."

"I can't do that."

"How come, Charlie?"

"Because you might tell," Charlie said, and he smiled, remembering that on October 12, 1969, the day that he and several of his followers were arrested at Barker Ranch in Death Valley, there was a girl who had not been hauled out of the desert and handcuffed, a girl who would never be prosecuted. She was camping a few miles west of Goler Wash, by the dry waterfalls in the Striped Butte Valley. She had driven out to this secret spot late the night before in a blue-flecked dune buggy, one of several that had been stolen from Palmdale Buggy Builders back in July.

On Sunday morning, this girl—Alice McMillan—ignored the heat and the spotter plane circling overhead as she hiked across Mengel Pass, where Carl Mengel, a famous local prospector, died in 1944. Two hundred yards northeast of his cabin, according to Charlie's crude map, there was a pile of red rocks shaped like a pyramid, surrounded by dozens of beer cans and spent shotgun shells. Buried underneath the rocks was an army-type pack containing a paperback copy of *Stranger in a Strange Land,* six canisters of 16 millimeter film, and $20,000 in small bills.

"The book is for you to read. The money you can spend," Charlie told Alice. "But keep that film hidden until you hear from me. Okay?"

"Okay."

"Promise?"

"I promise," Alice said. "It will always be safe."

That night Charlie masturbated for the first time in a month, and in the living space behind his eyes, where desire met absence, he saw a woman, her back toward him, walking barefoot through a field of pale green grass. Ahead of her was a lake, the blue surface shifting and rippling with the wind; and, as she approached the shoreline, she stripped off her white linen dress and dropped it into the wet sand.

This woman had appeared in Charlie's mind at other times when he touched himself. The landscapes were never the same, but she was always moving away from him, indifferent to his deep longing and the elaborate pain that had accumulated in his heart.

The following morning a new prisoner was moved into Charlie's cellblock. His name was Leonard Tisdale, and he'd been sentenced to death for raping and torturing seven women in the hills north of San Luis Obispo. Four of his victims were students at Cal Poly, two were nurses at the campus hospital, and one was a waitress at the local Howard Johnson. All seven were described as tall, thin, and very pretty.

"That's a lot of dead pussy," Charlie told Leonard later that day. "Seems like kind of a waste."

Leonard just shrugged his shoulders. "Once I trim the beaver, ain't no need to keep it alive."

"That's kind of selfish, Leonard."

"I do my thing. You do yours."

"Pussy is sacred. Am I right?" Charlie said, directing his question to Victor Zimmer, who was standing inside his cell with a weird smile evident around his lips. "What do you think, Vic?"

"Pussy is pussy," Victor said. In his mind was a picture of the last girl he slaughtered, her eyes gouged out and the red soup of her insides sliding through his fingers, soaking the ground beneath his feet. "Hot *or* cold. That's what I think, Charlie."

"Just checking," Charlie said, and laughed. "That's all I'm doin'. Just countin' up the votes."

Fifteen

While Gene

Was in Vegas:

Chris Long Returns

It was eight P.M., and Eddie Cornell had been sitting at the bar in Revells since a little before seven, knocking back double shots of tequila (from which he derived no pleasure) and chain-smoking Marlboros. In that time he'd maintained a brooding calm, breathing in and out through his nose, occasionally making a little grunting sound, while he listened to Patti Page sing ten straight songs on the jukebox. Chris Long was an hour late, and Eddie decided to give him until eight-thirty—no, make that nine—and if he had not arrived by then he was out the door.

(Although he was routinely late himself, Eddie treated tardiness in others with unreasonable anger, which was definitely a liability if you were a vice cop—as he once was—or a homicide detective, his current job with the L.A.P.D. Capturing bad guys required infinite patience, especially if you relied upon information supplied by snitches, who were notoriously undependable when it came to showing up on time for meetings, if they showed up at all. To Eddie, however, Long was not merely an informer but also a versatile con man and quite possibly a murderer, who had received a free pass on the streets only because he was useful to someone like Eddie and the people Eddie knew, both inside and outside the department.)

Eddie, his nerves strained, looked up and saw his pale heavy face in the mirror behind the bar, a face that discouraged levity and inspired fear. Then he lifted his chin and changed his expression to something more cheerful, knowing that he would be willing to wait all night for Long, if that's what it took to find out if he was telling the truth.

"This is it," Long had told Eddie that afternoon, when he called him at home. "This is what you've been waiting for."

"Don't bullshit me, Long."

"C'mon, man! This is real. I know this chick. She was there. She was center-stage."

"It isn't real until you've seen the film."

"Fuckit then. I'll go somewhere else."

"There is nowhere else to go," Eddie had said, after a shade of hesitation, indicating that he'd heard Long's threat and dismissed it. "Everything in this area goes through me."

"Look, Eddie—"

"My piece is half."

"Forty percent."

"Half."

A long silence. Then: "Okay, Eddie, it's a deal."

"Meet me at Revells at seven. And fuckin' don't be late."

The "Tennessee Waltz" came on the jukebox and Eddie glanced down the bar. Clyde Phoebe was drawing a stein of beer for a thin black man with a sallow complexion. He was wearing a cheap leather jacket and a fancy gold Rolex that was probably fake.

Eddie said to Clyde, after the song ended, "Did you ever dance with her?"

"Dance with who?"

"Guess."

Clyde flicked Eddie a look that suggested annoyance. "I don't know what you're talking about," he said.

"Sure you do. Miss Patti Page, the singin' rage."

Clyde put the stein of beer on the bar in front of the black man, who said, with a little giggle, "Come on, boss, tell us the truth. Did you dance with her or not?"

Clyde looked at the black man disapprovingly for a few moments, paying special attention to the surgical scars above his eyes, then he limped back to the register. "Ain't none of your business, Jimmy," he said, after he rung up the sale. "Ain't neither of your business."

The black man was now looking at Gene. "Clyde still in love. Ain't that something?"

Eddie nodded slightly, agreeing in silence. Then, as he watched the black man drain half his beer, he felt a sudden change of awareness. Jimmy. That was it. His name was Jimmy Hilton, and he'd been a boxer in the fifties, a slender welterweight who went undefeated in his first thirty-two fights. Gene remembered sitting ringside on the night Jimmy fought Felix Escobar, the pride of East Los Angeles, knocking him out cold in the eighth round with a devastating left hook.

Eddie said, "I saw you fight Escobar."

The black man looked at Eddie for a long time, his eyes showing puzzlement. "Escobar, huh. You were there?"

"Ringside. I was sitting with Jack Havana and Carl Reese."

"You bet on me?"

"Yeah, I did."

"Then you made a bundle."

The fight was fixed, Carl Reese told Eddie ten minutes before the bell sounded for the first round. Escobar's contract was owned by Jack Havana, and Hilton's career was guided by Joe Monument, a black loan shark from Detroit, Hilton's hometown. Monument was the front man for the Trapani crime family, specifically Joe Carbo, the gangster who controlled boxing on the East Coast. In his next bout, Hilton fought Kid Gavilan for the title. Hilton was brutally beaten over fifteen rounds, surviving six knockdowns to go the distance.

Eddie rocked back and forth on his bar stool with his eyes closed, drawn into himself, trying to remember the year of the Escobar fight— 1956 or '57, he wasn't sure. Either way, he was only a couple of years out of high school and already on the take.

"Jesus Christ," Eddie said softly, shaking his head when he felt a tiny flutter next to his heart. Then he opened his eyes and ordered another drink, hoping to quench this moment of inarticulate sorrow.

At Los Angeles High School, Eddie was an all-city football player, a lean, vicious linebacker who was recruited by Notre Dame, Ohio State, and every major university on the West Coast. He was even more highly sought after than Jon Arnett, the speedy halfback from Manual Arts who went on to star for U.S.C. and later, professionally, with the Los Angeles Rams.

"Fuck school. I hated studying. And I always wanted to be a cop," Eddie told Gene after they had worked together for a while, their partnership held together more by their mutual anxieties than any intertwining trust. "I was tough, relatively bright, and I had a passion for justice. It was a good fit."

Eddie played it by the book for his first two years on the force, and he was even cited for bravery twice, the second time for the arrest of Lenny Simic, a Peeping Tom and serial rapist who was terrorizing the residents of Hancock Park, a fancy residential district that was located a few miles east of downtown. Responding to the report of a prowler, Eddie spotted Simic kneeling in a flower bed outside a house on Mansfield and Sixth, a Tudor mansion owned by the actress Rhonda Fleming. With his right hand he was holding a small pair of high-powered binoculars to his eyes, raptly staring through a downstairs window, while he used his left hand to satisfy his ferocious lust.

"When I told him to put up his hands, he dropped the binoculars and just stared at me like he was in a trance, continuing to yank on his dick until he shot his wad. When he came, it was like he pissed this long silver rope. It was fucking unbelievable," Eddie told Gene. "I was so weirded out that I didn't see him pull the knife. Fucker cut all the tendons in my bicep before I could take him down."

Gene later learned that Lenny Simic had died in the back of the ambulance taking him to Hollywood Presbyterian Hospital. The official cause of death was a massive cerebral hemorrhage produced by blunt-force trauma to the head. Apparently Eddie beat Simic to death, the first of three people he would kill on the job, in circumstances that were later described as suspicious.

The arrest got heavy play in the newspapers, and with this publicity Eddie emerged as something of a celebrity around town, sought out for interviews on radio and television. At city hall, when Police Chief Parker awarded him the medal of valor, he extolled Eddie's exploits as a schoolboy athlete and called him "a homegrown hero and a model policeman, a young man I would be proud to have as a son."

And it was during this time, when Eddie was on paid leave, recovering from the deep wound in his arm, that he met Carl Reese at the Ambassador Hotel. Singer Julie London and comedian Shecky Greene were appearing at the Coconut Grove, the hotel's famed nightclub, and Eddie had received complimentary tickets to the dinner show, courtesy of William Morris, the talent agency that represented the grateful Rhonda Fleming. Reese was dining at an adjacent table. Sitting with him were two women around twenty, maybe even younger, and in both their faces was the element of boredom, a studied indifference that was used to hide their cunning and their desperation.

Eddie's date that night, Stephanie Kohler, worked for Art Morales, a bail bondsman with an office in North Hollywood. Eddie had met her at Jimbo's, a piano bar on Lankershim, and he'd fucked her that first night on the fold-out couch in her overheated living room.

Between shows, Carl Reese tapped Eddie on the shoulder. "Just want to shake your hand. That fucking prick Simic got what he deserved. Excuse the language," he said to Stephanie, who smiled and rolled her eyes. "Don't worry. I've heard a lot worse," she asserted confidently. "I work for a bail bondsman."

"I know."

"I didn't think you recognized me."

Eddie looked at Stephanie, reacting with surprise. "You two know each other?"

Stephanie continued to smile, a smile that now held some pride. "Mr. Reese sends Art some clients now and then."

"I operate a few clubs," Reese explained, and the women with him were now both glaring at Stephanie, unhappy that his attention had become divided. The boredom on their faces was gone, replaced by something hard and more aggressive. "Sometimes things come up."

Minutes before Shecky Greene took the stage, Frank Sinatra entered the Coconut Grove, looking sleek and carefully groomed. Actress Ava Gardner was hanging on his arm, gazing straight ahead as she walked across the dance floor, keenly aware that she was the most desired woman in that smoky room. Also in their party was Darryl Zanuck, the president of Twentieth Century Fox, Zanuck's current girlfriend, a pretty young woman with tan, smooth skin and silver hair, and two massive bodyguards, both with expressions that were professionally blank.

"Frank's here," Carl Reese said, and the women sitting with him followed his gaze. Whatever gloom was in their dull faces instantly disappeared, and their eyes now gleamed with the thrill of possibility. "Be good and I'll take you over after the show."

Halfway through his act, Shecky Greene stopped to introduce the many celebrities who were sitting in the audience. Jockey Johnny Longden was there that night and so was Betty Grable and her husband, bandleader Harry James. When Shecky pointed to Frank Sinatra, the audience roared and Ava Gardner urged him to stand up, which he did a little reluctantly, his shyness in this moment enhancing his boyish charm.

"Ava's gorgeous," Stephanie said. "Isn't she, Eddie?"

"Yeah. She sure is."

"I bet you dream about screwing her," Stephanie said, as the applause began to die. "I would if I were a guy."

Eddie was momentarily caught off guard. Before he could think of a response, Shecky Greene said, "We have a special guest here tonight—a cop who's a real hero. Most of you have read about him in the newspapers or heard him being interviewed on radio and TV. His name is Eddie Cornell."

The audience "oohed" and "aahed," and once more the applause began to build as Shecky Greene stepped off the stage, the spotlight following him as he made his way through the packed house. When he came to Eddie's table, Shecky's face was filled with admiration.

"Go on, Eddie. Stand up," Stephanie squealed joyfully. "They want to see you."

The audience cheered as Eddie rose to his feet. "Eddie Cornell. Here he is," Shecky Greene shouted into the mike. "One hell of a cop. Listen to them, Eddie. They love you. Go on, say something!"

Eddie took the mike and waited proudly while the audience grew quiet. Then, with a modesty that seemed unexaggerated, his slick black hair picking up the light, he said, "I just want to thank everyone for being so nice the last few weeks. Especially Miss Rhonda Fleming, who invited me here tonight."

Shecky Greene said, "She wanted to be here in person, Eddie, but she's shooting a picture in Mexico."

"What I did wasn't special," Eddie said, his impulse now to tell the truth, but only part of it. "Cops I work with do things just as brave every day of the week, so I feel a little strange being singled out. And I'll be a lot more relaxed when this whole fuss is over."

Shecky Greene took back the mike. "Eddie, before you sit down, would you like to introduce your pretty date?"

"Yes, I would," Eddie said, and Stephanie pushed her chair back and stood up, smiling shyly while her heart pounded with excitement. "Her name is Stephanie Kohler."

Shecky Greene leaned in and gave Stephanie a peck on her flushed cheek. "Come on," he said, giving both Eddie and Stephanie an appreciative look. "Let's give these two kids another round of applause."

After the show, Carl Reese excused himself and Eddie watched him stroll confidently through the quietly murmurous crowd, acknowledging people with a wave, a handshake, or sometimes a pinch on the cheek. When Frank Sinatra saw him approach, he quickly stood up and clasped Reese's shoulders before he pulled him into an embrace. It seemed to Eddie that Sinatra's face contained some odd joy while Reese whispered softly in his ear.

One of the women at Reese's table, looking at Sinatra with an expression of mindless sexual craving, said, "What I wouldn't give for one night with that man."

"Wouldn't that be heaven?" said her friend, her smile both childish and sly. "We'd give him a time that he'd never forget."

"For fun and for free."

"As long as he sang just one song."

The women laughed together as Sinatra returned to his seat. Reese, now grinning contentedly, his left hand resting comfortably on Ava

Gardner's elegant neck, reached across the table to shake Darryl Zanuck's hand.

Eddie said, "That guy knows everyone."

"Everyone that matters," said Stephanie.

"Did you screw him?"

Stephanie lifted up her glass of champagne and paused for a second. "No, Eddie. I didn't."

"Have you ever fucked a celebrity?"

"Just you," she said, half-jokingly. "Any more questions?"

"Nope. That's about it."

"Good."

"For now."

In a few moments the maitre d' appeared in front of Reese's table. He was tall and skinny, with an authoritative manner and sad-looking eyes. In a quiet voice, as if not to embarrass them, he told the two women that a limousine would be arriving shortly to take them home.

"Home? What do you mean?" one of the women said. "We're with Carl. We're all going home together."

"He was going to introduce us to Frank," her friend said, her eyes swinging toward Sinatra's table, which was now unoccupied.

"I'm sorry. I'm merely passing along what I was told," said the maitre d', looking at the two women patiently but also cautiously. "I'll notify you when your driver is in front of the hotel. Come with me," he said, turning to Eddie and Stephanie. "I've been asked to escort you backstage."

Carl Reese was sitting in a deep armchair by the door inside Julie London's dressing room, drinking scotch out of a tall glass. Balanced on his knees was a plate piled high with cold cuts from the sumptuous buffet. The curvaceous singer and ex-wife of actor Jack Webb was seated on the couch with her legs crossed at the knee, sharing a joint with Frank Sinatra and James Bolden, the black drummer in her band.

"I saw Frank sing for the first time in Chicago," Julie told Bolden, her speaking voice almost as soft and sexy as her singing voice. "He was working at Johnny Roselli's place on Wabash. I was appearing across town at the Carlton."

"I backed up Dinah Washington at Roselli's," James Bolden said.

"But now you're backing me," Julie London cooed, patting him on the thigh. "Right, James?"

"That's right, Julie."

Frank Sinatra smoothed his hair with a pocket comb and stood up to make another drink. His eyes looked tired, and the bright light in the room gave his complexion an unhealthy sheen. "Ava said she was sorry she couldn't stay for the second show. She's got an early call tomorrow."

"She's a gorgeous broad," Julie London said. "Better than you deserve."

"I'll drink to that," Frank said, holding up his glass.

"And not just her face is perfect, either. Tits. Ass. The whole package," Julie London said, and the room was quiet for a second.

Then Carl Reese said, "But she can't sing like you, sweetheart."

"I'll trade my voice for her face any day."

"Never," Frank Sinatra said. "You've got gold in those pipes."

"I'd rather have men fight over me than listen to me."

"Bullshit, Julie. I know you better than that."

"You don't know me at all, Frank."

The maitre d' knocked twice on the dressing room door, and one of Sinatra's bodyguards ushered him inside. Trailing behind him, looking eager but uneasy, were Eddie Cornell and Stephanie Kohler.

Rising to his feet, Carl Reese said, "Well, look who's here. Come on in, you guys. Make yourself at home."

Eddie's eyes were wide as he gazed around the room, and for what seemed a long time he didn't speak. Finally, after the maitre d' retreated into the hallway, Eddie stepped forward and stuck out his hand. "It's really an honor to meet you, Mr. Sinatra."

"Thanks. But you're the big cheese tonight," Frank Sinatra said, before he dropped Eddie's hand and shifted his attention over to Stephanie, who leaned forward to show off her cleavage.

"And this is Miss Julie London," Carl Reese said.

"As you can see," Julie said, looking a little annoyed at being ignored, "we're smoking some Mary Jane."

James Bolden stood up. He looked tense. "I think I better be goin' now."

Frank Sinatra snagged Bolden by the wrist to stop his progress toward the door. "Sit down, James. Relax," he said, making eye contact with Reese. "This kid's cool, right?"

Reese gave Sinatra a wink. "He's cool. Right, Eddie? You're not on duty tonight."

Eddie glanced at Stephanie and wondered whether she saw the guilt in his face. "No," he said, trying to laugh off his nervousness. "I'm not on duty."

Eddie smoked his first marijuana cigarette that night in Julie London's dressing room, becoming so high and disoriented that he recalled only random fragments of the events that followed. He remembered shadowboxing with Sinatra, a slapfight that nearly got out of hand, until both of Sinatra's bodyguards quickly and skillfully wrestled him to the floor. In his memory somewhere was Julie London singing "Cry Me a River," but he didn't remember seeing her show, only hearing her sultry voice. Also, there was a period of time—an hour, two, three, he couldn't tell—that he had no memory of at all, just a shameful silent darkness. But he knew that somewhere toward the end of the night everyone piled into Sinatra's limousine and drove to a home in the Hollywood Hills.

Carl Reese was already there when Eddie arrived, sitting out by the lighted pool with Jack Havana and B-movie producer Max Rheingold. A girl with bright red pubic hair and even redder nipples was in the pool swimming laps naked, and Stephanie quickly threw off her clothes and joined her.

On a patio filled with couples dancing, Eddie tried to dirty-boogie with a black woman wearing silver lipstick and a detached smile on her strong face. After a few clumsy steps, he tripped and fell, cracking his forehead on the corner of a white wrought-iron table set with food. He was unable to stand, and blood ran down his cheek from a deep gash above his right eye. The actor Nick Adams and another man carried him into a guest bedroom, where his wound was dressed by one of the bartenders, a pretty girl with long, straight, white-blond hair and thin gold bracelets on each wrist.

Before he passed out, Eddie thought he might have kissed her, but he wasn't sure. The next morning he woke up and lay motionless for several minutes with his eyes closed, trying to remember where he was. When he raised his arm to scratch his cheek, he heard the sound of birds and felt someone's breath tickle his neck.

"A woman was sleeping next to me," Eddie told Stephanie when he called her at work. "At first I thought it was you, but when I opened my eyes I saw that her hair was darker and cut short. She was laying on her side, facing the wall."

"I hope you had fun with her."

"If I did, I don't remember."

"What a shame."

"What about you?"

"What about me, Eddie?"

"Did you have a good time?"

"What a silly question. I had a great time."

When she didn't elaborate, Eddie waited a few moments before he asked her how she finally made it home. She said she begged a ride from a guy named Herb Stelzner, a record producer she knew from Jack's Sugar Shack, a rockabilly club in Van Nuys where she occasionally hung out, playing darts and quarter pool. Of course, Stephanie left out the end of the party and the twenty minutes she spent upstairs in a locked bedroom with Frank Sinatra and Carl Reese.

"What about you?" she said. "How did you get back to your car?"

"I had to call a cab. I was late for my shift. I'll probably be written up."

"Sorry."

"Yeah, well . . . No big deal."

There was a short pause before Stephanie spoke again, and her voice seemed strangely formal. "Check in with me later in the week. Okay?"

Before he hung up, Eddie said he was worried about some of the things he'd done the night before—that by using drugs and openly carousing with known racketeers, he might have compromised his future as a cop.

"Relax, Eddie. This is Hollywood. You were having fun," she told him, responding with some amusement. "That's all you were doing."

But looking back, Eddie knew that the night at the Coconut Grove was the night that everything changed. The door to another life was opened, and he stepped through it without hesitation, unaware that he was entering a world of treachery and multiple contradictions, of desperate and single-minded men, where it was always cold and darkness ruled.

Sixteen

Alice in Phoenix

Dear Alice:

    I'm writing you from Phoenix, Arizona. It's after midnight and I'm staying at the Carefree Inn, this funky little motel on Van Buren Avenue, the main drag that runs straight through the center of town. Next door is this rowdy bar called the Silver Peso, where there are always pick-ups idling in the parking lot and the favorite song on the jukebox is "Goin' Up to the Country" by Canned Heat. Across the street is the Navajo Lanes, a bowling alley that's open twenty-four hours.

    In the room next to me a young mother lives with her five-year-old daughter. I met them out by the ice machine this afternoon. The mother dances topless at another bar across town called the Pepper Tree Lounge. She says she's trying to save enough money to get to Las Vegas. She wants to be a showgirl at Caesars Palace. That's her dream. She's pretty, but not that pretty.

    I only mention her because the red bikini with the blue trim she was wearing around the pool reminded me of you. You had a swimsuit just like that in high school. And Penny's body—that's her name, Penny, short for Penelope—is kind of like yours too, only your boobs were real and Penny carries a little more weight in her butt.

    Anyway, Penny's husband left her and Daph—that's her daughter's name, short for Daphne—a couple of years ago while they were living in Flagstaff. He ran off with another woman. They rode out to L.A. on his motorcycle and he joined the Gravediggers, this biker gang that started up in the Antelope Valley back in the 1950s. And how's this for weird? Charlie spent time in prison with a bunch of Gravediggers, and they used to hang out at the ranch with us all the time, getting high.

Of course I didn't tell Penny any of this, because I didn't want her to think I fucked her ex, which was certainly possible. Plus I didn't want to slip up and mention anything about Charlie. I have to be careful what I say about him. Even though I've broken loose, I can sometimes feel his presence brushing up against me like a ghost.

By the way, I may be going home for a few days. I spoke to my mom and she said it would be okay, even though my dad doesn't really want to see me. She says he's still mad because I took off and never said goodbye. But that's not the real reason he's angry. He was pissed because he couldn't sneak in my bed anymore and molest me.

He was as bad as Mister Keegan. Worse, because he was my dad. You know, if it wasn't for Charlie, I would've never learned how to enjoy sex again. Do you enjoy sex? I wonder.

Also, I wonder if you kept my letters a secret or turned them over to the police. They could be looking for me right now for all I know, although I'm not that easy to find. And what if they did arrest me? What could they prove? That I left my family for another family? So what? We were all just gullible girls with separate selves, part of a creepy chain of hope that carried the wrong message.

Hey Alice, my dad was a pervert and your mom was crazy. How come you ended up so good, and I ended up like . . . me.

Your friend,
Alice

Seventeen

Spahn Ranch

Alice McMillan first met Chris Long backstage at the Sunshine Sideshow, a three-day pop festival held outside at Devonshire Downs in Northridge, California, in the latter part of June 1969. Spahn Ranch, where she was living at the time, was located only a few miles west in Chatsworth, and she and Susan Atkins, along with several other members of the Manson clan, attended the sold-out Saturday concert, which included appearances by the Grass Roots and Jethro Tull, Alice's favorite band.

Spindizzy, a multiracial blues group similar in style to Canned Heat, took the stage around dusk, and midway through their set, when the lead singer noticed Alice in the audience, riding topless on Tex Watson's shoulders, he signaled one of the roadies to invite her backstage. Remembering Charlie's edict to "use your pussy to make friends," Alice and the girls provided sexual favors for anyone who asked, no matter how drunk or stoned, using the air-conditioned motor home that had been reserved for Donovan, who was scheduled to close the festival on Sunday evening.

Spindizzy's manager, Chris Long, fucked Alice twice that night with a crazy hunger, the second time while Sandra Good massaged his hard shoulders, which were red and glistening with sweat. Afterwards, Long agreed to drive Alice back to the ranch, but as soon as they pulled out of the parking lot she unbuttoned his Levi's, and his dick popped up like a jack-in-the-box, red and rigid.

"Wow!" Alice said, laughing. "You really get hard fast."

"I'm glad that makes you happy."

"Sex makes me happy."

"I've noticed that," Long said, looking down at her bobbing head.

After he came in her mouth in three little thrusts, Long, who was high on mescaline, told Alice that his real name was Christopher Von Lang, and that he was born in Germany in 1941.

"My father was a nuclear physicist," he said. "He was a Catholic, but my mother was a Jew. The U.S. smuggled us out of Berlin right after I was born. They wanted my father to help build the atom bomb. He was a genius."

"Did he?" Alice asked.

"Did he what?"

"Work on the atom bomb."

"Yeah, he did," Long said, with a slight, embarrassed hesitation. Then his face became confused. "I can't believe I'm telling you this stuff."

"Why? Is it a big secret?"

"Yeah, it is."

"Is that why you changed you name?"

"No," Long said. "I did that later."

In his junior year in high school, Long lived with his parents and younger brother in Sherman Oaks, a pleasantly unpretentious suburb in the San Fernando Valley. By this time his father had become a senior scientist at the Jet Propulsion Laboratory in Pasadena, supervising the development of long-range ballistic missles. But his career ended suddenly on a summer Sunday afternoon in 1959, after he was caught shoplifting a set of screwdrivers from the hardware department in the local Sears.

"The day after he was released from jail he was fired, and the F.B.I. revoked his security clearance. That night he shot himself," Long said. "The story made the front page the next day, with his picture. Herbert Von Lang commits suicide. In the article they made it seem like he was a spy or something."

"But he wasn't."

"No. He was just a fucked-up guy that made one mistake. Two weeks later we packed up and moved out of the neighborhood. In the fall I started going to a new high school in Hollywood. *That's* when I changed my name."

After Long stopped speaking, he and Alice sat in silence for a few miles, the warm wind rushing past their faces, exchanging the complicit glances of lovers or coconspirators.

"I've got a secret, too," Alice finally said, sounding frank and forthright.

"Tell me."

"I killed someone."

"Who?"

"This guy from my hometown. I didn't do it alone. I had help."

In the summer of 1967, Alice McMillan was on the corner of Haight and Page, pacing the sidewalk, hawking copies of the *Oracle,* San Francisco's most widely read underground newspaper, when she noticed a bright blue bus packed with tourists pull up to the stoplight. In a window toward the back, a middle-aged man looked down at her and smiled, a smile that was more sinister than playful. She stared back at him coldly, holding his little grey eyes, and then a giddy excitement made her whole body vibrate as she recognized his gold-capped teeth, his oily side-parted hair, and his boggy face.

It was Mr. Keegan from Cedar Rapids, a responsible member of society and the owner of Keegan's Wash and Dry, the Laundromat in which Alice's ripening body and those of other hometown girls were flagrantly abused.

"He didn't know who I was at first," Alice told Chris Long. They had left the freeway by now and, as they approached the gates leading into Spahn Ranch, Long's headlights picked up a boy armed with a rifle, speaking into a walkie-talkie. When he recognized Alice in the passenger seat, he dipped his head and waved them through. "I was older and thinner, and my hair was all different. Shit, I was a hippie chick now, not some corn-fed hick with hay in my ear. You should've seen the look on his face when I knocked on his window and shouted out his name. He went, 'Alice, my God! Is that you?' and right away he jumped off the bus, telling the driver that he'd take a taxi back to his hotel. Boy, did he look excited. I bet he thought he was gonna fuck me or something. Actually, I did let him fuck me."

"Before you killed him?"

"Yeah. That's right. Park over here," Alice said, pointing at a wooden bunkhouse surrounded by deep weeds, one of several decrepit, proplike buildings that made up the remnants of this fake western town. "You don't believe me, do you?"

Chris Long remained silent after he cut the engine and switched off the headlights. Off to his right, in a small clearing ringed by tall white oaks, a squatty clump of people dressed like cowboys and Indians were sitting around a campfire, talking softly while they passed around a pipe filled with potent local weed.

Alice reached for the door handle. "No. Don't get out. Not yet," Long said. "Finish your story first."

"I'll tell you everything except the very end."

"No. I want to hear everything."

"You can't. Charlie has to say it's okay."

"Who's Charlie?"

"Charlie's God."

"Yeah, right."

" He is," Alice said, looking at Long with serious eyes. "You'll see."

Alice escorted Mr. Keegan into the Bourgeois Pig, a coffee house on Fillmore Street where Charlie hung out in the late afternoon, dealing speed. Over a tuna sandwich and a glass of iced tea, Alice learned that Mr. Keegan was in town for a convention, and that he was scheduled to fly back to Cedar Rapids the following morning.

Alice made a pouty face. "That's too bad. It would be fun to spend some time together."

"We could spend some time together today."

"You mean now?"

"Sure."

"Doing what?"

"You tell me, Alice," Mr. Keegan said, and his mouth worked itself into a meaningless smile.

Alice leaned forward and lowered her voice. "I'm more experienced now."

"I bet you are."

"But I have to get paid," Alice said. Then she took Mr. Keegan's hand and held it between both of hers. "Is that okay?"

"Sure."

"Can we go back to your hotel?"

Mr. Keegan shook his head, his stare now fixed on her ample chest. "No. That's not possible. My wife is with me."

Alice thought for a moment, glancing at Charlie, who was sitting at a table in a darkened corner, playing chess with a black man named Johnny Fletcher, a local actor who appeared regularly in X-rated films. Then she smiled and sat up, her body taut, her breasts pushed out. "I've got an idea. But first I have to make a phone call."

Alice signaled Charlie with her eyes as she crossed the room, and he waited for a few moments, his brow knitted and his hand poised over a chess piece, before he made his move and casually stood up. After giving Fletcher a thin, almost condescending smile, he followed Alice down a short hallway that led to the restrooms and the pay phone.

"That's him. Mr. Keegan. He's here," Alice told Charlie, rushing at him, unable to contain her excitement.

"Keegan?"

"The guy I told you about. The one who molested me."

"The Laundromat guy?"

"Yeah!"

"Wow."

"He wants to give me a hundred dollars. What should I do? Where should I take him?"

Charlie thought for a moment, rocking back on his heels as he ran his hand through his scraggly hair. "Take him back to our place. You'll be cool there."

"Are we gonna punish him, Charlie?"

"Yeah," he said. There was a glint in his eye. "Probably should."

* * *

"We crashed at this house on Carl Street in the Haight. Five of us lived there, four girls and Charlie," Alice told Long, after she led him inside the bunkhouse. There was no electricity, and they were stretched out on a lumpy mattress, covered by an old gray army blanket that carried a rank smell. "Those were cool times."

"Did you all screw him?"

"We still do," Alice said. Then she unbuckled Long's belt and fiddled with his crotch. "What about you? You ready to go again, handsome?"

Long stopped her hand. "Just tell me what happened."

"I told you. We killed him."

"How?"

"Charlie stabbed him in the back while he was balling me. He used his hunting knife," Alice said, reaching into Long's pants. "Mr. Keegan died with a hard dick. But you—"

"Don't." Long's grip tightened on Alice's arm.

"What's wrong? You scared of me?"

"Maybe."

"That man hurt me. He deserved to die. I don't want to hurt you."

"Glad to hear it."

"That's why we're sharing secrets. Because we trust each other," Alice said, and she took his face in her hands and kissed him on the lips. "Right, Chris?"

Long drew in a deep breath as he leaned back a little and stared into her eyes, trying to decide whether he really believed her. "Yeah," he said after several moments. "That's right."

When Long woke up the next morning, Charles Manson was squatting on the weathered wooden floor in the center of the bunkhouse, studying him with a sly intensity. Although there was a sense of great peace in his body, his hair was wild and he was dressed in filthy jeans that were patched to cover the holes in both knees and in his crotch.

Long propped himself on his elbow. He looked over at Charlie and they stared at each other for a moment. Then, with a guileless smile that seemed to be directed inward, Charlie said, "I bet you could use some coffee."

Long nodded. "Yeah, I could."

"Alice is making you some right now."

Long threw off his blanket and a puff of dust rose up through the late-morning sunlight, then slowly settled around his head and shoulders like sprinkles of pollen. "Who're you?"

"Me?" Charlie squinted his eyes but continued to regard Long with a smile. "My name's Charlie."

Long pulled on his T-shirt and eased himself back just a little. "You're the guy they call God," he said, as sort of an aside. "Right?"

Charlie made a shrugging motion. "Who told you that?"

"Alice."

"I did not." Alice entered the bunkhouse carrying a metal cup filled with steaming coffee. She stared at Charlie expectantly until he looked up and gave her a wink, which Long caught. "I told him that *I* thought you were God, not anyone else."

Alice handed Long his coffee while avoiding his eyes. Outside a baby cried out and a fat gray dog passed by the open door in a half-trot, followed by a naked child holding an ear of corn.

"Alice is good people," Charlie said, keeping his voice low as she walked outside. "She digs you. But sometimes she gets to yakking too much when she's stoned. So whatever she told you last night, you should probably take with a grain of salt."

Long looked relieved.

"I'm not sayin' it was bullshit, only that you should forget you heard it."

Once Long was dressed, Charlie took him on a tour of the ranch, showing him the stables and the mock-up cowboy movie street. Inside the Long Horn Saloon there was a long wooden bar and a working jukebox stocked with 45's. Charlie played "Never Learn Not to Love," the B-side of "Friends," a Beach Boys single that sold poorly in the summer of 1967, never rising above 64 on the Billboard Hot 100.

"I wrote that," Charlie said, peering at Long closely, while they sat at the bar listening to the complex harmonies. "It was one of my tunes. I called it 'Cease to Exist.' Dennis Wilson changed the title and a bunch of the words."

Long was staring at Charlie's reflection in the long mirror behind the bar. "You wrote that? Really?"

Charlie withdrew from his back pocket a greasy piece of lined white paper that was folded into a small square. "These are the original lyrics. See for yourself," he said, and he placed the paper on the bar. "I've written a bunch of tunes. Hundreds. Songs that will change the world when they end up on the radio. And that's why you're here, mister. You've been sent to help put things in motion. It's all part of the plan."

Long unfolded the paper, and while his eyes raced over the lyrics, he occasionally nodded his head to indicate that he was impressed. After a minute, he looked up and said, "If you know the Beach Boys, how come you need my help?"

Charlie gazed at Long with a new intensity. "I don't need anyone's help."

"I didn't mean—"

"Right now you're the one who's here. You fucked Alice. You're part of the family. This is what's supposed to happen. It's the way it is. Karma. That's all."

That afternoon Long joined Charlie and several of his submissive women on a hike into the woods behind the ranch. As if by agreement no one spoke a word, and Charlie seemed withdrawn, almost hostile, as they trudged single file through the yellowish haze. Cresting a scratchy hillside, Charlie suddenly stopped and settled into an apelike crouch, pointing at a thick brown snake that was curled in a swatch of grass, sleeping next to a long hollow log.

In a movement that was almost too swift for the eye to see, Charlie sprang forward like a fox and seized the snake behind the head; and with a witless smile on his face and no sound at all in the air except the humming bees, he did a funky childish little dance, waving the writhing snake above his head in his clenched hand.

"What do you think about that, Mister Snake? Caught you napping, didn't I?" Charlie said, giggling, and threw a glance over his shoulder. "Didn't I, Gypsy?"

One of the silent women, a chunky blond wearing glasses with golden wire frames, stepped out of line and Charlie handed her the slim hunting knife he kept fastened in a leather scabbard on his belt. With her face ruminative and peaceful, and with the light catching her eyeglasses and the tip of the knife, the woman, using a quick slashing stroke, cut the snake in half.

"Nice work," Charlie said solemnly, staring down at the twitching tail and the black blood pumping into the dirt by his feet. After a long time he lifted his head, and Long saw in his face a kind of nameless rage. "Let's move on."

After a while the trail ended in a small glade, and Charlie stopped and took a seat on a stump with his back to the sun. The girls sat before him on the ground in a semicircle, watching quietly while he used his knife to draw various geometric symbols in the dirt by his boots: a cone, a pyramid, a square, etc. When he was done, he sat staring at them with grim bemusement, ignoring Long, who was standing in the shade with his arms hanging loosely at his sides.

After a prolonged silence, Charlie began talking about the secret meaning of "Helter Skelter," the Beatles song off the *White Album,* repeating the final stanza three times while he pointed to the recondite symbols in the dirt. "Helter-skelter is comin' down. It's the niggers versus the whites, and it's all gonna happen soon," Charlie said in a tone of quiet amazement. "Open revolution in the streets. All it needs is just one spark to set it off. That's what the Beatles are saying, if you listen carefully." Charlie stopped speaking and gazed at Long with the faintest of smiles. "Am I right, Mr. Long?"

Almost as one, the girls snapped their heads around and stared at Long. His face didn't change, but his voice sounded anxious when he said, "I don't know, Charlie. I never heard that in the song."

"Not everyone can. But it's there for people like me to decipher," Charlie said, slowly running his finger down the blade of his knife. "I've been chosen to be the messenger. Just like I chose you, Mr. Long. That's the way it works."

One of the girls, a redhead with a thin face, raised her hand to speak. Charlie nodded and she said, "What happens when the killing starts?"

"People die, little sister. That's what happens."

"Everyone?"

"No." Charlie shook his head and closed one eye. "Not everyone."

"Do the Beatles want the revolution?" another girl asked.

"Of course they do. Listen to the words, "Charlie said, and he quoted more lyrics from the *White Album,* from the song "Revolution." "They're asking me for advice. They want me to sing out, tell everyone the plan. That's why Mr. Long is so important. I got the keys to the kingdom, but he needs to open the lock."

There was no movement for almost a minute. Then a tall girl with long blond braided hair stood up and turned around to face Long. She was wearing ripped tennis shoes and a white flowery cotton shift that ended six inches above her knees.

Charlie said, "This is Leslie. She's gonna show you her pussy."

Leslie, her face never losing its calm, pulled the shift over her head and dropped it into the dirt by her feet. A few of the girls began to giggle, peeking over their shoulders to sneak a quick glance at Long, who was staring straight ahead, his attention fastened on Leslie's beautiful slender body.

Charlie said, "She wants you, Mr. Long. She wants you to fuck her. Don't you, Leslie?"

"Sure," Leslie said, preserving her set expression. Then in a lower, shyer voice, she added: "If he wants to."

"Of course he does. Don't you, Mr. Long?"

There was a pause. One of the girls said, "He's worried about Alice. He thinks she'd be jealous."

"Is that it?" Charlie asked.

Another girl said, "He's afraid of us. He thinks we're weird."

Leslie abruptly stepped forward and stood in front of Long, still keeping her features immobile. Then, appearing to gather herself, she took his hands and placed them on her breasts. "We'll go someplace private. It'll be fun," she whispered. "Just do what Charlie wants."

"What do *you* want?" Long said, as he moved his hands down to her smooth belly and her slim boyish hips.

"To make Charlie happy."

Long and Leslie made love on the downhill slope of a small meadow, surrounded by blood-red poppies in the tall dry grass. Afterwards, the blades of his back were scratched and raw, and the twisted shadow of a nearby tree stretched over their bodies, signaling the end of the long afternoon. On the way back to the ranch, Leslie took Long's hand and told him that he was a wonderful lover.

"Not like most of the guys I've been with," she said, in a voice that contained an element of self-loathing. "Up and down, up and down, in and out. They treated me like a machine."

Leslie then went on to tell Long about all the famous men she'd slept with, the movie stars and rock-and-roll musicians who came out to the ranch in their long black limousines. She said Charlie turned her—turned all the girls—into swooning sex machines. And these girls, she said, were not ugly or retarded, but ordinary girls from the white middle class who became strangely unfazed by their persistent desire.

"Alice is the worst. She has to have everyone," Leslie said in an angry voice. "I know I'm prettier, but she makes me so mad sometimes that I want to hurt her. Slice her to pieces like Gypsy did that snake. But if I did, Charlie would be angry. I don't want Charlie angry with me."

Leslie looked quickly at Long, who said, "Do you think Charlie scares me?"

"Are you kidding?" Leslie said without irony. Then she stood up. "Charlie scares everyone."

As they walked back to the ranch, Leslie told Long about Steve Taylor, a local news reporter who visited the ranch on an oppressively warm day in the early spring, when the temperature was driven up by the Santa Anas, those fear-quickening winds that occasionally blow in from the desert. Taylor had heard about this scruffy, little, self-styled guru and his mostly female followers, and he came out with his camera crew to film a segment for the evening news.

"A bunch of us were sunbathing nude when they drove up," Leslie said, as she and Long walked along, their eyes on the ground as they crossed a small stream, then stepped around a branch from a downed tree. "They were all kind of cute, and right away we started coming on to them, flirting and rubbing up against them like a bunch of horny cats. Charlie came out and watched for a while, hanging back near the bunkhouse with this tricky smile on his face, like he was putting together a plan.

"Before he agreed to be interviewed, Charlie told Taylor that he wanted to take him on a dune-buggy ride, show him around the ranch. They were gone about an hour, and when they came back Taylor wasn't acting normal. His eyes were bugged out and he was talking all weird, saying that he saw a blue snake with two heads and a jackrabbit that was as tall as a man. That's when we knew that Charlie had dosed him with acid.

"His camera crew knew something goofy was happening. Before they could do anything, Charlie said, 'Let's show these people how to make love,' and then he passed around this fat joint laced with mescaline and PCP. He said he wanted to stage and film an orgy, which was cool with Taylor, because he was so stoned and sexed-up that he couldn't see straight. By now, all of them were.

"The whole night became like a big sex circus, with Charlie acting as the ringmaster, leaping around like this horny little elf, telling everyone what to do, who to fuck, who to suck. Everything was cool until this Taylor dude started coming down off the acid. When his mind finally came back, and he realized that Charlie had him on film screwing a bunch of hippie chicks, some who were probably underage, then he freaked out.

"He tried to grab the film, but Charlie punched him in the face, giving him a bloody nose. Charlie said that not only was he keeping the film, but he was also taking the camera and whatever equipment they had

in their truck. His line was, 'You came out to my house. You fucked my
women. And for that I need something in return.'

"Taylor started yelling and screaming, calling Charlie all sorts of bad
names, but there was nothing he could do. Charlie let him rant and rave
until he got bored, then he asked Tex Watson and Clem Grogan to escort
everyone off the property."

Long and Leslie walked in silence for the next thirty minutes,
listening to the random notes of the birds passing through the trees
overhead. Alice was waiting for them by the stables. She told Leslie
that Charlie and Susan Atkins had gone into Hollywood to run an
errand.

"They want everyone to stay on the ranch until they get back. That
doesn't include you," Alice said to Long. "You can split anytime you want.
But Charlie wants you to stay in touch."

"I'm not sure I can help him with his music."

"What do you mean?"

"I'll have to hear his songs first."

"Charlie's music is going to save the world," Alice said with a tone
of finality. "That's all you need to know. It's your job to get it heard."

Long's voice rose. "My job?"

"Yeah." Alice looked at Leslie. "Right, Les?"

Leslie shrugged. "I don't know. I guess," she said, offering Alice a
timid smile, and then she walked away without saying goodbye.

Alice followed Long over to his dented, rusted-out VW van. He
looked surprised when she told him she would be leaving Los Angeles in
a few months, by September at the latest. Everyone was moving into the
desert north of Death Valley, where they planned to wait out the war
between the races that Charlie expected to erupt before the end of the year.
That was the reason he went into town, she said, to close a monster drug
deal that was going to finance their move.

"Charlie thinks you're good people. The girls liked you, too," Alice
said, giving him a coy smile as he climbed behind the wheel of his van.
"They were all jealous when I told them you had a huge cock."

"Thanks for the compliment."

"It's true."

Long started the engine. "Leslie told me about the home movies you made," he said, staring at Alice but not smiling back. "I'd like to see them sometime."

Alice's face went blank. "What movies?"

"The skin flicks."

Alice shook her head. "I'm sorry," she said with a note of displeasure. "I don't know what you're talking about."

"Leslie said—"

"Leslie makes things up."

"That's what Charlie said about you."

Alice was staring at Long with a grim mouth. He looked back at her unsteadily while he gunned the engine. Then, without speaking again or offering a parting wave, he put the van into gear and drove out of the ranch.

Two days later, when he got up to pee in the middle of the night, he felt a burning sensation shoot through the shaft of his penis, followed by a thick liquid discharge the color of tapioca. He knew, of course, that he'd contracted a venereal disease, a particularly virulent strain of gonorrhea as it turned out, and it took three visits to the L.A. Free Clinic and a wide range of antibiotics before he was symptom-free.

"We've been seeing some weird stuff lately," the doctor, a dour-faced woman in her mid-forties, told Long on his last visit. "The GI's are bringing it back from Vietnam and spreading it around. All this free love is wonderful, but sometimes there are consequences to pay. Be careful."

Toward the latter part of July, Long received a phone call from Alice McMillan, which took him by surprise, since his number in Hollywood was unlisted and he had no memory of giving it out while he was at the ranch. She said, happily, that Charlie wanted to meet with him that weekend.

"On Saturday or Sunday, whatever's good for you, " Alice said. "He wants to play you his songs."

"I can't do it. I've made other plans," Long said, explaining that one of the bands he managed, a country-rock quintet called Fiddlefuck, was opening for the Jefferson Airplane in San Diego.

"Charlie's gonna be bummed."

"Tell him I'll do it some other time."

"That's not the way it works."

"What do you mean?"

"Didn't you read the newspaper today?" Alice asked in a different voice, a colder voice.

"No. Why?"

"There was a story about this guy who was stabbed to death up in Topanga Canyon. His name was Gary," Alice said. "He was a musician, a guitar player who sometimes jammed with Neil Young at The Corral. He used to come out to the ranch and fuck the girls. He fucked me, like you did, and he said he could help Charlie get a record deal. But he didn't do shit. Now he's dead."

Half-startled, Long said, "I never said I could get Charlie a record deal."

"Charlie thinks you did."

"He's wrong."

There was a moment's pause.

"Really? Well, I'll pass that along" Alice said, and there was another pause, a longer pause, before she quietly said goodbye.

That afternoon Long had his phone disconnected, and the following morning he abandoned his apartment on Carlton Way, leaving no forwarding address. And for the next two weeks he lived in a suffocatingly small room at the St. Francis Hotel on Hollywood Boulevard, departing on August 10, the morning after actress Sharon Tate, hairdresser Jay Sebring, and three others were stabbed to death in the hills north of Sunset.

Because Long was already an elusive, almost cryptic presence in the local underground music scene, his absence over the next twelve months went unnoticed, except by the bands he deserted and the people, mostly women, who had loaned him money.

■

Alice felt her muscles tense when she picked up the phone and dialed Chris Long's number. It had been sixteen years since they'd last spoken, and when she heard his voice—a voice that was thickened and stupefied by drugs and booze—she tried to contain the rush of excitement that erupted inside her.

"Hello, Chris. This is Alice."

"Alice? Alice who?"

"Alice McMillan."

"I don't know any Alice McMillan."

"Sure you do," Alice said. "Spahn Ranch. Summer of 1969. You remember?"

There was silence. Alice waited, enjoying Long's uneasiness. Then he said, "How did you find me?"

"How do you think? Charlie."

"That's bullshit. Manson's in the fucking slam."

"Of course he is. But he's up there with people who know a lot about you, Chris. People you snitched on."

More silence. Then, suddenly on the edge of panic, Long said: "What do you want?"

"What do I want?" Alice's voice was detached, almost chatty. "Well, let's see, Chris. I guess I want to make you rich."

Six hours later, when she saw his sharpened face and they looked at each other with a pretense of familiarity and trust, Alice told Long that Charlie had sent her and Susan Atkins over to his apartment on the day he moved out.

She said, "We had orders to kill you."

"Would you have done it?"

"Maybe."

Long stared at Alice, who gazed back at him with unflinching eyes. She was sitting with her legs folded on the rumpled bed inside her room at the Tropicana Motel. Long sat in the easy chair opposite the bed, occasionally glancing over his shoulder at Eddie Cornell, who stood guard by the door, swaying slightly, his face both cold and tranquil.

Long said, "Why don't we talk about the film."

Alice reached for a cigarette. "What do you want to know?"

"Where is it?"

"It's here."

"Where?" Long glanced around the pseudo-friendly room. "Here?"

"No."

"Where?"

"Close by. It's safe." Alice lit the cigarette and flipped the dead match into the metal ashtray on the nightstand. "Don't worry."

Long said, "Nobody's worried, Alice. But Eddie has to see the footage before money can change hands."

Alice shrugged. "I'm cool with that."

"She's cool with that," Eddie said in a mocking tone. "Give me a fucking break."

Long turned his head toward Eddie. "What's the problem, Eddie?"

"The problem? I'll tell you what the fucking problem is," Eddie said, and his sudden anger made a vein throb in his forehead. "I don't like sitting around this shithole motel. I didn't come here for a meet and greet. I came here to make a deal."

"We're making a deal, Eddie."

"You were two hours late," Alice said and took a drag off her cigarette.

"No. *He* was two hours late," Eddie said, jerking his head in Long's direction. "Mister queerbait over there."

"Fuck you, man. I'm not queer," Long said, looking to Alice for confirmation.

"Okay. Then you're impersonating a queer."

Alice said, "He wasn't queer sixteen years ago."

"Oh really? I take it you fucked him good back then," Eddie said, and when Long started to stand, Eddie pushed him back down in his chair.

"Yeah, I fucked him good."

"Did whatever Charlie told you to do."

"That's right," Alice said comfortably. "That's the way it worked."
Alice put out her cigarette with an air of nonchalance. But when she looked
over at Long, she was unable to control the quiver in her lips. "What's
going on here, Chris? You told me this guy was okay."

Glancing back at Eddie, Long said, "Easy, man. You're freaking her
out."

Eddie ignored Long. He was smiling at Alice in a way that showed
his hate. "Let me ask you something," he said. "What if I told you I wanted
you to suck my dick? How would you react to that?"

Alice studied Eddie for a moment, and then she swung her feet off
the bed and stood up. She looked both terrified and incredulous. "This
was a mistake, Chris. I'm sorry," she said and grabbed her purse. "I'm
leaving."

"You're goin' nowhere," Eddie said.

"Fuck you, mister."

Alice stepped back and turned to go. But she was only able to take
one step toward the door before Eddie's right hand shot out and caught
her in the mouth, sending her crashing to the floor. "I want the film, and
I want it now," he said, as he dropped into a crouch and seized her by the
throat.

"Okay, Eddie. That's enough," Long said in a normal voice.

Eddie looked up at Long with a puzzled frown. "Since when do you
tell me what to do?"

"Back off."

"Kiss my ass, punk."

Long stood up and removed a silver pistol from the pocket of his
leather jacket. "Take your hands off her," he said with an inner seriousness, aiming the long barrel at Eddie's head, "or I'll blow your fucking
brains out."

There was a pause, in which a smile spread across Eddie's face. "Okay,
I get it. You wanna be in charge. That's cool. Everything's cool," he said,
standing up and taking a step backward. "Just relax."

"Give her the money," Long said, more urgently now.

Eddie looked at him, and Long could see the muscles tighten in his jaw. "What're you talking about?"

"Give her the fucking money and she'll bring back the film." Long glanced sideways at Alice. Tears rolled down her cheeks, mingling with the blood that already coated her lips. "Am I right? No way you're gonna fuck us."

"No way," Alice said, starting to sob out loud.

Eddie reached into his pocket. He took out a thick roll of bills and dropped them on the bed. "Ten grand. She gets the rest when she gets back."

Keeping the pistol still pointed at Eddie's head, Long reached down and took Alice's hand, pulling her to her feet. "Go wash your face."

Alice took her purse into the bathroom and closed the door, leaving Eddie and Long standing in the center of the small room, facing each other, their bland—almost disinterested—expressions saying nothing about what they might be feeling inside. They remained in these postures for an awkward minute, until Eddie nodded at the gun and said, "When are you going to put that thing down?"

Long kept silent, listening to the toilet flush and then the water running in the bathroom sink. Without meaning to, he recalled the conversation he'd had with Eddie on the ride over from Revells, a conversation that still made him feel slightly aggrieved.

Eddie said, "I checked out your file this morning. I had some time to kill, and I wanted to refresh my memory. And guess what? I saw something in there that I never noticed before. Long's not your real name, is it? Von Lang's your real name. You're a fucking kraut."

"That's right, Eddie."

"And guess what else I found? Your father had a rap sheet, too," Eddie said, and he went on to reveal that he'd discovered Herbert Von Lang's arrest report from the summer of 1959, a twelve-page document in which he admitted that his brother Luther, Long's uncle, had been a Nazi war criminal—a guard at Treblinka, according to evidence presented during the Nuremberg trials—and that he was living in Mexico City at the time of the arrest. "But I guess you already knew that. Right?" Eddie let out a stupid little laugh—"haw haw"—but Long remained silent, his irritation building as Eddie swung his new Camaro into the parking lot of the Tropicana Motel. He found an open space in front of room ten and doused the lights. "So, you want to know what happened to your uncle?"

"I know what happened to him, Eddie. He was shot and killed in Mexico City, outside the main post office," Long said. His mother had seen the article in *Time* magazine, clipped it out, and saved it, and Long found it in her desk a few weeks later while he was scrounging around for cigarettes and loose change.

"I guess having a Nazi for an uncle is something you'd like to forget?"

"I had forgotten about it, Eddie. Until tonight."

Fifteen minutes after Alice entered the bathroom, Long called out her name, and when there was no response, Eddie said, "What the fuck's going on?"

"I don't know."

Under the door Long could see the light was on, and through it he could still hear the sound of running water.

"Maybe she split."

Long gave Eddie a quick, sideways glance. "No way. How?"

"The window."

"She wouldn't do that."

Not waiting for Long's next move, Eddie used his foot to splinter the hollow wooden panel next to the doorjamb. Reaching through the jagged hole, he quickly opened the door.

"Empty. What did I tell you?" Eddie said. "Now what, asshole?"

"Just this."

"What?"

Long raised the pistol. His mouth was smiling, but his eyes held no feeling. "Goodbye."

Alice McMillan heard the gunshot a split second before she peeled out of the parking lot and fishtailed into the right lane, nearly colliding with a city bus moving west on Santa Monica Boulevard. Although her heart was racing, she found herself playing with a smile when she realized that it made no difference whose life may have ended back in room ten: Whether it was Long or Cornell was inconsequential, because whoever survived would still be looking for her, along with the police.

Like Charlie said to her the night before he was captured, "Even if it ain't your fault, they'll come after you like a pack of mongrel dogs, pursuing you until your skin catches fire like burning paper. We live in an occupied territory, sister, in a hopeless world that could care less, waiting to send us away or just shoot us. And if you're alone, you're fair game, so just keep walking and stay alert, and don't stare at the corpses hanging in the trees."

As she drove through West Hollywood, her expression somewhere between repulsion and amused resignation, Alice once again tried to understand how she came under Charlie's spell; how he became so real inside her, as though before him she only half-existed; how when she did see the madness it was too late. It didn't matter that what he did was wrong, and that despite what he preached it was death, not life, that he knew best. It only mattered that he perceived her pain and knew exactly how she felt inside, and how she needed to be cherished by someone's hands.

Eighteen

All That They Wanted

The morning after he drove in from Las Vegas with the desert dust still on his skin, Gene stood by the open window in his kitchen reading the *L.A. Times,* deeply preoccupied with the front-page story describing Eddie Cornell's murder. He couldn't say that he was shocked or even mildly surprised. On the contrary, he experienced a vague sense of comfort, a reestablishing of balance, as if something inevitable had been brought to closure.

For years it was common knowledge—both in and out of the department—that Eddie was a rogue cop with a looted spirit, a soulless mayhem artist who obsessively and blatantly worked both sides of the law. The enemies he'd made were numberless—gangsters, pimps, drug dealers, cops, ex-cops, ex-lovers—and any one of them might have wanted Eddie off the planet. Gene himself could have provided the names of several suspects, and he would, with little hesitation, if he were asked.

After he finished the article, Gene put down the paper and stood staring out the window for several seconds, his face displaying no sign of feeling as he listened to the wind outside moving the leaves. Then, acting on impulse, he grabbed the phone off the wall and called Melanie Novack in Las Vegas, leaving no message but just his name and number on her service. When he had not heard back by four that afternoon, he phoned the Desert Inn and was told that she could not be paged, that she was in the middle of a shift.

"Have her call me back. It's extremely important," Gene instructed the switchboard operator, and once more he rattled off his number. "If she wants, she can call me collect."

Thirty minutes later, while Gene was napping on his cool leather couch, the phone rang, jarring him awake. His hand shot out, seizing the receiver. "Hello."

"Miss Novack would like you to stop calling her." It was a man's voice, bad-tempered and slightly hoarse. "Is that understood?"

"Who is this?"

"Leave her alone, Mr. Burk. That's what she wants."

"I'd like to hear that from her directly."

"Don't be a jerk-off," the man said, speaking with a persuasive force. "The lady ain't interested. Goodbye."

Gene put the receiver back in the cradle and stood up, feeling drowsy and diminished. Still dressed in his bathrobe and slippers, he walked outside and down the brick steps to his mailbox, a large yellow wooden duck that Alice found at a flea market in Redondo Beach. Inside, along with the usual bills and applications for new credit cards, was a thick manilla envelope with his brother's name and address printed neatly in the upper left-hand corner. It contained, Gene knew, the final draft of *The Last Hope,* the screenplay Ray had written for Columbia Pictures.

"This is it. This is what they're gonna shoot," he told Gene, when they spoke on Friday. "I nailed the cocksucker."

Gene said, "I thought you were off the picture."

"I was. Then I decided to sell out and do the changes. Better that I fuck it up than some hack. Plus they're paying me for an extra set of revisions."

But the surprising news came later on in the conversation, when Ray, clearly drunk and stumbling over his words, told Gene that Louie had been cast in the pilot for *Cool Heaven.* "You believe that shit? My kid's gonna be a television star," he said, sounding tremendously excited. "Is that fucking amazing?"

"Yeah, it is," Gene agreed.

"They start shooting in September, at the same time my movie goes into preproduction. He's renting a house in Beachwood Canyon," Ray said. "But he said he didn't want to hang out with me if I was drinking."

"I can understand that."

"Yeah. So can I."

Gene, making his voice completely free of tension, brought up the name Melanie Novack, asking his brother if he'd ever heard of her.

"No. Why? Who is she?"

"She used to have a script-typing service. She worked out of her apartment in West Hollywood. It was called Melanie's Place."

"Melanie's Place." Ray made a thinking sound. Then after a moment, he said, "Yeah, I remember. She used to advertise in the trades. What about her?"

"She lived below Bobby Fuller, in the same apartment building on Sycamore. She was home the night he died."

Ray, his voice both deadpan and teasing, said, "Here we go again. Fiction and fact from Gene's almanac."

Gene also wanted to disclose that Melanie was an alcoholic who was now sober, but he decided not to break her anonymity, even though their paths could have easily crossed back in 1967, after Ray's second arrest for drunk driving, when he was court-ordered to attend ninety A.A. meetings in ninety days or risk going to jail.

"Gene?"

"Yeah?"

"I gotta split. I'll send you the script. I'd like to hear your thoughts."

"What if I think it sucks? Can I be honest?"

"I would expect nothing less."

Gene closed the mailbox, turned away from the tree-shaded street, and started back up the steps to the front door. Before he was halfway there, his shoulders tensed and a flash of fear—like a warning light—streaked through his abdomen, warming his neck. Call it intuition, a cop's sixth sense, whatever, but he was absolutely certain he was being watched.

Gene turned around slowly. A car was parked across the street, a dark blue Buick Regal that was a stranger to the neighborhood. There was a woman sitting behind the wheel, her gaze breaking away from Gene as the door swung open and she stepped out, shrugging uneasily as she took up a position by the front fender with her hand resting lightly on the sun-warmed hood.

From where he was standing, his eyes still bleary from sleep, Gene saw nothing about her that looked even remotely familiar. Mid-thirties, average height and weight, lank brown hair that needed to be washed: a plain woman with downcast eyes, her oval face half-shadowed by a bushy branch that leaned over the street.

Gene walked back down to the curb. Ten feet separated them, no more, and as he looked at her, she looked down at the ground. They stood silently for several moments, enough time for Gene to select a chunk of memory and give it shape: Her face, in profile, was framed by the open window of a different car, an older foreign model with a dent on the left front fender.

"A Volvo," Gene said out loud, and the woman lifted her head. "Green."

"Yes."

"You were driving a green Volvo."

"I said *yes.*" The woman moved away from the car, stopping when she reached the center of the street. She was staring at Gene with a fierce intensity. "Do you know me? Do you know who I am?"

Gene's mind was racing, and he felt a wetness underneath his arms. He answered with a quiet voice. "I saw you in Cedar Rapids, after the funeral. You were parked outside Alice's house."

"I was an intruder. Or I would have been, had I gone inside."

"You said you knew her."

"I did. I knew her," the woman said, pausing briefly to watch a car roll by, a battered old VW bug, the sunlight glancing off the cracked wind-shield. After it sputtered around a curve and disappeared, the woman turned her attention back to Gene. "My name is Alice, too. Alice McMillan."

Gene watched the woman scan his face for a reaction, but he remained impassive, trying with great effort to hide his fear and neutralize his sur-prise. Gradually, though, the woman's face seemed to soften; then a vul-nerability appeared around her mouth and her pallid cheeks took on a gentle shade of pink, a blush of shyness that Gene didn't trust.

"Did your Alice ever talk about me?" said the woman, moving forward to close the interval between them.

"No, she didn't."

The woman instantly seemed crushed. Her voice was low, choked down in her throat. "Not once?"

"No. But I know who you are."

"You do?"

"I read your letters," Gene said, trying now to picture her in the summer of 1969, one of Charlie's tribe of antiangels, a naïve, self-blaming flower child who was fully ready to participate in helter-skelter, the terrible nongame that ended in the heat of August. "What are you doing here?"

"In Los Angeles?"

"No. Here. At my house."

"I'm in trouble," said the woman, almost apologetically, her voice torn and her eyes scared. "I need your help."

Her story? It took two hours to tell and was too strange to be disbelieved. But when she was done, when her voice was no longer coming out of her mouth with a stale applelike smell, Gene asked her to start over.

Alice McMillan, the Other Alice, said, "From the beginning?"

"Yes," Gene said. They were inside his house now, in the living room, the light almost gone, just a piece of sun on the legal pad he was using to take notes. "But you don't have to rush."

"I feel like I do."

"There's all the time in the world."

"Not if you're dead."

Born in Cedar Rapids, Iowa, and like Alice Larson—of whom she was the opposite in every way—an only child. However, this time, in the retelling, the Other Alice added a brother to her family, Arlen, a boy who was born early by six weeks with a hole in his heart, a life that was canceled before it began.

"He was buried in this tiny casket," said the Other Alice, as she stood up and moved around the room with an easy sleepy motion to her hips. "No bigger than this." She pointed to a small rectangular tin box on the mantel that was filled with loose change. "I was eight. My dad didn't go to the funeral. He was drunk. Why do I need to repeat all this?"

"So I can get the facts straight."

"You should have gotten them straight the first time," said the Other Alice. She had stopped by the sliding glass doors and was peering out at the backyard and the scrubby hillside beyond. The house was very quiet. "There's a cabin down there a mile or so, off Old Topanga Road. Back in '68 I screwed the guy who lived there. I stole his watch and gave it to Charlie."

The Other Alice turned to look at Gene. Her mouth was set hard. He said, "Why didn't your father come to Arlen's funeral?"

"I told you. Because he was *drunk.*"

Her father, Boyd McMillan, was a landscaper for the Department of Parks and Recreation. He was also a boy scout troop leader and coached Little League, a volunteer position that he held until the spring of 1970, when the Other Alice appeared on the nightly news, her chin thrust out and her arm outstretched, giving the finger to the camera.

She told Gene: "I was standing out in front of the courthouse with Squeaky and Gypsy, just fuckin' with the news guys. They loved it when we acted all crazy like that."

Not long after that incident, Boyd McMillan lost his job with the city. His wife, the Other Alice's mom, began drinking heavily. And driving back from the liquor store one rainy evening in her top-heavy Oldsmobile, she lost traction and drifted across the interstate, bouncing off the concrete center island and plunging into a ditch.

"Mom spent the next seven weeks in the hospital. She had to walk with a cane until 1982, the year she died of cirrhosis of the liver. My dad died the following spring. Heart attack. Both under sixty."

In this new version of her story, she told Gene that her father fucked her when she was fourteen and still a virgin, making her first ride on top, then taking her from behind, his big male hands squeezing the smooth cheeks of her ass. This went on—this violation of his daughter, this night after night of nonlove—until the Other Alice left home.

"Does this story turn you on?" she asked Gene.

"Not really."

"Do you think I'm lying?"

"No."

"I'm not."

Jumping ahead but looking squarely into her eyes, Gene said, "When was the first time you saw her?"

"Who?"

"Alice."

"The very first? When I was at Delano Park, watching my dad get the field ready for a Little League game. She was playing on the slide with her mom. She had the cutest laugh, didn't she?"

Gene nodded, answering slowly, "Yeah, she did."

"I even remember what she was wearing. Overalls, a pink T-shirt, a floppy pink sun hat, and white plastic sandals."

"How old was she?"

"Around eight or nine, I think."

"And the first time you spoke to her was—"

The Other Alice groaned loudly. "I already *told* you."

"Take it easy."

"Fuck you. You take it easy. Why don't we talk about Chris Long? He's probably out there looking for me, wanting to kill me, and you're writing my goddamn biography! What kind of a stupid cop are you?"

"Ex-cop."

"Stupid ex-cop," said the Other Alice, and smiled.

Gene stared at her until she blinked, and then his mind, almost against his will, was pulled suddenly and spontaneously backward into the recent past. He thought about the very first A.A. meeting he'd attended in Hollywood—an experience he'd approached with a mixture of curiosity and apprehension—while he was trying to locate Melanie Novack. It was held in a small church basement on the corner of Yucca and Gower. The lead speaker that evening, a skinny paint salesman from

Glendale, a man with a squarish head and a sizable birthmark on his neck, had compared life to a three-level chess game.

He'd said, "We're all down here on the lowest level, moving the pieces around, figuring out this great strategy, lining up everything just right: wife, kids, job, all part of this grand plan we've cooked up. And guess what? It don't mean shit, because God's up there on the third level laughing his ass off. See, we're all sober—which is a miracle—so that means He's already made the right moves, and all we have to do now is show up and be amazed. You know what's the first thing I say when I wake up? I say, 'I wonder what's going to happen today.' Stay in wonder, my friends."

In a while Gene's mind came back to Chris Long. His name had appeared twice in Bobby Fuller's file, both times in connection with Melanie Novack. No mention was made of Long's father, the suicide, or his Nazi uncle. That strange part of his family history, along with his shadowy life as a police informer, was detailed in a different file, one that would be found later by detectives in Eddie Cornell's doleful, dimly lit apartment.

"His mother was a librarian," the Other Alice was saying from the kitchen, where she had gone to get a beer out of the refrigerator. "Either that or she just worked at a library. I'm not sure. But Chris read books all the time while he was growing up. He was smart as shit. In high school he said he won a statewide contest for an essay he wrote about his dad. He called it 'The Death of Science.' I thought that was a pretty cool title." The Other Alice came out of the kitchen, yawning, the can of Coors pressed to her cheek as she stepped around the coffee table and padded over to the bookcase. A gentle but not quite sincere smile softened her face as she peered closely at the row of framed photographs. In one, Alice Larson was standing by the ocean with her eyes closed and the wind sweeping her hair across her face. "God, she always looked so pretty in a bathing suit."

Gene, who had gotten up from the couch, was now standing behind the Other Alice, staring silently at the picture. After a while he said softly, "Ask me what I loved most about her."

The Other Alice turned around slowly, her face controlled and composed. "What?"

"Ask me."

"What did you most love about . . . Alice?"

"Not what you think," Gene said. "Not her vitality, her intelligence, her values, her essential goodness. None of those things I loved the most. I loved most what I couldn't see, what she concealed, the mystery that disappeared from my life when she died."

"What if you knew everything?" said the Other Alice. "Then what?"

"Then she wouldn't be Alice anymore. She would just be—"

"Real. Like me."

The Other Alice told Gene that she needed to take a shower. Personal hygiene, she said, was extremely important to her; twenty-four hours without soap and water made her feel shamed and tainted by the world. Back when she was a hippie things were different. In the desert with Charlie she lived like a wild animal, going weeks without bathing, the grit and grime filling every wrinkle and crevice.

"I let the filth of the world disguise who I really was," she told Gene, following him as he turned on the hall light and pointed to the bathroom. "But I'm not that person anymore."

Gene hesitated for a moment, surprised by the intensity of her last statement. Then, looking away from her face, he said, "I'll find you some clean clothes."

"That would be nice," the Other Alice said. Then, as Gene continued up the hallway, she added: "You haven't had a woman in your house since she died. Have you?"

Gene turned around but didn't look surprised or troubled. "No. I haven't."

Before she stepped inside the bathroom, the Other Alice plucked off her earrings and drew her sweater over her head, exposing her narrow hips and her heavy breasts. Gene turned away from her body and she said, "There's part of me that knows I shouldn't be here."

Gene, moving into the shadows of his bedroom, said he thought that made sense.

"But sometimes it's important to be where you're not supposed to be."

In the bottom drawer of Alice's dresser, Gene found a fresh pair of faded khakis and a navy-blue T-shirt with a school of smiling dolphins pictured on the back, leaping out of a galloping green sea. He put the folded items outside the bathroom door, wincing a little as the touch and smell of Alice's clothing made his grief return, a grief that gave way to a rising anger, then a rage that seemed limitless.

"*Oh Alice! Come lie down with me!*" he wanted to scream, as his memory released a moment of affection, a moment that could never be recovered. "*Why aren't you here?*"

Gene sat in the living room with the lights off, feeling disconnected in the silent darkness, knowing that he could change his mind right now, that he didn't need to go forward to the very end, that he could send her away as soon as she was clean. What did she say to him earlier, while they were sitting on the patio, smoking, a neighbor's cat prowling around their chairs, playfully pawing their ankles? She said that her dream in high school was to have every boy in her class want to fuck her.

"I wanted to be like your Alice," she said. "I wanted those turned heads and furtive glances. I wanted to be noticed, followed, kept track of. I wanted to be an object of desire."

She said all of Charlie's girls felt that way: Susan, Squeaky, Patricia, Gypsy, even Leslie, who was the most attractive. And it was Charlie's admiration and affection that opened their hearts and fed their damaged spirits, rendering them subservient.

"We felt our lives would be purposeless without his love and protection. He made it good for us."

"What? Sex?"

"Everything. Being alive."

"You mean nothing you could do was wrong."

"You don't understand, Gene."

"I'm trying to."

"We were girls who were tender, with hurt places all over. Charlie gave us our pride back. He made us feel wanted. He gave us a dream."

"That wasn't real."

"We thought it was," said the Other Alice. "Or we wouldn't have done what we did."

And that's when she told him about the LSD-induced fuckfest with the news crew from KNBC, the sophisticated equipment that Charlie confiscated: the lightweight 16mm Bolex cameras and the Nagra sound recorders that they all learned to use, their training connected to their constant orgies.

According to the Other Alice, prior to the night of August 9, 1969, they had accumulated upward of fifty hours of film, a lot of it just casual partying, but there were at least five hours of torrid sex—sex that was greedy and forgetful and conferred no pleasure, involving people who were well known.

"In which you participated," Gene said.

"Sure. It was cool," she said. "It made me feel special."

"And you're talking about celebrities, major movie stars."

"Rock-and-roll stars too. Lots of those."

Gene remained skeptical. He said, "You know how many detectives worked on the Tate-LaBianca murders? Upward of fifty, maybe closer to a hundred, not counting the investigators who were hired by private parties and the district attorney. And there was not one piece of evidence that such films existed."

"Well, they were just plain wrong," said the Other Alice.

"Then what happened to it?"

"Whoever searched the ranch took it away and stashed it somewhere."

"You're talking about the police."

"Of course. Who else? Then they sold it back piece by piece to anyone who would pay the right price, meaning whoever didn't want their career to go in the toilet."

"But they didn't find all the film."

"No."

"Why?"

"Because there were six reels buried in the desert."

"That you were willing to put up to the highest bidder. Why now?"

"I guess it just seemed like the right time."

"But it didn't turn out that way."

"I'm here, Gene. I'm with you."

"What's that supposed to mean?"

"Maybe this is how it's all supposed to end."

The Other Alice appeared in the living room, fully dressed and smiling the smile of someone who was awkward wearing borrowed clothes. Her hair was still wet and unbrushed, but her face seemed to glow with genuine good feeling, with some inner satisfaction that Gene didn't understand.

"It must feel weird to see me dressed in her clothes," she said, after a short silence.

Gene nodded, looking back at her. "Yeah, it does."

"Does it make you feel sad?"

"I'm not sure."

"I would be," she said, as she drifted across the room. She took a seat in an armchair by the window, her gaze looking out past the fruit trees on the front lawn. "We don't look anything alike, do we?"

"Not really."

"Our eyes, our lips, our hair, our facial structure, the way we carry ourselves, it's all different, everything, except we're the same size. Now. Before I was way chunkier."

"Your breasts are bigger."

"Hurrah, hurrah." The Other Alice laughed a little, then stopped. To her right was a small table with a telephone balanced on a pile of magazines. She picked up the receiver, holding it in the air until she heard a dial tone, then put it back. "I spoke to Alice back in February."

Gene sat without moving. "What do you mean you spoke to her?"

"Just what I said."

"On the telephone?"

"No. In person."

"I don't believe you."

"Don't. You don't believe me about the film, either."

Gene shifted his weight. He seemed to lean forward, trying to see her eyes in the dark. "Where?"

"Where did I see her? Back home. In Cedar Rapids."

The Other Alice stood up and came toward the couch. She took a cigarette from Gene's pack, let him light it for her, and then sat down next to him.

"We talked for a long time."

"What about?"

"Lots of things. The past. The present. Girl things."

"Did she talk about me?"

"Sure."

"What did she say?"

The Other Alice smiled elusively. "You want to know everything, don't you?"

Gene looked at her seriously. His voice shook a little when he said, "I want to know what she said about me."

The Other Alice sank back into the couch, adjusting her body so their thighs were resting against each other. Then she reached down and took his hand, squeezing it lightly before she placed it in between her open legs. "What will you do if I tell you? What's in it for me?"

"What do you want me to do?"

"Treat me like I was . . . her."

Gene looked at her face, dull and ordinary, gleaming with desire. "I can't do that."

"Sure you can."

"No. It wouldn't be right," Gene said. " I couldn't . . ."

"Couldn't *what,* Gene?"

"I couldn't make you feel good."

The Other Alice, smiling miserably, said, "If you wanted to, you could. Right? I mean, you could try."

"I would just hurt your feelings."

"Try," said the Other Alice, her clammy hand squeezing his fingers. "Please."

Three months later, when Gene told his brother what happened over the next twenty-four hours, he neglected to mention his sexual misadventure with the Other Alice: the crush and pounding of their bodies, unrestrained and seared with shame. And then there was that crippling moment when his arc of desire ended, that great fall back down into blackness, the wish for death, Gene quietly cursing this woman still slithering underneath him, this dirty double: an Alice that wasn't and a fuck that was shaped and reshaped by need and loss; a fuck that should have been illegal, the plug pulled, stopped completely, stilled.

"Why are you crying?" she said. "Do you always cry afterwards?"

"Sometimes. And sometimes I don't cry for hours."

Nineteen

Alice Twice

Six months before her plane crashed down in the hills of Indiana, exploding like a giant cauldron, sending flames through the ancient iron-colored trees, Alice Larson came back home for a short visit. Her father had suffered a mild heart attack while she was on a one-night layover in Atlanta, and she quickly caught the first available flight to Des Moines. From there she rented a car and drove to Cedar Rapids, stopping for an hour in Westhaven to visit her mother, who had been confined to the Westhaven State Mental Hospital for the past twelve years.

"I'm not sure she even knew who I was," Alice told Gene later that night. "When the nurse told her my name, she just stuck out her hand, and when I tried to hug her she pushed me away. She looked so angry I thought she was going to slap me in the face. After she calmed down, I sat with her in the day room while she smoked cigarettes and drank Diet Cokes."

"Did you guys talk at all?" Gene asked her.

"Not really. She wasn't making any sense. There was this other woman in her thirties sitting by the window, rocking back and forth in her chair, chanting, 'I'm wanted by the Utah State Police' over and over, then she'd collapse into a giggle fit. Mother said she was Karen Black."

"Karen Black? You mean, the actress?"

"Right. From *Nashville.* She wasn't, of course," Alice said. "Mother insisted that all these famous actors drop by to visit her, and that she takes them into her room, where they have sex. She said a bunch of wacky stuff like that. Toward the end she fell asleep in her chair. One minute she was awake, the next she was snoring. Just like that."

"It sounds like a sad visit."

"It was, Gene. She used to be so pretty. Now she's all fat and gray, and her face is filled with wrinkles. I wish I had more compassion, but I don't."

"What about your dad?"

"He's better. I'm gonna stay with him through the weekend and fly back Monday."

"Alice?"

"Yeah?"

"I love you."

"I know. And I love you, too."

"I'm horny."

"Too bad."

"Can we have phone sex?"

"No. We can't."

"Why not?"

"Because I'm in the house where I grew up and—"

"In your bedroom?"

"No. I'm in the living room."

"On the couch."

"Yes."

"Hmmm."

"And my father's sleeping right down the hall."

"What're you wearing?"

"Gene?"

"What?"

"Beat off."

"Okay."

"Good night, sweetheart."

"Good night."

Alice put down the receiver and took a deep breath before she got to her feet. On her way out of the living room, the phone rang and she quickly retraced her steps. When she picked up the handset, the line was open but no one answered when she said hello. Over the next twenty-four hours this would happen six more times.

On Saturday morning, while Alice and her father were eating buttermilk pancakes in the breakfast nook, they heard a letter drop through the mail slot and land on the floor in the foyer. Alice's father looked confused, scratching his chin as he squinted at the clock mounted on the wall above the sink. "Barely nine o'clock. Rex don't usually bring the mail on Saturday until at least noon."

Alice stood up and moved into the foyer. On the floor by the faded blue rug was an envelope with her first name printed on the front, but there was no return address in the left-hand corner and no stamp. Alice picked up the letter and brought it back into the kitchen.

"It's for me," she said, as she sat down across from her father. "It didn't come through the mail. Someone delivered it by hand."

"Are you gonna open it?"

"I know who it's from."

"You do?" Alice nodded, unable to look at him full in the face. "Who?"

"Someone I knew growing up," Alice said, her voice sounding nervous as she glanced down at the familiar handwriting. "A girl."

"Do I know her?"

"No. She wasn't a friend."

"Is she the one who's been calling?"

"I don't know. It might be her," Alice said, getting to her feet to clear off the table. "Do you want some more orange juice?"

Alice's father shook his head. He let a few seconds pass. Then he said, "When are you gonna read it?"

"When I'm done with the dishes," Alice said from the sink, looking at him teasingly, hoping that her coquettish grin would mask her alarm.

"You want to tell me her name?"

"No. I'd rather not," Alice said, watching her father's face become annoyed and fretful. "I'm sorry, Dad."

"No need to be sorry," Alice's father said, as he dropped his napkin on the table and rose slowly from his chair. "Just all this seems a little odd."

Alice's father shuffled out of the kitchen, trying not to look offended. In the living room he turned on the television, and Alice could tell by the

music that it was some kind of game show. When she was finished drying the plates and silverware, she hung up the dish towel and wiped her
damp fingers on the front of her jeans. Then she went back to her bedroom and ripped open the envelope.

Alice,

*I saw you the other day picking up medicine at the pharmacy for your
father. I was buying shampoo. Even if you saw me you probably didn't recognize my face. Very few people do, which is just fine, considering all the things
that have been said.*

*I very much need to talk to you, Alice. I will be at the Shoney's on I-80
at 4 o'clock this afternoon. I'll be sitting in a booth in back, wearing jeans and
a plaid shirt. Please come.*

Thanks,

A

Alice quickly folded the letter and slid it back inside the envelope.
Outside she heard a neighbor mowing his lawn, and through the bedroom
window she could see a fat orange cat crawl carefully along the slanted
roof of the house next door, stalking a tiny bird with white wings. Before
he could pounce, Alice rapped her knuckles loudly on the window, drawing the cat's attention away from the bird, who suddenly burst up into
the clean blue air.

Alice continued standing by the window for a few moments, staring out at the street and listening to the familiar neighborhood sounds,
then she craned her neck to watch a pack of boys walk up the sidewalk,
their shouts and laughter muffled by the window glass as they passed by
in front of the house.

Alice was smiling now, reminded of an afternoon in the spring of
1965, when she was fifteen and purposely stood naked in front of that
same window. The shaggy boys who saw her that day were working on a
car in the driveway next door; and the one she had a crush on, Tommy
Spindell, froze when he caught sight of her plump breasts and her hun-
gering gaze. His buddy Eric looked bewildered, almost panic-stricken,

his fingers gripped tightly around a Phillips screwdriver, the silver tip
shining brilliantly in the white sunlight. When Alice closed the curtains,
she could still see them staring at the window, their reddening faces flooded
with desire.

That night, when Tommy called and asked Alice to the movies, she
smiled and secretly hugged herself, feeling the excitement rise from her
throat as she accepted the invitation. On Saturday afternoon they sat in
the back row of the theater and kissed until their lips hurt, and then Alice
let him push up her sweater and squeeze her breasts. She moaned softly,
her mouth upon his, and across the aisle a girl turned and stared at them,
her eyes strangely hostile as they swung from face to face.

"What's she lookin' at ?" Tommy asked, suddenly tense before the
girl's wild gaze. "Turn around, you."

For several more seconds the girl remained looking backward; then,
abruptly, she turned away and slumped down into her chair, her eyes
streaming tears in the darkness. Eventually the sound of her violent weep-
ing became so loud that she was asked by an usher to leave the theater.
On her way out, she stopped at Alice's row and said, with a smile that
looked a bit crazy, "You want to know something, Alice? Right now you
may be happy, but one day you'll find out how much it can hurt."

"It was called *The Chase* with Marlon Brando. He played the sheriff," said
the Other Alice, grinning to herself as she cast her eyes around the restaurant. Alice Larson was sitting across from her in the red Naugahyde booth
by the window, leaning slightly forward, trying to remain calm while her
heart was banging against her ribs. "Robert Redford played this escaped
convict. Jane Fonda was his wife, but she was this other guy's mistress,
this oilman."

"I don't remember the story," Alice Larson said.

"Of course you don't. You were too busy making out," said the Other
Alice, still glancing away. "That looks like Marty Newman over there. It's
probably not, but it looks like him. He went with Sue Harris, didn't he?"

"I don't know," Alice Larson said without looking over her shoulder. "I didn't go to your high school. Remember?"

The Other Alice tapped an ash off the cigarette she was smoking. "Yeah, that's right. But everyone knew who *you* were," she said. "You were one of the popular girls."

"I never thought I was that popular," Alice Larson said. "Maybe at the time—"

"Did you save my letters?" interrupted the Other Alice, and there was a pause, a gathering of anxiety as her watching eyes looked directly at Alice Larson's face for the first time.

"Yes. I saved them. And I would have written you back if I'd had a return adresss."

"I'm not sure I believe you."

"At the time I thought I would," Alice Larson said, and the Other Alice put out her cigarette and gazed outside. Two teenage girls in prefaded blue jeans walked past the window with tiny smiles on their disobedient faces. They were followed by a thin, vain-looking couple around forty, wearing matching army fatigue shirts with corporal stripes sewn on their sleeves. "What do you want, Alice? Why did you ask me to come here?"

"I wanted to see you. I wanted you to see me."

Alice Larson drew back a little. She wanted to tell the Other Alice that she'd grown more attractive through the years, that there was a glow in her skin and a gentleness in her face that had not been there at fifteen. But the words stayed inside Alice Larson's mouth, and they both fell silent, staring past each other, until finally the Other Alice said, with a look of concern, "Are you scared of me, Alice?"

Alice Larson shook her head slowly. "Should I be?"

"No. But I should be scared of you."

"Why?"

"You have my letters. I told you secrets."

"Maybe. But nothing that . . ."

"What?" The Other Alice leaned forward and tossed her hair away from her eyes. "Finish your sentence."

"There was nothing in your letters that was incriminating. You never said you did anything bad."

"But you think I did. Right?"

"Do you want the letters back?" Alice Larson said, ignoring the question.

"I've done bad things, Alice. I admit it. But I'm not a bad person," said the Other Alice, and she put her hands on Alice Larson's elbows, gently pulling her forward until their faces were only inches apart. "What's the worst thing you've ever done?"

Alice Larson felt her heart jump, a clench of fear as she surveyed the Other Alice's round smooth face, trying to decode the message hidden behind her wide-open eyes. In this pose of stillness, which lasted for almost a minute, Alice Larson tuned out the voices chattering around her and ignored the large emerald fly that jittered against the windowpane by her ear.

When she started to speak, nervous lines appeared in her forehead and the words came slowly, listlessly, as if she were drugged. She spoke about her childhood, the good times with her parents before her mother became ill: the barbecues in the backyard on her birthday, the trips to the zoo and the county fair, and especially the summer Sundays at Lake Ballard, where the sunshine was everywhere and they flew kites and fed the ducks. She got a lump in her throat when she told the Other Alice how much she loved to feel her father's touch, the way he stroked her hair and massaged her shoulders, an intimacy that was spontaneous and deeply satisfying but never took place in the dark.

"When I was seven," she said, "I asked my dad to show me his penis. He laughed, and then he took me into the bathroom so I could watch him pee. When he was done, I said I wanted to touch it, and he let me."

"Did he get hard?"

"Yes."

"Then what?"

"Nothing. He just looked embarrassed."

Alice Larson spoke about her mother too, the journal she kept and the lovers she wrote about in those pages: Ted worked in a tollbooth on the interstate; Jack was a cashier at the Montgomery Ward; Bill was a trucker who called her dirty names and took pictures of her naked. She said all three were married. And the sex, she wrote, was "boring as hell."

"But your father never found out."

"No."

"How many men do you think she had?"

"I don't have any idea."

"I bet I've fucked hundreds of guys," said the Other Alice, and Alice Larson opened her purse. She found a picture of Gene that she kept inside her wallet and placed it on the table between them. "Who's that?"

"My boyfriend. We've been going together for six months. We're planning to get married."

The Other Alice stared at the picture without any visible envy. "Are you officially engaged?"

"Yes."

"What does it feel like?"

"Feel like? What do you mean?"

"To know you're going to be married to someone you love?"

"It feels like . . . like a beautiful dream that repeats itself every day," Alice Larson said with a grin that widened her cheeks. After a moment she glanced down at her watch and said that she had to leave soon. She had to go back to her house and pack, then drive to Des Moines, where she was booked on a nine o'clock flight back to Los Angeles.

"Is your fiancé going to meet you at the airport?"

"Yes."

"It must feel good to have someone to fly home to," said the Other Alice, her voice absent of sentiment. "I've never had a man meet me at an airport."

Alice Larson put down her coffee and reached across the table, briefly touching the Other Alice's wrist. In a voice that was gentle but slightly seductive, she told her that Gene was only the second man she had ever loved. Her first sweetheart—his name was Nick Fitzpatrick—she'd also met on one of her flights.

"It was only my third week with the airline. I was based in Chicago, and he was flying to San Francisco after spending two weeks covering the Democratic Convention for *Life* magazine. His pictures were on the cover," Alice Larson said, and her voice was underlaid with a kind of melancholy. "He was on his way to Oakland to photograph the Black Panthers. But what he really wanted to do was cover the war in Vietnam. When *Life* wouldn't send him, he quit, and the Associated Press hired him as a stringer. He left the day after Christmas, and we spent his last week together in Los Angeles, where his family lives. His dad was a movie director," Alice Larson said, and stopped speaking. There was a sad, faraway look in her eyes. After a short silence, in which she was staring at the Other Alice without seeing her, she said in a soft voice: "I've never talked about Nick before, not like this. My dad never even knew his name. I told Gene only a little, because I could tell it made him uncomfortable. It's been almost fifteen years since he died, and I still think about him every day."

The Other Alice was sitting perfectly still, but her eyes moved nervously. "Did he die in Vietnam?"

"He was with a Marine platoon that was ambushed near the Cambodian border. Out of seventy-two men only four survived."

"I can tell you really loved him."

"I did."

"That's the way I loved Charlie."

"It's not the same thing."

"How do you know?"

"Because Nick was a good person."

The Other Alice made a severe face. "Charlie wasn't always bad."

"You can't compare them," Alice Larson said. She suddenly looked pale and tired. "Look, I'm sorry, but I can feel myself starting to get irritated."

"You're just upset because you know we're not that different."

"I've never hurt anyone," Alice Larson said, in a tone that suggested she was insulted. After an extended silence, she stood up and said, "I have to leave now."

In the parking lot, the Other Alice reached for a hug after Alice Larson unlocked her rental car and turned to say goodbye. In their wordless embrace, Alice Larson felt a space open up inside her chest, a space that offered comfort but could also fill with pain.

Stepping back from this clutch of confusion, Alice Larson told the Other Alice how glad she was they'd met and talked, and she thanked her for her openness. The Other Alice smiled and, in an enthusiastic voice, she said that she didn't feel jealous or resentful anymore. But she also said that they would never become real friends.

"So don't expect any more letters," she said, still smiling.

"I won't."

"And just for the record, I didn't tell you everything."

"I know," Alice Larson said. "And neither did I."

Driving home, Alice Larson found her mind returning to that warm gray Christmas day she'd spent at Nick's house in 1968, the day before he flew overseas. A western directed by his father had just opened that week to mostly negative reviews, causing a sour mood to hang over what should have been a festive occasion. By noon, when the first guests began to arrive for the family's annual holiday brunch, Nick's father was already drunk and out of control, reeling through the house in torn Levi's and a filthy, grass-stained tennis sweater, raging about the "fucking, dimwit, faggot critics who fucking want to ruin my fucking career."

Alice, overdressed in a royal-blue skirt and sweater that she'd bought the day before at Saks Fifth Avenue, was sitting at a poolside table, chatting with a young British screenwriter, when Nick's father staggered outside holding a fifth of brandy, his wet lips pulled into a strained smile.

"I want to propose a toast to my son. Nick, get over here!" he bellowed, and Nick, who was standing by the buffet, put down his plate and moved over to join his father, who threw his arm around his shoulder to steady himself. "Unlike myself," he continued, clearing his throat, "and most of you liberal assholes who can only make pictures about war, this young man has the guts to pick up the gun."

Nick said, "What're you talking about, Dad? I'm not picking up any guns. I'm a photographer."

"Bullshit! You're going to see action. You're a fucking hero," his father said, looking out at the assembled crowd, most of whom seemed to have difficulty meeting his eye. Then he turned his attention to Alice. "And sitting over there by the pool is his beloved, Miss Annie Larson—"

"*Alice,* Dad—"

"—the girl he's leaving behind. They just got engaged. Is she a gorgeous piece of ass or what?"

Nick gave his father a furious sidelong glare. "Dad, that's not cool."

"Come on, let's hear it for these two."

After a smattering of applause that seemed unnecessarily polite, Nick's father lurched back inside the house, where he continued drinking throughout the afternoon, alone, until Nick found him passed out on the Oriental rug in his study, surrounded by black-and-white stills from his latest film. With the help of Lee Marvin, Nick carried his father upstairs, washed his face and neck, and put him to bed.

Before he left the party, Marvin pulled Nick aside. "I was a Marine in the Pacific," he said, staring straight at him, his voice broad and deep. "It's no picnic in the jungle. That shit's real. Keep your head down, and watch your ass."

Alice and Nick were staying in the guest house by the pool, and that night after they had made love for the second time and Nick had dozed off, Alice heard a loud splash. Peeking out through the curtains, she saw Nick's father backstroke the length of the pool. The lights were on underneath the water, illuminating his body, and she was surprised to see that he was swimming nude.

After five or six laps, he stepped out of the pool in the shallow end and stood facing the guest house, his hands resting on his hips. Between his legs she could see his semierect penis begin to lengthen, straightening itself out. And when he tugged it gently, she knew he knew she was watching him.

The complex look on his face while he masturbated—wide-eyed, unblinking, self-admiring—reminded Alice of *her* father's expression when she touched his penis with her hand; and when Nick's father ejaculated, she thought she heard him say her name once, looking skyward, while the scattered drops of his semen fell on to the water like soundless rain.

Twenty

The Boys

and Their Blood Ties

Jacob Reese sat tensely and silently as he and Larry Havana drove east on Hollywood Boulevard. Havana had his eyes closed and was singing along to the oldie playing on the radio, a beautiful soft ballad by the Dells that made Billboard's top ten in the summer of 1957. The record, "Oh What a Night," unclogged a chamber in Havana's mind, a chamber that was stuffed with memories from his teenage years, most of them profoundly painful.

"I never got to dance," Havana said, glancing over at Reese, who gave him a questioning look. "You get polio when you're five, you can put away your dancing shoes forever." Havana laughed to himself, and when he was done there was a bitter smile left on his face. "You just try to forget about it, but you can't. And the first time I heard this tune I wanted to dance so bad that everything inside my body seemed to hurt."

"Where was this?"

"At this party up at Zuma Beach. All the coolest kids on the west side were there. I got invited because I paid for all the booze. Fuck, I paid for the hamburgers and hot dogs, too. I paid for everything," Havana said, with a look of pretended indifference. "You know who else was there?"

"Who?"

"Gene Burk."

"Burk? Really?"

"He was with this chick from Venice High. Barbara Westbrook. She was so pretty she kept me awake nights. And when I went to sleep I dreamed about her," Havana said and paused, looking sad. "When this song came on, they got up to dance."

"Everyone?"

"No. Just Burk and Barbara. They were off by themselves, underneath the lifeguard tower, their feet barely moving in the sand, not paying attention to anyone, not to me that's for sure, the creep in the wheelchair with the dead legs, sitting by the fire roasting the hot dogs.

"I got drunk that night for the first time. Whoever took me home left me in the wheelchair at the bottom of my driveway. It must have taken me an hour to roll myself up the hill, but I never made it inside the house. Instead, the next morning my dad found me passed out in the backyard. Somehow my wheelchair ended up at the bottom of our swimming pool. I didn't remember shit. I must have blacked out."

Reese glanced at Havana. "So what happened to the chick?"

"Barbara? She went off to college and became a hippie."

The song ended on the radio as they coasted up to a red light. Two underage whores, both white and pathetically thin, were posing on the corner in matching pink satin hot pants, their every movement watched by a black pimp who was standing in the doorway of Popeye's Chicken, his face locked into an exaggerated expression of menace. When he noticed the Eldorado, the pimp threw down the cigarette he was smoking and raised his fist in a black power salute.

When the light flashed to green, and they were once again moving east, Havana said, "That nigger is not happy paying me twenty percent."

"I don't blame him, since he's out there doing all the work."

"Excuse me, Jake. But I think the pussy is doing the work."

"But the nigger owns the pussy."

"But I own the street."

"You inherited the street, Larry."

"Same deal."

Reese didn't agree, but it was stupid to argue the point, since his business was also handed down from his father, although his turf was no longer in Hollywood, where his dad and Jack Havana were once partners, not equal partners exactly—*never* equal partners—but partners nonetheless. Now Jacob Reese was operating out of the West San Fernando Valley. He owned three strip clubs and a bookmaking business that netted him five grand a week. And once in a while, for the right price, he would move a kilo of cocaine.

Reese turned left on Argyle and parked in front of the Argyle Manor. Chris Long lived in 208, a furnished single on the second floor, and several winged insects were circling the yellow porch light outside his room.

"So?" Reese was looking at Havana's profile with a vague stare. "What do you want me to do?"

"Find out where the fuckin' film is."

"What if he sticks to his story?"

"Then be creative."

"He's no good to us dead. He knows that," Reese said and saw that Havana, his head turned, was now glaring at him with undisguised contempt. "Take it easy. I didn't fuck this up. This was your idea." Which was true, since the fifty thousand dollars that Eddie Cornell brought to the Tropicana Motel was money that came from Larry Havana's safe in the House of Love. "Am I right?"

Havana seemed embarrassed as he looked past Reese, concentrating on the Argyle Manor. "Yeah, you're right."

Long, who had called Havana minutes after the shooting, insisted that he'd been double-crossed by Alice McMillan. "That bitch killed Eddie," he'd said, his voice shaking with rage. "No matter what it takes, Larry, I swear to God I'm gonna find her and get your money back."

"What about the film?"

"It was bogus. The murders were never filmed. We were set up."

"Are you telling me this fucking cunt—"

"Not her. Manson. He planned this whole thing from his cell in Vacaville. He figured you would go for it."

Havana knew Long was lying by the mere fact that he was alive. But he also knew that Manson had a long-standing grudge against his father, dating back to the mid-1950s, when Jack Havana co-owned a nightclub called The Wipeout, a thieves bar on Western where Charlie started out as a pimp. He was eighty-sixed one night after he pulled a knife on a cocktail waitress, a college girl from Glendale, who laughed in his face when he offered to turn her out.

The morning that Manson was arrested for the Tate-LaBianca slayings, Jack Havana told his son, "The guy was a scum, but I never figured him for anything like that."

Reese was nervously tapping his finger on the steering wheel. He didn't want to be here, on this unnaturally quiet street. He wanted to be back in Marina Del Rey, inside his condo, getting his cock sucked by Amanda from Atlanta, the chocolate-brown chick with the splendid body who lived downstairs. Unfortunately, daydreaming about Amanda made Reese recall the dismaying day he turned sixteen, a day ripped out of time and the day his father—a man with an old body and tin-colored flesh—bought him a black prostitute with round hips and dark eyes that were so cold Reese could not look at her face. And while his son got laid for the first time in their complimentary suite at the Desert Inn Hotel, Carl Reese stood naked in the doorway of the adjoining bedroom, jerking off.

"Did it bother you?" his father asked him the next morning while they were sunbathing by the pool.

"That you were watching?"

"Yeah."

"Sort of."

"I'm sorry."

"That's okay."

"But after all, it was my dough."

"Did you screw her, too?"

"Of course. But I think she enjoyed you more."

"I don't think she cared."

Carl Reese made a laughing sound that was less than heartfelt. "I wouldn't be so sure. From what I saw, she was getting her rocks off."

"Dad?"

"Yeah."

"Can we not talk about this?"

"Pussy, Jake. That's what men are supposed to talk about."

When his father dropped dead back in 1978, Jacob Reese was living at the Regency Arms, a newly built apartment complex in Studio City, not far from Universal Studios, where he sold drugs and worked as a union grip. After the funeral, which took place at Hillside Memorial Park, Jack Havana pulled him aside. He said there was a problem.

"Nothing major. Just a business matter that needs to be cleared up," he said, and they made an appointment to meet later that afternoon at the House of Love.

That's when Jacob Reese learned that his father—a man who kept all matters of business carefully to himself—died owing Jack Havana $200,000, money that had been paid out to the Aryan Brotherhood, the Mexican Mafia, and the leaders of several other prison factions, ensuring Carl Reese's safety while he did a two-year stretch in Folsom for federal income tax evasion. And Jacob Reese found out another piece of bad news that afternoon: All the businesses that his father had supposedly owned— the bars, dry cleaners, and valet services that had his name on the deeds and titles—were, in reality, controlled by Jack Havana.

"Your dad worked for me," Jack Havana said, and he rapped his knuckles twice on his cheap wooden desk. "Plain and simple."

"And so what you're saying is—now I work for you?"

"For me and my son, Larry."

Reese turned and aimed his eyes at Larry Havana, who was present at this meeting, sitting quietly in the corner, grinning throughout. "This is bullshit."

"It is what it is, Jake."

"What if I don't go along?"

Jack Havana looked intently at Jacob Reese for several seconds, and then he smiled. "Then you'd be making a big mistake."

And that's how Jacob Reese, seven years later and still $25,000 in debt, ended up parked outside the Argyle Manor on a warm and breezy Sunday evening, weighing his options while his heart went crazy and he watched the densely green and red lights suddenly blink on atop the Pantages Theatre, brightening up the poisonous darkness.

Larry Havana lit a cigarette, using the lighter in the ashtray. He took several puffs without inhaling before he said, in a low voice, "You take care of this thing, then we're even."

"This thing. You mean, take care of Long?"

After reflecting for several moments in silence, Larry Havana reached over and jiggled Reese's knee. "Let me ask you something. Can you feel that? Yes or no?"

"Yeah, I can feel it."

"I can't. I don't feel anything from my knees to my neck. Maybe a little buzz in my chest once in a while, but that's all. Toes, nose, eyes, ears, tongue, yes. I can feel things with my tongue. I can eat pussy. But nothing happens between my legs. That's not to say I don't get turned on like you. I do. I just don't feel it in my hangdown. You following me, Jake?"

"Sort of. But I'm not sure—"

"Where I'm going?" Larry Havana said. "You don't have to know. You just have to follow me. Say to yourself, 'Listen to Larry. He wants to explain something to me.' You didn't listen three years ago when my father died, and what happened?"

"Larry, come on. I—"

"You told me how your debt was over. You said goodbye to your family obligation."

"Look, I made a mistake."

"And what happened? A guy came by your apartment in Studio City, a big ugly guy with a big ugly knife. And what did he do? He gave you a scar. He put a fucking zipper in your back. And why did he do this? Because he worked for the guys my dad worked for in Chicago, the guys I work for now. So you *had* to pay up. Am I right?"

Jacob Reese closed his eyes for a moment. He was obviously agitated. Then he said quietly, "Yeah, that's right. I had to pay up."

"You can *feel* everything, Jakey. But you don't *know* everything," Larry Havana said, and he flicked his cigarette into the grass next to the curb. "Here's what I know. Number one: It's not a good thing that Eddie Cornell is dead. Eddie alive was protection. Now I'm exposed. We're all exposed. Number two: Eddie knew secrets, too many secrets. Number three: Chris Long knows what Eddie knows. And number four: It doesn't matter if he's lying about the fucking film. Because if it does exist, which I think it does, I'll know about it ten minutes after it surfaces."

Jacob Reese caught sight of his frightened face hovering in the rearview mirror. Then he let his eyes wander back over to the Argyle Manor. "So I go up there and do what?"

"You fuck with him. You threaten him. You do what it takes to find out where the film is."

"If he stonewalls?"

"You take him out. Either way you take him out."

Chris Long was sitting on his studio couch with his heart jumping and his eyes clouded with a muted melancholy. On the scarred coffee table in front of him was a pack of Camels, some crumpled bills, a half-empty glass of tequila, a loaded pistol, and a glassine envelope that contained three grams of uncut heroin.

Long had just gotten off the phone with his mother. For the last three years she'd been living in Laguna Niguel, a retirement community situated in the low rolling hills just north of San Diego. After a long period of self-imposed silence, Long had recently started calling her every other week, usually on Sunday evenings after *Sixty Minutes,* and that night he'd promised to drive down soon and escort her to a San Diego Padres baseball game. A lifelong fan, she'd switched her allegiance from the Los Angeles Dodgers to the Padres when she'd relocated down the coast in 1980, the year she retired as the head librarian at the Culver City branch of the Los Angeles Public Library.

She said, during their conversation, that she remembered a toy she bought him on his tenth birthday, an electronic baseball game that he only played once or twice before he pushed it under his bed to make room for his Lincoln Logs and other toys.

"I wasn't a baseball nut like you," Long said.

"I know. And your father didn't care much for sports either. I was the only one in the family who had any interest."

"But you never pushed. You bought the game, and when I got bored you never said a word."

"Didn't I buy you a mitt, too?" his mother asked him. "I think I did. All the kids in the neighborhood were trying out for Little League, but you refused to go. You liked going to the beach. You liked looking at the girls in their sexy swimsuits."

"In high school I used to bring girls back to the house while you were at work. I bet you didn't know that."

"Oh, Chris," his mother sighed. "I'm your mother. I did the laundry. I washed the sheets and towels. I knew what went on."

Long laughed. "Yeah, I guess you did," he said, and there was a long silence.

Long's mother, aware that she was still getting used to speaking to her son and not wanting to drive him away, found herself communicating in tones that seemed unnatural. At times she was hesitant, unsure of which subjects were off-limits, like his drug problem, a problem he never denied, or the life he lived in Hollywood: a life of carelessness and unconcern, an unsavory life that was filled with danger, where the line between innocence and guilt had been erased.

Long, who had snorted a line of heroin, said, "You remember when I was fourteen? You bought me a pair of bongos for Christmas."

"You wanted a drum kit, but I knew you wouldn't stick with the lessons."

"You were right."

"What else did I get you?"

"A portable typewriter. A Smith-Corona. I wrote my first published article on that typewriter. It was an interview with Screamin' Jay Hawkins that was printed in the school newspaper."

"You were a very smart boy," Long's mother said. "But you never stayed with anything. You lacked discipline."

"That's what happens when you take drugs. Your potential goes out the window. You lose focus."

"And you get in trouble."

"Yeah."

"Are you still in trouble?"

"Yeah, Mom. Big trouble."

In the lull that followed his admission, Long stood up and walked the phone over to the window facing the street. He saw the Eldorado parked on Argyle with Larry Havana and Jacob Reese sitting in the front seat, their faces looking quite grim. The top was down and Reese's hair, heavily greased, looked more blue than black in the moist night air.

Long's mother said, "I wish I could help you, Chris."

"I know."

"If you need money—"

"I got lots of money, Mom. I got lots of drugs, too. I just don't have much time."

Long's mother waited for him to go on, to clarify his last statement or give it an ironic twist. Then, sounding more bemused than frightened, she said, "Will you still take me to a Padres game?"

"Of course."

"I look forward to that."

"Maybe we'll go across the border."

"To Mexico?"

"Yeah."

"Maybe," Long's mother said. "If you want to."

Neither spoke for several seconds. And in that silence a precisely detailed picture was formed in Chris Long's mind, activated by a memory that he thought was lost:

A portly man in his forties steps out of a one-story adobe building with a tile roof and the flag of Mexico suspended over the front entrance, fluttering gently in the midday breeze. Clutched in his hand are several letters that he sorts through nervously as he walks toward a car waiting by the uneven sidewalk, a blue Chevrolet with a blond-haired woman behind the wheel, her face hidden by a red scarf and very large dark glasses.

The man is wearing black pants and a short-sleeved white linen shirt, the same outfit worn by another, much thinner, man who emerges from the gray Mercedes parked behind the Chevrolet. This man is holding a gun, a pistol with a silver grip that is aimed at the portly man's head; and when the bright flame leaves the barrel, the heavier man falls forward, the thin air around his face filled with three shades of blood.

Long said to his mother, "Did you ever meet Uncle Luther?"

"Your father's brother? Yes, of course."

"What was he like?'

"I didn't like him," she said. "And he didn't like me."

"Because you were Jewish?"

"Yes."

"Are you glad he's dead?"

"Chris," his mother said, sounding a little annoyed, "why are you asking me this?"

"I just want to know."

"Yes," she said without any guilt or doubt. "I'm glad he's dead."

Reese was now standing outside the Eldorado, still talking to Havana, occasionally glancing over his shoulder at the Argyle Manor. Havana said something that made him laugh, a sound that was both exuberant and completely false.

"I wish you were here," Long said into the receiver.

"Here?"

"Here with me," Long said, as he watched Reese move away from the car, his body screened by a long hedge as he angled toward the steps leading up to the landing on the second floor. "Now. I wish I could turn around and see you sitting at the little table in my kitchen. We could talk."

"We're talking now, Chris."

"I know. But there are so many things I don't understand."

"Like what?'

"Like how I got from there to here," Long said, and there was a brief silence. "I want to tell you a story, Mom. It's my favorite childhood memory. Will you listen?"

"Sure."

"It was October 6, 1958. I remember the exact day because the World Series started that afternoon and you were really excited. That morning I got up early and washed the car before I drove to school. On the way I picked up Susie Foreman, who was my girlfriend that semester. There was a commercial playing on the radio for Pall Mall cigarettes, the brand Susie smoked. When it was over, she scooted over right next to me, and the DJ, Jimmy O'Neill, came back on the air and said, 'Kids, the promotion man for Brunswick Records came into the booth while we were on that break. His name is Lenny Deluca, and he just handed me the new single by Jackie Wilson. And guess what? You and I are gonna hear it for the first time right now.' The song was 'Lonely Teardrops,' and we knew—me, Susie, and whoever was riding to school that day—that Jimmy O'Neill was telling us the truth, that we were all hearing it together for the first time."

Long was grinning when he turned away from the window and moved back to the couch. Telling his mother that story gave him the momentary reassurance that everything might still turn out alright, that he could be that boy again, riding in a car with a girl's hand resting on his thigh, the untamed music pounding on the radio, the windows shuddering, and his body charged with a dizzying freedom.

But this mental fiction, this split second of illusory well-being quickly disappeared, crowded out of his mind by the brutal facts of his life, a life that, put simply, might soon be over.

Long's mother said, "That was a nice story, Chris."

"Yeah, I know. It was fun being a teenager in the fifties," Long said. He was sitting in the center of his couch, his eyes fixed hypnotically on the front door. "What about you, Mom? Do you have a favorite childhood memory?"

"Several."

"Tell me one."

"I'll tell you when you come down to visit. It'll be something to look forward to."

Long didn't respond. His attention was focused outside, on the sound of footsteps—intimate and merciful—that were approaching his room.

"Chris, are you still there?"

"Yes, I'm still here."

"When will I see you?"

"Soon, Mom. You'll see me soon."

Long hung up the phone and sat still until Reese appeared in silhouette outside the curtained window. There was a long uneasy silence that was broken by Reese's knock, then quickly followed by his stern voice: "Long, open up!"

There was an expression of reliability and not fear on Long's face as he leaned forward to pick up the pistol. He flicked off the safety and took a deep breath, holding the barrel steady in his soft strong hand. Then he said, almost apologetically, "Come on in, Reese. The door's unlocked."

■

Larry Havana felt his eyes get tired, but he was too tense to sleep. It was not quite eleven P.M., which meant that forty-five minutes had passed—way too much time, he thought—since Jacob Reese had entered Chris Long's apartment. Experiencing a wave of profound unease that caused a sharp pain to flare across his forehead, Havana silently berated himself for entrusting Reese with this job. He could have easily farmed it out to Joey Caruso in Phoenix or Norm Wheeler up in San Francisco, both seasoned professionals with solid resumes, but guys like that didn't come cheap. These days a contract hit went for ten, sometimes twenty grand, and Havana, facing a temporary cash-flow problem due to I.R.S. liens, had decided to use Reese.

A breeze came up and Havana shivered a little in the evening air. Down the block he heard someone whistle, and a huge gray Airedale bounded across the street, his slippery shadow vanishing into a darkened yard. A moment later a screen door slammed, the sound echoing throughout the neighborhood like a gunshot.

Then, with his thoughts beginning to disintegrate, Havana closed his eyes, and into his submissive mind his father's voice arrived, chiding him:

> "I told you to always go first class, and what do you do? You hire a lightweight to handle an important matter, a matter of extreme delicacy. You're a moron, Larry."
>
> "I'm not a moron. I'm saving money."
>
> "You're not saving shit. You're buying trouble."
>
> "Yeah, we'll see. You'll be singing a different tune when I get hold of that film. I'll be so rich it won't even be funny."
>
> "Rich, maybe. But you'll never be happy."
>
> "I'm happy you're dead."
>
> "Is that the way a son talks to his father?"
>
> "Go to hell."

This anger and counteranger continued throughout the night, the quarreling interspersed with fragments of memory that Larry Havana carried around in his mind, pictures and clippings from a long-hidden family album.

Larry, in his wheelchair, is pushed down Vine Street by Gene Burk. They spent the morning together at Nate's News, reading comics in Nathan Burk's office. Now they are selling maps to the homes of movie stars, maps which are stacked in Larry's lap. He is nine years old.

■

Larry, at twelve, is sitting in the back of the Vogue Theater, his wheelchair occasionally bumped by the crush of bodies moving down the narrow aisle. They are all here to watch *The Thing*, Howard Hawks's sci-fi shocker. Gene Burk, who is Larry's paid companion that summer, is somewhere in the crowded theater, sitting next to Carla Bloom, a girl from their seventh-grade class, a girl whom Larry yearns for but pretends not to like.

■

Larry is fourteen. The year is 1955, right before the Christmas holidays. Gene and Larry are at Larry's house, in Larry's bedroom, listening to *Harlem Matinee,* the rhythm and blues show on KGFJ. Earlier that day Gene had dropped by Nate's News, and, while his father's back was turned, Gene swiped two copies of *Sunshine and Health,* a magazine depicting naked men and women engaged in outdoor activities, like swimming or playing volleyball.

The pictures give Gene an erection, and he decides to beat off in front of Larry, who stares at him, unblinking, feeling his heart pound but feeling nothing in his groin. The phone rings while Gene is in the bathroom cleaning up. Larry wheels himself into the front hallway and grabs the receiver. A woman is scream-ing on the other end. She wants to speak to his father.

"He's not here," Larry says.

"Tell him to send me money," she screams. "Tell that cocksucker he owes me. He ruined my fucking life."

"Who should I say called?"

"Mona. You tell him Mona said to send her money or else. You tell him that."

Gene is buttoning his Levi's, getting ready to leave, when Larry pushes himself back into the bedroom. He tells Gene that a woman just called his father, yelling and cursing like a crazy person.

"She wanted money," he says. "She said her name was Mona."

"Mona was my mom's name," Gene says.

Larry says, "Maybe that was her."

"Why would my mother be calling your dad?"

"I don't know."

"I'm going home," Gene says, sliding the nudie magazines back inside his school binder before he walks out the door.

■

Larry in high school is not part of any crowd. During lunch hour he usually sits alone in the cafeteria, eating the same unhealthy meal every day: a sloppy joe with a side of macaroni and cheese, and peach cobbler for dessert. Most kids who know about his father (or have heard rumors) keep their distance, but there are some who are intrigued, girls mostly, and the more adventurous come by his table to ask him questions:

"Is your father really a gangster?"

"No. He's a businessman."

"We heard he's killed people."

"My dad is so gentle he wouldn't hurt a fly."

"Have you ever been to Las Vegas?"

"Yes."

"What's it like?"

"Fun."

"At night I heard the stars are so bright that you get dizzy looking at the sky. Did that happen to you, Larry?"

"No."

"Will you be paralyzed all your life."

"Yes."

"Does it make you mad?"

"Yes."

■

Larry, at seventeen, is escorted off the high school grounds by the principal, a jowly man named Mr. Elliot. Larry has been expelled for extorting money from several students, including a girl named Norma Rudman, the daughter of a rabbi, Max Rudman, who accompanied her to school that morning, and was now, after accomplishing his mission, pulling away from the curb in his black Buick Roadmaster.

Larry is left alone on the sidewalk to wait for his father. He is still sitting there, slumped in his wheelchair, at three o'clock, when classes end for the day. None of the other students speak to him as they rush to their cars or pile into the yellow school buses parked by the curb.

Gene Burk drives by in his '50 Oldsmobile. On his face is a smile that is too wide. But Larry could care less about Gene Burk. He's thinking about his father, knowing that he'll be proud of him for not breaking down, for denying all the charges during the two-hour interrogation by the principal and the rabbi, no matter how much he was shouted at or harangued.

The street is dark when Jack Havana's silver Coupe De Ville pulls in front of the high school. Carl Reese is riding shotgun. He helps Larry into the backseat, then folds the wheelchair and slides it into the trunk. No one speaks on the way home. In their immense living room, his mother, who will be dead of a drug overdose by the end of the year, is passed out on the couch in her bra and underpants.

Larry goes to his room. He wants to cry, but he can't. He will never go back to school.

And then, finally, his eyes snapped open. It was just before dawn and Havana turned his head toward the sound of small breathing noises: The Airedale from the night before stood trembling on the curbside grass, staring at him with saliva drooling down his chin. Standing behind the dog, holding him tightly on a thick red leash, was a tall black man wearing an out-of-date Afro and a blue terry-cloth bathrobe.

"You been out here all night," the black man said in a suspicious tone. "You okay?"

Havana nodded, keeping one eye on the panting dog while he tried to clear his head. "I'm fine."

"Spike be up all night whining, looking out the front window. Now I know why."

"Sorry. I didn't mean to keep you up."

"Apology accepted," said the black man. Then he pointed to the wheelchair folded in the Eldorado's backseat. "That your chair?"

"Yeah. That's my chair."

"My brother Leon uses one just like it. He took a bullet in his back over in Vietnam. What about you?"

Havana, not used to such casual intimacy, looked up at the black man, his eyes slightly vulnerable. "I got polio when I was little."

The black man noticed his expression and said, "I didn't mean to get personal."

"That's alright. No big deal," Havana said quietly, frowning, his forehead creased. "Can I ask you a favor?"

"You can ask. I ain't saying I'll do it."

"Can you help me into my chair?"

The black man smiled, almost sadly. "Sure. I can do that."

"Thanks."

The black man pointed his finger in Spike's face, ordering him to lie down in the wet grass. Then, with little effort, he lifted the wheelchair out of the backseat, unfolding it on the sidewalk before he came back to the car and opened the passenger side door. "You ready?"

"Whenever you are."

Havana's legs dangled uselessly in the air as the black man, acting with a childish tenderness, picked him up and carried him over to the sidewalk. As soon as he was strapped into his wheelchair, a circular stain began to spread across the front of Havana's trousers, causing Spike to lift his head and sniff the odor of urine wafting in the air around his face.

Staring down with a guilty expression, the black man said, "You got a bad deal, mister."

"I don't feel sorry for myself."

"Leon don't either. But I would."

Havana just shrugged as he aimed his wheelchair down Argyle, away from the Argyle Manor and whatever happened inside Chris Long's apartment on the second floor. Hollywood Boulevard was south three blocks, the House of Love another four blocks to the west. That was home now, the only place he felt safe.

Havana glanced at the black man. "Thanks for helping me out."

"Glad to do it."

Havana's thoughts were scattered as he pushed himself slowly down Argyle, his head turned away from a pair of headlights that swept across his face. On the opposite side of the street, a dawn-drunk woman dressed in red leather staggered up the sidewalk, loudly singing "With a Little Help from My Friends," the Beatles song off *Sgt. Pepper.* A man's angry voice came through an open window—"Shut the fuck up," he screamed—but she just laughed and sang even louder, the words garbled and devoid of meaning.

Havana watched the woman wobble across the street and disappear inside a small square white bungalow, the sound of her voice giving way to the echo of a siren pulsing in the distance, a siren that seemed to be growing near. Bewildered songbirds made a fuss in the trees overhead as he paused to rest in the shadow of a streetlamp, grimacing with the realization that he knew this woman, that she had worked for him briefly at the House of Love, playing the role of Susan Atkins in the staged reenactment of the Manson killings. Her employment ended the night she came to work loaded and too realistically attacked the "actress" playing Sharon Tate, nearly biting off her nipple.

Havana briefly closed his eyes after he felt a sharp pain near the base of his skull. When he opened them again, the sun, blood-red and incandescent, emerged—like an omen—from behind the buildings of the city looming downtown, blinding him for a moment, the blazing light filling every pane of glass with a small fire.

Maintaining an outer calm, his mind slowly yielding to the new day, Havana rolled forward in his wheelchair, soothed by a feathery breeze and the small cry of a child from a nearby house. You're going to be alright, he said to himself. Everything might have been different but you're still here. In another life your legs will work and you can play pirates and climb trees. You will grow up to be a handsome man, and girls won't turn their cheeks away from your lips. But most of all you will learn to count on nothing, so you will never be betrayed.

Twenty-one

The Morning After . . .

and the Night Before

In local news, two men were found dead this morning in an apartment on Argyle Street in Hollywood, apparently the victims of a murder-suicide. Although their names and the cause of death have not been released by the police, KNX sources tell us that the apartment was rented by Christopher Long, a reputed drug dealer and possible police informant.

Gene Burk first heard this KNX 1070 news report on Highway 91, thirty miles southeast of Furnace Creek, in the western boundary of Death Valley National Park. The Other Alice was still asleep, breathing quietly, her face soft and vulnerable and almost pretty. Gene decided not to wake her; he would tell her the news over breakfast. But thirty minutes later, when they left the interstate and pulled into the parking lot of The Pines, a greasy diner situated directly across the highway from a field filled with wind turbines and junked cars, Gene felt some uncertainty—a swell of confusion that caused him to consider acting against his best intentions.

After they were parked in front of the diner, the Other Alice sat up and reached into her purse for a cigarette. She was wearing a faded blue tank top and red gym shorts that showed off her long muscular legs, clothes she'd changed into at a Chevron station in Furnace Creek, after they had hiked back from Goler Wash.

She looked disappointed as her eyes wandered around the landscape. "Where the hell are we?"

"Just outside of Baker."

"You said we were going to drive straight through."

Gene shrugged. "I thought we'd get something to eat."

The Other Alice took a drag off her cigarette and rolled down the window. "There's too many cars here," she said. "I don't want to be around a bunch of people. Why don't we just get some donuts and keep moving."

"I'm hungry. C'mon," Gene said, reaching for the door handle.

"I know what happened."

Gene shifted in his seat and pulled the door shut. "What do you mean, you know what happened?"

"I heard," she said, pointing at the radio. "I heard the news report. Long's dead."

"It was his apartment. That's all they know."

"You don't believe it was him."

"It was probably him."

"Who was the other guy?"

"Whoever was looking for him," Gene said, gesturing toward the diner. "Let's talk about this inside?"

"They got him . . . " Her voice broke. " . . . They'll get me."

"No. They don't know who you are. Long and Eddie Cornell, they were the only ones who knew. And they're dead."

The Other Alice was biting her lip. "No. Charlie. There's still Charlie. He knows. Right?"

"Right."

"And you."

"And me. That's it."

Inside the diner, Gene and the Other Alice took a table next to a long horizontal window facing the gravel parking lot. At a table nearby, leaking malice, was a nervous-looking man around forty, with a shiny face and a twist to his small mouth. Sitting with him, her hand cupped to shield her swollen cheekbone, was a pale pretty girl no older than sixteen.

The Other Alice, ignoring the man's cruel black eyes, put down her menu and stared outside, past the highway, toward the inhospitable landscape beyond, the miles and miles of barren desert. "Now what, Gene? You go back to L.A. and what happens?"

"I don't know. I haven't thought that far ahead."

"Are you sorry about what we did?" said the Other Alice, and her gaze came back to Gene. She looked tired, withdrawn. "I'm not talking about the film."

"I know what you're talking about," Gene said. "No, I'm not sorry."

The Other Alice said assuredly, "Yes you are. I can tell. You're lying."

Gene didn't respond. He was watching the waitress, who was young and radiated an outer calm, thread her way gracefully through the crowded tables, stopping occasionally to pour coffee into an empty cup.

"Gene, did you hear me?"

"Yeah, I heard you."

The waitress arrived at their table, smiling good-naturedly. "Have you guys decided?"

Gene, glancing back at his menu, said, "I think I'll have the pancakes and a side of bacon."

"Nothing for me," said the Other Alice, as the waitress wrote down Gene's order. "Just coffee."

"You should eat something," Gene said.

"I'm not hungry."

"How about some fruit?"

The Other Alice shook her head. The girl with the bruised cheek was staring at her. In her eyes was a kind of desperation, a call for help that was eloquent in its silence. The man sitting with her reached out and poked the waitress in the hip. "How about some more coffee over here," he said, his voice flat and commanding. "And bring me the check."

"My Girl" by the Temptations came on the jukebox and the man began snapping his fingers loudly to the beat. The girl looked both embarrassed and disgusted as she pushed her chair back and stood up. "I have to use the bathroom."

The man smiled knowingly as he watched her walk across the room, her posture rigid but her tight teenage body drawing approving stares from the truckers seated at the counter. When the man turned back and saw the Other Alice staring right at him, he said, shaking his head, "Fifteen and she's already got their mouths watering."

The Other Alice looked surprised to be addressed directly. "Were you speaking to me?"

"Who else would I be speaking to?" the man said, his eyes moving over to Gene, who was pouring cream into his coffee. "You've been eyeballing me since you sat down. In case you're wondering, she's my daughter, and I'm used to men staring at her. You should've seen what it was like up in Vegas. She was getting hit on by every creep on the Strip."

"Where's her mother?" Gene said, keeping a casual tone in his voice.

"Riverside. We're divorced. I get her every other weekend."

The waitress came back with the man's check, acknowledging him with a nod as she placed it by his empty plate. "Your pancakes will be up in a minute," she said to Gene, who was looking outside, where a highway patrol car had just pulled into the parking lot.

"That's a mean bruise on your daughter's cheek," said the Other Alice, after a pause, and she saw that the man was clearly taken by surprise, although he met her stare equally. "What happened?"

"I don't think that's any of your business."

"Just curious."

Gene leaned forward and put his hand on her arm. "Cool it."

Ignoring Gene, the Other Alice said, "What did you do—gamble away all your money and take it out on her?"

The man turned away, then turned back. "What the fuck's your problem?"

"She's just worried about her," Gene said. His voice was soft and patient. "That's all. It wasn't personal."

"Yes it was," said the Other Alice, pointing her finger at the man's face. "I know that look. I've seen it before. You're doing bad things to that girl."

The man turned to Gene, who was watching him carefully. "You better shut this one up or—"

"Or what?" Gene said, as the girl came out of the bathroom and stood by the register with a slightly dazed expression.

The Other Alice said, "Are you gonna beat the shit out of me, too?"

The man, trembling with fear and fury, took out his wallet and dropped a twenty-dollar bill on the table. "You're crazy. Both of you," he said after an interval, then he looked around and made eye contact with his daughter. "Get over here, Juliet. We're leaving."

The girl looked at him with loathing as she nervously rubbed her arms. "No. I'm not going anywhere with you."

"Did you hear what I said, you little bitch?"

Conversations dropped to a whisper when the highway patrolman entered the diner, bringing in a breeze that fluttered some newspapers. He seemed to be aware of the diminishing voices as he calmly looked around the room. "Did anyone here call 911?"

"I did," said the girl in a steady voice, still looking at her father. "I don't want him to touch me anymore. I don't want him to hurt me."

Her father stood quickly. "This is nuts. I never laid a hand on her."

"He fucks me!" the girl cried out fiercely, and an undertone of disgust rippled through the diner. "He's been fucking me for years!"

"That's not true! She's lying!"

"Shut the fuck up," said one of the truckers at the counter, a bald guy wearing an Arrowsmith T-shirt and a thick turquoise bracelet. His face expressed a threat as he stood up. "Kids don't lie about shit like that."

"I never did nothing to her!"

The highway patrolman, moving slowly forward, his voice coldly even, said, "Just take it easy, everyone. We'll get this straightened out shortly."

In less than a minute, three more highway patrol cars arrived on the scene, and while Juliet was being questioned in the kitchen, her father was handcuffed and led outside. By the time his car was searched, revealing a 9mm pistol in the trunk, along with an ounce of cocaine and several pornographic videos, Gene and the Other Alice were back on the interstate, driving fast through a landscape wrapped in yellows and browns, dominated by sagebrush and windblown sand.

They were silent for several miles. Finally the Other Alice said, half to herself, "What that girl did took courage. Her whole life's gonna change. It's gonna get better. Don't you think so, Gene?"

"Probably."

"No. It will. It has to. Getting fucked by your father—it can't get any worse," she said. "And my life's gonna change, too. I know it. Everything's gonna work out."

Gene looked over at Alice, a side glance that seemed thoughtful and a little bit melancholy. "Tell me something else about her."

"Who?"

"Alice."

The Other Alice turned her head. Her eyes said, I've told you everything.

"There's more. I know it."

"Gene—"

"Making love to you I heard her voice."

The Other Alice closed her eyes. She looked like she was straining against some inner pain. "What did she say?"

Oh, Gene, nothing nothing nothing ever felt this good.

"Gene? What did she say?"

"She just said my name."

■

The night before—a night that was brilliantly clear and wild with stars— Gene and the Other Alice left his house in Topanga Canyon and drove east on the Ventura Freeway, turned off at the Van Nuys exit, then took Benedict Canyon over Mulholland to Sunset. Along the way, the Other Alice, smiling mischievously, pointed out houses that she had visited back in the sixties, both before and after she met Charlie.

She said, as they passed the driveway that curved up to Ryan O'Neal's hillside home, "That's where I took quaaludes for the first time. This older guy with gray bangs gave them to me. Dean of Jan and Dean was at this party, too. I think I gave him a blow job in the pool."

Gene mentioned that he'd gone to high school with Ryan O'Neal, and that his brother Ray used to hang out with Ryan's best friend and future stand-in, Joe Amsler, who, not long after they graduated, was one of three people arrested in the kidnapping of Frank Sinatra, Jr.

"Wow. That's pretty cool," said the Other Alice, and when they drove slowly past the turnoff to Cielo Drive, she looked toward the hills, toward the house where, in the summer of 1969, a force of evil took five lives, sending a cloud of fear over the city. "I met his sister Nancy up there once," she said, her voice deliberately calm. "It was at this humongous party that Charlie and a bunch of us crashed. Jack Nicholson was there, and so was John Phillips of the Mamas and the Papas. Charlie was looking for this guy Terry, Doris Day's son."

"Terry Melcher," Gene said.

"Yeah, right. He was a record producer. He came out to the ranch a few times to hear Charlie play guitar. He said he was going to record his songs, but he never did."

Gene said, "I think my brother was there."

"Where?"

"At the party. If Nancy was there, it was probably the same night."

"We came up with a big bag of drugs—coke, speed, acid—and we sold it all. Before we left, I went into the house to use the bathroom. Susan Atkins came with me and, while I was peeing, she went into the bedroom and stole some of Sharon Tate's jewelry. At the time we didn't know whose jewelry it was. We thought this guy Terry was still renting the place," said the Other Alice, and then her mind seemed to go off somewhere for several seconds. "When I came out of the bathroom, Dean Martin's kid tried to feel me up. I let him. I let him kiss me, too. His lips were perfect and so were his teeth. Everybody at the party had big, bright, shiny teeth."

The Other Alice smiled at this memory, a smile that was almost sad, and she and Gene remained silent until they reached Sunset. Then, waiting for the light to change and not wanting to look at her, Gene said, "Did you ever go back there?"

"Where?"

"Up to that house on the top of Cielo Drive."

"No," said the Other Alice. "No, I didn't. I never went back."

As they drove east on Sunset in the thick weekend traffic, the Other Alice reminisced about the first time she came out to Los Angeles, in the summer of 1965, when all the boys looked irresistible and excitement was everywhere. She told Gene about Archie, the bass player for Billy J. Kramer and the Dakotas, and the three days they spent together at the Continental Hyatt House Hotel.

"Every musician in town was staying there, all of them drunk or stoned on acid. It was crazy. And there were so many groupies," said the Other Alice, "girls that were all skinnier and prettier than me. But I knew what guys liked, and I gave it to them."

Gene spoke about the year he spent patrolling the Sunset Strip, when he was a rookie cop and Eddie Cornell was his partner. And he told her about Eddie's unlimited capacity for unkindness. "He hated hippies. He used to spend half our shift driving around Hollywood, harassing kids. If he found a joint in some girl's backpack, he'd toss her in the squad car and threaten to arrest her."

The Other Alice laughed with disgust. "But if they sucked his cock, he'd let them off, right?"

"That's the way it worked."

"Then he got what he deserved."

"I suppose," Gene said, and drew on the cigarette he was smoking. "His funeral's on Monday."

"Are you gonna go?"

Gene shrugged. After a hesitation, he said, "I'm not sure."

The Other Alice was going through her purse as Gene turned right on Vine Street and glided to the curb in front of of the Greyhound bus station. Standing by the entrance was a small, almost dainty-looking black man with a pencil-thin mustache and eyes that glittered with a kind of hypnotic conviction. On the pavement by his feet was a fake leather satchel overflowing with papers and, next to it, a beat-up boom box blasting Dixieland jazz.

The Other Alice held up a small silver key. "It's locker number 212. You want me to go in with you?"

"I'll get it," Gene said.

"You sure?" Gene nodded, and the Other Alice gently pressed the key into his outstretched palm. "Hurry back."

Gene got out and walked toward the bus station, slowing his pace when he heard the pay phone ring on the side of the building. A fat woman with a hopeful face rushed outside and grabbed the receiver on the third ring.

"Where are you?" she screamed, and, glancing at Gene, quickly lowered her voice to almost a whisper. "I've been waiting here all afternoon."

The black man grinned as Gene approached. Gene grinned back. The black man said, "I'm happy because I'm headed home. How come you're smiling, mister man?"

Gene shrugged. "I don't know. I guess I caught your smile."

"Smiling's good. So's happy. And pleasure—I likes pleasure a lot. Eatin', sleepin', sexin' it up with a good woman, that's pleasure," said the little black man, smiling wider now as he tapped his foot to the rhythm of the music. "You like Dixieland jazz, mister man?"

Gene looked over his shoulder. The Other Alice, was staring at him through the windshield glass. "I like all kinds of music," Gene said, and he started to move away. "Nice talking to you."

The black man chuckled. "We weren't talking. I was talking. You was listening."

"Well, then, nice listening to you."

"Now, *joy,*" the black man said, looking at Gene meaningfully. "That's different from happiness and pleasure. Joy is in a whole different category. Joy is a divinely given emotion. That's when you feel like doin' cartwheels."

Gene was paused by the bus station's front door, waiting for the black man to continue. The fat woman, now done with her call but still holding the phone by her side, was also listening.

She said, "What if you're too fat to do cartwheels?"

"Don't have to do them," said the black man. "You just have to *feel* like doin' them."

"Gene?" The Other Alice, her voice bewildered, was speaking to him from the car. "What's going on?"

Gene turned around. His face, in the half-light of the street, looked blank, uncomprehending. "Nothing. Nothing's going on."

"Joy contains three elements," the black man said, his voice now wrapped in a great passion. "Laughter. Gratitude. Honesty. You got those three workin' in your life—God's trifecta I likes to call it—then I will guarantee that you will feel joyful."

"Honesty, gratitude, and laughter. I like that," said the fat woman. "I'm gonna write that down."

"What about you?" the black man said to Gene. "You lookin' to feel joy in your life?"

Gene did not reply. The fat woman hung up the buzzing receiver and stared at his face. "He's talkin' to you, mister."

Gene stood frozen, the blinds suddenly drawn behind his eyes. Inside his head he was clinging to a memory:

He sees Alice back in June, on the morning she is leaving for the airport. She is waving goodbye to him as he stands on the front porch in the predawn light.

"I'll call you when I get in," she says, her gaze direct, without expectation.

"Have a safe trip, sweetheart."

"I will."

"I'm gonna miss you," he says.

"Yeah, I know. I'm gonna miss you, too."

And a moment later she backs out of the driveway in her red Honda convertible and drives away, her taillights disappearing forever, into the endless, aching darkness.

Gene turned and looked at the fat woman with a coolness that bordered on hostility, as though she were in some way responsible for Alice's death. "I know who he's talking to."

"He asked you if you wanted to feel joy in your life."

"Of course I do," Gene said, as he walked past the black man and through the double-glass doors. "I want to feel anything I can."

The bus station was empty, and the snack bar and ticket windows were closed. Gene walked slowly across the mopped tile floor, toward the row of lockers that were built into the far wall. And once more a door swung open in his mind, allowing a memory to escape:

He's a little boy, maybe eight or nine—his mother no longer lives with him so he's probably nine—and the stars light up the sky outside his bedroom window. Feeling thirsty, he slides out of bed and walks down a short hallway, past another larger bed-room where his father is sleeping on his side, breathing hard, his face turned away and his marble-white back almost shining in the darkness.

He walks into the kitchen and takes a glass out of the cup-board without turning on the light. He opens the icebox, pours milk from the bottle, and starts back to his room. Because it is dark and he is already taking a sip from the tall glass (which means his eyes are angled downward and not ahead), he doesn't see the half-open door separating the hallway from the kitchen. The col-lision causes him to stumble and drop the glass, and when he reaches out to break his fall, a thin shard pierces a tendon in his wrist.

His scream reverberates throughout the house, bringing his younger brother into the kitchen. Ray snaps on the light and quickly covers his mouth, his face going white with shock when he sees Gene sprawled out on the floor, the milk pooled around him, swirled with his blood.

From his bedroom, their father shouts, "What's going on out there?"

"Gene's hurt," Ray shouts back. "He cut himself bad. He has to go to the hospital."

And that's where they go at three in the morning, to the emergency room at St. John's in Santa Monica. The doctor, a man with a small sad smile, speaks to Nathan Burk when he's through stitching Gene's wrist.

He says reassuringly, "Your son will be fine. I will give him pills for the pain and a salve to help the healing."

"He's a good boy," Nathan Burk says. "Both my sons are good boys."

"Our mom left us last year," Ray says, and the doctor stares down at the little boy, who is holding on to his father's hand. "My dad's sad all the time."

Gene narrows his eyes at his younger brother and puts a warning finger up to his lips. Then a nurse enters their cubicle, gowned and masked. Her eyes tell the doctor that he's needed with another patient. Still smiling, he puts his steady hand on Nathan Burk's shoulder. "I'm sorry. I have to go," he says. "But I'm sure everything will turn out for the best."

Gene, as he stood in front of locker #212 with the key clenched in his right hand, burning his palm, wondered why a memory, locked in obscurity for so many years, had been retrieved on this night. Maybe it was the ceiling lights above, he conjectured, the same cold fluorescence that had buzzed and hummed in the emergency room at St. John's. Or perhaps it was the pale green walls or the two vending machines standing side by side, like those in the long hospital corridor, one for cigarettes and the other packed with candy and gum.

It could be any one of those things—or none of them—Gene decided, expelling a long breath as he inserted the key and turned it slowly, waiting until he heard the soft click before he opened the door. Inside the locker was a large metal box shaped like a hexagon.

Using the handle on top and projecting a businesslike air, Gene quickly removed the box and closed the locker. He was halfway across the lobby when he heard a toilet flush in one of the bathrooms. A moment later, a grim-faced woman in tight black leather pants walked into the lobby, swinging her hips. Both her eyes were blackened, and her hair was dyed the color of rust.

She said, in a twangy voice, "You want a date, tall boy?"

"No thanks."

"You don't know what you're missing."

Gene smiled over his shoulder. "You're right."

The woman laughed, but her thin face still looked depressed. Outside Gene heard the black man say, " . . . and there it will be on the other end of the rainbow, everlasting joy," and he walked back into the night.

The easiest way to reach Death Valley was to stay on 15, taking it northeast through San Bernardino and Barstow, the same route Gene took when he visited Melanie Novack in Las Vegas, only this time he would not cross the Nevada state line.

"We switch to 14 when we get to Mojave," said the Other Alice, once they had left the city and the desert was all around them. "At Randsburg, the road becomes two-lane. After thirty miles or so we'll reach Furnace Creek," she said, consulting the map unfolded in her lap. "Then it's about an hour northwest, past Mercer and Shoshone, into the Panamint Mountains. At Ballarat the road ends and we have to get out and walk."

"How far?"

"It's five miles from Ballarat to Goler Wash, then another three until we reach Barker Ranch. And it's not an easy hike, especially at night," said the Other Alice, and she looked at Gene. "You're still game, right?"

"Sure."

"Good." The Other Alice folded up the map and placed it on the dash next to her Marlboros. Then she closed her eyes and curled up with her hands between her thighs and her head resting against the window. "Because I wouldn't go in unless you were with me."

"Learn to trust the darkness. That's what Charlie used to say," said the Other Alice when they started out in the dead of night. On her back was a knapsack that contained a flashlight, a portable shovel, a bag of trail mix, a box of wooden matches, and a can of lighter fluid. Gene carried the oddly shaped metal box. "I don't want to use the flashlight unless we have to. Why take a chance attracting the park rangers or the highway patrol?"

As they walked single-file up the narrow trail that led into the desert foothills, the Other Alice spoke freely about the first time she came to Barker Ranch back in September of 1969, one month after the Tate-LaBianca slayings. Using credit cards that were illegally acquired, she and Charlie were able to purchase enough supplies to last for at least a year: tools, gasoline, cases of oil, sleeping bags, food, guns, knives (lots of knives), and camouflauge parachutes to hide the dune buggies and the other stolen vehicles.

Gene said, "I read where Charlie said he was looking for an underground city."

"Yeah. He was. It was this subterranean paradise he called the 'golden hole.' He probably dreamed it up on some acid trip."

"Didn't it sound crazy?" Gene asked her.

"What do you mean?"

"When he talked about this place."

"No," the Other Alice said, looking up into the sky and then down at the mountains ahead of them. "If you were here at the time, it sounded great."

In a way those months in the desert were like summer camp, she said, with cookouts and singalongs and dune buggy races across flat miles of deep sand. But everything wasn't perfect. There was also death: At least three people were killed, according to the Other Alice, two boys and a girl, backpackers from Holland who took the wrong trail and were suddenly confronted by several feral young women, all of them naked, their razor-sharp hunting knives strapped to their thighs.

The Other Alice said, "They were just innocent kids spending their summer vacation in America."

Gene stopped walking to get a breath. The muscles in his right arm were tense, and he released his grip, letting the heavy metal box drop to the earth by his feet. "That's fucked. That's really fucked."

"I know. A lot of fucked things happened out here," said the Other Alice, her pale features expressing sadness. Then she shrugged off her knapsack and sat down on one of the big rocks that crowded the trail. "I'm sorry I told you."

Gene raised his head in time to see a single vulture, swollen and black, float across the face of the moon, searching for death. "Did you have the camera while you were out here?"

"Uh-huh."

"What happened to *that* film."

"I don't know."

Looking down at the metal box, Gene said, "Maybe it's in there."

The Other Alice said nothing for several seconds. Around them the landscape was hushed and foreboding, the air dead still. Finally, she stood up. "Let's keep going."

"There's six hours of film. That's what you said, right? If—"

"Maybe I'm on that film." The Other Alice turned her face toward Gene, her eyes a little unstable. "Maybe I did something bad that I don't remember, because I was too stoned. Then where are we?"

"You're not on that film," Gene said, staring at her. "You would've never been willing to sell it."

"Maybe. Or maybe I wanted to get caught."

Several noiseless seconds passed. Then: "Did you?"

"Did I what?"

"Did you do something bad?" The Other Alice laughed, and Gene looked at her sharply. "Why are you laughing?"

The Other Alice answered through clenched teeth: "Listen to me, Gene. I've told you everything I know about Alice, including what she told me about you and secrets from her past that you didn't know. And I've told you my story too, as much as I feel you needed to know. But you don't get to know everything. Even if you knew everything—about me, Charlie, what really happened out here—even if you saw the film and your knowledge of evil was complete, you would still never understand why Alice died, because that's what you really want to know, what rips your heart apart. And there is no answer—no ending, no final knowledge—except the plane just crashed."

Gene stood there for some time without speaking, his face assuming a diffident expression. "So why am I here with you?"

"Because you're desperate and lost and longing for love."

"But I don't love you."

"I'm Alice from Cedar Rapids. I have her name. And when you fucked me, you saw her face in mine."

"For only a moment."

"Yet in that moment the pain you felt disappeared, escaped through me, and you no longer felt stranded or lost."

"But I betrayed her."

"You did. But in that moment you betrayed me, too. And that's why you're here."

The Other Alice shifted the pack on her shoulders and continued walking, but after a few steps she stopped and turned around, her mind suddenly reeling away from all she wanted to forget. With a look on her face that was both haunted and filled with unarticulated fear, she told Gene that they had traveled far enough, that it would be a mistake to hike all the way to Barker Ranch, where there were memories of a sun-stricken world of strangeness that she didn't need to rescue or relive.

Warning Gene to watch out for rattlesnakes and scorpions, the Other Alice left the trail and, with the moonlight grazing her shoulders, set out toward the mountains. "That's where Charlie liked to go and meditate," she told Gene after a mile or so, as they passed the entrance to an abandoned silver mine. "He'd stay out here for hours. Just him and the coyotes."

"Meditating about what?"

"Death. He said that's what you're supposed to meditate about in Death Valley. He said he could speak to the Devil in the desert. He said God and the Devil are the same thing, one was part of the other, that every human being had both inside him. To Charlie, what it really meant was that human life had no meaning: Killing someone—anyone—meant you were killing part of yourself, the Devil part. It makes no sense now, I know that, but he made it sound like it did.

"But the longer we were out here, the more paranoid he got. He became obsessed with violence and torture, and he bragged about all the people he'd killed and all the people he wanted to kill. Once he accused me of being a weak link in the family, a coward, and he threatened to kill me unless I could prove he was wrong."

"What did you do?"

"I learned how to handle live rattlesnakes. This girl Gypsy taught me. You did whatever it took not to be humiliated. That's what Charlie liked to do, humiliate us. He used to order some of the girls to give blow jobs to the park rangers and these old desert rats that lived around us. He called it 'buying health insurance with your mouth.' Only one girl—Randy from Reseda—stood up to him."

"What happened?'

"He nearly beat her to death."

The Other Alice stopped walking. She was standing next to a thumb-shaped cactus that came up to her hip. A few feet away, a red desert orchid grew out of what looked like a human skull, sand-scoured and bleached-out, teeth bared and grinning.

Gene, his fingers cracked and blistered, put down the metal box. "Have you been here before?"

"No."

"You sure?"

Without answering, the Other Alice opened her knapsack and took out the can of lighter fluid and the box of wooden matches. Then, kneeling, she unlocked the metal box and dumped out the six reels of 16mm film.

"What're you gonna do?"

"Burn everything."

"I thought you wanted to bury it."

"I changed my mind." Alice looked up at Gene. "Maybe you would like to help. Unless, of course, you're worried about being responsible in some way."

"Responsible? You mean for whatever's on that film? Hey, for all I know it's blank," Gene said, looking into Alice's unsmiling eyes. "This whole thing could be a hoax."

"You're right. It could be." The Other Alice reached inside the knapsack and removed the flashlight. She switched it on and held it out. "Here. Why don't you check out a reel."

Gene looked at the Other Alice's knowing expression, then past her face, toward the wide-open darkness. "No. That's okay," he said, after taking a few undecided moments. "I know all I need to know."

It took close to an hour to unreel all the film and pile it together into a hole that Gene dug in the dry ground. When he was done, his blisters were bleeding, and he was sweating and breathing hard. The Other Alice, who was waiting patiently, said, "I want to say a prayer before we do the rest."

"What are you going to pray for?"

"I don't know," the Other Alice said, kneeling down next to Gene, her big face revealing nothing as she bowed her head and closed her eyes. "For forgiveness, I guess."

After about a minute, the Other Alice opened her eyes and brushed her hair back from her face. Gene reached for the can of lighter fluid, and his hand shook slightly as he squeezed it over the fire.

"I think I should be the one to light it," said the Other Alice, once the can was empty. "If that's okay with you?"

"Sure."

The Other Alice struck a wooden match on her thumb and Gene saw the ruby flare doubled in her eyes, a red wick of light that barely trembled in the tame wind. "Now?"

Gene nodded. "Go ahead."

The Other Alice let the match fall, and the tangled film hissed like a nest of snakes before bursting into flames. Then she sat back from the heat and the smell of burning nitrate with an expression of some affection deep in her eyes.

Gene, watching her face, said, "What are you thinking about?"

"Movies."

"What kind of movies?"

"Movies I saw as a kid. Nice movies."

"Like what? Name some."

"I liked anything with Jimmy Stewart or Gregory Peck."

"To Kill a Mockingbird?"

"Yeah. That was good. I liked westerns too. *Shane. High Noon.* They were cool. And I liked movies that could make me laugh. Comedies with Laurel and Hardy made me laugh. And so did Buster Keaton."

Gene, feeling sweat jump out of his face, tilted his head away from the fire. "Yeah, Keaton was great."

"He used to live out near Spahn Ranch. We saw him once at the Hughes Market in Tarzana while we were Dumpster-diving for food. I should've gotten his autograph, huh? It's probably worth something. Not as much as Charlie's . . . but something."

Gene gazed off to the east, through the torrent of sparks that crackled in the air like kernals of popcorn. Along the horizon, penetrating the night sky, was a long vein of golden light, a light allied in Gene's mind with the end of his loneliness and sorrow.

When he turned back to the smoldering fire, the Other Alice reached out and took his hand. With her body rocking slightly, she watched a column of smoke rise up from the fire, smoke that didn't vanish into the air but that dipped and whirled into an updraft, forming disembodied heads with death glowing in their gutted eye sockets.

The Other Alice said, "Can you see them?"

"See what?"

"The faces in the smoke. The ghosts of the dead."

She then said their names out loud: Sharon Tate, Jay Sebring, Abigail Folger, Voytek Frykowski, and Steve Parent, the five who died at 10050 Cielo Drive on August 9, 1969. She said she also saw the soul of Sharon Tate's unborn child rising out of the wisps of smoke, a spirit lost and wandering aimlessly, unreachable and inconsolable, his insistent cries forever lost to the wind.

Gene said, "What does he want?"

"Just a name and a birthdate and a mother to sing him a lullaby."

"That's not much to ask for."

"You wouldn't think so," said the Other Alice, releasing Gene's hand. Then she stood up and slapped the dust off the back of her khakis. "Are you ready to head back?"

Gene didn't answer right away as he looked to the north, where the sky hung over the mountains like a rich blue canvas. Watching the dwindling lights of an airplane dip below the mountains and disappear, he thought of the woman he loved inside another aircraft, an aircraft that was doomed. He tried to imagine the pandemonium around her as gravity forced her to her knees and the unbreathable air strangled her lungs. The grief he felt was familiar but unreachable.

"Gene?" Gene looked over at the Other Alice. Her knapsack was back on her shoulders, and there was something in her features he had not seen before, an exalted innocence, a kind of rapture. "Are you okay?"

Gene nodded his head. As he slowly got to his feet, he felt the first rays of sunlight warm his cheek, and he turned toward the orange light expanding on the horizon. In the absolute stillness of this moment, he felt something that passed for peace, and a voice inside him spoke with fierce clarity: *Keep me in your heart. That's all I ask.*

"Should we start walking?" said the Other Alice.

Gene's smile was real. "Sure," he said, still nodding yes. "It's time to go home."

Part

Three

Twenty-two

Where Is Home?

Gene and the Other Alice were sitting in a row of blue plastic chairs facing the departure gate for Delta Airlines flight 453, which was scheduled to leave for Chicago in fifteen minutes, at two P.M. sharp. When they'd arrived at the airport, Gene had two quick Bloody Mary's at the bar while the Other Alice used the restroom to change out of her gym shorts and T-shirt. She was now dressed in the same outfit—light blue crew neck and frumpy corduroy pants—that she wore a few days earlier, on her flight into Los Angeles.

Sitting across from them was a pregnant woman around thirty and carefully groomed, flanked by twin boys who were too old to sit in her lap. Gene pretended to read the newspaper while he eavesdropped on the conversation she was having with the man sitting two seats to her right, a man she had just met, a businessman who looked disheveled and overworked, judging by his tired eyes and his wrinkled gray suit.

"We're on our way to Indianapolis. That's where we live," she told the businessman. Then she went on to explain that she and the kids had spent the weekend in Santa Barbara visiting her parents, who were celebrating their thirty-fifth wedding anniversary. Her husband could not accompany her, she said, because he was in the middle of a murder trial. "He's prosecuting a man who killed his estranged wife's boyfriend. It's one of those 'crimes of passion' things."

"My dad's gonna send him to the electric chair," said one of the twins, who stood up on his chair and shouted: "I now pronounce you guilty as charged!"

"Yeah. He's gonna fry," said his brother, as he twitched in his seat and made a loud buzzing noise.

"Okay, boys, that's enough," said their mother, when she caught Gene staring at her. "They can be so gruesome at this age."

The Other Alice glanced up from the *People* magazine she was reading and turned to look at Gene, but he didn't meet her eyes until she touched his arm. "You can leave if you want. I'll be fine."

Gene nodded but remained silent. The tired businessman and the pregnant woman were now sharing their views on the death penalty. He was against it.

"On moral grounds," he said.

"Believe me," the pregnant woman said in a superior voice, "if it was your wife or someone you were close to, you'd be singing a different tune."

Gene saw the flight crew pass through the gate and disappear down the walkway that led to the interior of the aircraft. A few moments later, a woman's voice came over the intercom, announcing that flight 453 was now ready to board, starting with the passengers in first class.

"That's us," said the pregnant woman. Then she stood up and threw her purse over her shoulder. "Time to go home."

Moving toward the gate, one of the twins said, "I want to sit by the window, so when it gets dark I can be close to the stars."

Gene rose with the Other Alice when her row was called, and when they looked at each other, she said, "Would you mind if I write you a letter now and then?"

"No. I wouldn't mind."

"Liar."

Gene smiled at this. Then he said, "Look, if you want to write, it's cool."

"But not all the time. And I won't expect you to write back," said the Other Alice, as she opened her purse and reached for her ticket. "Fair?"

"Fair."

"How about a final hug. Or am I pushing it?"

Showing no expression on his face, Gene stepped forward and the Other Alice wrapped her arms around the back of his neck, and for at least fifteen seconds they remained frozen in this embrace, ignoring the disgruntled passengers who were forced to move around them on their way to the gate. When the final boarding call came over the loudspeaker, the Other Alice withdrew her arms and kissed Gene gently on the forehead and the cheek.

"Thanks," she said. "I needed that."

Gene, looking relieved, said, "How long is your layover in Chicago?"

"An hour. With the time difference, I won't be back in Cedar Rapids until midnight. Tell me to have a safe trip."

"Have a safe trip."

The Other Alice smiled. There was nothing more to say. She started to move away but stopped before she passed through the gate. She was half-turned toward Gene, and he could see that her face had taken on an expression of satisfaction.

She waved. He waved back. And then she was gone.

Driving away from the airport on Century Boulevard, Gene found his mind returning to the night he sat outside Melanie Novack's condominium in Las Vegas, watching her fondle a male admirer while he listened to a late-night talk show on the car radio. In Gene's mind, what connected that night and this moment in Los Angeles was the city of Indianapolis, the destination of the pregnant woman traveling with the Other Alice and the birthplace of the man who'd spoken on the phone to Gil Dean.

"My dad and Charlie Manson's mom, they were really close back in Indianapolis," the caller had said. "My dad's even got pictures of her from those days. Sexy pictures. I think they might be worth something."

"To who?" Gil Dean had wondered.

"Folks who like that kind of stuff."

"Dirty pictures of Charlie Manson's mother?"

"Yeah. My dad wrote to Charlie in prison and told him what he had. Charlie said he'd like to see that, but my dad's scared to go up there. He doesn't trust him, even behind bars. I told him I'd go with him. I think it would be cool to meet Charlie. What about you, Gil?"

"I think you're both a little sick."

Shortly before dawn—by then Gene was already asleep in his room at the Desert Inn—Gil Dean had received a call from a girl named Emily. She'd said she was calling from a small town in the state of Washington. Gil Dean had asked her to name the town, but she'd refused, saying, " It wouldn't be fair to Thomas."

"Thomas who?"

"I can't give out his last name, but he's Charlie Manson's son. His mom lived in the desert with Charlie right before he got caught. She gave the baby up for adoption."

"How do you know he's really Manson's son?"

"His adoptive mom told him after he found some papers from the hospital with Manson's name on the birth certificate. I'm the only person other than Thomas who knows the truth. The reason I'm calling is just to let you know that Thomas is a really sweet boy. He's everything you would want in a boyfriend or a son. Nothing like Charlie. And wherever his real mother is, if she's listening, I want you to know you did the right thing by giving him up. You gave him a second chance. And everyone deserves a second chance."

"Does he ever want to see her?"

"No. He just wants to grow up and live a normal life."

Eddie Cornell was buried at Hollywood Memorial Cemetery, just a few yards away from Carl Switzer, the lovable freckle-faced kid who played Alfalfa in the *Our Gang* comedies. Switzer, a long-time customer at Nate's News, was shot to death in 1959, in a dispute over a fifty-dollar debt.

Gene came to Eddie's funeral straight from the airport. Among the dozen or so mourners gathered around the gravesite, he recognized only Clyde Phoebe, the former stuntman and bartender at Revells, and Richie Arquette, the dectective investigating Eddie's murder and the related deaths of Jacob Reese and Chris Long. No other members of the L.A.P.D. were present.

"Not much of a send-off," Gene said to Arquette, their eyes meeting briefly when Gene found a spot next to him on the freshly mowed lawn.

"What'd you expect, a fucking honor guard?"

Clyde Phoebe glanced at Arquette. "The man always paid for his drinks, which is more than I can say for most cops."

The minister, a stiff-looking young man with a round sweaty face, raised his eyes skyward as he spoke: "Although Eddie Cornell had no family of his own, no wife or children, he spent his life protecting the loved ones of others. This community was his family. We were his flock. He was a good man and a brave man. But he was not a perfect man. None of us can make that claim."

A young woman with damp, puffy cheeks said, "When I got sick and lost my job, Eddie let me stay in my apartment rent-free for six months, until I got back on my feet. I don't care what the newspapers say about him. He was a saint to me."

"We played ball in high school," said another mourner, a stocky man with strong-looking shoulders who was approaching fifty. "Not only was he a terrific athlete, but he was a darn good friend. Don't cross him, though. That's when things could go bad. You treat him right, and he'd do the same."

A woman wearing oversized sunglasses and a pink carnation in her graying hair stepped forward and held up a color snapshot. "This is me and Eddie at the Coconut Grove," she said in a voice that was balanced between nostalgia and sadness. "It was our second date. He was just a kid back then, a kid with a good heart. He just got mixed up with the wrong crowd."

The woman pulled the carnation out of her hair and dropped it into the open grave. When she stepped back, the minister, who was staring in Gene's direction, said, "Would either of you gentlemen like to say something?"

Richie Arquette shook his head. "I think I'll pass."

"I worked on the job with Eddie," Gene said, without looking at anyone, "but I can't say that I knew him. I know he helped a lot of people, and I know he hurt a lot of people, too. He was a complex guy."

"Because he was a human being," said the minister, with an expression of complete empathy. "And may his soul rest in peace."

Richie Arquette turned to Gene as the minister began to read from the Bible. "When this is over, let's meet for a drink."

"Where?"

"Revells."

When Gene entered the bar, Richie Arquette was already seated at a table against the back wall next to the cigarette machine. No one was behind the bar, and the only other customer, a dull-looking kid wearing a Stetson-style straw hat and excruciatingly tight jeans, was leaning over the jukebox in a girlish pose. He shot Gene a quick glance, blinking his long eyelashes twice before he dropped a quarter into the slot and made his selections.

Gene walked over to Arquette and sat down across from him. "Where's Clyde?"

"In back, changing out of his suit."

"With My Eyes Wide Open I'm Dreaming" came on the jukebox, and the cowboy moved back to his bar stool with his ass arched out and his face showing an expression of casual confidence. A moment later, Clyde emerged from his office with his hair smoothly combed and a long white apron tied around his waist. A bolo tie had replaced the dark blue knit that he wore at the funeral.

Gene, breaking the silence, said, "Do you know who did it?"

"Eddie?"

"Yeah."

"We got an idea."

"It sounded like a drug thing from the story in the paper."

"With Eddie you never know. It could be anything," Arquette said with a negative expression. Then he glanced at Clyde and upped the volume in his voice. "How about a couple of Stoli's, Clyde? And make them doubles." Clyde, who was counting the cash in the register, nodded his head that he heard but didn't respond.

Gene said, "In the papers they reported that a woman rented the room at the Tropicana."

"That's right."

"How does she fit in?"

"I was going to ask *you* that question," Arquette said. "You see, fortunately for us, she put the correct license number of the rental car on her motel registration card. We traced it back to the airport, and guess what? We found it abandoned across the street from your house."

Gene blinked in embarrassment and made a cramped attempt to smile. "No kidding? That's kind of a coincidence, huh?"

Arquette was staring at Gene irritably. After a short pause, he leaned across the table and spoke in a voice that was soft but firm. "Let me get to the point. Three people have been killed in Hollywood in the last forty-eight hours. One murder for certain, and probably a murder-suicide. We don't know for sure, but we think they're related. We know that you were acquainted with two of the victims, possibly all three, and this woman whose car was found across from your house—she may be a victim, she may be a suspect—we have a hunch you can help us find her."

"It's possible. Shit, anything's possible," Gene said, and he tried to make his face look vague as he rose from his chair. "Let me get this round."

On his way over to the bar, Gene noticed the cowboy staring at him while he moved his body languidly to the slow ballad playing on the jukebox. There was a smile on his face, and Gene was careful not to smile back.

Clyde pulled a bottle of Coors from the freezer and set it down on the bar in front of the cowboy. "Gene, this is Merle, my nephew. He's come down from Tulsa to spend a little time with me."

"Nice to meet you," Gene said, but did not put his hand out.

"Merle rode bulls on the rodeo circuit."

"Till I hurt my neck back in April," said the cowboy, slowly rotating his head to work out a kink. "I got thrown off at the national finals down in Houston."

"He may act a little sweet," Clyde said, "but don't let that fool you. This boy's tough as nails."

The cowboy displayed a muscle in his forearm as he raised the bottle of Coors. "I get along with most everyone," he informed Gene, "but don't be laughin' behind my back. If you do, you can expect to be hurt. I can be one mean faggot."

Gene nodded. "Well, I'll keep that in mind."

The cowboy, all smiles, said, "Just because a man don't like to lay with a woman, it don't make him less of a man. You ever been with a man, Dean?"

"Gene."

"Have you?"

"No."

"You should try it."

The cowboy laughed over the top of his beer bottle, and Gene, feeling his body fill with disgust, took out his billfold and put ten dollars on the bar. When he brought their drinks back to the table, Arquette said, "What was that all about?"

"Clyde's nephew. He came into town yesterday."

Arquette shook his head. His face had no expression. "Just what we need in Hollywood. Another fucking queer."

The song ended on the jukebox, and there was a blot of silence before "Dream," the B-side of Patti Page's hit "You Belong to Me," began to play. Gene took a sip of vodka while he gazed around the nearly empty bar. Then, without prompting, and under the guise of openness, he started to speak in a voice that was more relaxed than he looked.

From the beginning, however, Gene made it clear that he was not going to tell Arquette everything he knew. The prior connection between Long and Eddie was a matter of record within the department, and so was Eddie's long-time association with Jack Havana and Carl Reese. And Arquette already knew that, between these three men, there developed through the years a mutual distrust.

Gene said, "When Havana died, Eddie continued working with his kid. He brought Long in too, kept him involved."

"Long gave us some good information back in the sixties."

"You mean ratting out college kids who smoked reefer and were against the war?"

"Some of them were making bombs. Don't forget about that," Arquette said, lighting a cigarette. After he took two quick puffs, he put it gently in the ashtray. "You went to high school with Larry Havana, right?"

"Yeah. I've known him since we were kids."

"Were you gonna leave that out of your story?"

"I didn't think it was relevant."

"It could be," Arquette said, letting a short silence develop. "Keep going."

As Gene continued with his story—a story he told slowly but convincingly—Arquette nodded his head in avid concentration. A crooked cop (Eddie), a snitch (Long), and the mob (Havana, Reese) all working together, that made perfect sense. But when Gene introduced his brother into the already complex narrative, mentioning along the way that Ray's ex-wife Sandra did time in the Frontera Women's Prison, where she became friendly with Susan Atkins, Arquette's eyes started to glaze over, as if he were listening to a foreign language.

"When she got out," Gene said, "Eddie rented her an apartment in his building on Larrabee."

"This Sandra, she's not the chick we're looking for?"

"No, Sandra's dead. Like Alice, my fiancée. But they're both part of this story."

Arquette frowned and rubbed his eyes. "I'm lost."

"I'm gonna connect the dots for you, Richie. I promise."

"This is not about drugs, is it?"

"No."

"What's it about."

"Love. It's about love and death. And it's about Charles Manson."

"Manson?" Arquette's face lit up with anger. "Don't fuck with me, Gene."

"Charlie knew all the players: Havana from the fifties, Long from the street, and he was in Folsom with Reese. Eddie was the go-between. They all wanted something Charlie had—or said he had."

"And the chick worked for Charlie."

"So to speak."

Gene, ignoring the doubt in Arquette's face, returned to his story, telling it faster now as he backtracked to Alice's funeral in Cedar Rapids and the small wake that followed at her childhood home, where, among the journals and school papers that he brought back to Los Angeles, he found a packet of letters sent to her by a girl from the same hometown.

"Her name was Alice," Gene said, "the same as my fiancée."

"The Alice who registered at the Tropicana Motel under the name Linda Cooper. The Alice we want to speak to."

"She can't help you. You don't need to speak to her. That's why I'm telling you everything."

"Everything. I thought you said—"

"Everything you need to know."

It took Gene another thirty minutes to finish his story, and he told it in a voice that was almost intimate, adroitly weaving together all the intricate threads and unrecoverable moments into some kind of discernible logic, while the cowboy fed quarters into the jukebox, playing "Tennessee Waltz" seven times straight.

When Gene was done, Arquette said, still looking at him suspiciously, "You don't really expect me to believe you?"

"That's up to you, Richie."

"This chick from your fiancée's past, a former member of the Manson family, comes out to L.A. to broker—"

"The film of the Tate killings. That's right."

"Which you say was bogus, but you burned in the desert anyway."

"Correct."

"And for this three people are dead."

"But not sorely missed or mourned."

"True," Arquette muttered, and he very slowly shook his head. Then he finished his drink and glanced down at the luminous dial on his wristwatch. "So why're you protecting this broad, this . . . other Alice?"

"Because I said I would. If I thought she was guilty of something, it would be a different story."

"What's in it for you?"

"Someone who I loved died. I met someone who knew her before I did. She told me things I didn't know, and now I love her more. Simple as that."

Arquette looked at Gene, who met his shrewd gaze with something unspoken in his eyes. A moment later the front door opened, and a rather large, soft-looking woman stepped inside Revells carrying a big straw purse. She was wearing a peach-colored polyester pantsuit and gold sandals, and her soft, fluffy, gray hair was highlighted with blond streaks.

Clyde, grinning a good-time smile, said, "Well, look who's here. Merle, I want you to meet an old friend of mine. Peanut, this is Merle, my nephew from Tulsa."

"Pleased to meet you," said the cowboy, bowing slightly as the woman put her purse on the bar and took the stool next to him. "Peanut. That's a cute name."

"Well, I'm glad you like it," said the woman, and she signaled Clyde by holding up her pinkie. "Give me a Chivas in a brandy glass. Or should I say the usual."

The woman—her name was Barbara Jean Fowler—had met Clyde back in 1964, while they were both in Texas filming *Baby, the Rain Must Fall,* a contemporary western starring Steve McQueen, Lee Remick, and Don Murray. Barbara Jean was the script supervisor, and Clyde had been hired to choreograph two elaborate fight scenes that took place in a roadhouse, neither of which ended up in the final cut.

"Lee Remick was on a diet," Clyde told his nephew. "During the day all she would eat were peanuts, and Barbara Jean was put in charge of her supply. Drove McQueen crazy, because she took a handful after each take and her breath smelled awful."

Barbara Jean said, "Don Murray started calling me 'Barbara Jean the Peanut Queen,' and the crew picked up on it, eventually shortening it to just 'Peanut.'"

Gene told Arquette that he'd seen *Baby, the Rain Must Fall* when it was first released. Although the acting was fine, and he'd been moved by the story—McQueen played a trouble-prone rockabilly singer reunited with his wife and daughter after serving time in prison—he'd felt the musical numbers didn't ring true.

"You could tell he wasn't playing guitar, and he was lip-synching badly to someone else's voice. I didn't buy it."

Arquette said, "I liked him best in *The Great Escape* and that one about the cardplayers."

"*The Cincinnati Kid.*"

"That's the one."

As he glanced toward the bar, it crossed Gene's mind that Melanie Novack's mother, like Barbara Jean, had been a script supervisor. This fact alone did not seem significant, until he coupled it with his knowledge of Melanie's past and her friendship with Bobby Fuller.

Still looking away from Arquette, Gene said, "Bobby Fuller was from Texas. A little town called Goose Neck."

"Bobby who?"

"Fuller. He sang rockabilly in the movies, too."

"With McQueen?"

"In another movie, a stupid movie with Nancy Sinatra. But it came out around the same time. He died a year later, not far from here. You probably don't remember the case."

"I don't."

"Yeah. Most people have forgotten about it," Gene said. "But I haven't."

"What are you getting at?"

Gene hesitated for a moment, thinking he might offer an explanation. Then he shook his head. "Nothing. Forget I brought it up."

Arquette watched Gene for a while with eyes that were both remote and slightly restive. "I may want to speak to you again," he said, his gaze going back to his watch. "So don't leave town."

"I don't plan to."

After Arquette rose to his feet and walked slowly outside through the rear door, Clyde bought a round of drinks on the house. Then he opened the register and gave his nephew several quarters. "Play F-2, G-3, and A-9."

"Play D-11, too," Barbara Jean said, winking at Clyde. "You remember that one?"

"'Hush . . . Hush, Sweet Charlotte.'"

"Came out when we were on location," Barbara Jean said. She was speaking to the cowboy, who was over by the jukebox, but Gene knew she wanted him to hear this story too. "Clyde and I had a little fling on that show. Lasted for what—about a week?"

"About that."

"Can I tell them about your room at the hotel?"

Clyde took a cigarette from his shirt pocket and lit it with the gold lighter his nephew left on the bar. "Can I stop you?"

"Not really," Barbara Jean said, her eyes bright with nostalgia, concealing whatever sadness she might be feeling. "He had pictures of her all over the place: on the bureau, on the nightstand by the bed, taped to the mirror in the bathroom. It was a regular shrine to Patti Page."

"Tell him about the phonograph," Clyde urged her, clearly enjoying this trip back into his past. "Don't forget about that."

"That's right. He had his own record player up in the room," Barbara Jean said, as the first song came on the jukebox, "Too Young to Go Steady." "He had all her records in two big stacks. I mean, I liked her voice, don't get me wrong, and the whole setup was romantic and turned me on, but it was kind of strange, too," she said, glancing in Gene's direction. "Don't you think?"

"I don't know," Gene said. "I wasn't there."

"Uncle Clyde's a strange man. In fact the whole Phoebe clan is sort of strange, including me," said the cowboy, circling lazily back to his stool with his arms extended, pretending to dance the fox-trot with an imaginary partner. "Could I interest anyone in a dance? How about you, Miss Peanut Queen?"

Barbara Jean stood up. "I'd be delighted," she said in a sophisticated way, and her arms went around the cowboy's neck. "Clyde, are you watching?"

"Yes, I am."

"Do you remember dancing with me up in your room?"

"Yes, I do."

"Both of us a little drunk, holding each other close."

"I held you close. Yes, I did," Clyde said shyly, affectionately. "I never held Patti that close. Never even kissed her."

"Well, she missed out," said the cowboy, his hands on Barbara Jean's robust hips, then working their way over her ass. "That's all I can say. She plumb missed out."

Gene left Revells after listening to the opening bars of "Hush . . . Hush, Sweet Charlotte," feeling both isolated and helpless, as if every effort he might make to comprehend the recent events of his life would inevitably be in vain. Across the street, a woman with deep-set eyes and a face of assumed hardness stood on the sidewalk outside the House of Love. Behind her, in the semidarkness of the open doorway, was the bouncer, a small, short-limbed man wearing a white jumpsuit and white suede loafers with gold buckles. This was Nick, the jittery guy with the receding chin who Gene had first encountered in the offices of Big City Music, the company owned by Herb Stelzner, and later at the Pony Express, the poker club on Fremont Street in North Las Vegas.

Gene stopped in front of the doorway and stared at Nick, his expression conveying an impression of amiability. "I want to speak to Larry Havana," he said. "Tell him Gene Burk's outside."

"I know who you are," Nick said.

"Likewise."

"Larry's on vacation," said the woman standing next to Nick, and Gene noticed a trace of gray in her large bright blue eyes.

"When's he coming back?"

"That's hard to say," Nick said, his face all at once taking on a crafty expression. "Try back in a couple of weeks."

The woman was smiling at Gene, who smiled back, although inside he felt irritated and confused. She said, "Nick told me who you were while you were crossing the street. He said you used to be a cop, and now you're sticking your nose in places where it doesn't belong."

"His father owned the newsstand that used to be on this corner. Nate's News. Then he sold it to Larry's father. Jack tore it down and built the House of Love."

Gene said, "I thought you worked for Herb Stelzner."

"I work for a lot of people," Nick said, and now there was something volatile in his face. "Now why don't you move along. When Larry comes back, I'll tell him you dropped by."

Gene's expression looked outwardly friendly, but the woman, feeling something like hostility in the air, took a step backward, creating an open space between the two men.

Gene said, " Maybe I want to come inside."

"I don't think so," Nick said. "I think you should just leave."

"I heard about the show you put on. I'd like to see it."

The woman turned and looked at Nick. "What show?" she asked crossly. "What's he talking about?"

Nick looked at Gene in a way that suggested he was rapidly running out of patience. A second woman, slender and nondescript, emerged from the interior of the House of Love. She was wearing a red beret tilted at a rakish angle and a red knitted dress that clung to her boyish hips.

"I got a problem in room six," she told Nick. "Guy wasn't satisfied with the massage."

Nick made a masturbatory motion with his fist. "Did he get a happy ending?"

"I gave him two."

"Two squirts. Then he should be satisfied."

"Men are such pigs," the second woman said, and when she glanced at Gene, he saw only disapproval in her face. "What's this one looking for?"

"He's looking for Larry. Joyce told him he was on vacation. Now he wants to come inside."

"He mentioned a show he wants to see," said the first woman.

"A show? We do lots of shows. Describe it," said the second woman.

Before Gene could reply, a large black limosuine turned the corner and rolled to a stop in front of the House of Love. The chauffeur, his movements both robotic and restrained, slowly walked around the car and opened the rear door. The man who stepped out was in his late middle age, inconspicuously dressed, with an important face and a thin gray mustache that was neatly trimmed.

Nick said, "Good evening, Mr. Richards."

"Good evening, Nick."

"Joyce, why don't you and Rita take Mr. Richards into my office. I'll be there in a minute."

When Gene and Nick were alone on the sidewalk, Nick said, "Don't cause any trouble, Burk. Go home."

Gene said, "Larry and I go way back. If he was here, he'd let me in."

"Maybe. But he's not here. I am."

"And you're running things?"

"For now."

"The last time I was here," Gene told Nick, "a woman told me never to come back."

"She was probably right."

"I think she was. And I think this was a better corner when my dad owned it."

"That's a matter of opinion," Nick said, repressing any hostility as he glanced over his shoulder. "Look, I gotta take care of some business, so—"

"Don't worry about me," Gene said, already thinking of the profound relief he would feel once this long day was over and he was finally home. "I'm on my way."

Gene turned away and started up the street. There was more he wanted to say, but he knew it no longer mattered if he said the words out loud. What mattered now was that his relentless, single-minded search was about to end, that his heart's sorrow would finally be released, and that once again he could reach out to the world. Inside his head, a voice said softly, *You're almost there, Gene. You're feeling everything you need to feel.*

"That's it. I'm done. No more collecting," Gene told his brother the following morning, after he walked inside with the *L.A. Times* and picked up the ringing phone. "I boxed up all my records and put them in the garage."

"I think that's a smart move."

"Glad you approve."

"Give you more time for your business."

"Fuck the business. I'm gonna pack that in too."

"Then what?"

Gene hesitated for a few moments. "I don't know."

"Then I'd think it over."

"I'm not sure I asked for your advice."

"It was more like a suggestion."

"Work on your own life, Ray."

"I have been. I've been sober for thirty days," Ray said, and then he told Gene he was flying in on Friday. "I'll call you when I get to my hotel."

Gene, who was standing in the hallway, gave the phone a funny look when the line went dead. Feeling an inexplicable anxiety, he walked back into the living room and stretched out on the sofa. He sat up in a few moments and put his head in his hands, allowing his mind to push him slowly back to the conversation he'd had the day before with Richie Arquette. Gene had tried to question him on the deaths of Long and Reese, but he was reluctant to reveal any details.

"You said it was a murder-suicide."

"Yeah, I did. But I probably should've kept quiet about that, too."

Arquette did tell Gene that Jacob Reese had been shot three times, twice in the heart and once through the right eye. The gun he carried was still in the waistband of his jeans. Chris Long's body was on the floor in the kitchen. A syringe filled with blood was stuck in his neck. His right hand gripped the phone, and there was a woman on the other end screaming his name over and over: *"Chris! Chris!"*

But when the first cop on the scene picked up the receiver and asked the woman to identify herself, she quickly hung up.

Gene said, "Who do you think it was?"

"Someone who cared about him, but not enough to get involved."

Twenty-three

Alice Is Singing

Dear Alice:

*Okay, so here's the deal. I'm writing you from the Blue Diamond Café on
Interstate 80, just east of Flagstaff, New Mexico. I got dropped off here by
Jimmy, this Mexican dude with beautiful blue eyes who picked me up this
morning in Kingman, Arizona.*

*Because it's really hot today, Jimmy drove with his shirt off, and beads
of sweat ran down his neck and into the hairs on his chest, sparkling like little
jewels. He was really sexy, and I would've fucked him in the back of his truck
if he'd asked, but he was married and faithful to his wife, or so he said.*

*Right before he dropped me off, he took out his wallet and showed me a
picture of his four-year-old son. When I started to cry, he asked me what was
wrong, but I couldn't tell him, and I'm not sure I can tell you, either. Maybe I
can, but first I want to make a list of my five all-time favorite rock-and-roll
records. That's the reason I asked the waitress for a pencil and paper in the
first place. I had no idea that I was going to write you a letter.*

*(1) "All I Have to Do Is Dream" by the Everly Brothers. This was the
first record I ever bought with money I saved up from my allowance. When I got
home, I played it ten straight times. Years later I met Don Everly in Los
Angeles at the Whisky a Go Go. He was really sweet, and even though it
wasn't cool, I asked him for his autograph.*

*(2) "Lonely Teardrops" by Jackie Wilson. This record came out about the
same time as the Everly Brothers song, but my dad wouldn't let me buy the 45
when he saw Jackie's picture on the sleeve. He hated black people. He and
Charlie had that in common.*

(3) *"Don't Think Twice It's Alright" by Bob Dylan. This is more folk than rock and roll, but it's the way I lived my life—without thinking twice. There's a lot of stuff I wish I could do over, but I can't. I used to be bitter, depressed, insecure, and lonely. I looked creepy and acted weird. I couldn't see the good in the world. Now I can laugh in the movies, and I can cry too. I have dreams and hopes. I guess I simply want to go on living.*

(4) *"I Can See For Miles" by the Who. That's what happened when I left Cedar Rapids in 1965. The wind was blowing hard and I was definitely scared, but I could see for miles in every direction. It was a brand new beginning and the music made me feel free. And now where am I? I'm still free. Are you?*

(5) *"Mother and Child Reunion" by Simon and Garfunkel. This was the reason I was crying when I got out of Jimmy Santiago's truck. I was thinking about a boy—the son of my blood—who would celebrate his third birthday in a few days, on May 16. He was born on a clear spring night in the desert. And guess what? Even though he may be the only thing I've ever truly loved in my life, I don't even know his name.*

Goodbye,
Alice

Twenty-four

The Shadow

and the Real

On the day that Gene spoke to Deputy District Attorney Ted Babcock in his windowless downtown office, in a meeting that was arranged by Richie Arquette, who was trying to convince the D.A. to officially open the investigation into the death of Bobby Fuller, Larry Havana was arrested and charged with extortion, sexual battery, loan-sharking, and six counts of federal income tax evasion. During the closed-door hearing that followed his arrest, prosecutors also presented evidence linking him to the deaths of Chris Long and Jacob Reese. Bail was denied and, over his lawyer's objections, Havana was remanded to the L.A. County Jail until his appeal could be heard the following week. At noon on this same day, Gene learned that Melanie Novack had moved back to Los Angeles, and that she and his brother Ray had run into each other at a late-night Alcoholics Anonymous meeting in Hollywood.

"Actually, we spoke first a couple of weeks ago," Ray told Gene when they met for lunch in the Columbia Pictures commissary. *The Last Hope,* the movie based on Ray's screenplay, was already into its third week of production, and that day's scenes were being filmed on a nearby sound stage. "She said she almost fell off her chair when she heard me share. She couldn't believe our voices sounded so much alike. At the break she came over and introduced herself. Pretty weird, huh?"

Gene nodded as he leaned back in his chair a little, trying to look unimpressed when he saw Dustin Hoffman enter the commissary with Lily Tomlin and another, prettier woman who was wearing a black silk cocktail dress and heavy heart-shaped earrings. "So, have you two been hanging out?"

"A little. We go for coffee after meetings, that kind of thing. I invited her out to the set last week. We're just sobriety buddies," Ray said, and Gene continued to nod silently. "Look, she already told me you guys fucked, so it's no big deal. Anyway, I asked her to come with me on Saturday, if it's cool with you."

"Sure," Gene said calmly, his expression unmoved, and there was an uneasy silence. Saturday was their father's birthday, and Gene had arranged to take him out to dinner at Musso-Frank. Louie, who was also in town working on his television pilot, agreed to join them. "How come she came back to Los Angeles?"

"She said she was sick of Vegas, plus she wants to finish up her degree at U.C.L.A. She's really a neat chick," Ray said, and then added casually, almost as an afterthought: "That Bobby Fuller story would make a dynamite movie."

"No shit, Ray. I've been telling you that for years."

Ray shrugged. "Hey, what can I say? I didn't get it."

"Because you were always fucking stoned out of your mind on drugs and alcohol."

"Maybe. But when you get the story firsthand, from someone who actually knew him, it's different than reading a bunch of old newspaper articles."

Gene knew that his face couldn't hide the anger that was making his heart pound. "So what're you gonna do? Collaborate with her?"

"I thought we could all work on it together."

"We?"

"The three of us," Ray said. "I'll write it. You two can be part of the production team—associate producers or something. I don't know. It's just an idea. Fuck, who knows, if Louie starts to happen maybe he could star in it. He'd be the right age in a couple of years."

Gene reminded his brother that they had gone down this road before. "And not just with the Bobby Fuller story," he said. "How about the 'Hillside Strangler' case that you got so excited about. And remember Elizabeth Short?"

"Elizabeth who?"

"Come on, Gene! Elizabeth Short! The Black Dahlia murder in 1947. The most famous unsolved case in L.A. history."

"Oh, yeah. Okay. Right."

"I set you up with Lee Ahern, the last detective to work the case, and what happened? You met him at the Cock and Bull, got drunk, punched out some agent at the bar, and got eighty-sixed."

"It's different now," Ray said with recognizable pride. "I'm not drinking."

"For what? Seven weeks."

"Fuck you, man. It's a start."

"You're right. You're doing a good job," Gene concurred, nodding seriously, his gaze skimming over Ray's face. A moment later, their waitress came by and left their check on the table. "By the way, Dustin Hoffman's sitting behind you."

"I know. I saw him walk in. So did you, but you were too cool to say anything."

"He went to L.A. High," Gene said, ignoring his brother's lame attempt to put him down. "He and Eddie Cornell graduated in the same year."

Ray had to think for a moment. "You mean the detective who was shot to death."

"That's right. The same Eddie Cornell who covered up Bobby Fuller's murder."

"Oh really?" Ray said. His eyes looked amused. "You know this for a fact?"

"Yeah."

"Then you probably know who killed him."

"Pretty much."

Outside, after Ray paid the check and they were walking slowly toward the parking lot, Gene told his brother the same story he'd told Ted Babcock earlier that morning, before the haze had disappeared from the sky. And when he was done, Ray stopped walking and stared vaguely off at the Hollywood Hills.

"So?" Gene said. "What do you think?"

"Sinatra?"

"Yeah. But nobody's gonna believe it."

Especially Ted Babcock, who said at their meeting, after shifting nervously in his chair, "Let me get this straight. Nancy Sinatra meets Fuller on the set of this movie. They hit it off, start to go out, and Frank objects. He passes the word to Fuller's manager—"

"Herb Stelzner."

"—who Fuller ignores. So Frank has him whacked. Is that your theory?"

"That's not what Gene said," said Richie Arquette, who was also at the meeting. "He said the mob was already pissed off at Bobby. He wanted to break his contract with Stelzner."

"Stelzner owed Havana money. At least fifty grand," Gene said. "Stelzner, Havana, Carl Reese, they were all linked together in various businesses, most of them illegal, and they all had one thing in common. They wanted Frank to be happy. Because if he wasn't happy, he might pick up the phone and call his buddy Sam Giancana in Chicago, and then the shit-rain would start falling."

"So, you don't think anyone specifically ordered the killing?" Babcock asked Gene. "It just sort of . . . developed?"

Gene said, "There was no way it was professionally planned. Too messy. I mean, who kills himself by swallowing gasoline?"

"The word gets around that Frank's unhappy. Some guys, some low-level hoods trying to make their bones, they take Fuller out. Is that what you're saying?" Babcock asked Gene. "And because there were some people in the department that were on the take, they helped cover it up. 'They' meaning Eddie Cornell."

"That's it," Gene said. "More or less."

"Babcock didn't buy it," Gene said. He and Ray were standing in the parking lot next to Alice's red Honda convertible. It was the first time Gene had driven her car since her death. "Unless I could supply eyewitnesses or forensic evidence, he was not gonna lay his ass on the line. He said you'd have to be nuts to go after Sinatra, especially in this town."

Gene unlocked the Honda but made no move to get inside. "You remember the night we saw Bobby Fuller live?"

Ray nodded.

"I was still a cop, and you were drunk on your ass. I had to stop you from going over to Nancy's table. You still had the hots for her. Still do, for all I know."

"No." Ray shook his head. "I think I'm over that."

"But twenty years later, here we are, still talking about her."

"*You're* talking about her, Gene."

Gene unlocked the Honda and got behind the wheel. "High school," he said heavily, almost in a final tone. "Everything always seems to go back to high school."

Ray lingered by the car as Gene started the engine and lowered the convertible top. Before his brother drove out of the lot, Ray asked if he'd settled his lawsuit with the airline.

"Yeah." Gene took the last Marlboro out of his pack and lit it. "That's all over."

"How much?"

"A bundle."

"Did they—"

"Did they send me a copy of the cockpit transcript?" Gene finished the question, and Ray nodded. "I should get it in a couple of days." Gene put the car in gear but didn't move forward. He had another thought. "In A.A. you do this thing called an inventory, right?"

"It's called a fifth step."

"Where you tell someone your deepest darkest secrets, things that you've done that you said you would take to the grave. You haven't done that yet, have you?"

"No."

"But Melanie has."

"Probably. Why?"

Gene said nothing. His eyes slid sideways, away from Ray's face, focusing instead on the tall, sad-looking palm tree that towered over the front gate of the studio. "She was home the night Bobby was killed. I think she knows more than she told me," Gene said. "You just don't go from typing screenplays in Hollywood to working in a Vegas casino."

"She got sober and she wanted to change her life. I don't think there's some big mystery here," Ray said. "She's been pretty fuckin' open with me. Anyway, for this movie to work—"

"This is not a movie," Gene countered angrily, interrupting his brother but still avoiding his face. "We're talking about a murder."

"No it's not, Gene. It's a suicide that you've turned into some nutty crusade. If you think you've figured it out, congratulations. Just get on with your life."

Gene stubbed out his cigarette in the ashtray and glanced up at his brother, giving him a look of weary disgust. "We probably shouldn't work together, Ray."

His brother nodded. "You know something?" Ray said. "You're right. I'm sorry I brought it up."

"I mean, why would I want to spend my time around a bunch of pretentious Hollywood assholes."

"Thanks."

"Excluding you, of course." Gene laughed, but the laugh sounded meaningless. "I'll see you Saturday."

"Musso's at seven, right?"

"Right."

"And it's okay if I bring Melanie?"

"Hey," Gene said, assuming a too-cool-to-care tone. "I'm not your mother, Ray. I'm just your older brother."

After shooting wrapped for the day on *The Last Hope,* Ray joined the cinematographer and his camera crew for drinks and dinner at The Lucky Seven, a neighborhood bar and grill on Vine Street, just around the corner from the studio. But as soon as he walked inside and lit a cigarette, his desire for alcohol became so intense that he instantly spun around and walked outside. His voice, when he called Melanie from a pay phone on the corner, sounded desperate, and she urged him to meet her at an A.A. meeting that night.

"Where?"

"The Methodist Church on Mansfield and Melrose. At eight o'clock."

"I'll be there."

"I'm sober by the grace of God and the principles of Alcoholics Anonymous. And I'm a walking miracle," Melanie said to the alcoholics assembled in front of her, around sixty people altogether, equally divided between men and women, including some old-timers with over thirty years of sobriety. "By all rights I should be dead."

For the next forty-five minutes, as Melanie told her story—which was the very history of her heart—Ray, who came in a few minutes after the meeting had started, could feel something change in that overheated room. It was as if this personal confession, offered without rage or bitterness or self-disgust, released into that empathetic space a message of hope that embraced everyone present, cleansing them—all of them—with its honesty.

She spoke about growing up in Hollywood—"I went to grammar school six blocks from here," she said in a voice that was more than a little ironic—with a single mother who was ruled by her desires and always carried a bottle of Jack Daniel's in her purse. Melanie said she was already an alcoholic when she dropped out of high school, but her drinking and drug use started much earlier.

"When I was eleven, to be exact. At the time my mom was working at Paramount," Melanie said. "She was young and pretty, and she always had friends around that smoked weed. After parties I'd get up the next morning and find all those half-smoked joints, which I lit up when my mom wasn't around. Oh yeah, I forgot," she said, her voice cracking a little. "I got raped by one of my mother's boyfriends when I was thirteen."

He worked in the prop department at Warner Brothers, and, halfway through her sixth year of sobriety, Melanie contacted him at the studio. It had been fifteen years since the rape took place, and she was not surprised that he didn't remember her name—or if she was, she pretended not to be. When he asked her why she was calling, she said it was a private matter, one that she would feel more comfortable discussing face-to-face.

"He agreed to meet that afternoon at Norm's, this coffee shop in Burbank. He only vaguely remembered my mom," Melanie told her audience. "He said they probably only dated for a couple of weeks. When I asked him if he remembered me, he just shrugged a little and shook his head, without looking the least bit guilty. He really *didn't* remember me, because he was in a blackout when it happened, when he saw me naked and encouraged himself. 'That's what happens when I drink,' he told me."

And then he started to cry, Melanie said, a sobbing that was almost astonishing in its desperation, repentant tears that had been postponed for years, glittering on his cheeks before they splashed into his coffee. When he was through and his chest stopped heaving, she reached across the table and held both his freckled hands. She stared into his eyes—eyes that were permanently marked with pain and shame—and she said that she forgave him.

"That's when he told me he was sober," Melanie said, and inside that room Ray could hear everyone singing silent hallelujahs. "He'd been in Alcoholics Anonymous for four years."

When Melanie came out of the meeting, she saw Ray sitting on the fender of his rented red Mustang, staring at her with an expression that was slightly out of control. She said, moving in his direction, "I saw you come in late."

"Yeah. I had a little trouble finding the address."

"Oh."

"But I made it for your pitch. It was really awesome."

"Thanks."

"I don't know if I could be that honest in front of sixty strangers."

"Sure you could," Melanie said, "if your life depended on it."

"Too bad Gene couldn't hear your story."

Melanie shook her head. "Gene doesn't have a problem with alcohol, so he doesn't belong here. You belong here, Ray."

Ray felt himself sweating as he slid off the fender and stood in front of Melanie without meeting her eyes. He told her that he'd lied to her. "I was late to the meeting because I walked back inside The Lucky Seven after I spoke with you."

"I know," Melanie said. "I can smell the scotch on your breath."

Ray nodded. He was looking down at his shoes. "You want to get some coffee?"

"I can't, Ray. I'm sorry. I have an early class tomorrow."

"What about Saturday? Are we still on?"

Melanie reached in her purse for her car keys. As she was preparing to move away, she looked at Ray with a kind of sadness. Then she said, "I don't think that would be such a good idea."

■

Nathan Burk looked nervous, his head twisting from left to right as he stood on the sidewalk outside his house, watching for Gene's car. It was not yet dark and still warm, but there were no children playing on the street, nor any other signs of neighborhood life, except for a dog's bark and the steady chirp of a cricket from someplace nearby.

Back in 1947, when they first moved in, this was a precious time of day for his two boys—that hour before dinner when they were done with their homework and it was still light enough to ride their bikes or shoot baskets in their narrow driveway.

Dad. He could hear Gene's voice calling out to him from his shadowed past. *Come outside and watch.*

As he brought forth this gentle reminiscence, Nathan Burk was standing in a small patch of sunshine, half-expecting to hear the rattle of dishes inside his house, the sound of his wife setting the table for dinner. And if he turned around, he wanted her to be there in the kitchen window, gaily smiling, waving: *Nathan, dinner's ready, sweetheart. Call the boys.*

But alone in the reality of this lifeless street, his back to his horribly empty house, Nathan Burk put his hand into his pocket, and his fingers found the folded letter he'd received in the mail that morning, a letter he'd read and reread several times, a letter that he told himself he would not share with his two sons, but that he carried with him nonetheless, just in case he relinquished his timid resolve.

Minutes later, when Gene pulled in front of the house, he was surprised to see his father standing by the curb, staring into the oncoming darkness with a weird emptiness in his eyes. And throughout the drive over to Musso-Frank, he sat with his lips slightly parted, surrounding himself in a painful, almost self-diminishing silence that Gene was barely able to penetrate.

"Dad?"

"Hmm."

"Happy birthday."

"Thank you."

Silence.

"Should be fun, huh?"

"What's that?"

"Seeing Louie and Ray. The four of us having dinner together. It's been a couple of years."

Silence.

"Dad? Are you okay?"

"Yes."

"You sure? You're not usually this quiet."

Several more seconds passed in silence. Then Nathan Burk turned his head and looked at his son with a faint smile on his face. "When I was napping this afternoon, I heard the Good Humor truck come down the street, and when I woke up I was sure you guys were in the house. You and Ray. You used to swipe change from my coat to buy ice cream when I was asleep. Don't think I didn't know it. I counted my change."

"You did? Really?"

"Of course I did," said Nathan Burk, and then his smile became distant, remote. "I think about stuff like that a lot lately."

"You mean, the past?"

"Yes."

"So do I."

* * *

"Good evening, Mr. Burk. What a nice surprise," said the elderly maitre d', shaking Nathan Burk's hand as he stepped inside Musso-Frank. "We've missed you. You've been away much too long."

"I don't drive anymore, Jimmy. I can't get up here unless someone brings me. You know my son, Gene?"

The maitre d' nodded his head. "Of course. Since he was a boy," he said, glancing at Gene with a reserved smile. "Will there just be the two of you?"

"No. My other son, Ray, is supposed to meet us here with my grandson. Ray's a writer," Nathan Burk said proudly. "As we speak, a movie he wrote is shooting at Columbia Pictures. And his son, Louie, is a very fine young actor."

"I made a reservation for seven o'clock," Gene said, as his eyes discreetly surveyed the restaurant. At this early hour the counter was only half-filled, and there were several unoccupied tables in the center of the room. "I guess we're the first."

After he exchanged a look with a waiter hovering nearby, the maitre d' pulled Gene aside, out of his father's range of hearing. "Didn't we have a problem the last time you were here?"

"That was my brother. But he doesn't drink anymore. He'll be fine tonight."

"I'm sorry," the maitre d' said, shaking his head, his face utterly unsympathetic, "but I can't allow him to be seated."

"It's my dad's birthday. Nothing's going to happen," Gene said in a reassuring voice. Then he took a twenty-dollar bill out of his wallet and pressed it into the maitre d's palm. "I promise."

The maitre d' did not look convinced as he pocketed the twenty. Nathan Burk, who had been standing patiently a few steps away, moved forward. "What's going on? What's wrong?"

"Nothing," Gene said. "I was just deciding where we should sit." He pointed to an empty booth against the wall opposite the bar. "How about over there?"

*   *   *

Once they were seated, Nathan Burk's spirits seemed to rise, and even before their drinks arrived he began speaking in a lively tone, telling Gene about the first time he'd had dinner at Musso-Frank. "We'd been in Los Angeles no more than two weeks," he said. "You were six, and your brother had just turned four. We were staying at the Hotel Knickerbocker over on Ivar. It was a fancy hotel back in those days. George Raft was staying there, and I once saw Humphrey Bogart drinking in the bar. Your mother had a crush on George Raft. She went for that type," he said, frowning as he stared down at the table top, and, for a moment, it appeared that his cheerfulness was slipping away. Then, abruptly, he looked up and smiled, the animation returning to his face as he laid a hand on Gene's arm. "Your mom and I had some good times together."

"I know."

"The night we ate here we left the Knickerbocker and walked up Hollywood Boulevard holding hands, like we were newlyweds. Earlier that day I'd closed the deal on the newsstand and we wanted to celebrate. I loved this place as soon as I walked in. The dark wood, the leather booths, the gloomy-gus waiters, it was like Dempsey's or Toots Shor's, the joints I liked in New York. Movie stars, mob guys, writers, they all came in here."

"Does it still look the same?"

"Exactly. The lighting, the fixtures, the waiters' red jackets, everything but the prices. That night we each had a Caesar salad and the prime rib. Rare. Blood rare for your mother or she'd send it back. I think the bill was something like eighteen dollars for two, including drinks and the tip. Afterwards we walked up to C.C. Brown's for a hot fudge sundae. When we got back to the hotel, you guys were asleep. The radio was on, and the maid who was baby-sitting was reading a book, a mystery by Raymond Chandler. I remember that because Chandler used to come by the newsstand when he was working in Hollywood. I remember everything that happened that night."

Louie walked into Musso's around seven-thirty, and right away two women at the bar, both blond and exceedingly thin, turned and followed him with their eyes as he crossed the room. He was handsome, almost striking-looking, dressed like an English rocker in black satin jeans, a black silk shirt, and shiny black boots.

"Look at him," Nathan Burk said to Gene as Louie approached the booth, walking with an easy gait that disguised his nervous energy. "He reminds me of a young Richard Widmark."

"Hey, I'm sorry I'm late," Louie said, and Gene stood up. They exchanged a quick hug that seemed strained on both sides, before Louie slid into the booth next to his grandfather. "I spoke to my dad. He's still at the studio. He said to order and he'd catch up."

Nathan Burk shook his head, and the smile on his lips seemed half-irritated, half-forgiving. "Busy, busy, busy, that's your father. How long has he been in town? Over a month? And he comes to the house one time."

"He's in the middle of a movie. It gets crazy," Louie said.

Gene said, "How did he sound?"

Louie looked at Gene, eyeing him calmly for a few moments before he answered. "He sounded fine."

"What I meant was, did he—"

"I know what you meant, Gene. You meant, did he sound sober. I heard the question, and I said he sounded fine."

Gene smiled, a little bit condescendingly. "Relax, Louie."

"I am relaxed. You're the one—"

"All right! All right! That's enough," Nathan Burk said, giving Gene a sharp side-glance. "You shouldn't be talking behind your brother's back."

"I wasn't talking behind his back. I was just asking Louie, the new James Dean over there—"

"Hey, fuck you, Gene."

"Uncle Gene, to you."

Nathan Burk was glowering, his hands fisted on the tablecloth. "Stop! There will be no more arguing at this table. And no more cursing. Or I will leave and take a taxi home. Do you hear me?"

Louie nodded, hanging his head. "I'm sorry, Grandpa."

"Same here," Gene said, his face expressing remorse as he slumped back against the booth.

"All right. Good. That's settled," Nathan Burk said, looking at both of them. "Let's move on. Louie, tell us about your television show. When does it go on the air?"

"In September."

Nathan Burk smiled. "I guess that means in two months I'm going to have a celebrity for a grandson."

"I'm not interested in being a celebrity."

"Why not? What's wrong with being a celebrity?"

Louie leaned scross the table. "Grandpa, I just got lucky. Okay? I'm just a twenty-year-old kid that got a lucky break. And now I get to be on TV. It's not a big deal."

"Sure it is."

"No, it isn't," Louie said, shaking his head a little wildly. "It's all a bunch of hype. Anyway, the show will probably be canceled after one season like most shows. I just want to learn stuff. I want to learn to be a good actor."

"Of course you do," Nathan Burk said, taking in his grandson's determined expression. "But there's no reason you can't be a celebrity and a fine actor. Look at Henry Fonda. Or Gregory Peck. Both celebrities and Academy Award winners."

"Grandpa's just proud of you," Gene said, and then more emphatically: "So am I."

"And Sandra, your mother, she would've been proud of you, too," Nathan Burk said, and because Louie has his head turned away, no one at the table saw his mouth tremble or the tears that shimmered in his eyes.

Ray arrived at the restaurant over an hour late. As he crossed the room with his eyes fixed straight ahead, Gene noticed that the rigidity of his brother's body was counterbalanced by the expression on his face of exaggerated self-confidence—a self-confidence, Gene suspected, that was drawn from several ounces of alcohol, and could quickly turn aggressive or mean.

"Well, better late than never, as the cliché goes," Ray joked, as he sat down a little too vehemently in the booth next to Louie, waiting a second before he met Gene's eyes. "Always good to see you, Gene. And

Dad, you're looking great," he said, reaching across the table to squeeze his father's shoulder. "Happy birthday."

"Thank you, Ray."

"Oh, by the way," Ray said, turning back to Gene. "Melanie couldn't make it. But she said to say hello."

Nathan Burk looked at Ray, then back to Gene. "Melanie. Who's this Melanie?"

"A friend."

"A mutual friend," Ray said. "She moved here from Las Vegas. That's where Gene met her."

Nathan Burk said to Gene, "When were you in Las Vegas?"

"A couple of months ago. I was working on a case."

The table went silent as the waiter, looking a little annoyed, rolled the serving cart up the aisle and began dispensing their entrees. Both Nathan Burk and Louie had chosen the prime rib, while Gene had opted for the porterhouse steak. All three had ordered baked potatoes with sour cream and side orders of creamed spinach.

"I'll just have the Caesar salad," Ray told the waiter, but not looking at him directly. "And bring me a glass of red wine."

Gene said, "Why don't you forget the wine."

"Why don't you not worry about me."

Nathan Burk, sawing into his prime rib, said, "Gene told us you were on the wagon."

"That's right, I was. But I fell off," Ray said, turning away from his son when he scented Louie's disappointment. "Tomorrow I'll start over."

Louie said, "You can start tonight, Dad."

"I don't want to start tonight. I want to relax and celebrate my father's birthday with one glass of wine. Okay? Now would everyone get off my fucking case."

Nathan Burk put down his knife and fork and straightened his back before he spoke. "This dinner should be a happy occasion," he said, his face strong and filled with dignity. "If Ray feels he wants to have a glass of wine with his salad, that's his decision. All right? Now let's talk about something else."

Gene swallowed but said nothing. His attention had moved toward the front of the restaurant, where their waiter was standing by the cashier's desk, speaking in low tones to the maitre d', who had the expression of someone who was trying to restrain his anger.

Louie glanced at his father, trying not to look upset. "How's casting going, Dad?"

Ray turned his head. "Casting?"

"On your movie. You said they still needed to fill one part."

Before Ray could respond, their owlish waiter reappeared with his Caesar salad, kind of bowing a little as he placed the chilled plate on the table. As he started to leave, Ray said, "What about my wine?"

"I'm sorry," the waiter said with a kind of satisfaction in his voice. "I was told I cannot serve you alcohol."

"What're you talking about? What do you mean, you can't serve me?" Ray said, his face filled with indignation. "Why not?"

"Because they remembered what happened last time," Gene said. "The maitre d' only agreed to seat us if I promised you wouldn't drink."

Ray glanced at his son. "Can you believe this shit, Louie? My brother gets to decide when I can drink and when I can't."

"Don't make a scene, Dad. Please. Just forget about the booze tonight. You don't need it."

For a moment Ray looked ashamed. Then he shook his head and smiled, as if he were thinking of something else. "This is some family, isn't it? Look at the four of us."

Nathan Burk said, "What's wrong with the four of us?"

"We're alone. That's what's wrong," Ray said, and his smile, little by little, turned into a grimace. "There's no women here. How come?" He glanced at Louie. "Where's your mother? Shouldn't she be here?"

"She's dead. She died drunk two years ago," Louie said. "Like you will, if you don't stop drinking."

There was a long silence. Then Gene said, "What's the point, Ray?"

"The point?"

"Why bring up Sandra?"

"She was my wife. I can't bring up my wife? I can't wish she was here? That's not allowed? I need your permission to miss her?"

Nathan Burk shook his head. "No, Ray. You don't need anyone's permission."

"Good. Thanks, Dad. What about you, Louie? Is it okay if I miss your mom?"

"Sure. That's fine with me," Louie said, and he stood as if he'd decided to leave. "I miss her, too."

Gene said, "Are you taking off?'

"Yeah. I have an early rehearsal tomorrow."

"If you miss her so much," Ray said, speaking to Louie but staring at his father, "how come you're scared to talk about her?"

Ignoring this question, Louie shook hands with Gene and leaned down to kiss his grandfather on the cheek "I'll see you, Grandpa."

"Call me."

"I will," Louie said. He started to move away, and then, after taking two steps, he stopped and wheeled around. His father's head was now turned, staring up at him. "And I'm not scared to talk about my mom. I talk about her with my shrink and friends I'm close to. Just not with you, Dad."

Ray shrugged, looked away. "Well, maybe someday you will."

As Louie turned and made his way toward the front door, he was stopped by a tall, thin man with tight black hair who was standing in a line near the reservations desk. They shook hands and spoke briefly, but the man's mobile face suddenly changed, turning hard and filling with helpless anger when Louie quickly separated himself and moved outside.

Gene said, "That guy looks familiar. Doesn't he, Ray?"

Ray shrugged. "He looks like an agent."

"No. He's Maury Geller's kid," Nathan Burk said.

"Who?"

"Maury Geller. He owned World Wide Fashions, the dress store on Hollywood and Cahuenga."

"That's right," Gene said. "Ronnie Geller. I went to high school with him."

After Gene signaled the waiter for the check, Ray stood up and excused himself, saying he needed to use the restroom. But once inside a locked stall, he quickly broke out the gram of cocaine he'd purchased earlier in the evening, before he'd left the studio. It was the best shit in town, pure "Peruvian flake," according to the gaffer who'd sold it to him, and Ray had waited until now to try it, knowing that once he snorted the first line—like taking that first sip of alcohol—his ravenous craving would kick in, and he would not be able to stop.

While he fashioned a straw out of a crisp ten-dollar bill, it crossed his mind that he'd not had anything to drink so far that day, and if he could just muster the courage to flush the coke, he would most likely wake up the next morning with one day of sobriety. For close to a minute Ray sat on the toilet seat, staring down at the black and white tiled floor, while he silently debated his decision. And what it came down to, finally, was this: More than anything in the world, he wanted his son's respect—he knew he could never provide the trust and safety that was absent from Louie's childhood—but that would only happen if he could first begin to respect himself.

"So I dumped the blow," Ray told Melanie Novack the following day, when he called her from the studio. "That's a first."

"Congratulations."

"I think I'm gonna make it this time."

"How'd the rest of the dinner go?"

"Okay."

"Probably better that I wasn't there."

"True."

"Out of curiosity—did my name come up?"

"Briefly."

"He still thinks I know who killed Bobby."

"Probably. We didn't talk about it."

"What do you think, Ray?"

"Well, you know what they say in A.A. You're only as sick as your secrets."

"Go on."

"If you knew, Melanie, and you never told anyone, I don't think you could stay sober."

"So, it follows that either I don't know, or I know and told someone."

"Or you're not really sober."

"Aha! Never thought of that."

"Which is it?"

Melanie laughed. "Take your pick."

Ray was not aware that, after he'd left Musso-Frank, while Gene and his father were still seated in their booth, talking softly and sipping coffee, they were approached by Ronnie Geller. Exuding an air of superficial sincerity, he first apologized for interrupting their conversation. He then went on to explain how he'd met Louie on a recent flight from New York to Los Angeles, after having just seen him perform off-Broadway in Sam Shepard's *Tooth of Crime.*

Geller said, "When I saw him here tonight, I realized you were all together. What's it been, Gene, twenty-five years?"

"Somewhere around that," Gene said.

"Louie told me what happened to your fiancée. I'm sorry," Geller said, making his face look appropriately sad. "That's a terrible tragedy."

Gene gave Geller a long quiet look. Then, with his face devoid of expression, he said, "Thanks for stopping by, Ron."

Geller, his natural volubility cut short, reached for his wallet. He took out a brand-new business card and put it on the table next to Gene's hand. "Here's my number. Give me a call sometime. We'll talk over old times."

After Geller moved away, back to the bar area, Gene signed the credit card receipt and slipped the copy into his wallet. He looked like he was about to stand up. "Are you ready to go?"

"In a second," Nathan Burk said, as he picked up his napkin and gently dabbed his wet upper lip. His other hand was resting on his thigh, and through the weave of gabardine he could feel the letter folded inside the front pocket of his slacks. "Have you thought about what you're going to do with the settlement?"

Gene nodded slightly. "Pay off the house. Maybe travel a little."

"Where?"

"The Caribbean. I always wanted to go to Jamaica," Gene said, and his voice had a thoughtful quality. "Alice and I had planned to go there on our honeymoon."

Nathan Burk smiled with a careful kindness. "She was a great girl."

"She liked you too, Dad."

"She reminded me of your mother," Nathan Burk said, and he gave Gene a knowing wink. "In little ways, like the way she smoked, and the way she closed her eyes when she laughed. And like Mona, she was high-strung." Nathan Burk leaned sideways a little as his fingers went into the pocket of his slacks. "Your mother wanted to go to Cuba on our honeymoon, but I couldn't afford it. So like a schmuck I took her to Niagara Falls. If I had to do it again, I would've borrowed the cash. It was a bad start." Nathan Burk looked more wistful than sad when he raised his hand to show Gene the letter he was hiding in his lap. "I got this in the mail yesterday. I didn't know whether to tell you."

"Who's it from?"

"Your mother."

Gene didn't move as he stared at the light blue stationery that was bordered with pink and yellow daisies. Then he looked into his father's eyes. "Can I see it?"

"Why don't I read it to you," Nathan Burk said, his fingers shaking as he reached for his glasses.

Dear Nathan,

Happy Birthday. I am writing you . . .

Nathan Burk's voice dropped to a bewildered murmur when the black shape of the words went out of focus, blurred by the tears that swam into his eyes. "I think you better read it, Gene."

Nathan Burk placed the letter on the table between them, and Gene, trying to disguise any doubt he might be feeling, looked away for a second. Then he picked up the letter and began to read out loud, in a voice that was rhythmic but curiously distant.

Dear Nathan,

Happy Birthday. I am writing you this letter after spending the whole morning looking through all the pictures I've saved, pictures of our life together in Los Angeles. I don't know why—your seventy-fifth birthday probably—but right after breakfast I felt compelled to walk into our basement and haul up the box containing my mementos from another life.

If you noticed the pronoun "our" in front of basement, then you know I'm living with someone. We've been together for the last seven years. His name is Stan, and he runs a company that builds swimming pools, which is a profitable business in this neck of the woods. If you checked the postmark, you know I live in Tucson, Arizona.

Right now I have some pictures spread out on the table in the kitchen where I'm writing this letter. The first picture is you and the boys posed in front of a sand castle you've been building at the beach in Santa Monica. All three of you guys are looking at the camera with big smiles on your faces. My men! My big strong men!

It's hard to believe that in five years I would be gone, into another life, surrounded not by what was wholesome, like my family, but by other men, shady characters with underworld connections who would soon be done with me. I ran away. I made a mistake that I'm still paying for. And that's the honest truth.

I can't understand it, Nathan. Why didn't I think I belonged there?

Gene put down the letter and looked across the table at his father, who nodded solemnly. "I remember that day at the beach. That's when I saw those kids body surfing for the first time. I wanted to go in the ocean, but Mom wouldn't let me."

"It was rough," Nathan Burk said, "and you were not a strong swimmer."

"Mom was a good swimmer."

"She was good at all sports. Tennis, swimming, softball, you name it," Nathan Burk said. "She was a natural athlete."

Gene nodded without speaking. Behind his eyes he found an image of his mother. She was walking out of the ocean in a white, one-piece bathing suit with the straps falling off her shoulders. When his father stood up to meet her, she wrapped herself in the towel he was holding and kissed him lightly on the cheek. Neither seemed to be smiling.

And with this snapshot in his mind, Gene picked up the letter and resumed reading out loud, knowing that there was already something wrong with this picture of his family, something half-glimpsed and intolerably sad.

Here's a good picture of you, Nate. Actually, it's you and me, and it was taken at the Coconut Grove, on the seventh anniversary of our marriage. We had ringside seats for . . . who? Eartha Kitt, that's right. And there we are, our faces turned toward each other, our foreheads almost touching, the flash from the camera making our smiles shine like . . . like we were movie stars. Why not? We could've been movie stars, because later that night, waiting for our car, Henry Fonda gave you a big hello and a handshake, treated you just like an old friend, and not like some nothing who owned the newsstand that carried his hometown newspaper.

"She hated the newsstand," Nathan Burk cut in very calmly. "She thought I should do something else."

"Like what?"

"Oh, she thought I should involve myself in the picture business. She'd say, 'All day long you talk to big shots. Why don't you ask them for a job?' Like all of a sudden Henry Fonda or John Huston is going to snap his fingers, and the next morning I'm going to be sitting in an office over at MGM. And doing what? Being someone's flunky? No chance. That's not me. Besides, I liked the newsstand. That's where I felt comfortable."

"I thought it was cool. So did Ray," Gene said. "We could read all the comics free."

"She wanted me to sell the dirty stuff under the counter. I wouldn't do it," Nathan Burk said, shaking his head. He sat silent for a moment, then he touched Gene's arm. "Keep reading."

Here's a picture of me, just me. I think you would remember this one. It's—how can I say this—a little racy. I'm naked, not a stitch. I'm standing by the window in the living room of our new home. I'm drinking a Coca-Cola from the bottle. We just got through making love on the couch, and you caught me by surprise after I walked out of the kitchen. It was a Monday morning—you went to work late on Mondays—and the boys were at school.

Even though my hair is a mess, I look good in this picture, smiling and satisfied. Do you remember how we got the film developed? You didn't want to take it to a regular drugstore. You were afraid you'd get arrested for making dirty pictures, not that a naked woman—your wife—standing in her own living room was dirty. Finally, I had to ask around, and Maury Geller gave me the address of a photo lab that would do the job, no questions asked. It seems really silly now, but back then I guess you had to be careful.

Before I tell you about the last picture, I think there is something you ought to know. I haven't been entirely unknowledgeable about your life over the last twenty-five years, or since I saw you last in Los Angeles, when we spent that weird and confusing afternoon together at the Hollywood Knickerbocker Hotel. You see, I've spoken to Ray several times, not in person but only over the phone.

Gene stopped reading and raised his head. His face wore a look of shock. Nathan Burk said, "So you didn't know?"

"No."

"I don't believe you, Gene. You and your brother are too close, and Ray couldn't keep a secret that long."

Now Gene was grinning. "You're right."

"Continue reading, please."

I called him after Pledging My Love *was released, which I enjoyed very much. I never realized that he'd become a writer until I saw his name up there on the screen. I was really surprised, and I felt proud too. He wasn't listed anywhere in Los Angeles, so I called the Writers Guild and made up this phony story. I said I was a long-lost friend or something, and they gave me his number in Berkeley.*

He was shocked to hear my voice, and angry, really angry, and he hung up on me before I could even finish one sentence. A few days later I called back and we spoke for about twenty minutes. I didn't tell him anything personal, only that I lived on the East Coast, which I did at the time, and he never expressed any desire to know more.

I asked him if I should contact Gene, and he said no.

Nathan Burk said, "You didn't want to speak with her?"

"Not then. No."

"Why?"

"Because she left us."

"But you could've forgiven her."

"I wasn't ready."

Ray told me about his wife, her drinking problem and his, and of course I was shocked to learn that she'd killed a man and gone to prison. When she died, he called me and cried his eyes out. I came to the funeral, but Ray never saw me or knew I was there.

I also saw Gene and your grandson at the gravesite (Ray told me later that you couldn't be there because you were recovering from a heart attack). Louie sure is a good-looking boy, but I'm worried that he's decided to become an actor. That's a rough career. I would've steered him away from that occupation, but what do I know, I wasn't around to give advice to either of my two kids.

A year after the funeral, me and Stan came out to L.A. for Aquarama, the national convention of swimming-pool builders, and while he was schmoozing at the hotel, I took the car and drove through the old neighborhood. I parked in front of the house and thought about the years we spent together, the good times and the not so good. I sat there for about an hour, waiting for you to walk outside, but you never did.

When I think about it, it's better that I remember you from the pictures I've saved, and vice-versa. You know what I mean? We're not exactly young-sters anymore, although I'm sure you've aged quite nicely.

But enough of that! Here's the fourth and final picture. It's a Polaroid of Gene and Ray that was taken at a July 4th barbecue up at Gene's house in Topanga Canyon. They both look happy and a little bit drunk, and Gene has his arm around Ray's shoulder. Off to the side, almost out of the frame, is a woman with a very pretty face that is partially blurred. I know that this is Alice, Gene's fiancée. Ray sent this picture to me after her plane crashed, along with a long letter. He said that Alice was a wonderful girl—she was certainly beautiful, I could see that—and that he'd never seen his brother as happy as when he was with her. He'd thought that the family's run of bad luck had ended, and that finally, for one of you guys, the right girl had come along. I felt so badly that it had to end the way it did. I wanted Gene to be happy, and I think he knows this in his heart.

"She called me," Gene said, as he looked up from the page. "Ray asked me if he could give her my number, and I said it was okay."

"So you spoke to her after all?" Gene nodded, and Nathan Burk said quietly, "I can't believe you boys hid all this from me."

"We didn't think you'd want to know," Gene said cautiously. "Are you angry?"

"With you and Ray? No, of course not," Nathan Burk said. He shook his head. "I'm just confused. Did she say anything about me?"

"She asked how you were feeling, and I said you were fine. I told her what a great dad you are. I'm sure Ray told her the same thing. It was just a short conversation, and a lot of it was spent crying."

"You were crying?" Nathan Burk said, a little nervously.

"No. She was."

"She wanted you to forgive her?"

"She didn't say that."

"She wouldn't call me," Nathan Burk said in a bitter voice immediately. "This I'm sure of."

"If she did, would you talk to her?"

"No."

"Ever?"

Nathan Burk didn't answer. After a while he just sighed and said, "Finish the letter, Gene."

Nate, I know what you're thinking. You think I'm using the boys to find a way to sneak back into your life, but that's not the case. There is no way back after what I did, and the boys are men now, with lives that have passed me by. But if I look back to our days together in Los Angeles, I know I acted like I was in love, but I felt more like I was just a friend or your roommate. That was not your fault, and we should've talked, but it was too late to catch up, like it is now, because my love just turned cold, that's all. I say this not to make you sad, but to tell you how it was, or how I decided it was thirty-five years later.

But if you have a picture of me in your mind, standing naked in our living room drinking a soda, available to you and only you (with the emotional crossroads still yet to come), that's how I want you to remember me—as a girl with good posture and a shapely body, a girl who loved you, then gave you up before you could find out what she was really like.

Once again, happy birthday.

                                                                Mona

When he and his father left Musso-Frank and walked up Hollywood Boulevard, Gene found that he was not indifferent to the rudimentary faces of the pedestrians who made up the evening crowd, the timorous escapees from their silent and lonely rooms, intent on their private concerns. These sluggish individuals, with their blank and silent masks that he usually considered benign, now appeared stern and condemnatory, their cool clinical eyes pierced with suspicion. Only the gangs of nosiy, colorfully dressed teenagers that charged up the sidewalk did not make him feel conspicuous or profoundly paranoid.

On the corner of Hollywood and Las Palmas, Nathan Burk paused in front of the House of Love. An official notice was taped to the padlocked door, declaring that the building had been sold.

Gene said, "They're tearing it down. I guess that's it."

"That's it?" Nathan Burk said, looking at his son in a puzzling way. "What do you mean?"

"Larry Havana's in jail. The rest are dead. It's the end of an era."

"And now life can go on. Is that what you mean?"

"No. I didn't mean that."

"*This corner was my life!*" Nathan Burk shouted, swinging out with his foot and kicking the door ferociously three times, an act of violence that was acknowledged by the passersby with a sly, almost delighted detachment. "*Bastards! Dirty rotten bastards!*"

Gene put his arm around his father's shoulder. "Take it easy, Dad."

"She was your mother! And they took her away from me!" Nathan Burk screamed without any restraint, and more curses fell from his mouth. Then, bowing his head, he began to cry with an intensity that Gene was unprepared for. "Take me home, Gene. I want to go home."

Driving back to Mar Vista, Gene was still concerned about his father's emotional state, and therefore he paid little attention to the hourly news that was broadcast on the oldies station where the dial was set. Only when he heard the name of Manson family member Leslie Van Houten did he lean forward and turn up the volume:

> *Although she has expressed deep remorse for her part in the Tate-LaBianca murders, and has been a model inmate, Van Houten was denied parole today for the third time. She said, at her hearing, "I wake up each day and know that I am the destroyer of the most precious thing, which is life, and living with that is the most difficult thing of all. And," she added, "that's what I deserve—to wake up every morning and know that."*

After he dropped off his father, whose tears had dried on his disconsolate face, Gene elected to drive home using U.S. 101, better known as the Pacific Coast Highway. It was probably faster to take the Ventura Freeway and cut over Topanga from the valley side, but the traffic was light at this hour and he was not in a rush. Still, he was quite surprised when he saw the sign for Zuma Beach and realized suddenly that he'd overshot the Topanga Canyon turnoff by five miles. But instead of spinning a U-turn and continuing back down 101, Gene pulled into a deserted parking lot on the beach side of the highway and flicked off his headlights.

Gazing past the lifeguard tower to the ocean—flat and black and reaching to the end of sight—he felt soothed by the salty smell and the repetitive roar of the waves breaking on the shoreline. When he looked to his right, he saw the snack bar, a square cement building that was painted pink, flanked by the restrooms and the outside showers.

In high school, when he was a senior and the surf was up, Gene and his buddies would cut school and speed north on 101 to Zuma, stopping first to buy a six-pack of Cokes and a quart of rum. In those days, there was a jukebox inside the snack bar that was stocked with the latest hits, and one of Gene's favorites, "Do You Wanna Dance" by Bobby Freeman, was the oldie playing now on the radio in his car.

"We used to dance with the waitress," Gene told Alice one night, when they were parked in this same lot. "She was this slutty Mexican chick who already had a kid. After her shift, she used to hang out with us down on the sand, drinking rum and Cokes and playing hearts. She had a crush on this buddy of mine, Matt Rowe, and one afternoon he fucked her in the back of his Chevy."

"Where was her kid?"

"Who knows? Probably with the chick's mom."

"Did you fuck her?"

"No. She didn't have a crush on me."

"Have you ever fucked anyone at the beach," Alice asked him, "not counting tonight?"

Gene told her the truth, describing a party at this beach or one close by, where he and Barbara Westbrook, his girlfriend for one semester, snuck away and made love in the hard wet sand by the ocean.

"Were you a virgin?"

"No."

"Who was your first?"

"She was a whore."

"How did that happen?"

"I fucked her in this motel on Sunset. Me and a couple of other guys. This kid I knew arranged it. Larry Havana. His dad was a gangster," he said, leaving out that Larry was also at the beach party, a sad presence among the merriment, and when it turned out that Gene had knocked up Barbara Westbrook, it was Larry who had also arranged the abortion. "It wasn't all that great."

"You didn't care about the whore. How could it be?"

"I care about you."

"That's why it feels so good."

Striking a match to check the clock on the dash, Gene felt an odd dizziness, as if he were coming down with a fever. It was past midnight and "All I Have to Do Is Dream" by the Everly Brothers came on the radio, the opening chords of the song followed closely by the sound of a plane's engine off to the west, a plane that was not yet visible over the darkly breaking waves.

At first a low ghostly hum, the sound grew louder and louder, a thunderous drumbeat that pressed down on Gene's lungs and resonated along his spine, vibrating the darkness around him. This avalanche of noise made Gene feel both terrified and calm; and when the long silver fuselage appeared phantom-pale against the black velvet backdrop of the night, hovering just over the ocean, he experienced an uncontrollable surge of excitement.

> *Whenever I want you*
> *All I have to do is dream*

The aircraft and the faces in the windows were frighteningly close. These were ordinary people, tourists and businessmen, intimate strangers ticketed on a journey clothed in mystery, a journey that would end on a fog-thickened hillside in the middle of America.

And then Gene saw her, striding slowly up the aisle, moving (it seemed) in slow motion, her shiny blond hair parted in the middle and swinging softly on her sweet shoulders. Never had Alice's face looked so beautiful and at peace.

The passenger she was looking for was a young boy seated on the aisle, and she knelt down so she could speak into his pale green eyes. She said something and the boy laughed, and she laughed at his laughter. And before he realized it, Gene was laughing too, laughing so hard, through his tears, that it was impossible to believe he would ever stop.

Twenty-five

Last Words

This is a transcript from the cockpit voice recorder aboard TWA flight 232, which crashed in the woods north of Greencastle, Indiana.

04:15:18–Captain Ted Stewart: "Mayday! We are inverted! We gotta get it! Push!"

04:15:20–First Officer Lee Doerr: "I'm pushing! I'm pushing!"

04:15:24–Stewart: "Okay. Now, let's kick rudder. Left rudder! Left rudder!"

04:15:31–Doerr: "I can't reach it! I can't reach it!"

04:15:40–Stewart: "Jesus Christ! You gotta help me here! We're going down!"

04:15:55 (Banging sound)

04:16:07–Doerr: "Oh God! Here we go!"

04:16:14 (Unintelligible screams)

04:16:21–Attendant Alice Larson: "Please . . . please . . . please . . . everyone . . ."

04:16:35 (Unintelligible words, screams, followed by a series of crashing sounds)

04:16:48–Alice: " . . . JUST . . . HOLD . . . ON!"

04:17:06 (Recording stopped)

Acknowledgments

I am indebted to the following authors and books: Vincent Bugliosi and Curt Gentry, *Helter Skelter;* Ed Sanders, *The Family;* John Gilmore, *The Garbage People.* I am also grateful to my agent Amanda Urban for all her encouragement and helpful comments, and above all to my editor, Amy Hundley, for her patience and her clear-eyed editorial judgment.